IN KNIVES WE TRUST

IN KNIVES
WE TRUST

GEOFF BROOKES

Matador
9 Priory Business Park,
Wistow Road, Kibworth Beauchamp,
Leicestershire, LE8 0RX
Tel: 0116 279 2299
Email: books@troubador.co.uk
Web: www.troubador.co.uk/matador
Twitter: @matadorbooks

ISBN 978 1789016 055

British Library Cataloguing in Publication Data.
A catalogue record for this book is available from the British Library.

Printed and bound in Great Britain by 4edge Limited

Typeset in 11pt Minion Pro by Troubador Publishing Ltd, Leicester, UK

Matador is an imprint of Troubador Publishing Ltd

TO ELIZABETH

Chapter One

When Daniel Guy came back from America, he was as embittered and angry as he had been when he had left Swansea five months earlier. The difference was that this time, he had a revolver.

It had been a cold and wet March day, and the evening was showing no improvement. Daniel had drunk his way steadily through that miserable Tuesday afternoon, just another successful investment in the relentless destruction of his marriage. He sat in the darkest corner of their mean rooms at 32 Little Gam Street, drinking beer from a chipped earthenware jug, and looked around him in disgust that after thirty-eight years, his life should have come to this.

He was tall, with a straight well-defined nose and thin lips. In other circumstances, he might have been described as handsome, but his features were tainted by grime and dominated by hooded eyes, which gave him a brooding, dangerous appearance. He was a restless man, impatient and heartless, and others were always very wary of him.

His wife Mary sat close to a smoking oil lamp in the kitchen, the dark room barely illuminated, struggling to see whilst she finished an untidy repair to the frayed hole in the knee of a neighbour's trousers. She wore an apron which may once, long ago, have been white, with a ladder of dull and bent pins threaded into the left-hand side, along with long strands of cotton hanging from blunt needles. Her unruly hair was tethered by a filthy rag in a grey-streaked ponytail. Her eyes, narrow with distrust and disappointment, peered with difficulty through air that was heavy with smoke and recrimination. Their relationship had become an angry exchange of unanswered questions. They had argued earlier, of course. They always argued. Usually, it was about money. Tonight? There was no food in the house – because there was no money. Daniel, who had made no attempt to find work since his unexpected reappearance, had drunk it all away.

Mary earned what little she could through her sewing but, now her husband had returned, there was never enough. They had married in youthful haste and had plenty of time in which to consider the mistake they had made. Now they were chained together in a marriage which brought happiness to neither of them. Daniel Guy had once worked as a haulier, with his own horses and cows pulling his own carts. A fortunate position indeed! He had a yard and stables; he was his own boss. Daniel was so much more advantaged than many others who surrounded him. But he was, by nature, sullen and unpleasant. He worked with no enthusiasm and displayed a poorly disguised contempt for those who employed him. They had rarely employed his services a second time, and the business had failed when he couldn't find the money to feed his animals. Mary blamed him for the failure, and he blamed everyone else.

Unexpectedly, after fifteen years of mean-spirited domestic argument and confrontation, he had deserted Mary and left for America to start a better life. But whatever release Mary might have felt when he disappeared had been only temporary.

Daniel Guy returned to Swansea after five months: a simmering confusion of barely suppressed rage. There were no cows this time. There were no horses and there were no carts. But this time he had brought a gun with him. He had a small tin in which he kept the cartridges, and he spent some time every evening loading and unloading the gun, testing its mechanism, feeling its weight.

He hated, truly hated, relying upon the generosity of Mary's brother John Phillips, who had given them a bedroom and allowed them the use of his house. Guy found it demeaning to accept charity in this way, particularly from someone he did not like, but made no attempt to change his situation. After all, to pay rent on a room elsewhere would have been impossible.

Mary threw her work onto the table and rubbed her strained eyes. 'Why have you brought that gun home? How could you afford to buy it? Where did the money come from?' Again, Mary snapped her familiar questions. Again, he declined to answer them.

'Everyone must have one in America. And this is the best. A Colt.' He flicked the cylinder with his fingernail, watching it spin.

'Is that so? So what are you going to do with it in Swansea? Who do you think you are going to shoot with it?' she sneered. Mary stood up and stretched her back.

'You. I have told you before,' he said, and pointed it at her, his arm straight out, sighting along the barrel at her forehead.

'You have threatened to shoot me every day since you came back. Why don't you do it now?' She stared at him defiantly, bending closer towards him. 'Put it out of sight. I do not wish to see it,' she said scornfully, knocking the gun from his hand. It fell with a clatter on the floor.

'Pass me my gun, woman.'

'Get it yourself.'

'I said, pass me my gun.'

She held his gaze for a long moment, then picked up the tin of bullets and emptied those too onto the floor. He watched them roll under the table.

'I have to return these breeches. Feed yourself, if you can. I am going out.' She maintained her contemptuous gaze for a moment and then turned and left.

The door slammed and Daniel stared vacantly into the gloom, wondering why he had allowed himself to be persuaded to return to Swansea. In a few moments, Phillips came into the kitchen to see about the noise. He was carrying in his hand an empty wine bottle and had been standing outside talking to his neighbour, Mr Gallivan, when Mary had pushed past him. He looked at Guy. Experience told him that it would be better not to say anything at all when his brother-in-law looked so grim, and he returned quickly to the doorstep.

Daniel picked up the gun and the bullets and fiddled with them once more. This American revolver was all he had. Everything else had gone. His hopes and his schemes had disappeared; all he had left was a futile existence in a shabby room in a neglected town. He should never have come back. He should have stayed in New York. Another day here in Swansea would surely follow this one, without meaning or purpose, just as it had always done. He sat in the chair with his eyes closed, spinning the cylinder. How many bullets had he loaded? Was the gun full? Or were there only five? Or four? He couldn't remember. Perhaps he should put the gun against his head and take a chance. What did he have to lose? He practised it, to see what it felt like, but with his finger well away from the trigger. Should his eyes be open? Or closed? Perhaps closed would be better. He wasn't sure. Then he saw a mouse moving across the floor so he pointed the gun at it instead, wondering whether it would be worth the bullet. He smiled. It would be his choice. At least with the gun he was someone, he had influence, he possessed the power of life and death, even if it was merely over a mouse. With the gun he could decide who – or what – lived or died. The gun brought him hope; it gave him status. It offered him an escape and he was going to take it. He watched the black beetles as they emerged from beneath the sink and began to click along the floor, spreading across the room. A few black shapes climbed steadily up the wall.

∾

He may have fallen asleep because he was suddenly aware that Mary had returned. She was lighting a candle. 'I am going to bed,' she said. She swayed slightly as she climbed the stairs. 'Where have you been? Someone has been buying you drink. I can smell it. You said you had no money. What did you offer in return? Tell me.'

'Wouldn't you like to know,' she said, without turning round.

'I have a right to know. I am your husband.' He wished to command authority but instead sounded impotent, feeble. 'It is Sam Grove, isn't it?'

'And why, pray, is it any of your business? You give me no money. I have no obligation to you. None at all.' She put the candle down on a chair in the bedroom and took off her dress.

'You have a duty to obey me. You must do what I say.'

She stood defiantly in front of him, naked, with her hands on her hips and shook her head. 'And does this mean that I must submit to you once more? Is that your desire? You desert me and then return because you can find no one else, and so once more I must do your bidding? Well, Daniel Guy, the answer is no.' She picked up her nightdress from the bed and began to put it on.

He took the revolver from his pocket and shot her. It surprised him how quickly it happened. Three bullets in quick succession. She was spun around by the impact and fell to the floor panting, unable to breathe properly.

He stared at what he had done, his ears ringing with gunfire, rather shocked by this unexpected turn of events. Was it really that easy?

Phillips rushed upstairs from the kitchen and saw Guy standing near the open bedroom door with the revolver in his hand. 'Oh my God, Dan! What have you done?'

Guy turned towards him. 'I'll serve you the same, you bastard!' he shouted, and fired. The bullet ripped past Phillips's chin and embedded itself in the wall. Phillips, acting before Guy could fire again, leapt forward, grabbed hold of him and threw him down the stairs. Guy tumbled to the bottom but held on to the gun. He turned himself around and pointed the revolver back up the stairs at his brother-in-law, who stood looking down, frozen in fear.

Guy stared at him. He aimed the revolver carefully and pulled the trigger, but there was only a click. He had loaded only four bullets. 'Damn you! Damn you!' He scrambled to his feet, threw open the door and disappeared into the night.

Chapter Two

It was after midnight when Inspector Rumsey Bucke met with Constable Sprague at the Central Police Station on the corner of Tontine Street. Although his turn of duty had been completed for the day, Bucke had come back into work to meet Sprague before he started the second circuit of his long and difficult circular beat, which stretched around Greenhill, Hafod and Brynhyfryd. He stood before the desk in the small office of shining brown wood, which smelt lavishly of polish. It received the very best of attention from the cleaners, who devoted much more time to the room than any other part of the building. Bucke appreciated their efforts and told them so, though in truth he would have preferred a less highly polished floor. He placed his elbow on the desk, cupped his chin in his palm and studied the constable carefully. He sighed inwardly.

Robert Sprague was one of the most recently appointed constables, and his short record was already far from distinguished. He was standing in front of the window, a square of thick darkness since almost all the gas lamps outside, rather like the constable, were unreliable. He had his hands clasped behind his back and was staring straight ahead. His face, badly scarred by smallpox, showed no emotion. In the lobby, behind the counter, there was a large clock which ticked loudly, to the solemn rhythm of which Sprague tapped his boot on the parquet, something Bucke found especially irritating, though he was determined not to be provoked. He did reflect, however, that if it hadn't been for clocks, the meeting would have been unnecessary.

The constable listened without interruption to what Inspector Bucke had to say. When he had finished, Sprague cleared his throat. 'You can be sure that I would be a constable to be proud of, Inspector, if I was able to work with a better class of people.'

'I see,' Bucke sighed. 'Unfortunately, I am unable to change the nature of the area in which we must work.'

'I came here from Newport, Inspector. You will recall that the Superintendent found that my testimonial was satisfactory. Before that, I worked for the Glamorgan force. I was not dismissed. I resigned to go to Newport to better myself. I did the same when I came to Swansea. I was told I was faultless in the execution of my duties. But in recent weeks, sir, I have started to believe that the criminal classes here in this town are intent upon my destruction.'

He knew that Sprague was not being entirely honest. There had been a credible affiliation order in Newport; there had been accusations of extortion and assault. Bucke remained calm and controlled. 'What gives you the impression that you are the particular target of their anger, Constable Sprague, rather than any of your other colleagues, all of whom have, on occasion, found themselves in difficult situations?'

'Because they are forever attacking me, Inspector, and I am disappointed that my fellow officers have done nothing to address this.'

There was an element of truth in this, he had to agree. Sprague had been stabbed in the hand when arresting Patrick

Clarke on the High Street and then beaten with a poker by Euphenia Williams on Jockey Street when he tried to intervene in a domestic brawl. He still carried that particular scar on the side of his head. But Sprague himself was more a school bully, rather than a police constable, and not much different from those people he was trying to arrest. He was eager to resort to violence himself and rarely brought a calming presence to his duties. This had been especially evident in his early-morning dealings with Mrs Farrell, who lived in Dolphin Court, a ragged collection of run-down houses on Ebenezer Street, a short distance from the police station. She had been so incensed that she had walked down to the Town Hall in the middle of the morning, where Bucke was attending the Police Court, to complain about Sprague. That was why Bucke needed to see him.

She'd got out of bed just after midnight and gone down to look at the railway station clock to check the time. Like most others who lived in the area of Swansea known as Little Ireland, she had neither a watch nor a clock, and visiting the station to check the time was the only way she knew to ensure that her husband got out of bed in time to catch some casual employment on the docks, unloading the ships coming in on the early-morning tide.

Inspector Bucke knew this was common practice and asked her why she went down to see the railway station clock when there was a perfectly good one in the police station, where normally the lighting was better. She had shrugged. Some of the policemen, like Sprague, wouldn't let them come in to look at it, she said.

As she had walked down Ebenezer Street, where the pavement was uneven and inadequate, and where gas lighting had yet to be installed, Constable Sprague had loomed out of the darkness, grabbed her and pushed her against a damp, uncomfortable wall of uneven stones.

'And you are sure it was Constable Sprague, Patsy?'

'Of course I am sure, Inspector. It was dark but, begging your pardon, I recognised his poxy face, sir, and his number. Like the one on the station clock. PC Number 9. He told me that it was too late for a woman to be out on the street, sir. He called me a bad word, sir, and slapped me across the face. And he tore my shawl as well. Look, see; here it is. It will be a devil to mend when you look at what he done to it. And then he hit me with his staff and caused me a wicked bruise on my leg here, sir. And then, when I told him I would report him to you because you have always been an honest and true policeman – begging your pardon, sir, but it is true – and when I said that to him, sir, he grabbed me again and threw me to the ground. Sorry to have to say, sir, but I think he had been drinking. So I lay on the ground until he had gone and then I went to look at the clock and then I went home, sir. I have not told Mr Farrell about this because I do not wish him to become agitated and act in a way that he might have cause to regret later on, sir.'

'I think that is a very wise decision, Patsy. Did your husband find work this morning?'

'Certainly, sir. He was first in the queue,' she said with pride. 'He is a good man.'

'Of course he is, Patsy, because you make sure that he remains so. You have done the right thing in coming to see me and I thank you for it. I hope you are prepared to leave the matter with me, Patsy.'

'To be sure, without a doubt, sir. I wanted to tell someone but I didn't want to tell no one but you.'

As everyone in Greenhill said, a policeman could be many things and not many of them especially pleasant. But Inspector Bucke? Well, he was straight, and what greater accolade could there be for a policeman than that? If they had a problem – and there were many – they knew they could talk to him and he would treat them with proper respect and do something, if something could be done.

But of course now, when he questioned Sprague about this, he denied it. She was lying, he said. Bucke knew whom he believed.

'Swansea can be a difficult place to be a policeman, Constable Sprague. But I urge you to resist the temptation to use your fists. I have squared it with Mrs Farrell and I can assure you the matter will go no further, but it is unlikely that I would be prepared to do so again. For now, the Watch Committee do not need to hear of this. But if it happens again, things could be more difficult – for both of us. Because they would ask me why I had not reported previous incidents to them and they would then be informed of issues which you might prefer to keep hidden.' Bucke did not feel there was any reason to go into any greater detail.

'I see, Inspector.' Sprague began to rock up and down on the balls of his feet. He paused and collected his words. 'I have to tell you that I am disappointed that you have chosen to accept the word of a common prostitute, rather than the word of a fellow police officer.'

'Mrs Farrell is not a prostitute, Constable Sprague. She is an honest, hard-working wife and mother.'

'So you say, sir. But for what other reason should she be on the streets after midnight, sir? Such a thing we should not permit.'

'She went to check the station clock, Constable Sprague. I did explain that.'

Sprague offered his finest sneer. 'Even though she cannot tell the time?'

'She can tell the time well enough, Constable Sprague, and she could certainly identify your own number when she compared it to the figures on the clock,' replied Bucke patiently. 'When you must try to survive as she does, feeding her children and paying her rent, you would soon learn to tell the time if your income depended on it.'

'This is a further example of the way I am being singled out for persecution by criminals, Inspector. It is an attempt to undermine the rule of law in this town. For this reason, Inspector Bucke, I think I should be immediately reassigned to the west side of Swansea where I would find greater sympathy from residents who would appreciate the way in which I endeavour to carry out my duties.'

Bucke quickly calculated his motives. Sprague wanted to be transferred to the part of town where there would be more things to steal. He chose his words very carefully. 'Should the Chief Constable consider a reallocation of duties, Constable Sprague, I am sure he will look for guidance to inform his judgement. You may be sure that I will be very clear in what I say.'

'I thank you for that, Inspector. As I recollect matters pertaining to the incident in Ebenezer Street, it may be that during the course of our conversation the woman in question slipped and fell to the ground on account of her being drunk, sir. The time being after midnight shows she had been attending an illegal drinking den.'

'An interesting judgement, though, in truth, rather more speculative than I would have liked. You have no evidence at all that she was drunk. But perhaps, in the circumstances, the best advice I can offer would be that should you see Mrs Farrell on the streets again after midnight – or indeed any of the other women of the area – walking in the direction of the station, that you do not become involved, but rather watch closely and then report your observation to me. In that way, we may be able to identify the location of this secret drinking den. If you have nothing further to add, Constable, then I think it is best that you resume your beat.'

'Immediately, Inspector.' He gave a half-hearted salute.

'Thank you for your consideration,' he said with a palpable lack of sincerity.

As they walked towards the front door, Bucke heard the faint sound of police rattles and the sound of distant voices.

'Sounds like trouble to me, Inspector. It is going to be a hard night indeed,' Sprague said, shaking his head.

As they paused on the steps, straining to identify from which direction the sound came, Constable Gethin Lewis ran into a pool of light cast by the only operative gas lamp at the far end of Tontine Street.

'Inspector Bucke! 'he shouted breathlessly. 'Come quick. There has been a murder!'

~

When he had reached Castle Street, Bucke realised that he was suddenly alone. Somehow, in a short distance, he had lost Constable Sprague, which did not surprise him at all. He continued as quickly as he could along Oxford Street, though it was particularly difficult. The paths through and around the mud pools in the streets where the gas lamps had never been installed were intricate enough in the daylight, but in the dark it was dirty work. When he got to Little Gam Street, he saw Constable Ball and was pleased to see that he was holding his lantern, guiding Bucke to the doorstep.

There hadn't been a murder at all, although it seemed that two had been attempted.

Mary Guy was lying on the bed, her nightdress bloody. She was pale, her features were knotted together by pain, but she was alive. Bucke asked her how she was, but she was unable to reply. Another woman with Mary was holding her hand tightly, as Dr Beynon worked at one of her wounds.

'Good evening, Doctor Beynon. How is your patient?'

'As well as can be expected, in the circumstances. It is serious, Rumsey; do not doubt it. She is shocked at the moment. I would venture that she has been extremely fortunate, but I am confident that she will survive.'

Bucke looked over the doctor's shoulder and watched him gently teasing away at something in Mary Guy's shoulder with a pair of forceps.

'She has endured a bullet in her left shoulder and another which is lodged in her groin. It appears that no vital organ has been pierced. Mrs Guy has a wound on the upper right side of the chest near the collarbone from which I have now extracted this.' He turned and held up a small conical bullet. 'The two other bullets are still present, but I do not think that their extraction will prove too difficult. However, I need better light.'

'It would seem, Doctor Beynon, that you are right. She has been very fortunate,' said Bucke.

'Indeed. She is not about to die, so I can see no necessity for taking her deposition immediately. That can wait. She would benefit from rest, and you will have the testimony of John Phillips, her brother, in any event. He was unharmed. The bullet intended for him missed entirely and is lodged there in the wall. I do not think that the case should prove too difficult, even for the Swansea Constabulary. There is only one person whom you should detain.' He yawned. 'I will extract the other two bullets tomorrow in the hospital. It is too late for me now and I cannot see well enough. Mrs Gallivan here, who lives next door, I believe, has kindly agreed to look after her. The police ambulance would find it difficult to attend anyway, given the state of the street lights down here. Mrs Gallivan will fetch me if there is any further blood loss, but it is not something that I anticipate. The deed was inexpertly done.'

He put his equipment in his bag and Bucke went with him downstairs. 'I fervently hope that you and your men can catch him soon, Rumsey. We do not need a man like that, apparently with an American gun, in Swansea, no matter how bad a shot he is.'

'It is certainly an unwelcome development, David. Thank you for attending to Mrs Guy. I would be obliged if you would let me know when you think she will be in a position to speak to me.' They shook hands and Constable Ball saluted the doctor as he left.

Bucke clarified the sequence of events with the constable. He had been patrolling his beat in the lower part of town and Mr Gallivan had found him on Western Street. Ball was an unimaginative man but a dependable officer, and Bucke knew that he could rely upon the accuracy of his report.

'Mr Gallivan brought me here and I went upstairs where Mrs Guy was being attended to by her brother. I could smell gunpowder in the room, sir, and there was blood everywhere. So I went to get Dr Beynon whilst I was swinging my rattle.'

'Thank you, Constable Ball. And you saw no one else?'

'No one at all, sir. The streets were dark and there was no one that I could see. '

'And do you know Daniel Guy? Would you be able to recognise him?'

'Yes, sir. I have had occasion to speak to him once or twice, but I saw no sign of him tonight. He likes to stand outside Nellie Tits's house, waiting for the fights to start, but it has been quiet down there since she went inside for a spell.'

'Very well, Constable. You have done well. You must resume your patrol; but if you see Daniel Guy, you must not approach him on your own. Do you understand?'

'Yes, sir. If I see Daniel Guy, I must summon assistance.' Ball tapped his trouser pocket. 'Do not worry, Inspector. I have got my handcuffs with me.'

'Remain alert and circumspect, Constable,' said Bucke as Ball took his lantern away into the night. He thought it unlikely that Ball would find him; he had had plenty of time to get away and limitless places where he could hide.

It was a bare and mean house, dirtier than it should have been but bigger than many. There were two rooms downstairs: a meagre kitchen and a room which others might have called a drawing room which was entered directly from the street, with two bedrooms above. There was enough space for the three of them to live tolerably together, with the pavement of Little Gam Street serving as a communal space with the neighbours on those occasions when it wasn't raining.

He found John Phillips sitting calmly in the kitchen, drinking tea from a saucer. When Bucke appeared, he started to shift uncomfortably in his chair, perhaps unhappy with the idea of talking to a police officer in his house, amongst his own things. He put down his saucer and placed the empty bottle, resting in his lap, beneath the table as casually as he could. 'It is a shocking state of affairs, Inspector,' he declared.

'Shocking indeed.' Bucke sat down at the table. 'I don't think I have ever met your brother-in-law. What should I know about him, in your opinion?'

'He is a wild and wandering man, sir. Difficult and argumentative. I found him bitter and envious, right from the off. Daniel never seemed to take no pleasure in his marriage to my sister. I have been renting them a room here in my house for two years, and in that time I have seen from him few signs of affection or tenderness. He left her last year. But then he come back.'

'Was he especially troubled tonight, Mr Phillips? Did anything occur which might have made him angry?' asked Bucke.

'Not that I was aware of. I knew they were not very good friends this evening, though I could not hear what was said. I was talking to Harry Gallivan when Mary went out. I saw Daniel sitting in the chair, and his gun and the bullets were on the floor. I did not feel that he wanted company.'

'Where did your sister go?'

'I cannot be sure, Inspector. She probably took the breeches she was repairing back to Sam Grove, the landlord at the Builder's Arms. He might have given her a drink. I think he is fond of my sister – but all innocent, like. It was after midnight when she come home. She and Dan went upstairs and I could hear talking and raised voices, but could not work out what it was about. I did not take the least account of them, like.' He shook his head. 'It was not an unusual occurrence. Then I heard the gunshots, and when I ran to the room, I saw my sister was in her nightdress. She was covered in blood as you see her now. I threw Daniel downstairs in my temper and he fled into the street. Harry from next door had heard the shots too and he come to see what had happened. He went for the constable.'

'Last year, Daniel disappeared, did he?' asked Bucke.

'Well, Inspector, one day he was here, see, and the next he was gone. We looked for him around the town but we could not find him. Mary settled to a new life and earned a little from her sewing. Then someone told us he had gone to America, so we thought he wasn't coming back. Can't say we were unhappy. But I am telling you now and I don't care what no one says, she did not stay out in the nights, Inspector. She lived quietly and she was alone. We were very comfortable together, see. Then a few weeks ago, Daniel suddenly come home. Said when he run away, he'd stowed away on a ship. It was two days before they found him, so they gave him a job, stoking the boilers, he said. In America, he worked on the docks.'

'So why did he come back?'

Phillips shrugged. 'Daniel said he didn't like it there. Never had no money. He's always been changeable and contrary, as I see it.'

'And how had he come back? Was he a stowaway again?'

'No, sir. Come on a ship to Liverpool this time. Then he took a train.' Phillips shook his head. 'Mary was not best pleased to see him.'

'And he had a gun?'

'Yes, Inspector. And it puzzled me, like. He said he had no money, see, but he had a gun and a box of bullets. Didn't go looking for a job. I could have got him a job, see. I deliver for Morgan the Baker on Castle Street and I could've found him some work, but he wasn't interested. Just sat in the chair and played with his gun. Mary used to call him Wild Bill Hickok.'

Bucke raised his eyebrows. 'Did Mary goad him?'

'No more or less than he deserved. He took her money and spent it. Then blamed her when he was hungry.'

'I see. Do you have any knowledge of where he might have gone tonight? Did he have a particular friend who might help him?'

'No one I knows about,' replied Philips. 'He did not go out very often, sir. Just to get his beer in the Builder's Arms. Or he went to Nellie Tits's on account of him liking to watch the fights. Mary accused him of consorting with Annie Taylor all the time before he went away, like, but I don't know if he has seen her since he come back.'

'He won't be with Annie tonight, Mr Phillips. She is in gaol.' Sprague had arrested her for being drunk and disorderly in Waterloo Street and, in her rage at the injustice of it, she had broken five panes of glass in the window of the police cell. Her reward was fourteen days in gaol.

By now, it was after 3.00 am. The history of Daniel Guy was much less important than where he and his revolver were presently located. He had probably gone to ground somewhere. There was not much else Bucke could do. He asked Phillips to inform him if there was any change in Mary's condition, bid him goodnight and began his walk home through the cold and empty streets, a thin drizzle clinging to his beard. He was exhausted, and the prospect of painstakingly running Guy to ground filled him with apprehension.

When he got to Orange Street, Bucke stopped and leaned his back against the wall in shadows beyond the reach of the inadequate gas lights. He was abandoned and alone. A stray cat, with wet, matted fur, took some nervous steps towards him and opened its mouth but made no sound. It was a silent cry for help which he understood so well and he could not hold back the tears. He wept, the futility and irrelevance of his life expressed in the uncontrollable, shuddering sobs which had come to visit him once again.

Chapter Three

He awoke with a start, shaking from head to foot. He hadn't slept well for a long time now, haunted always by his dreams, and this morning had been no different. In the short time he had been asleep, Anna had been to see him again, holding out her rag doll towards him. He remembered trying to speak to her; he had something really important to say, but the words would not come out. He remembered wanting to reach out to her, but his arms seemed locked and immobile. He had to watch her fade away to nothing, powerless to prevent it. He had tried to hold on to sleep, to maintain contact with his daughter, but there was nothing he could do to prevent himself waking up.

He was exhausted. Sometimes it was Anna, sometimes it was Charles, and sometimes it was Julia. They seemed to take it in turns. There was one memorable night when Julia had come to him and cradled his head in her lap, stroking his hair. She had whispered to him, 'Everything shall be well, do not worry, everything shall be well.' And every night since then he had tried so hard to go back to that moment, and yet the more he tried, the more elusive it became. He knew that he would never recapture that fleeting moment of serenity; it was impossible.

He sat up in bed and looked around the simple room. Anna's doll and the wooden sword with which Charles always irritated his sister were still there, propped up on the chair, symbols of a happiness that he had lost, forever.

He had lived, he had done many things, he had seen parts of the world that had once been a mystery to him, he had been happy. And now it had all disappeared. Every day he did what he had to do, but there seemed no purpose to any of it. He must monitor weights and measures, he must prevent the adulteration of milk, he must investigate William Johnson who was found in Pentre Mawr wearing a pair of wet trousers which were not his own, he must detain boys for swimming naked in the South Dock, he must arrest Nancy James and George Jones for an act of indecency in Gloucester Place – but no one had ever told him that he must one day attend the funerals of his wife and his children.

Anna and Charles had been taken in a measles outbreak in August. Their deaths within days of each other were terrible blows from which Julia never recovered. She had watched her children die; and when she contracted diphtheria, she hadn't had the strength – or perhaps even the inclination – to fight back. Bucke had found her dead in bed when he came back from duty late one night in October, five months ago, and that image never left him.

A life-changing moment. Bucke had moved out of the house on Henrietta Street, where they had started to build a home, and took a room at 9 Fisher Street, above Mr Scott the dentist, close to St Mary's Church. The tolling of the church bells outside his window marked out the passing of his futile hours.

He splashed water on his face at the washstand and then sat back down on the bed. As he bent down to put on his boots, he stopped and stared at the floorboards, sighing. 1879 had been the grimmest of years and had given him little appetite for 1880.

There was no reason at all for him to stay in Swansea. It contained too many memories eager to ambush him when he least expected it. Everything now seemed without purpose. Perhaps he should return to Islington where he had been born. But to do what? He could rejoin the army. He had once resigned in order to marry Julia and start a new career as a police officer, a husband and then a father. His military background and bearing had been more impressive than those of the other candidates, including Constable Lewis's father; and so the job was his. Swansea had seemed ideal, a place where he could achieve advancement on merit and where the family could become an integral part of a small town by the sea. But that had turned to dust. Now might be the time to enlist again, and then, in some distant part of the Empire under a hot sun, a tribesman with a stolen Enfield rifle might release him from his dreams.

Everyone in the small town knew his history, but he knew, too well, that the tragedy he had confronted was not unique. People in every part of Swansea had to manage terrible bereavements. For some, a second marriage was the only solution to urgent economic necessity. But Rumsey Bucke believed that his situation was different. He had lost everything he had ever loved, in a town which was not his own and where he had no family, and was now entirely defined by his grief. He had always been honest and compassionate, but his cheerful humanity had been replaced by sorrow and cynicism.

In a town of short men, Bucke appeared tall, though in reality he was little more than average height. His hair was neat and his beard was light and kept carefully trimmed. It was not there for fashion, for it helped to cover the scar which ran along his jawline, a souvenir of his service in India on the North West Frontier. In the same incident, he had lost most of his left earlobe, though the beard usually obscured the injury. His face had the potential for happiness and there were times he seemed to be on the edge of a smile, but those brown eyes, which previously others had noted for their warmth, had seen far too much; and now their light had been extinguished and he had been defeated and diminished.

He walked through the town, distracted by his thoughts. There was something about Daniel Guy that was gnawing away at him, something that wasn't quite right. Why had he returned from America? Why had he brought a gun with him? Were these important questions or were they irrelevant? He was too tired to decide. But if Guy had stowed away once before, then what was there to stop him doing so again? Perhaps even now he was far out to sea, stoking boilers.

When Bucke arrived at Tontine Street, two constables, Lewis and Davies, were, as usual, waiting behind the counter, hoping that by being seen there regularly, one of them would eventually be given the job of Desk Sergeant, a position currently in possession of the efficient Sergeant Flynn. Bucke sent them off to search the docks and requested they deliver a message to the harbourmaster, asking him to be particularly vigilant of intruders and stowaways. Unfortunately, he could never be sure that his instructions would be followed properly. Lewis was invariably hostile and Davies deeply and often worryingly simple. He had also requested that Sprague should make enquiries in the copper works in Hafod, where a large number of foreigners were employed, when he went out on his beat, but he was not confident that would happen either.

His first task was to meet with John Allison, the Chief Constable, a man for whom prosperity had created a body much too big for his narrow head. Bucke always regarded the watch chain which stretched across his waistcoat as the final, vulnerable restraint for an expanding belly. He was a large and aggressive man with narrow eyes beneath heavy brows and a vindictive nature. Bucke would never describe him as intelligent, but he knew that the Chief Constable was immensely cunning and devious. He had a large and unpleasant wart sitting in the corner of his nose, which had become increasingly noticeable in recent months as it started to darken. Allison picked at it constantly and Bucke had a disgusted fascination with it.

He had left his previous post as Head Constable in Lancaster with an impressive reference, though there were rumours about some unpleasant business relating to the receipt of an unexpected and valuable legacy of property, acquired from a reclusive but wealthy widow. Lancaster had breathed a sigh of relief, and Swansea soon began to realise that his reputation for confrontation and intolerance was well deserved. Bucke recognised him, above all else, as a skilled politician, endlessly manoeuvring to his own advantage. Swansea Corporation wanted to spend as little as possible on the police force, and Allison always gave them exactly what they required. So they repeatedly slashed the budget and Allison smiled, ignored the inadequacies of his force, and produced spurious evidence of improved crime fighting – for which he was then personally rewarded. He was, truly, the perfect Chief Constable, and Bucke had no intention of emulating him.

'So where is the bugger? Can't have gone far. Someone will know where he is. You has to ask the right people. If he's not hidin' in a shed then there's a trollope looking after 'im. Haven't you got any clues at all?'

'He has stowed away on a ship before. Perhaps he will try it again,' replied Bucke carefully.

Allison glared at him. 'Well, get down t' docks then. Turn place upside down. Trail's gone cold. This won't do, Bucke. It won't do at all.'

'I have constables down there conducting a search at the moment. I must attend the Police Court this morning, but it is my hope that I will be able to speak to Mrs Guy later on today.'

'I am telling you now. You need an arrest. There will be people in town thinkin' you can't do your job. No room for incompetence in my force, Bucke. There are others eager for this job and likely better than you. So think on,' he said, tapping his desk with his finger for emphasis.

Bucke nodded – he knew who that was – Allison's son. 'If he is still in the town, we will find him.'

'You best get on with it then. I'll be watching. And don't forget that meeting tonight at the Institution. Find out what the daft sods are up to. I have got an appointment.'

'I have not forgotten. How could I ever forget, Chief Constable?' he said with a sigh.

When he arrived at the Police Court, he was surprised to see that what was normally a depressing parade of human frailty had become a celebration of unexpected, though measured, hilarity because Punch had turned up dressed as a sailor. Her real name was Catherine Owen and she managed to keep herself alive through petty theft and prostitution. On the day when she was eighteen and had been caught stealing and thus sent to gaol for fourteen days, her descent into relentless poverty had been irreversible. She was known to everyone as Punch for one very good reason. She was a skilled street fighter and had an extremely effective right hand which she employed frequently to resolve any dispute she had – and she had plenty. She lived in a single grim room on the Lower Strand – one of the most notorious locations in town –a nest of brothels and illegal drinking dens; a celebration of robbery, threats and violence. Alcohol would sometimes offer Punch a temporary escape from her surroundings and whenever she had money – like her neighbours – she drank, and the drink usually brought trouble. And Punch was always ready for it.

To be fair to Constable Sprague, which was not something that Bucke found particularly easy, on this occasion he had had little choice about what to do. He had been drawn down to the Strand by the raucous sounds of a disturbance. He found Punch in the process of resolving a professional disagreement with Mrs Bird about the temporary possession of a Belgian seaman, who was slumped and insensible against the wall, which was just how Punch preferred her clients. A large, generally good-natured, crowd had gathered, which Sprague, with no evidence at all, said was over 300, a crowd full of 'drunks and low-bred females.' He had dragged Punch away from Mrs Bird and arrested her, managing to extricate himself from what might have been a very difficult situation with merely the loss of his reinforced hat, which was later found decorating a gas lamp.

This was her twenty-ninth appearance in Swansea Police Court and she was becoming bored with it. Where once there had been fear and apprehension, now it was nothing more than routine, a tiresome and meaningless ritual. It needed something to break up the tedium.

So today she had turned up in court dressed as a sailor, in a large white shirt trimmed with blue tape, a large cloth cap with blue ribbons lying down her back and – most shocking of all – white canvas trousers. Where she got it all from, no one bothered to ask. When she was sentenced to seven days in gaol, she replied, 'Aye, Aye, Captain!', saluted the magistrate, and then, as she was escorted away to the general merriment of the court, she shouted, 'Man overboard!' Bucke couldn't help smiling.

His own case was less dramatic and less entertaining. In his capacity as Inspector of Weights and Measures, he had tested the scales of Elizabeth Dacey, a meat seller in the market. She had a hook which she attached underneath her scales which enabled her to sell short measures and thus defraud her customers. She was fined £3. It was a simple, uncomplicated case, but the look in her eyes when the sentence was delivered persuaded Bucke never to go near her if she was skinning a rabbit.

Back in the police station, he received a message from Dr Beynon informing him that he had removed the other two bullets from Mrs Guy and, later in the afternoon, Bucke went to the hospital to see her.

He had the opportunity to look at her more closely this time. He saw a thin, malnourished and deeply unhappy woman. Bucke noticed her twisted mouth, which to him expressed not hope, but hatred for the world which had stamped upon her dreams. She was sitting up in bed, with Mrs Gallivan by her side, and could add little to what he already knew about the attempt on her life. She hated her husband, wished to see him dead. She told him, unbidden, that her only child had been stillborn after a long and difficult labour which she had barely survived. Bucke could see that the experience had scarred her and suspected that an unacknowledged part of her wished that Daniel had been more efficient in his shooting. If he was right, then he understood perfectly.

Although she was still weak, her deep-seated anger was undiminished. 'I should never have married him. I knew after two days. It was a shocking mistake. Then he went off with a young girl, no more than a child, and I took him back, stupid cow that I am. I had a chance to get rid of him and I didn't, and I have been paying for it ever since.'

'Bastard,' said Mrs Gallivan emphatically.

Inspector Bucke promised to keep her informed of any developments there might be in the search for her husband, lying when he told her he was certain he would be detained very soon, and went off to check on his constables. The docks and the wharves were a confusing collection of sheds, stores, offices and abandoned equipment, rusting through neglect. There were narrow alleys and hidden yards. And, of course, ships; lots of them, held in place by a complex web of ropes along which the agile could climb. The two constables had searched as diligently as they could, although their enthusiasm had been dampened by the persistent rain. They had found a stolen, unopened sack of sugar under a tarpaulin in a shed, clearly waiting to be collected, and had chased off a couple of young boys who were prowling around, searching for whatever they could find; but of Daniel Guy there was no sign at all.

He ate his bread and cheese slowly, dreading the evening in front of him. The Swansea Society for the Acquisition of Useful Knowledge? How his heart sank at the prospect. During his military service, he had once, alone, come face-to-face with a Pathan tribesman on a narrow path cut into the side of a mountain – and survived the brutal encounter. He would rather be back then, taking his chance in the swirling mist once more, than trudging along wet streets to the Royal Institution building in the Burrows to listen to a lecture by a retired vicar on "The Phenomena of the Ocean".

The Society was a tedious group of self-important men who regarded themselves as the intellectual powerhouse of Swansea. They met occasionally in order to parade their knowledge in front of each other and to congratulate themselves on their achievements and status. The lectures were generally brief, often esoteric, sometimes plagiarised and much less important than the subsequent conversations. It was an opportunity for uninformed opinion to rage unchecked, where simple solutions to complex problems were routinely paraded, where elderly men of substance could express their frustrations at the madness of a badly run world, one which only their wisdom could redeem.

Bucke was greeted at the top of the Institution steps by Herbert Jenkins, a minor industrialist with a small factory near the river in Llansamlet where he made copper-plated accessories for ships. He was a spare but powerful man, aggressive and confrontational, an expert on every possible topic. In conversation, he asserted and bullied, believing, it seemed, that in all aspects of life there could only ever be winners and losers and that always he deserved to triumph. He wore a fashionable – and expensive – tweed jacket and his hair was invariably parted and combed precisely, though sometimes thin, unruly strands escaped over his shirt collar. He seemed oblivious to the apparently independent movement of his expensive, but ill-fitting, artificial teeth. On the rare occasions he had met him previously, Bucke had been unable to take his eyes off them. Jenkins leaned casually on a thin cane with a distinctive handle, a polished oriental dragon's head. Bucke had the impression he had been waiting for him, but did not feel in any way flattered.

'Evening, Inspector. Shocking news about the shooting. Most alarming. As I was saying to the Chief Constable this morning, we need an arrest. Maintains confidence in our civic arrangements. Seems to me there is a moral deformity in our midst, Inspector, and you have an obligation to root it out. Gentlemen of standing, such as you see here, are rightly alarmed at the prospect of a gun-toting maniac stalking the streets of Swansea.' He stared at Bucke with the slightly protruding, blank eyes of a lizard. 'The villain must be found so that respectable families can sleep safely in their beds. My advice? Your number one priority. Look to it.'

'I have constables working diligently, following up every piece of information we receive. It is only a matter of time,' he said hopefully.

'Hope so, Bucke. And whilst you're at it, arrest a few of these foreign sailors loitering about on the High Street. Come on in,

Inspector. Rogers is speaking tonight. Good man. Terribly dull.'

Bucke followed him reluctantly into the lecture theatre.

The driving force behind the Society was a local headmaster, an irritating man of remarkable arrogance and vanity. Vaughan Bristow had appeared in Swansea a few years ago and established a school called The Rugby College in a three-storey terraced house at 25 Mansel Terrace. He was forever writing to the newspapers in energetic and shameless self-promotion to establish himself as the intellectual leader of the town. He was overweight and was easily identified by an unruly nest of blond hair. He was clean-shaven, although he wore expansive side whiskers. But even with his expensive clothes, there were times when he resembled an overstuffed scarecrow. He habitually wore a bow tie, and his open jacket displayed an elaborate waistcoat and a gold watch chain. He took great pride in both his appearance and his status and, on occasions like this, he enjoyed swirling around in his academic gown, glowing in his self-importance. Bristow nodded to him as he entered and looked at him over the top of his glasses with those eyes which, to Bucke, were nothing more than the calculating eyes of a liar.

'Ah, Inspector Bucke. I am pleased that you have been able to attend our small gathering. I shall be announcing a truly historic moment for the town. Welcome and thrilling news, and you and your officers will have an important part to play in our arrangements.'

Bucke inclined his head faintly in response and sat down, noting with surprise the size of the audience. It appeared that the prospect of this "thrilling news" had galvanised the educated classes in the town. Reverend Rogers might think it was his lecture that had drawn such an impressive audience, one willing to brave the evening squalls with eager anticipation, but there was another reason which explained why both the local French and German Consuls were also in attendance, staring vacantly at the ceiling. The Society had invited Ferdinand de Lesseps, the French engineer, diplomat and creator of the Suez Canal, to speak to them. His new project was the building of another canal, this time through Panama, to link the Atlantic and Pacific Oceans; and he was planning a speaking tour to galvanise support from investors and industrialists.

Bucke could see that it would appeal considerably to the Swansea ship owners, traders and captains who regularly sailed their vessels dangerously around Cape Horn. Even so, it had seemed a ridiculous idea for a small town like Swansea to invite him to speak, rather like the idea of digging a canal across Central America itself, but remarkably he had agreed to come.

The Chief Constable had already been given the news and that was why he had sent Bucke here tonight. The visit of a man with an international reputation, no matter how brief that visit might be, had significant implications for the police. They needed to be involved from the beginning. Bucke turned slightly and looked around him at this pompous collection of middle-aged men and groaned inwardly, picking briefly at a protruding splinter on the back of the seat in front of him.

The next hour disappeared in a vague muttering about tides, icebergs, the Continental Shelf, the swaying weeds of the Sargasso Sea and the fascinating lifestyle of the European eel. Bucke drifted away into a welcoming void. For the first time in weeks, his mind emptied and he rested. Suddenly he was wide awake, startled by applause in the lecture theatre led enthusiastically by Bristow, who then waited for silence to settle once more.

'Thank you, Reverend. Fascinating. Completely fascinating. I am convinced that you will soon excite in the young men of our town a wish to emulate your understanding and your commitment to knowledge. Be assured that I myself will lose no time in throwing a bottle from the pier to await news of its perilous adventures upon the sweeping currents of the ocean.'

There was a smattering of polite laughter.

He continued. 'In two weeks' time, Mr Terry will deliver a paper on Acoustics, with diagrams. *Non scholae, sed vitae discimus*, indeed.' He smiled, enjoying his own erudition, then ostentatiously withdrew his watch from his pocket and flipped open the cover. 'But now, as we close our proceedings for another evening, I have exciting news for you all. As many of you are already aware, I am delighted to report that Monsieur le Comte Ferdinand de Lesseps has agreed to include Swansea in the itinerary of his tour of the British Isles, and will be speaking to us in early June of this year. We are indebted to Monsieur Follet, our respected French Consul, for helping with our invitation.'

Follet forced a thin smile and nodded.

'*Merci, Monsieur Follet. Votre contribution est très appréciée.*' Bristow cleared his throat and then dramatically threw his arms wide. 'My friends, Great Britain is proud to have brought civilisation to the world. Enlightenment, leadership, parliamentary democracy and, of course, unrivalled education.' There was a ripple of approval and Jenkins said, 'Hear, hear,' which Bristow acknowledged with a self-satisfied nod of the head. 'Our Empire has put an end to primitive ways and banished the heathen. Our Empire is the greatest achievement in human history and as such is the wonder and envy of the modern world. Monsieur de Lesseps, a highly respected gentleman and a visionary, has realised that such a project as he proposes, to link the west and the east, will never succeed, not just without Great Britain, but without the great men of Swansea.' There was a round of applause. 'We will listen to what he has to say and then Swansea will bring the substance to his ideas! I shall of course immediately forward the letter to the Lord Mayor and arrangements will be swiftly put in hand, but I was anxious that you should know of our tremendous success as early as possible.'

There was more applause and the meeting broke up into small groups which constantly expanded and shrank, like bellows of hot air.

It was a considerable achievement to have persuaded such an eminent international figure to visit Swansea rather than Bristol or Cardiff. An audacious move. But not everyone was happy. Herbert Jenkins, as Bucke soon discovered, had been agitated for a number of weeks because de Lesseps, as an innovative engineer, was a keen supporter of a tunnel beneath the English Channel. Most of the members of the society had little interest in it, other than as an unexpected curiosity, but Jenkins was extremely exercised by the idea and took particular objection to the approval that de Lesseps had given it. This evening, Jenkins once again was eager to recruit support for his opinions and intruded into a group of members exchanging casual pleasantries with an angry tirade, with which many of them were all too familiar.

'Don't forget, this Frenchman is a supporter of this ridiculous notion of a tunnel beneath the waves. The man is no engineer, whatever he claims. He is not a captain of industry. He is nothing more than a politician. What business is it of his, this ridiculous and foolhardy enterprise?' Jenkins demanded angrily. 'I warn you all now; it is the greatest threat to our sovereign nation and it troubles me considerably if his approval should be regarded as an instruction to lift the shovel. It must not be allowed to proceed! The Frenchman needs to know that it is not something that we in Swansea will permit,' he declaimed. 'By all means, we will lend our expertise to the development of the canal through Panama to boost trade and profit. But we must disabuse him of this ridiculous notion of a tunnel to France. Let us keep the foreigner as away from these shores as much as we can. The Latin seaman is responsible, in my considered view, for the moral degeneracy which hangs over some parts of the town like a noxious cloud. We have all seen them. Base creatures, driven by their perverse desires. Lowest form. Don't you agree, Inspector?' he said, turning to Bucke.

'I cannot say that I find foreign sailors worse than our own people, Mr Jenkins.'

'You surprise me, Bucke. Ridiculous notion to me,' replied Jenkins, turning to the others for support.

Bucke had no inclination to humour him. 'I do apologise, Mr Jenkins. But all men at sea for weeks on end feel trapped by the waves. It is not a surprise that they should become excitable when they reach the shore. Our own men are the same. I saw it in India.'

Jenkins snorted at him, contemptuously. 'I am concerned to a considerable degree that we seem to have an inspector of police who is a supporter of the devious southern European. Mightily concerned. Need to examine the contents of the police cells in the morning, Inspector. Whatever you are doing just isn't working. Learn the lesson.' He tapped him firmly on the shoulder with patronising emphasis.

Bucke controlled his response, choosing his words carefully, unwilling to be publicly bullied. 'We offer temporary lodging to everyone, whenever we need to. Nationhood is no barrier, Mr Jenkins, and neither is social standing or position. Perhaps you need to consider the nature of those who find themselves before the courts. I am sure you will remember the Chief Constable's most recent report. Last year, we detained fifty-nine foreigners for various crimes, and over three hundred Welshmen.'

Jenkins narrowed his eyes and thrust his head forward, ready to reply, but was interrupted by Bristow, his gown a black swirl of self-regard. 'You see, Herbert. I told you that we would be successful. A great day for investors across the town. Prosperity beckons to us all.'

Bristow took centre stage and the conversation quickly moved on.

~

When Bucke finally managed to slip away towards the door, Mr Glascodine, a solicitor he knew from the courts, stopped him. He laid a friendly hand on Bucke's arm, squeezed it gently and whispered, 'Frightful man.'

Bucke sighed and raised his eyebrows.

'Good night, Inspector. I can see busy times ahead for you, I fear,' added Glascodine.

'Such are my duties, Mr Glascodine,' he replied wearily and slipped out of the door.

Bucke walked down the steps. A group of sailors, spilling out of the Queen's Hotel and singing a song in a language he could not understand, staggered off towards the South Dock. As Bucke turned left towards home, he saw Joseph the Matchboy standing by the railings.

'When are the gentlemen coming out, sir?'

'Shortly, Joseph. Don't stay out too late. These are cold and inhospitable nights.'

Joseph had a threadbare jacket that was too big for him, long since abandoned. He wore a dirty collarless shirt but, somewhere or other, he had found an old bow tie, without which he was never seen. His shoes did not match and his lice-ridden hair was matted, uncombable. Around his neck there was an old belt supporting a wooden apple box, in which he displayed his matches. Men in pubs would buy from him matches which they did not need. But Bucke could see an undeniable brightness in his eyes. He was uneducated. He was illiterate. But he missed nothing.

There was a loud crash from Victoria Station behind the Institution, where goods wagons were being shunted, wagons in which, Bucke suspected, Joseph sometimes slept. His was a vulnerable life.

'Don't worry, Inspector, when these gentlemen have gone home, I shall go back down to the Strand. It is much warmer there.'

It was a cold Good Friday and Bucke, declining the matches, gave him a couple of coins, though not enough to change the destiny of another lost soul.

Chapter Four

The search for Daniel Guy continued throughout the Easter weekend but with no success. A man arrested for throwing stones at his mother-in-law's house on Aberdyberthi Street in Hafod on Saturday night, said he was sure he saw Guy dodging into a dark alley that ran through the middle of a terrace of houses. But he had been drunk and Bucke was impressed that, even in the condition in which he found himself that evening, he could still remember where his mother-in-law lived. The constables searched the area dutifully but could find no evidence of Guy anywhere. They questioned men at the copper works as they finished their shifts, but most of them just shrugged, eager to get home. Neither shopkeepers nor landlords had seen him. It was obvious to Bucke that someone was sheltering him somewhere and keeping him out of sight.

The increased police presence in Hafod had an unfortunate consequence because on Monday morning, Edward Coleman, a painter who lived in Mysydd Terrace, was found sitting in the outside toilet with his throat slashed.

Bucke arrived at the house at 7.30 am to find Constable Sprague sitting in the small kitchen with his head in his hands. He glanced up. His face was completely drained of colour. 'Sorry,

Inspector, but I was sickened at the sight of that. There is blood everywhere.'

Bucke went outside, where PC Lewis was standing by the door to the closet. 'Morning, Inspector. Be careful you don't get your uniform dirty.' Lewis was nothing if not fastidious.

'What do we know?' Bucke asked.

'The name is Coleman, Edward Coleman. He and his wife have been renting rooms in the house for about a year. No children. He is unemployed. A painter, they say. She takes in washing. They found him in here about an hour ago. A neighbour, Mrs Jones, comes to use the closet. Opens the door, doesn't much like what she sees and so runs for his wife. She comes down. Takes a razor from his hand. She has identified the body. It is her husband and he is dead, Inspector. They calls for a policeman. They gets Constable Sprague. He throws up and so they send for me. This is what I finds. Good start to the week all round. And it stinks in there as well.'

He opened the door for Bucke to see. The man was sitting on the seat with his head thrown back against the wall. His mouth was wide open and Bucke could not help noticing that his few remaining teeth were brown and scattered haphazardly across his gums. He would have to stop looking at people's teeth, he decided, but, in such circumstances as this, it was easier to focus on a detail like that. There was a terrible wound across his throat, stretching virtually from ear to ear, exposing the trachea. His clothes were drenched with blood. Someone was going to have to clean out the closet and he hoped that one of the neighbours would do it, rather than his wife. It would be an awful job. Would she ever be able to use that closet again, he wondered?

He turned away. 'And his wife has taken the razor?'

'Yes, Inspector. Identified it as belonging to her husband. Did it to himself, I reckon. Not done a bad job of it either. Can't have been easy. To be honest, I can't see this is anything to do with our man Guy, sir. Hardly enough room in there for one person, let alone him and a murderer.'

'I am sure you are right, Constable. Wait here until we get the body moved for the inquest.'

Constable Lewis grimaced, and for the briefest of moments, Bucke had some sympathy for him. Lewis would have to help to manhandle the body into a cart, when by rights it should have been a job for Sprague.

Inside, some of the colour had returned to Constable Sprague's face. He was drinking tea whilst Ena Coleman stood with her arms folded, looking out through the greasy window down towards the closet. She was clearly in shock and Bucke wondered how much of the detail of her husband's death she had registered. More than the poor woman could remember at the moment, he thought. He knew it would all come back to her over the next few days as she tried to come to terms with the suddenness with which her whole life had changed.

He sent Sprague home and told him to return to the station to do the night shift instead and sat down with her, released for a moment from his own unhappiness by the despair that had taken root in this mean little house. There could only be one question, the one which he knew Ena Coleman had already asked herself – why had her husband chosen this moment to kill himself? Bucke listened in sympathy and knew very quickly that the Inquest could only ever find one verdict: that of "Temporary Insanity". Overwhelmed and filled with self-loathing, Coleman had decided that death was preferable to life.

Eva's story had a grim familiarity, one that Bucke saw almost every day. Edward's problem had been drink. He had lost his job and had been forever travelling around the area looking for a new one. Yesterday, after he had returned home from yet another unsuccessful visit, this time to Llanelly, he had taken what little money the couple had down to the Hafod Inn. When he had come home later that night, Edward told Eva that he had seen the police in the streets and that he knew they were intent on arresting him for negligence and vagrancy, a delusion Bucke ascribed to a sense of hopelessness and alcohol. Then, early in the morning after a restless night, he had gone to the shared closet in the yard with his razor.

As he walked back to the police station, Bucke looked at the long rows of houses stretching down to the copper works and the dirty river. Did he really want to know what these houses contained? The secrets they held – the misery, the guilt, the grinding unhappiness? The air was heavy with soot and sulphurous smoke. Beyond the pall which sat permanently above the east side of Swansea, he was sure that it was a pleasant morning, suggesting the imminent arrival of spring. But here at this moment he had slipped suddenly into hell, where the sun never shone and distress and anguish would last for eternity.

Of course, the whole area was suddenly in a state of terror and excitement. In the Vernon Arms, it was soon obvious that Edward Coleman had been killed by Daniel Guy, who was on the loose, ready to strike again; a madman seeking out those in their most private moments so that he could slice open their throats. They wanted bobbies on the street and in their privies. Why couldn't they catch him? Even though an accurate summary of the death of Edward Coleman would eventually appear in the *Cambrian* newspaper, there was little Bucke could do to calm anxieties fanned by rumour. He arranged for Constable Ball to be sent as an additional officer to Hafod; his calming and avuncular presence might help. Bucke hoped that added watchfulness in the area might flush Guy out, if indeed that was where he was.

~

The area unexpectedly managed to pass a peaceful night, although those with access to a chamber pot felt considerably safer than those without. Inevitably perhaps, the increased police presence failed to uncover the whereabouts of fugitives of any kind.

The search for Daniel Guy, however, was interrupted in a most unexpected way. The following morning, Bucke was in the police station looking at a report from the public analyst on the adulteration of milk by a local farmer, when Sergeant Flynn told him that a young woman had arrived in order to report a theft.

'Can't you deal with this, Sergeant?' he asked, indicating the papers scattered across his desk. 'I really need to finish off this milk business so I can get down to the docks to look at the shipping registers.'

'With respect, sir, my advice is that you do see her. On account of who she is and because of what she has to say,' said Flynn with careful emphasis. 'She is the domestic servant to Mrs Jenkins, the wife of the factory owner, Herbert Jenkins.'

Bucke sighed. 'Very well, Sergeant. Bring her through.' He closed his eyes briefly and tried to disguise his frustration.

She wasn't what he expected. She was an attractive woman, perhaps in her mid-thirties. She was poised and confident and sat with her hands folded neatly in her lap. She was well dressed. Her light brown hair was parted in the middle and pulled into a bun at the back of her head. She had a fashionable Paisley shawl around her shoulders, not the traditional Welsh one. Her name was Elinor Roberts and she had worked for Mrs Jenkins for about ten years. She looked steadily and calmly at him as she spoke, clearly and precisely.

'I carry out general duties, Inspector. Whatever it is that Mrs Jenkins might ask of me. And this morning, she requested that I come to the police station in order to speak to a senior officer. This is why I am here. To report a crime.' She waited for Bucke to respond.

'I see, Miss Roberts. So what is it you would like to say?'

'We have a comfortable residence on St James' Crescent. Mrs Jenkins has lived there for a number of years. We live quietly, in what we have always believed is a respectable area. However, I must report that during the early hours of this morning, an intruder entered our garden and stole a tablecloth from the washing line.' She was controlled and measured.

Inspector Bucke sighed. 'I am very sorry to hear of this. I shall ask Sergeant Flynn to begin an immediate investigation. Now if you will excuse me...'

She looked Bucke firmly in the eye, exasperated perhaps by his failure to understand the implications of what she was saying. 'I am not here to waste your time, Inspector Bucke. I saw the thief take the tablecloth very clearly. It was one of your constables.'

Bucke leaned back in his chair, putting his hands briefly over his eyes. 'Please go on, Miss Roberts.'

'It was two o'clock this morning, Inspector. I was in the kitchen, which is at the back of the house. I looked out into the garden and saw a man removing the tablecloth from the washing line. I did not light the lamp in the kitchen for fear of attracting attention to myself. I watched him take the tablecloth, roll it up and push it inside his coat. He was wearing a policeman's uniform and he was using a policeman's lamp. Then he left the garden through the gate which leads towards Belgrave Lane. I was shocked and frightened by the intrusion.' Elinor Roberts looked straight back at him, obviously aware of the difficulties she had brought to him. 'Mrs Jenkins is anxious that something is done immediately, Inspector.'

If she really had been frightened, she had certainly recovered her poise, thought Bucke. 'I am sure it must have been distressing. May I ask you, Miss Roberts, why you were looking into the garden at that time? Were you disturbed? Did a noise draw you from your sleep?'

'No, Inspector. I had risen from my bed to deal with Mrs Jenkins's needs. I looked out of the kitchen window and saw the man, as I have told you already.'

'You were required at such a time?' he asked.

'Yes, Inspector. I must always perform my duties as requested,' Elinor said patiently.

'And does Mrs Jenkins often call upon you at such a time, Miss Roberts?'

'There are occasions, Inspector, when my attentions are required. Such is my life as a domestic servant.' She shrugged her shoulders, as if she regarded the question as unnecessary.

'Did you open the door of the kitchen? To get a better view perhaps?'

'No. I did not consider it wise to confront an intruder committing a felony. As I have already told you, I had no wish to draw attention to myself. Mr Jenkins is overseas on business, and Mrs Jenkins and I were alone in the house. I believed it best to act as I have described. I had no wish to put either myself or my mistress in danger, Inspector.'

'I am sure it was the correct form of action, Miss Roberts. But it must have been dark in the garden. Could you see clearly? And you are sure it was a constable?' He realised he was clutching at straws, seeking out a mistake which he knew in his heart was not there.

She sighed. 'Of course. He was carrying a police lantern and it shone on his uniform. I know it was a constable. I would not be here if it were otherwise, Inspector Bucke. If it had been a pedlar or an urchin, then I should have attended our local police station, which would have been more convenient.'

'Did you discern any distinguishing features that may help me identity this man?' asked Bucke.

'No, Inspector.' She sighed once more, exasperated by his questions. 'I would have thought that his uniform would have been suitably distinctive. I saw nothing of his face. Mrs Jenkins is of the opinion that it is your duty to identify who the culprit might be. She expects an imminent arrest, so that we may sleep more securely.' She stared straight at him, her face expressionless.

'Of course, Miss Roberts, but I must gather whatever information I can to help us with our work. Can you tell me the nature of the missing tablecloth, Miss Roberts, so that I can identify it, should we find it?'

She nodded. 'It is white damask. I believe that it has Mrs Jenkins's initials worked into the design in the corner. *VJ* – Virginia Jenkins. I do not read, Inspector, but that is what I am told. This alone should make it sufficiently distinctive.'

Bucke thanked her and promised to report his findings once his investigation was complete. He asked Sergeant Flynn to escort her to the door.

He knew immediately, of course. It had to be Sprague. Who else could it be? Bucke was aware that he had asked Sergeant Flynn if he could exchange beats for the evening with Constable Plumley, who normally included the Uplands in his patrol. He made the request, he said, as an aid to his recovery following the unpleasantness of the body in the toilet. Bucke was irritated, feeling tricked, knowing that Sprague had manipulated the circumstances for his own ends, to get his own way in defiance of his inspector's comments in their meeting. The habitually morose Plumley had been reluctant apparently, but in the circumstances, Sergeant Flynn had agreed. And now this. Bucke left his desk and went to the front of the police station where Flynn was on the street, watching as Elinor Roberts walked away down the High Street, stepping carefully around a smouldering pile of ashes at the end of Ebenezer Street.

'Good-looking young woman, Inspector. And a very proper way of speaking if I may say,' said Sergeant Flynn.

'Indeed, Sergeant,' said Bucke. 'She told you why she was here, I presume?'

'I am afraid so, sir. Said that she had come to report a theft by a man in a policeman's uniform. Unpleasant business, sir, but we have a duty to perform. I am sure we know who it is. I don't wish to speak out of place, Inspector, but I have to say that something like this was bound to happen. In my view, the young man is not suited to employment in the police force. We should be thankful that it is only a theft that he has committed.'

'I know, Sergeant. But there are occasions when my duties sadden me. If Sprague has done it, and we both suspect that he has, then he will go to gaol. And that is never a happy place for an ex-police constable to find himself. But we have no choice.'

It was one of the easiest investigations they had ever had to carry out. When Sprague came on duty, Sergeant Flynn went to his lodgings. He had a room in the Section House on Caer Street where the single policemen lodged, and Flynn found the tablecloth after a brief search, hidden unimaginatively between the sacking which acted as a mattress and the unstable bed frame beneath.

Inspector Bucke waited for Sprague in his office and confronted him when he called in between his circuits. It was not a surprise that his version of events was different in some important respects from that reported by Elinor Roberts, but that made little difference now that there was the incontrovertible evidence of a white damask tablecloth, with the initials *VJ* embroidered in a corner, hidden within his bed. Sprague tried his best because of course his future depended on it, but his position was desperate. He had heard a noise, he said, as he walked along Belgrave Lane. So he looked surreptitiously over the wall into the Jenkins' garden and saw the kitchen door open.

'I saw a man come out, sir. He walked out into the garden and then into Belgrave Lane. A distinguished-looking man, if I might say. God's honest truth, sir. May the Lord strike me dead here and now if I am lying.'

Bucke raised his eyebrows and looked directly into his eyes. He could sense the constable's discomfort. 'Did you recognise him, Constable Sprague, this distinguished-looking man?'

'No, sir. It was dark. But he was a large gentleman, sir. Fat, you might say. There was a light on in the house so that is how I saw him when the door opened.' He now spoke to the wall above Bucke's head. 'It has always been my belief that people should not be parading through the streets in the night. It is an indication of disorder. So I tried to follow him secretly, but he disappeared in the dark when I tripped and fell into a hedge. I can show you the graze here on my neck which I sustained when I fell. It might be that the noise startled the fellow and allowed him to make good his escape. As a result of that, I returned to the garden to observe whether it was the scene of any further villainy and saw the tablecloth on the washing line, so I took it for safe keeping. If there was one man walking the streets in a respectable area, there may be others. I was doing my duty, sir.' He seemed to Bucke to be a man surprised and impressed by the power of his own invention, but the clock ticking loudly at the front of the police station was counting out the final seconds of a disintegrating career.

'I see, Constable Sprague. But if that was your intention to secure the item, which indeed should have been your duty, then I am forced to ask why you didn't return it this morning,' he asked.

Sprague continued to avoid eye contact whilst his pock-marked face twisted with the effort of invention. 'I forgot, sir. It had been my intention to hand it in at the station. The considerable demands of the duties I must perform every day sometimes make me forgetful. There is so much that I must remember.' He was so impressed, once again, by this unexpected idea which had leapt into his head and apparently offered a possible escape from his predicament, that a nervous, momentary smile touched his face.

Bucke leaned across the desk and rested his chin on his intertwined fingers. 'Constable Sprague, if that is the case then I do not understand why Sergeant Flynn found the tablecloth bunched up beneath the sacking on your bed. You must agree, as a serving police constable, that this places you in a difficult circumstance.' Bucke paused. 'You must agree that it looks very suspicious.'

'I didn't want anyone to steal it, sir. I live amongst dishonest men...' said Sprague, his words tailing off as he saw the edifice of lies he had tried to sustain falling in pieces. His eyes flicked around the room. 'Inspector, please! I am a single man living in the Section House. What use is a tablecloth to me? Why would I steal such a thing? It is useless to me.' He saw Bucke shake his head. 'You have to understand, Inspector,' he added desperately, 'that if it was in another part of town you might think otherwise of that house on St James' Crescent, sir.'

Inspector Bucke drew himself up in his seat. 'It doesn't matter where in the town a house is situated, Constable Sprague. Theft is a crime and it should be dealt with in the same way, in east Swansea or in the west of the town, no matter whether the item is large or small. You have taken a tablecloth belonging to Mrs Jenkins of St James' Crescent and I have no alternative but to arrest you for it. A felony committed by a man charged with upholding the law is a very serious crime. You will be required to appear before the magistrate as soon as possible. Sergeant Flynn, please escort Constable Sprague to the cells.'

Bucke sat back in his chair and rubbed his eyes with the heels of his hands. Everything – the crime, the culprit, the excuses, the law—all of it, at that moment, was unutterably pointless.

Chapter Five

They stood in the shadows in a passageway on Cwm Road, close to the bridge. It was a dark and unsavoury corner. They could smell the scum-laced, slimy river nearby, slipping away in its rank oiliness on the ebbing tide towards the sea.

'Because you were so impetuous, our plans we have had to change. Now we have this complication that you have created. Now the police are looking for you very much, I think. They are working hard to find you. It is because of you that the police are searching the streets of Hafod. This is not my doing. Please remember this, Daniel.'

Daniel Guy grunted and shrugged.

'It was easy. It was my job to make it so. You came back and a man of Swansea you became again, that is what we said. You were given a job. In the copper works. You are found that job to make you safe, but you don't go to work. You do not like the job, you say. Then you shoot your wife. So now we must change our plan. So we will hide you for a few weeks, I think. But you must not try again to kill your wife. I am very clear about this and I hope that you understand.'

'Damn her, the bitch. By rights she should be dead,' said

Daniel Guy from the shadows of the doorway. He had a dirty woollen muffler tied tightly around his neck against the damp, a cap pulled firmly on down to his ears and a dirty, old coat which smelt of neglect.

Pieter Moitch was extremely irritated. The job was a difficult one but their plan should have worked. As was so often the case, however, it had been undermined by human frailty. He wasn't surprised that Daniel Guy had let him down, even if the arrangements were simple. All he had been required to do was to go to work quietly in the copper works and not draw attention to himself. It would have been the perfect cover for their task. But Guy was dishonest and dishonourable. Moitch could only ever rely upon his unreliability.

'If you are in difficulties with the changes we now have to make, then you must need to think about what you have done. It is your fault entirely. Let me be quite certain of this, Daniel. You should have been working quietly. This is what we said. But you would not go to work. So you tried to kill your wife. So you let everyone know you had a gun. So you have the police looking for you. And this is my fault? I think you are very wrong, Daniel. This is very absurd. So now we must have a different plan.'

Daniel looked at him carefully. He had been a good friend on the docks in New York. They had worked together, drank together, and then Moitch had come up with this scheme. Some people he knew wanted a job doing, back in his old town. What a happy coincidence. It was possibly a dangerous job, but he would be well paid, especially well paid. But once he had agreed to the deal, he had changed. Less of a friend, more of a master. He wasn't sure he cared for that, and he didn't really know what to make of Moitch, but then no one did.

Who could be sure what or who he was? He could have been Russian. Or German. Someone in New York had said he was

Polish. Someone else Latvian, whatever that was. He could have been none of those. Or all of them. But he was undoubtedly a man of whom it was sensible to be wary.

Pieter Moitch had the gift of looking anonymous, an important attribute in his work. He looked in some ways like just other seamen, though he was clean-shaven and generally presentable. He was short and stocky, with a bearing which suggested controlled strength. He was always dressed in dark trousers and a dark jacket, buttoned up to his chin. He wore a dark sailor's cap pulled low to shade those quick eyes that were always alert, always attentive to every small detail. He was a man made for the shadows, with a face that knew other people's secrets, which he held as tightly as his own. He worked for an unacknowledged bureau, within a barely acknowledged ministry, within the German Government; and he was a murderer, one with an instinctive understanding of the skeleton, which allowed him to guide his blade untroubled through the frame to the vital treasures within.

'I am telling you now, Pieter. I will not rest until the bitch is dead. I have to finish what I have started.'

'No. It is more important that you understand. Your rage I appreciate, but it might have been better if you had not tried to kill her at all. Not now. We did not give you the gun so that you could to yourself draw attention. This was an error. But be sure it can be corrected, Daniel. We must move you to a new location, I think. Martin Willrath is a reliable man and you can be sure he will have said nothing to anyone. He and Eva have been looking after you very properly. I am sure that you will agree. But about you the police have been asking questions in the copper manufactories. So for you it would be better to move away and, I think also, for Martin Willrath and Eva. But we have a good place for you now, for a short time. But you must stay hidden, on this I insist. This you must do but we believe not for much longer and then you will be paid and you can do as you wish.' Moitch moved his face closer to Daniel's and whispered, 'But remember. For your wife you must save your last bullets if that is your wish. It was a mistake to use your first.'

Daniel, knowing he had been wrong, tried to make light of it. 'I had to practise shooting the gun, Pieter, didn't I? I need to know what it feels like.'

'I must hope that when it is the right time you will be more efficient.' He paused and then added, 'In New York you told me you could shoot.'

'Don't you worry, Pieter. I will get closer next time.'

'Be sure that this is what you do.' Moitch suddenly grabbed hold of Guy and pushed him further back into the shadows and placed a strong hand over his mouth. A policeman walked past the entrance to the passageway, swinging his lantern and whistling softly. Moitch stretched down his other hand and withdrew a long knife from his boot. He was tense and poised, but the constable hadn't seen them and continued with his measured walk along the dark street. Moitch and Guy watched him gradually disappear into the dark.

'I shall need some money, Pieter,' Guy said.

'I am not sure that this is so. All your needs will be taken care of, truly. The professor is expecting you and has made provision for your needs. It will only be a short time that you will be staying with him. We will then be finding you somewhere else.'

'I will still need some money. A man must live.'

'You are not to be drunk, please, Daniel. Of this we have spoken. About this I have been very clear, I think.'

'For Christ's sake, I am not a bloody monk!' Guy hissed.

'I remind you again. Of this we have spoken before. You will do your duty and then you will be rewarded.'

'I need some money now.' He paused. 'Or I won't be doing your bidding.'

There was a long pause and Moitch looked at him steadily. He bent down and returned the knife to his boot. 'This, my friend, is a dangerous thing for you to say. You have two courses of action only. One is that you must stay in hiding until the time is right. If this is difficult for you, then it is because of what you have done. The other alternative is not one which you would wish to consider, I think. There is no way out for you. Our people are very unforgiving.'

Guy was distinctly uncomfortable. He could sense the power of the threat. He knew that this was no bluff. He was trapped. 'Look, I am sorry, Pieter. The police are looking for me. I am not sure what to do.'

Moitch smiled. 'There will be no money. Your side of the bargain you must complete, please. It is then that you will receive what we agreed. This you knew. This does not change. But you will be comfortable, I think. The professor is expecting your arrival. He is a man of many books. You will have plenty to read. He is expecting us.'

'I cannot read, Pieter.'

Moitch shrugged. 'Perhaps now is the time to learn, I am thinking.'

As they began to walk away, Moitch laid a hand on Guy's forearm. 'Please, Daniel. It is important that you do not underestimate the professor, I am thinking. He is an important man for us, but he is also a very strong man. You would be impressed by his power. He is a well-trained man. He is today a teacher of languages and there will be many visitors. But you will not enjoy if you are provoking him. You understand, I think. You have met him already, after all.'

Guy nodded. He would get money somehow. Willrath and his wife had watched him constantly throughout the few days he had been with them in their house in Hafod. Perhaps the professor would be less attentive. He hadn't liked him when they had met. He seemed cold and disapproving. Clever too, not easily deceived. The idea of being imprisoned in his rooms was just too much to bear.

Chapter Six

Bucke considered the house carefully before he approached the door. It represented a way of life entirely different from his own and one to which he knew he could never hope to aspire. He knew too that it was his responsibility to offer the same protection to those who lived here as he did to those who, in his mind, most needed it.

6 St James' Crescent was large and comfortable, the sort of house that agents described as a "very desirable family residence", with fine views towards the church. There must have been at least six bedrooms, as well as servants' accommodation. There was an attractive front gable and tall elegant windows on the two upper floors. He walked up the steps and stood beneath the porch, his attention drawn to the stained glass in the door and a shadow behind it. He sensed that there was someone waiting there. When he knocked on the door, it was immediately opened by Elinor Roberts, who nodded respectfully to Bucke and invited him inside.

At the foot of the wide staircase which led to an impressive landing, there was a large hatstand containing a number of walking sticks, including the cane with the dragon's head handle he had seen with Herbert Jenkins at the Royal Institution. There was also a table on which there was a large pile of unopened letters, and Bucke noted that the one on the top had the word "Urgent" written boldly beneath the address.

'Miss Roberts,' he began, but she did not allow him to continue.

'I presume you are here to see Mrs Jenkins. I believe you may attend her in the drawing room, Inspector. Please follow me.' She led him across the hall. To the left, Bucke noticed the open door to the library, though it was dominated by a large billiards table.

'Inspector Bucke, Madam,' she announced as she opened the door to the lounge.

'Thank you, Elinor. You may attend to matters elsewhere.'

'Of course, Madam.' She offered an almost imperceptible curtsey and closed the door.

Mrs Jenkins was sitting in an armchair close to the fireplace, a small fire glowing within its brown marble surround. A small dog was asleep on a rug in front of it. There was a table by her side on which rested an embroidery hoop and a basket of threads. She nodded to him, 'Please sit down, Inspector.'

Bucke was immediately aware that the contrast between Mrs Jenkins and her husband could not have been any greater. He was much older than her, coarser and clearly much less sophisticated. Her dark red dress was tight-fitting, hinting at the generous body constrained beneath, with a high neckline and sleeves trimmed with white lace. The opulent mass of her dark hair was dressed in thick curls. Her skin was white and her face, clear and open. She was a beautiful and self-assured woman, of that Bucke had no doubt. And yet he sensed a coldness about her; and in her eyes, he identified an intelligence which calculated the effect of everything she said or heard.

The room was crowded with furniture, and, where the walls were visible, Bucke could see that it was fashionably decorated with dark green wallpaper in an elaborate and intricate leaf design. There was a series of paintings hanging from the dado rail, showing apparently semi-naked Polynesians reclining amongst lush vegetation.

'I see you admire our wallpaper, Inspector. It is a most contemporary design. I ordered it from Paris,' she said with pride.

'Indeed, Mrs Jenkins. It is most striking. The paintings too demand the closest attention.'

'Alas, they are merely prints, Inspector, but impressive nonetheless. *The Savages of the Pacific Islands.* They were recommended to me by a gentleman in London.'

When he studied the prints with closer attention, he saw a fine display of nakedness, in which the young men were allowed a greater degree of privacy than their sisters, who were painted relaxing by springs and waterfalls, combing and arranging their hair, with their modesty only occasionally preserved by unfeasibly large leaves and fronds which dappled the sunlight and cast strategic shadows. Bucke was not at all sure what to say about them. 'Very artistic, Mrs Jenkins,' was the best he could manage.

It was, however, sufficient.

'Indeed, Inspector Bucke.' She sighed. 'They are images of another world far, far away. A world without conventions or obligations. Images of the Garden of Eden, of a time without sin or guilt. Who would not wish themselves there?'

'Perhaps the reality is somewhat different, Mrs Jenkins. Perhaps these young people who look so carefree might even prefer to live their lives amongst the filthy smoke of the east side of Swansea, rather than in the South Seas.'

'And perhaps it was ever so. But, Inspector, I thank you for coming this morning. I must assume you have come here because you have news.'

Bucke delivered to her the results of his investigation. A police officer arrested for stealing was sure to feature in the *Cambrian* newspaper, and her social standing, as well as his own sense of responsibility, demanded that she should be told first. He told her how Sprague had admitted to taking the tablecloth, probably with the intention of selling it, and since the tablecloth had been recovered, he was in a position to report that his questioning of Constable Sprague had been concluded. Now it was a matter for the courts.

Mrs Jenkins was relieved. 'I must confess that Elinor and I were most alarmed by the occurrence. It is worrying to think that even in the respectable part of town, there are thieves peering into the gardens of prominent citizens such as ourselves. Is the tablecloth to be returned, Inspector?'

'Eventually, Mrs Jenkins, but for the moment we will require it as evidence,' replied Bucke.

'It is of little consequence, Inspector. We have others that we can employ.'

'There is something else that I must ask you, Mrs Jenkins, something about which I need clarification.'

Mrs Jenkins looked at him sceptically. 'Indeed? How may I help you?'

'The constable who took the tablecloth said that he saw a light from your kitchen, which showed a prosperous-looking man leaving the house and using the garden gate into the lane. He tried to follow him. I need to be sure that this is not the case, that you have not been the victim of a more serious intrusion.'

She sighed. 'Elinor tells me that you questioned her carefully yesterday and she has also told me what she said. She has told you there was no one else in the house that night, nor yesterday, nor indeed this morning. My husband is away in Germany on business. She has told you that she saw your constable from the darkened kitchen. The gas lamps were not lit at that late hour. My maid has complete integrity and I trust her implicitly.'

'You must understand my concern, Mrs Jenkins,' said Bucke patiently. 'I need to be reassured that there was not another man in your garden. You have already indicated that you might be vulnerable.'

'Inspector, there was no other man on my property. Only your wretched constable.' Mrs Jenkins was becoming exasperated. 'This constable of yours. Would you describe him as intelligent? Does he have an honest disposition? Ah, but of course, I have answered my own questions.' Mrs Jenkins looked at him with scorn. 'He is a thief. He stole a tablecloth. God only knows why, but that is what he did. Why then should you believe a word that he says? He steals. He tells lies. Is that not abundantly clear? Please tell me your reasons for accepting the word of a thief. I am curious to know how your mind works.'

Inspector Bucke was patient, methodical. 'Constable Sprague committed a crime, Mrs Jenkins, and for this he will be punished. His actions have shocked us all and they are a betrayal of all of us who work in the police force. But it does not mean that everything he said was a lie. He may have mentioned the idea of an intruder to present his actions in the best possible light. On the other hand, parts of his story could be true and others false. I cannot be sure. That is what I must ascertain.'

'I am impressed, Inspector, by your diligence.'

'Everyone should be granted that courtesy, Mrs Jenkins. Even those who do not deserve it. He has said that he saw the door open and a man leave. I have a duty to establish the truth.'

'Inspector, this is tiresome,' said Mrs Jenkins belligerently. 'He is lying. I was alone here in my house, together with my domestic servant Elinor Roberts. We have no male servants, Inspector. Therefore, there was no one else here, no man anywhere in the house. How could there be? And yet you seem ready to believe your constable who has, do not forget, already confirmed himself to be a thief and a liar. No man was here in this house and therefore, when he reported that he saw a man leaving, he is lying. Unless of course there are secret rooms beneath the house in which men, unknown to myself, live and come and go as they wish. Frankly, Inspector, this is ridiculous and insulting. You have a decision to make about whom you believe, Inspector Bucke. Many would be surprised if you should find it hard to do so.'

Inspector Bucke remained calm. 'I can only make a judgement, Mrs Jenkins, when I have established the truth. When does your husband return, Mrs Jenkins?'

Her tone softened slightly. 'My husband is in Hamburg, Inspector, attending to his business interests in that city. I believe that he is due to return on Friday. I will be alone in this house until then; in the company of my maid who is always available should I require her. Apart from Thursday afternoon, of course, when she has business elsewhere.' She looked directly at Bucke and then raised her hand to her collar and unfastened the top two buttons at the neck of her dress. 'You should understand that my husband has his business, which is of no interest to me. I concern myself with my own affairs.' She paused, long enough to make Bucke feel uncomfortable, then added, 'Inspector Bucke,' smiling but without warmth or pleasure.

The dog stretched out in the hearth, stood up briefly and shook its head so that saliva fell into the fire and hissed, before it resumed its sleep. Mrs Jenkins raised her eyebrows briefly.

Bucke knew that she was trying to unsettle him, perhaps even to intimidate him. What possible reason could she have for doing so? he wondered. Perhaps she enjoyed flirtatious behaviour as well as embroidery. Or perhaps, more worryingly, she had somehow recognised his own vulnerability. There were no other witnesses to this conversation, and he knew precisely what sort of witness Elinor Roberts might prove to be. Whatever Mrs Jenkins might be doing, he found her behaviour unusual and puzzling. She was playing a game and he was not sure what it was. Why was she trying to make him uncomfortable? Did she really have something to hide? What was she trying to stop him finding out? That was, almost, interesting, he thought with surprise.

He knew that since Julia's death he had not been comfortable in the presence of women, but then he found the company of most people, male or female, particularly unwelcome. He recognised that a world-weary cynicism for the motives of others had settled over him, but he saw no possible release from it. Consumed by his exhausting unhappiness, he could see no light in the darkness, no selfless giving, no solace, no love. All he could see in Mrs Jenkins was self-interest and the instinctive necessity to survive. He returned her gaze just long enough for her to know that she was wasting her time.

'I am sure, Mrs Jenkins, that during your husband's absence you will be completely safe, although you may wish to speak to him concerning your anxieties, should he venture abroad once more. Thank you for your time this afternoon, Mrs Jenkins. I am sure that you have much more interesting things with which to occupy yourself.'

She spread her hands, as if such a thing was not possible. 'And what will become of your constable, do you think, Inspector?'

'He will be sent for trial at the next quarter sessions. The court will not treat him with any sympathy. His crime draws into question the judgement of the chief constable who first appointed him. So he will go to gaol. If he is lucky, it may be three months with hard labour. I would anticipate that it will be more. There are other unfortunate issues on his service record.'

'So Swansea is not a more dangerous place without him then?'

'Far from it. There are those who might think that the efficiency of the police force will improve now he has gone.'

'Hmm. Then you should be grateful to us for what we have done in resolving such difficulties for you. Good afternoon, Inspector. Elinor will show you to the door. I shall ring for her.'

~

He did not immediately return to the police station. Instead, he went on to Belgrave Lane and looked at the back of the house. It was as Sprague had described it. There was a narrow, uneven path with bushes into which he could certainly have stumbled and a gate into the garden opposite the back door, which presumably opened into the kitchen. And, as if deliberately done to complete the reconstruction, another tablecloth was fluttering on the propped-up clothes line, in defiance of the occasional showers which pushed in from the bay. As he turned to leave, Bucke saw the kitchen door open and Elinor Roberts go to the clothes line to unpeg the tablecloth.

It was something which continued to puzzle him as he walked slowly down the gentle slope of Walter's Road, through the impressive prosperity of its substantial buildings, back towards the town centre. He knew that he should feel relieved. The case involving Sprague and the tablecloth he could now dismiss from his mind and return with vigour to the search for Daniel Guy. Yet there was something which troubled him about his meeting with Mrs Jenkins. He didn't think that either Virginia Jenkins or Elinor Roberts had been completely honest with him. Perhaps the simplest explanation for her secrecy was that Mrs Jenkins had been involved in a liaison with another man and wanted to keep it hidden. If that was the case, then it need not trouble him. But he could dismiss neither the house nor the women within it from his mind. Something wasn't right there, but perhaps you could say that about any of the houses he walked past. He was sure that they all contained secrets of one kind or another. All houses were deep wells of hidden frustration and sorrow.

His priority had to be the Guy case. The first thing he needed to do was to check the shipping registers himself. He had sent Constable Lewis to look at them in the harbourmaster's office, but he never regarded him as being particularly diligent and it was quite likely that he would miss something. He thought it probable that Guy had left the town almost immediately and a ship would be the simplest route. It might have taken him to Europe or merely to the West Country or the north of England. Some destinations would be easier to deal with than others. And then unexpectedly he found himself at the top of Henrietta Street.

He realised that he hadn't been back here since he moved out of the house after Julia's death. He stood looking down the long rows of neat terraced houses which lined both sides of the street, leading down to St Helen's Road. Such memories he had here. He remembered sitting at the bedroom window with Anna, who giggled helplessly at three cows and a number of sheep rampaging through the small front gardens, which had escaped when been driven to the market. A cow had wandered through Mrs Evans's open front door and appeared in her kitchen as she stood at the sink, washing carrots in a bucket. For weeks afterwards, Charles was forever trying to open the door in the hope that he could have a cow too. He remembered when Sanger's Circus had come to town and paraded along St Helen's Road. Charles had been awestruck by the camels that slobbered casually and deposited copious amounts of manure in the road with haughty distain. It was, without doubt, the funniest thing Charles had ever seen. There was then a lot of explaining to do when their neighbour Mr Jones, a keen gardener, collected the waste with shovel and bucket. More explaining was then urgently required to prevent Charles scurrying next door to help Mr Jones with the fertility of his soil whenever the need was upon him. He smiled wistfully. Anna and Charles had loved animals. He liked to take them down to the tram depot on St Helen's Road. He would lift them up, one at a time, so that they could stroke the necks of the horses and sometimes feed them apples.

Bucke gazed sightlessly along the street, lost in memories of a happy family, full of hope and expectation, travelling together into a bright, shining future, building their own history. It was impossible to believe that those beautiful, unique children were not there anymore.

'Good afternoon, Inspector. It is good to see you here again. Are you well?'

He turned round, startled. It was Martha Price, a neighbour and close friend of Julia. 'I believe so, Martha. It is very good to see you again. Please excuse my distraction; I was thinking of the old times.'

'And why not? They were good times,' she replied. She was carrying a basket of groceries from the shop on Humphrey Street and he took it from her as he walked her home. He asked after her daughter. Alice was now in service at the Tenby Hotel on Walter's Road, where Bucke and Martha's husband, John, a hospital porter, would sometimes drink together in happier times. Sadly, John was quite reclusive now. Their son Henry had been knocked down by a horse and cart when he was nine years old at the junction with St Helen's Road. Julia, hearing the commotion, had been one of the first on the scene and had cradled Henry as he died, his blood flowing on to the road from an ugly wound in his groin. Henry had run into a horse and, tangled in its legs, had fallen beneath an iron wheel that had passed over him. A foolish accident – and it had happened so quickly. He was a boy just being a boy, running carelessly across the road. Nothing more than a simple miscalculation, but there had been a deadly price to pay. John had taken it very badly.

'You must come back some time, Rumsey. John would be very pleased to see you. Perhaps you might like to go with him to the Tenby Hotel as you used to. He does not get out as much as he should.' There was a plea in her eyes.

He said that he would do so, knowing that he would not, and Martha was ready to accept the politeness. He returned the basket to her, bid her good afternoon and walked to the end of the road, as he had done so many times before. It was then he realised that, whilst speaking to Martha, he had walked past his old house without noticing. He was not sure whether he should be guilty or relieved.

Bucke was very close to Little Gam Street so he thought he would visit Mary Guy to see how she was and to see if she had any information to add to the little he had already learned. He doubted whether she had, but he had nothing to lose. As he turned the corner into the untidy street, he was seen almost immediately by Mrs Gallivan, who quickly took hold of a wheelbarrow and pushed it with practised skill through the narrow opening of her house and closed the door. Mary Guy was sitting on a chair in her own doorway, presumably to catch the daylight as she worked carefully to repair a tear in a shirt. By her side there was a basket, full of clear glass wine bottles, which looked as if they had been recently washed. She looked up from her work as he approached.

'Have you caught the bastard yet, Inspector?'

'Not yet, Mary. We are still looking. Have you heard anything of him?'

'If I had, you would have been the first to know, you may be sure of that.'

'Can you think of anywhere he might be hiding, Mary? It is really important.'

'Well, if he isn't with that cow Annie Taylor, then I have no idea. He ran away once before, so he's done it again by the looks of it. If he is on a ship, I hopes he falls off and drowns.' She spat copiously on the street, but the effort made her cough and she held on to the wound on the right side of her shoulder, grimacing with pain.

Bucke helped her back inside the house and then brought the chair in for her. It had been almost a fortnight since she had been shot. He saw how pale her face was and how any sudden movement still caused her to gasp out loud, but she had had no alternative other than to resume her work; he understood that. How else was she to live?

'People have been very good, sir. Sammy Grove at the Builder's Arms has let me have this chair to sit on, and the neighbours keep bringing me bits of work for me to do with my needle, but I am very slow on account of my shoulder not working properly, but they say it will get better in time.' She tried to make herself more comfortable and screwed her face in discomfort at the effort. 'Mrs Gallivan brings me a bite to eat of an evening, and I am washing bottles for her to earn a few pennies, but I can't get about much. I will get better, Inspector, I know that, but not fast enough when a body's got to eat. But I do worry about Daniel coming back. I shall sleep better once I know you have got him. I keep thinking he is going to be coming through the door. Once my brother John is home, we lock the door and put a chair under the handle.'

When Inspector Bucke left the house and turned the corner of Little Gam Street, he walked straight into John Phillips, Mary's brother. He noted immediately how uncomfortable Phillips was with this unexpected encounter, his eyes casting nervously about, thought Bucke, as if searching for additional constables hiding with handcuffs in the shadows. As he was about to wish him a good evening, Phillips suddenly blurted out, 'What's she done? Is she in trouble, Inspector?'

Bucke reassured him, of course, telling Phillips that it was merely a call to enquire after her health, but he was surprised by the nature of the question, in the circumstances of her recent wounding. He seemed apprehensive, and Bucke was sure that he had something to hide. Phillips blundered on, saying very little of any consequence, until Bucke decided to put him out of his misery by ending the conversation and bidding him a good evening. Phillips nodded nervously and hurried the short distance home, closing the door firmly behind him.

Bucke speculated idly as he watched him go. Who would he have rather seen? Daniel Guy or a police officer? At that moment, he was sure that Phillips would have much preferred to have bumped into his brother-in-law.

Chapter Seven

There was much civic excitement at the laying of the central stone of the new East Docks. Its construction would surely act as a significant boost to trade and profit and so there were ceremonies and celebrations right across the town. However, Bucke's immediate concerns about the new dock were different. Itinerant workers brought in for projects like this formed part of a deep reservoir of lawlessness, convinced that they could easily escape the consequences of their actions by moving on – and they frequently did. The problems had started already.

Patrick Rourke, an Irish navvy, had assaulted Constable Lewis on the High Street, after he had been accused of being drunk and disorderly.

'Gave him a proper backhander across the face, sir. Shocking it was, I can tell you,' reported Constable Ball, who had responded to the call for assistance.

'Did any words pass between them?' asked Bucke.

'Not that I heard, Inspector. But it took the two of us to get him back to the station and there were plenty of words said then. I had my handcuffs so I used 'em. Sergeant Flynn put him in the cells.'

Bucke went down to speak to Rourke. Assaults on the constables disturbed him. There seemed to be more of them in recent months and he was alarmed by how much harder it was to police the streets of Swansea. Second-rate and dishonest police officers were a particular problem, but, of course, unsolved crimes did not help either. He could not be surprised that many held the force in contempt, as a result of their generally accepted incompetence.

Rourke was still belligerent, though he calmed down slightly when Bucke arranged for the removal of the handcuffs. He hadn't been drunk, he said. It was impossible. He only had ten shillings, and in the afternoon he had spent 7s 6d on a new pair of boots. Then he had gone to the Duke of Wellington on St Mary's Street, and his remaining money was hardly enough with which to get drunk. The problems on the High Street had started when Constable Lewis had called him a "stinking Paddy" and he had lost his temper.

Bucke believed him. Lewis had done this sort of thing before, and half a crown was certainly not sufficient to get drunk, especially in the Duke of Wellington, where the landlord's prices were higher than elsewhere. The landlord had his own problems, though. Bucke had identified his nine-year-old son, Herbert, as Swansea's own pocket crime wave. Yesterday, he had been caught thieving again, his eighth arrest so far in 1880. This time he had taken nine shillings from the till of Mr Trew, the grocer and biscuit maker in Nelson Street. Bucke noted that it was only a little less than the navvy Rourke originally had in his pocket. The Irishman was on his way to court, and he would need more than that if he hoped to pay a fine rather than go to gaol.

He continued to find these day-to-day responsibilities irritating, however important they were in themselves, since they took him away from his other investigations. He went to the harbourmaster's office and endured a long afternoon of frustration; their meeting interrupted by sailors who sang interminable, obscene songs as they prepared to cast off from the dock and then loudly traded insults with an Italian vessel waiting to take their place. Ernest Leyshon, the superintendent, was organised and authoritative. No potential stowaways had been spotted last week. There was the inevitable petty theft, a daily occurrence all around the docks, but nothing significant. All the ships' complements had been correct, with no late additions made. There had been no desertions from any of the ships. It had been a quiet week. Of course, it didn't mean there hadn't been stowaways – being a stowaway meant you did your best to remain hidden for as long as you could – and the high tide had been just before dawn, which would have helped Guy. But the departing ships on the night of the attempted murder had been heading for Fowey in Cornwall and Newcastle, places from which Guy could be easily returned, if he could be found. Bucke tried to simplify it in his mind. Guy was either in Swansea or he wasn't. And if he was asked to say which one was most likely, then he would have to say that he was somewhere in the town. The harder question was where that could be.

He walked around in the acrid smoke belching from the dirty funnel of a trawler, lost in such thoughts, until he found himself at the wharves along the river. He stood by the mooring posts, looking across at the black mass of Kilvey Hill, where the streets of terraced houses edged a little further up its slopes every year. All those houses, all those rooms. Guy could be hidden in any of them. Bucke knew that at the moment, the search for Guy was going nowhere. He was reliant upon someone coming forward to say that they had seen him or that they knew where he was – a nosy neighbour perhaps, or a chance encounter. Until then, he wasn't sure what he could do or indeed where to begin.

He wandered rather aimlessly back into the town, planning to get a slice of ham and some bread for his supper but instead, inspired by the warmly appealing smell, buying a baked potato from Dai Potato who had placed his cart and oven at the bottom of Wind Street . He ate it from a newspaper and watched the trains in Victoria Station.

It was early evening by the time he reached Salubrious Place, the narrow and usually congested alley which would take him home to Fisher Street, when he heard a loud and familiar voice calling to him.

'Oi! Rum! Inspector! It is me!' It was Punch, falling out of the door of the Shades public house.

'Well good evening, Punch. You are out of gaol, I see.'

'Oh yes, and there is one of them Italian boats fresh in, so Punch has got money. Poor buggers have been at sea for more than two weeks an' won't leave a girl alone. It's going to be a good night!' Fuelled by gin, she hugged him enthusiastically, despite his polite resistance. 'Anyways, I was wonderin' if you were getting over your troubles, Rum. Chin up. We don't want to lose ya. The only decent one we got. The rest is bastards. They say you got rid of the poxy one. Good work.'

He extricated himself from her grasp. 'It takes a while to recover, Punch, when you have lost those dearest to you, but thank you for your concern. Promise me you will be careful tonight. Don't get yourself into trouble. You need to stay out of the court or you will find yourself marooned in Swansea Gaol like Robinson Crusoe.'

'Very funny, Rum. But don't you worry about me. I can look after maself. It is you us girls are worried about. You is the one what needs lookin' after, Rum. Need to find yaself a nice decent girl. Not like me a'course! I mean, I can do ya decent if you wants. But not for long!' She laughed; her eyes bright with freedom.

'Thank you for your advice. But please listen to mine – and carefully too. Don't drink too much and don't start any fights. Because if you do, you will be arrested. You know that.'

Who? Me? You is talking to the wrong girl, Rum. Changed character, me. Tell you what, though, that name of yours. Must be good to be named after a drink. Next time I am up in front of the judge, I'll ask him to change me name to Gin. Yeah. That's what'll do, boy. Virginia, see? A good name for a posh tart!' She laughed again, though this time less raucously, as she briefly considered the chaos that always surrounded her.

'Do ya know what? Praps we should get together, Inspector. I wouldn't buy you no earrings for a wedding present, though!' She laughed loudly at the thought. 'But just think about it. Together we could be Rum Punch.' She laughed once again. 'I know your sort, though. I suppose you'd want to call me Catherine and go all la-di-dah. Posh buggers like you always do.'

'Never,' smiled Bucke. 'You will always be Punch to me.'

'Don't be soft. See you around, Rum. It has been a week now since the bastards put me inside. Need to make sure my new name will suit me.' She turned towards Wind Street and bounced off into the evening, waving to him with the back of her hand as she walked away.

He never saw Punch alive again.

When she emerged from the Adelphi at around about midnight, all those things at the edge of her vision were a bit fuzzy, though she did know where she was and would be able, if she paid sufficiently close attention, to make her way home. The last week in prison had been hard. No matter how often they locked her up, she never got used to it. But tonight had been a good night. It almost made it all worthwhile. There had been some business which thankfully she could only barely remember and then plenty of drinking and laughter. Now it was time to go home. Her rented room was dingy and squalid but it was all she had – and indeed was all she was ever likely to have. She walked slowly down the slippery cobbles of Green Dragon Street, putting her hands against the walls occasionally to steady herself and stepping with exaggerated care over the prostrate figure of an unconscious drunk. When she reached the bottom, she turned right and saw the shadowy figures of two men in front of her. The taller one walked briskly past Punch and turned up Green Dragon Street. She immediately recognised the shorter one who had remained behind.

'Ohmigod! What are you dewin' down by yere? Ain't seen you in weeks. Tell you what. If you is looking for some assistance, I'm sure I can oblige. I can remember what to do.' She swayed backwards, wiping her sleeve across her mouth in an attempt to clean it. Suddenly she stopped, finally processing the details of what she had just seen. 'Hang on! I remember! That's Dan Guy, ain't it? The one that's just gone? Bloody hell! He used to be sweet on ma sister!'

∾

In the early hours of the morning, Constable Davies found Punch sprawled out in a doorway at the bottom of Green Dragon Street. She had been murdered.

∾

Punch was lying flat on her back, her hands clenched into claws on either side of her head. Her shabby, tattered clothes were like rags, soaked with the blood which had seeped from a single stab wound to a heart expertly pierced. Her eyes, wide open, still held that final look of surprise. The smell of stale gin hung over her like a poisoned mist over the river.

Dr Beynon knelt by her side. 'Given her profession, Rumsey, I would be unable to say whether or not she had suffered an outrage. But I think we must assume that she was working last night. And a death such as this is a hazard of her occupation. If you put yourself in these circumstances often enough, then one day something like this is likely to happen.'

'She had been working. There is no doubt about that. And she was stabbed only once, David?' Bucke asked.

'Yes, she was transfixed. The blade emerged to the right of her spine. I would suggest that he was right-handed, but that matters little in these circumstances. It was either a highly trained assassin who knew exactly what he was doing and slipped the blade expertly between her ribs, or he got lucky. I know which version I favour, Rumsey. It was nothing more than the final act in a drunken transaction with a sailor. He is probably on a ship not thirty yards from here, with no memory at all of what he did last night or why his knife is bloodstained. Find him if you can.'

'You don't send an assassin to kill someone like Punch.' Bucke shook his head at the absurdity of the idea.

'You are the policeman, Rumsey, but there was nothing in the pockets of her skirt, other than a few small coins, all English. So I cannot imagine that robbery was a motive. If she had been working as you say, the money she'd earned she'd spent. You can smell how she spent it.'

'We will make a policeman of you yet, Doctor Beynon,' nodded Bucke.

'Heaven forbid that such a horror should be inflicted upon me.'

He looked down on her in the dim pool of light from Constable Davies's lantern. She seemed exactly what she was – small, malnourished; old before her time, in death a victim as she had been for most of her life. All the resilience and defiance which had defined her had gone. Now she was an unimportant bundle of grubby rags which once, oddly, had breath and hope. But now, the light which had shone briefly on Bucke last night had been snuffed out forever.

As dawn began to break, he watched a handful of dockers, diverted from their work so early on a Sunday morning and with pipes clenched between yellowed teeth, carry her body respectfully to a room across the road in the Pelican Inn for the inquest, the final station in Punch's personal Way of Sorrows which would end, appropriately at Easter, at an unmarked grave in St Mary's Graveyard , where Bucke would watch the vicar shake his head once again over a chaotic life without purpose and a death without reason. He knew he should attend, for who else would go? But he dreaded the prospect of another funeral and those recollections he would be unable to suppress.

News soon spread of her murder and her old friends gathered outside the pub to pay their respects to one of their own, dead on the Strand. She had now become a reminder of the dangers of the life choices they had all made. Everyone knew her, had examples of her unpredictability, had experienced her fists, her temper and her generosity. Inspector Bucke moved amongst them sensitively, asking questions, trying to piece together the last hours of a wasted existence.

The last confirmed sighting of Punch had been in the Globe Inn on the Strand, one of Swansea's most notorious public houses. Everyone had seen her there since she had made a typically expansive entrance, calling out 'Splice the main brace, Captain!' and receiving sustained applause in return. Her appearance in court had already achieved legendary status and the story was now certain to outlive her. That small ineffectual moment of defiance in the face of authority, would one day come to represent the unquenchable spirit of a whole generation of lost souls.

But it was crowded in the pub and no one could be sure who she had been with or when she had left. Generally, those who frequented the Globe Inn would never have spoken to the police. This was different, and Bucke urged them to remember the details of what, for them, had been a routine sort of evening, but he could learn little that was helpful.

However, Eliza Keast, one of her professional rivals, did tell Bucke something useful. Punch had asked her if a reward had been offered for information about Daniel Guy.

'Said she knew him, din't she? Said Daniel Guy and her sister had once been intimate. That's the word, innit? Anyway, said she could recognise him.'

'And do you know who her sister is, Eliza?' asked Bucke.

'Nah, she never said. Me? I din't know she had a sister.'

It might one day prove to be an important detail, though it was the sort of coincidence that was hardly surprising in a town as small as Swansea. Older or younger? He didn't know. Perhaps it was important. Perhaps not. But he added it to his list of unanswered questions. Who was Punch's sister, who had once had a relationship with the elusive Daniel Guy?

~

By midday, the Coroner had returned the only possible verdict – "Murder by a person or persons unknown", and then everyone was ready to move on.

He called on the Chief Constable to inform him of the murder, as was his duty, but he showed little interest. 'A sailor's done it. I know it. You probably won't find the bugger. Get on with summat else. It is not as if we've got a shortage of tarts, is it? You've got more important things to deal with, Bucke. Fact is, we are regarded as rubbish. A laughin' stock. Lots of questions bein' asked and I am runnin' out of answers. An attempted murder you can't solve and when we've gotta real murder, bugger gets away. Not good enough. Mayor were asking me the other day, when will there be an arrest? What can I say? To my mind, the job's too much for thee.' He stared at Bucke and dabbed with his handkerchief at a film of blood seeping from his picked wart.

Soon a ridiculous situation suddenly became a whole lot worse. The arrest of Robert Sprague, now, as far as everyone was concerned, an ex-constable, had naturally left a gap in personnel in the force. Chief Constable Allison took the view that an additional appointment was not necessary and that the force could be strengthened most effectively with redeployment from within, with little additional expense. Bucke found himself curiously detached as he heard Allison explain that he had persuaded the Watch Committee to promote his son Thomas to the position of inspector and move him to Swansea from his post in Gorseinon on the fringes of Gower, with Sergeant Flynn moving in the other direction. Constable Ball was promoted to sergeant in his place. Bucke was then relieved of some of his duties, such as the Inspector of Weight and Measures and the licensing of traders, tasks which were transferred to Thomas Allison, ostensibly to allow Bucke to concentrate on criminal investigation.

He said nothing at all when the Chief Constable told him, but merely nodded politely. When he got back to his room in Fisher Street, he laughed and laughed. He really did have to go somewhere else now. He had to do anything, anything at all, to get away from Swansea. It was the town which contained so much of his past but which could no longer offer him a future.

Bucke knew, without a doubt, that he was being outmanoeuvred by those who were far more adept than him, but he didn't care very much, which was the most revealing thing of all. He stared out of the window, watching Dai Potato wheel his cart noisily up Fisher Street to take up a position for the evening outside the Theatre Royal. At least it had helped him to make up his mind, and he tried hard to feel some sort of relief. He would leave Swansea and make a fresh start somewhere. Perhaps in the Army. Perhaps in the Colonies. If the Allisons were what Swansea wanted, then it could have them with pleasure. What were those dimly remembered words? As you sow, so shall you reap? Well, whatever they were, so be it.

But as he considered the injustice of it all, he also realised that he was determined to solve the Daniel Guy case – he didn't want to leave his post and be branded a failure – he still had his self-respect after all. And he also very much wanted to find Punch's killer, even if he was already at sea and enjoying the privileged anonymity of an itinerant seaman.

Chapter Eight

Bucke made his way reluctantly to the Royal Institution, passing through the arch of Salubrious Place on to Wind Street, deliberately wasting time by taking a circuitous route. The rain had fallen incessantly once again until the late afternoon when it finally stopped, apparently exhausted. Tuesday had never been his favourite day of the week, and today he was required to Acquire yet more Useful Knowledge, which he would never use. However, he was granted an unexpected moment of good fortune. There had been an incident on Wind Street, and, whilst the constables had already been called, Bucke, even though he was already late, responded to a pressing need to lend a hand and thus encourage his men.

A market trader called Richard Preece, from Neath, who dealt in fruit and vegetables, had managed to overturn his cart and had become the source of considerable entertainment for a crowd of drinkers from the Adelphi, who had a grandstand view as abusive carters edged their way around the confusion. Preece had been drinking and would inevitably face a charge of being drunk in charge of a horse and cart. The horse stared blankly down Wind Street and relieved itself copiously, whilst the driver scrabbled around on the road trying to recover his stock of apples, some of which had been squashed into the road and many more had being smuggled into the Adelphi – a bonus not to be overlooked. In the end, Preece gave up and sat down on the pavement, looking bewildered.

'See, Inspector, it is like this, mun. I suffers from fits, don't I? It is the doctor, like. He told me that if I starts to feel unnecessary, I has to take a glass of brandy. So that is what I did.'

It must have been a particularly generous glass of medication, thought Bucke. He would probably get more sense from the horse.

'I is dreadful sorry, but the horse was going to bolt so I pulled on the reins, like, and it all fell over.'

Constables Davies and Lewis arrived to escort Preece back to the police station, and together, the three of them pulled the cart upright, in spite of the helpful advice offered by the spectators who regretted the conclusion to the evening's entertainment. Bucke heard something rattle and, looking under the seat, he found an almost empty bottle containing a small amount of brandy. It was a clear glass bottle, unlabelled, with no cap or cork, but secured merely with a screwed-up rag. He knew where he had seen a bottle like that before.

When he finally ran up the steps of the Royal Institution, he was relieved to learn that he was sufficiently late to have missed the talk on Acoustics. However useful that knowledge may one day prove to be, and no matter how he might then regret not acquiring it, it was not likely to make his current difficulties any easier. He stood at the back of the room whilst the proceedings were concluded. The members were listening politely whilst the German consul, Herr Dahne, expressed the view that in the interests of fairness, they should follow the meeting with the

Frenchman de Lesseps with a meeting with a figure of substance from Germany. There was polite agreement and Herr Dahne resolved to contact the German Ambassador for guidance. Bristow, standing at the lectern, flipped open his fob watch as usual and, satisfied, carefully arranged his academic gown before grasping his lapels with both hands, which, thought Bucke, made him straighten his back, as if called to attention.

'Gentlemen, may I thank you for your attention. At our next meeting, in a mere two weeks, we shall enjoy a presentation upon "The Study of Science and the Cultivation of the Intellect" by Mr Arthur Dean. Our pulses are racing already, Arthur.' There was a murmur of laughter and Arthur Dean nodded in acknowledgement. 'But of course events move on quickly amongst us, as you might expect in the engine room that we have now become, in the vibrant intellectual soul of Swansea.' He looked around pompously.

'I am delighted to tell you that our Lord Mayor is energised by the visit of Monsieur le Comte Ferdinand de Lesseps and is determined to do all in his power to make it a success. I know I can say with confidence that the whole of the town is behind our bold invitation. We will provide for Monsieur de Lesseps a sympathetic but challenging audience – one that could not be bettered anywhere. Great men with exciting ideas need a great town to bring their plans to reality. We are that town!' he declaimed dramatically. 'Last week's announcement of the new East Dock confirms that Swansea will remain the centre of the commercial world.' There was vigorous nodding and sustained applause. Bristow took a moment to tame his unruly hair but with little success. When the applause had ended, he went on.

'Let us greet our visitor, this great diplomat and engineer, with the honour befitting the man who had the vision to construct the Suez Canal and who is now planning to make the world an even smaller place, with a canal through Panama. Consider this, my friends. His canal would halve the voyage to the west coast of South America and remove the necessity for our brave Swansea sailors to battle around Cape Horn. What a boost for our copper trade with Chile.' He paused again whilst the audience murmured their approval. 'Let us make no mistake. We will support his momentous canal through the isthmus. The world is ready for bold endeavours and we are ready to lead them. We are, by nature, endowed with instincts and understanding beyond all other European races. Our chief attributes are common sense, energy, self-reliance and a readiness to assume any and every role which conditions may present. But let us make clear, in no uncertain terms, that he should drop his support for this ridiculous idea for a tunnel beneath the English Channel. It is not what we want and it is not what we need. He should be reminded that it is called the English Channel for good reason. It is not now, nor has it ever been, and indeed nor will it be in the future, the French Channel! It is ours and it provides a welcome and, indeed, essential barrier.'

Herbert Jenkins added his own support for Bristow. He stood up and threw out his arms expansively. 'He should keep his snout out of our affairs. Bring Europe closer to Great Britain for their greater good perhaps, but not at the cost of bringing Great Britain closer to Europe.'

'Thank you, Herbert, trenchant as always,' Bristow replied, offering Jenkins a thin smile. 'As for the arrangements, I have left the matter in the capable hands of the Lord Mayor's office but, in short, our guest will arrive from Liverpool on the afternoon of Tuesday 3rd June at the Mumbles Road Station, where he will be greeted formally and then allowed to relax and refresh himself. In the evening, there will be a dinner at the Mackworth Hotel, after which Monsieur de Lesseps will be invited to speak. One hundred tickets for the dinner will be available for the modest fee of one guinea for those wishing to attend. Our business is of no interest to the lower classes and we should endeavour to keep away the riff-raff and the merely curious. That, I fancy, will occupy our fine police constables, Inspector Bucke; those sturdy rocks against which the turbulent tide of Swansea's streets constantly surges,' he said, nodding in his direction. 'At the conclusion of the evening, he will be boarding the mail train to take him to the Channel. He has a speaking engagement the following evening in Amsterdam, which illustrates beyond measure how daily our world becomes smaller.'

'No bloody tunnel for him then,' muttered Jenkins loudly, provoking wry smiles from those around him.

'Herbert, please,' said Bristow, irritated by the interruption. 'I am sure you will have every opportunity to tell Monsieur de Lesseps exactly how you feel.'

'Vaughan, you know as well as I do that it is a ridiculous idea. It will open up the country to an epidemic of villainy. We will see the consequences of such madness every day along the High Street, even more so than we do today.' Jenkins was in voluble form, his wet eyes twisting their way around the audience. 'We need to confront the scoundrel. The promotion of this ridiculous tunnel should be no concern of his, and all Englishmen are duty-bound to oppose it.' He paused and pushed back at his teeth, which his excitement had briefly dislodged.

Bristow was pleased to be able to conclude his address. 'Gentlemen. There is much that remains for us to discuss, but we should not underestimate the great honour we have been granted. Through the very presence of the French monsieur, we will be mentioned in the same breath as some of the greatest cities in the country. We have a right to be proud. And this heralds a new dawn of prosperity for us all! Remember, gentlemen, the words of the Bard: *There is a tide in the affairs of men. Which, taken at the flood, leads us on to fortune!* Now is the time. Let us seize it!' The members got to their feet to offer applause and to stretch their legs, offering a smattering of "Hear hears!" and two "Bravos!"

The members started to move around, stretching their legs and gathering to talk in small groups. Bucke listened in to their conversations, hoping to gather useful information he might be able to pass on to someone when he resigned.

'Please excuse my ignorance, Mr Jenkins,' he heard Reverend Rogers say gently, 'but perhaps this colossal undertaking of the tunnel which the French gentleman supports will, in the future, serve to unite the United Kingdom and our Empire in India.'

'Stuff and nonsense, Rogers!' snorted Jenkins. It will merely serve to bring the Ottoman ever closer to us, along with the Greek and the Latin. What do we see in Swansea? The curse of the foreigner at every turn. A few days past we had another example: the murder of that unfortunate woman, without doubt the filthy work of the Latin, a race always ready to slide the blade between your ribs – anyone's ribs! Man, woman or child! They have a terrible love of the thin-bladed knife. Stiletto, call it what you will; it is a secret, dishonest tool.' He turned to Bucke for support. 'As Bucke here will confirm; it is not British, it is craven and cowardly. When an Englishman must kill a scoundrel, he confronts him, face-to-face. You are a military man, Bucke. You will understand.'

Bucke tried to remain measured. 'I think that murder is the same however it is delivered, Mr Jenkins. Someone is killed and the reason is rarely honourable.'

Jenkins chose to ignore him. 'I tell you now, Rogers, unless we act, Swansea will be forever cursed by the foreign criminal.' He emphasised his point by tapping firmly on the floor with his polished dragon-headed cane. 'And answer me this too, if you will, Reverend. We claim to be the most Christian land on earth, and yet we are so busy looking after natives overseas, we are neglecting the filthy heathens who live in our very own slums. God knows, they are crying out for salvation...'

Bucke was sure that Jenkins believed all the things that he said, but there was something about the way he said them that seemed almost pre-prepared, coached, staged. But his own fragile resolve had faded away. He couldn't listen to any more of it and he began to move slowly towards the door whilst a half-remembered quotation came back to him – *The longest sword, the strongest lungs, the most voices, are all false measures of truth.* The door and salvation were within his grasp, but he was cruelly intercepted.

'Ah, Inspector, I was explaining to my friends here,' Bristow said, gesturing to the group gathered around him, 'how best to handle those irritating little domestic frustrations which can disrupt the smooth running of an otherwise ordered household.' He laughed. 'Never forget. Women are like a walnut tree. Need to be beaten for the best results.'

The group broke up in laughter and, pleased with himself, he put an arm around Bucke's shoulder. Bucke glanced at the door, knowing how a notorious murderer must feel, detained by the police when stepping on a ship about to sail to freedom.

'As I think about it, Inspector Bucke, perhaps you should attend one of my lectures. I intend to offer the Society, at the very earliest opportunity, my reflections upon Prince Madog, the Welshman who without a doubt discovered America. As you will know, there are those overseas who strive to claim that honour but, rest assured, I will show conclusively that such an honour rests alone with the Ancient Britons.'

'I would be honoured to attend,' he lied.

'Good man, good man. I think I can safely say that I have some success in making my talks entertaining. As I am sure you know, my letters to *The Times* and the *Daily Telegraph* are well regarded and have, I am told, a loyal following.' He went on, as he finally steered Bucke towards the door, 'You are a man of the world. From London, I am told. I don't mind telling you I am trying to drag Swansea into the current century. A backward sort of place. It has its engaging businessmen like Herbert Jenkins – a fine man – but Swansea needs to do more about its education provision for the classes on the west side of the town. Their children will eventually be required to sustain and grow the Empire, and it is my duty to educate them to do so. As Seneca would have it, *non progredi est regredi*, don't you agree?'

'Without doubt,' said Bucke, for want of something else to say. What a dreadful place this was.

'Good man, good man!'

Bucke took the steps two at a time and then paused at the bottom. Above him, the once-elegant pediment and the columns were deeply engrained with heavy black soot, darker than the dark night, as if the building was disguising itself out of shame for what it had become on nights such as this. He looked right, towards the lights of the Queen's Hotel, glowing in the darkness. The members of the society were leaving – some indeed, like Bristow, were heading there. Perhaps it was free of sailors tonight, he thought – and others were strolling down York Street towards the town. He watched Jenkins striding out purposefully with his walking cane until he turned right into the darkness of Little Wind Street, where Bucke could no longer see him. He didn't want to go home to that lonely room and to those agonising dreams, but he had nowhere else to go.

It had become another restless and disturbed night, bringing Inspector Bucke no peace. Leering faces, bloated limbs, inhuman figures, threats. And when he heard the sound of the police rattle close at hand, he wasn't sure whether he was awake or asleep. But it didn't stop, and when his room took a shadowy but familiar shape in the darkness, he knew he was awake and that it was real.

He got out of bed, opened his window and looked down into the street. Sergeant Ball was standing directly below. 'Begging your pardon, Inspector, but you better come. I regret to have to tell you that there has been another murder, sir.'

It seemed to him that he had been expecting it. 'I shall be with you directly, Sergeant.' He did not ask who it was. After all, what will be, will be. Bucke was exhausted. He was convinced he had been hearing a police rattle all night, an insistent accompaniment to those intimidating dreams. He stood at the washstand and inaccurately splashed water on his face. There was more misery to come; he knew it. The rattle was an insistent call to something else he wouldn't be able to solve. He dried his face. Perhaps one day the constable would come and tell him that Rumsey Bucke was dead. And so then, at that moment he would be dead and it would be all over. He dressed and then walked down to the front door, like a man walking to his own execution.

'Good morning, Sergeant. Where are we going this time?' he asked.

'The Uplands, sir. St James' Crescent. Mr Jenkins the factory owner, sir. Dead in his garden, so they say.'

They walked steadily up Walter's Road in the dim light of the gas lamps. Bucke said nothing, whilst he tried to control a mind in turmoil. Jenkins dead? He was daunted, bewildered. It was his responsibility to solve the crime, but he did not feel capable of doing so. But he was no longer sure if that was what people truly expected of him. Did they want him to succeed? Did they want him to find the truth? Or did they want him to wrap it up, put a label on it saying "Solved" and lock it away so it could be forgotten?

They arrived at the house at 2.30 am and were directed by a constable away from the front of the house and on to Belgrave Lane, in order to access the rear garden. Bucke noticed that there wasn't a tablecloth on the line.

The cold April breeze made the trees sway, and the two police constables hunched inside their capes looked in envy at the lights in the house, which offered them comfort and warmth. Instead, they held their lanterns to illuminate the details of the scene that had drawn them all here.

Herbert Jenkins was curled up tightly, like a man sleeping uncomfortably. Whatever qualities Jenkins had once possessed, they were long gone. Now he was merely a corpse. His essence had faded away with the blood that had seeped into the wet grass. Bucke thought about Punch whom he had also seen lying dead on the ground. In life she and Jenkins had been so different. Now in death they were united.

Bucke saw that Jenkins's teeth were a couple of feet away, as if they had been forcibly expelled from his open mouth. He was lying on the lawn on his left side, with his knees drawn up to his chest. His feet were on the path. A long dagger or sword protruded from his chest and he was clutching at it with bloodied hands, seemingly too terrified to let the blade go. At the hilt was the ornate oriental dragon which Bucke had seen before and which now sparkled in the dim light from the lanterns. He wondered whether the Balinese craftsman who had spent hours making that striking decoration, had ever realised that it was destined to decorate a dead man's chest far away.

Bucke switched his attention to the dead man's socks, thinking about how Jenkins would have put them on with every intention of taking them off later. Someone had obviously planned the murder, but it had certainly come as a surprise to the victim. Jenkins could have had no expectation that he was to die on his own lawn, next to his own greenhouse. One of the panes was broken and there were shards of dangerous-looking glass sparkling in the light.

Dr Beynon was there, once again kneeling by a body. He looked up as Bucke approached. 'It occurs to me, Inspector, that if we are truly so eager to meet, we could at least choose occasions more convivial than the discovery of a murdered citizen.'

'Good morning, Doctor. It is always a pleasure to see you, no matter what the circumstances. Nonetheless, I do not need the expertise of an eminent surgeon such as yourself to recognise that this was no accident.'

He leaned back on his haunches. 'Indeed, though I have no wish to speak out of turn, it is undoubtedly the case that more effective police work would ensure that I remained warmly in my bed, where fate has decreed I should be. Mrs Beynon is starting to believe I am keeping an insatiable doxy in Greenhill.'

'There could be no greater incentive for us to improve policing than the restoration of domestic harmony in the Beynon household,' Bucke replied.

'Flora will be delighted to hear the good news.' He stood up and stretched his back. 'Not quite as messy as the last one, Rumsey. At least the blood has soaked into the grass, but he is dead just the same. Another stabbing, I am afraid.'

Bucke again examined the blade sticking out of Jenkins's chest. 'Is it the same sort of wound as the one which killed Punch? The same weapon?'

'It has similarities, certainly, though it would be difficult to say they were identical killings. They were both stabbed with a thin blade which penetrated the rib cage. As you remember, it slipped cleverly between the ribs of Catherine Owen. In Mr Jenkins's case, it seems to me that there were three blows. The first two, I imagine, hit a bone. It was the third which dispatched him. You will have already noticed the large contusion in the middle of his forehead here.' Dr Beynon pointed to an ugly discoloration. 'He might have fallen, I suppose, but it is my opinion that he was struck by a heavy object. This would have been enough to disorientate him so that the stabbing could take place. A piece of wood, an iron bar, a piece of kitchen equipment – anything heavy enough would have had the desired effect. He would have been unable to defend himself. I will dress it up in the correct words at the inquest, Rumsey, but that is what I will say – he was stunned and then stabbed to death. Jenkins had been drinking; I can smell it. I do not think he was drunk, but the inquest should confirm that or otherwise.'

Inspector Bucke was lost in his thoughts. What had Jenkins said a few hours earlier? *This terrible love of the thin-bladed knife*? He carried one with him and now it was protruding from his own chest, the cause of his own murder.

David Beynon picked up his bag. 'It is not my place to anticipate your conclusions, Rumsey, but in both cases the victims appear to have been stabbed from the front; and it might be that they were both acquainted with the person who killed them. Naturally, that is for you to determine. I can only speculate, particularly with the case before us. There is money in his pockets. I do not think that he has been robbed. It will be interesting to see what conclusions you do eventually come to, Inspector. We need to get the body to a room for an inquest. I would suggest the Tenby Hotel. I have used it before. I won't be saying anything I haven't already told you. You have a dead body to consider, Rumsey, but I have to offer my attentions to a patient who still lives.'

The doctor went into the house and Bucke walked around the garden. The path to the kitchen door was clear to see, even in the dark, and there was nowhere he could see where a murderer could hide. Perhaps behind the greenhouse was a possibility, but it was hardly ideal. There was nothing growing inside it to obscure the view. He saw no substantial bushes, apart from those on either side of the gate. Had he been struck there and staggered down the path before someone picked up his sword-cane and ran around to the front to stab him? Or had an intruder emerged from the kitchen and confronted him face-to-face, driven him backwards with a blow to the forehead, picked up the cane and finished him off by the greenhouse? If you wanted to kill Jenkins specifically, why wait until this point? It wasn't a well-chosen spot. Why not do the deed in the darkness beyond the garden? It would have been some time until anyone found the body back there, giving you more time to get away. To the left of the kitchen there was an outhouse, perhaps a coal shed. That might be an effective hiding place. He tried the door. It was locked. The ground around it was in shadow, though the grass appeared to be flattened. There would have to be a proper search in the daylight. He examined the garden carefully, but he could see neither the outer case of the sword-cane nor Jenkins's hat.

One of the constables went to get a cart to take away the body, and Bucke asked his remaining colleague how they had discovered the murder.

'From the maid, sir. Elinor Roberts. She heard sounds of breaking glass and was drawn into the garden in fear for the greenhouse. She saw the gentleman on the ground, as he is now. She found me on the corner of Westbury Street and I raised the alarm. I came here directly. I saw no one else in the vicinity. Sensible woman that one, if I may say, Inspector. Didn't get hysterical or anything. Had the presence of mind to get a tablecloth off the line so we could properly see what was going on.'

Bucke went into the kitchen. There, a bucket standing in the sink in which clothes were soaking, ready to be washed. There was that tablecloth, neatly folded, cold and damp to the touch. A kettle was bubbling gently on the stove, next to a small frying pan. He closed the door and looked through the window. Yes, there was a clear view along the path to the back gate. Anyone inside would have seen Jenkins enter the garden. But he thought that behind the outhouse might have offered more effective concealment. No door to open, and the murderer could have taken him completely by surprise.

He went through to the drawing room, where he had met Mrs Jenkins previously.

Mrs Jenkins was wearing a long red paisley dressing gown with blue velvet trim, held together inefficiently by a cord belt, which gaped occasionally to reveal a white nightdress as she walked around the drawing room. Her hair was loose and untidy as Bucke would have expected for someone who had only just risen from her bed. She kept dabbing at her brow with a red handkerchief wrapped tightly around her right hand. She was flushed; struggling, it seemed, to understand the enormity of what had happened. Elinor Roberts was standing dutifully to one side, dressed for work – a clean apron, a black skirt, a fresh mob cap; her hands crossed in front of her, waiting. Doctor Beynon sat in an armchair, watching Mrs Jenkins closely.

Mrs Jenkins dismissed the offer of Bucke's condolences with a wave of her hand. 'Thank you, Inspector, but that is not necessary.' She appeared agitated, angry, obviously shocked, but he was a police inspector and he knew what he had to do.

'These are difficult times, Mrs Jenkins, but it may be that if we are able to act quickly, we will be able to apprehend the murderer. I wonder why your husband was in the back garden early in the morning, Mrs Jenkins? Your own safety is my primary concern and I would be alarmed if your husband had disturbed an intruder,' he said. 'We would urgently need to know why your husband was there.'

'It was not unusual for my husband to enter through the kitchen on his return home, Inspector. Apparently he liked to inspect his property. He would have used his key to the kitchen door. It was his house, after all. If it had been his wish to enter his own house via the drawing room window, who are we to question it?'

'Did you hear anything, Mrs Jenkins? Was there any sound of an intruder?'

'Inspector, don't be ridiculous. I was asleep.'

'The dog did not bark?' asked Bucke.

'No. He is a contented animal. Perhaps the only one in the house. But even if Towser had barked, I would not have heard him from my bedroom. Did you hear him, Elinor?'

'No, Mrs Jenkins, I heard nothing until I heard the breaking of glass. This is what attracted me to the garden and that is when I discovered Mr Jenkins. I saw no one else.'

She turned on her heels and spread her arms in an agitated way. 'Such a stupid, stupid man. Why die here in your own garden? It makes everything so much more difficult. He could have arranged his murder so as not to interfere with one's domestic arrangements.' She twisted the handkerchief more tightly around her hand and ground her teeth.

Bucke watched her carefully. 'I did speak to you on my previous visit about the possibility of intruders. You have seen nothing to alarm you at all in recent days?'

Doctor Beynon recognised that it was time to bring an end to the proceedings. 'I think, Inspector, that what is most important at the moment is that Mrs Jenkins gets some rest. Perhaps you should return tomorrow when the shock of the night may have retreated slightly and you may receive answers which will offer you the assistance you require. Mrs Jenkins, you may find it helpful if I was to offer you a mild sedative.' She paused in her walk, looked at him and nodded.

'Of course, Doctor,' said Bucke. 'My concern remains that a murderer was waiting for him in the garden, that there was a brief struggle during which the greenhouse window was broken and Mr Jenkins met his death and that the murderer may still be in the vicinity. We will leave a constable here until morning, in order to offer you some security, Mrs Jenkins.'

Elinor Roberts opened the door to the drawing room and Bucke waited in the hall whilst the doctor administered the medication. Bucke saw there were a number of walking sticks in the hatstand, any of which could have concealed a weapon. Why would anyone need so many? he wondered. When Elinor escorted Doctor Beynon from the drawing room, she unlocked the front door and the two men left together.

At the bottom of the steps, Beynon yawned. 'Time for bed, I think, if only for a short time. You know, Rumsey, I think we would all appreciate a holiday from these midnight murders.' He patted his hat onto his head, they shook hands and they parted.

~

A murder in east Swansea, amongst the desperate poor, generally created a vicarious thrill across the whole of the town. The death of Punch had been a fine example, with the victim condemned as much as the shadowy perpetrator. But a violent murder amongst the trees and wide avenues and clean air where the prosperous people lived? Suddenly something must be done. Families deserved better policing and the Chief Constable would want a prompt and reassuring arrest. On the east side, death was the inevitable consequence of drink and dissolution, the fate of the undeserving poor. On the west? A madman was on the loose, one who knows exactly where you live, and every night he is waiting for you in the shadows, grinning and with a deadly blade.

There had been two murders within a short time, both stabbings, both late at night. Where next would he strike?

This was the obvious question that troubled the press and the residents alike. It was more comforting to think in terms of one murderer rather than the prospect of two lurking in the streets. The victims were so apparently different. The inevitable conclusion was that he was choosing his victims at random – which was hardly reassuring, unless of course there was something as yet unknown which linked Punch with Herbert Jenkins, which Bucke believed was highly unlikely.

The location of the murder and the method employed created considerable unease. Had the victim been followed from town, or was the murderer lying in wait for him? And the biggest question of all was why? What had Jenkins done to warrant his murder? If Bucke could unravel that, then the identity of the murderer should become clear.

Bucke had to establish Jenkins's movements after he left the Royal Institution and turned into Little Wind Street at about 9.30 pm. He was found dead at 1.30 am. So where had he been?

He began by speaking to town centre publicans, who were always keen to cooperate with the police, especially when their licence was due for renewal. On this occasion, no one could remember seeing Jenkins, though that was not a surprise in those crowded public houses. For Bucke, the strangest thing was that Jenkins was there at all. What was he doing in this part of town? There were times when it was a dangerous place, even for those who knew it well. The best lead he had came from Eliza Keast. She had seen two men in conversation on Castle Bailey Street at about midnight. One of them was a toff with a walking stick. She had seen him hanging around on the High Street before. The other? Well, she didn't think she knew him.

The night watchman at the Music Hall on Cradock Street had seen a man answering his description walking up Mansel Street, the direction Herbert Jenkins would have taken, sometime after midnight. There was no one else around, and there was no sign that the man was being followed.

It wasn't much but it was a start. He needed to speak to Mrs Jenkins about what he was doing at that time of night, since this might indicate who could want him dead. Her husband was an unpleasant man, opinionated and aggressive; but was that sufficient to kill him?

Bucke returned to St James' Crescent later in the morning. Two constables from the Sketty station had been conducting a search of the garden and the lane behind. His heart sank. Constables Smith and Williams were notorious for their inefficiency and for what Sergeant Flynn had once described as a "lack of mental agility", which was far more polite than they deserved. Bucke was never really sure which one was which, but at least they had the reputation for being honest, if nothing else. The gate was closed, and, as he went into the garden, he saw some clothes drying on the line – a brown flannel shirt and black corduroy trousers. He wondered who they could belong to. They didn't look like the sort of thing that Herbert Jenkins would have worn, and there were no other men in the house – or so he had been told.

The taller constable leaned casually on a garden rake. 'Don't worry, Inspector, we have tidied it up. The gardener, Mr Pettigrew, came and helped out, like. Didn't find anything but we have picked up all the glass. Didn't want the ladies cutting themselves, did we? Mr Pettigrew tidied up the bushes and washed out the grass. It is all as good as new.'

Bucke closed his eyes briefly. The garden had been effectively sanitised and the memory of the events of the early hours wiped clean. He was depressed, most of all, by the evident pride which the two constables had taken in their work.

He tried to be patient. 'And what about behind the coal shed? Anything to report?'

'Well, Inspector, it was a bit untidy back there, I got to be honest. So I raked it out and Mr Pettigrew did some weeding, so it doesn't look too bad at all. He did a good job, fair play.'

'And the greenhouse? Any clues, Constable, why the pane of glass was broken?'

His companion looked at Bucke and wrinkled his face, surprised by his superior officer's obvious stupidity. 'It might have got broken in the fight, Inspector. Don't you think?'

'And what fight might that be?'

The constable spoke carefully, as if Bucke was unfamiliar with the intricacies of English. 'The fight when the gentleman got killed, sir.'

'I see.' Bucke took a deep breath. 'Did you find anything? Any objects that should not have been in the garden? Anything that we might think of as evidence?'

'Mr Pettigrew found a hat, sir, by the back gate; but don't worry, Inspector, he handed it in to the lady's housemaid. She was very pleased to see it, let me tell you.'

'And the bit of the walking stick,' the other constable reminded him. 'Don't forget that. She told me it has washed up nicely. Good as new. She is a proper lady, that one. Very polite.'

He sent them back to Killay and they left with heads held high after a good morning's work, then sat for a moment on a garden bench and closed his eyes. He may as well resign now, he thought. He walked around the well-manicured garden. If Jenkins had been hit with a tree branch, there were plenty of them about. He noticed that there had been a small garden fire behind one of the large oak trees and the embers were still glowing. He poked at the fire with his foot. There was wood there and something which could be fabric of some sort. Inside the greenhouse there were a few stones which might have broken the glass, but then again, might not.

He gathered himself and went into the kitchen. Everything was neat and stored away, apart from that small iron frying pan still sitting on the range. There was a smell which suggested some clothes had recently been washed. The tablecloth he had seen earlier was now in a basket, ready for the line.

'Good morning, Miss Roberts,' he said as Elinor appeared through the internal door. 'I hope you have managed to sleep a little after all the distress of earlier this morning.'

'Thank you, Inspector. I managed to sleep for a while. Mrs Jenkins was sedated and did not require my attention. I am tolerably well this morning.'

Bucke nodded his pleasure. 'I noticed two garments hanging to dry outside. Who do they belong to?'

'Mr Pettigrew the gardener, Inspector. He attends most morning and I sometimes wash clothes for him when there is an occasion to do so. Mrs Pettigrew passed away last year. I believe he found Mr Jenkins's hat and the rest of his cane in the garden, by the gate. They are in the hall if you wish to see them. They have been properly cleaned.'

'Thank you,' he said, shaking his head, 'but it may not be necessary.' If Jenkins had drawn the blade from his walking cane, then he must have seen someone. What had happened to the hat? Had it been knocked off? Taken off?

'Was the greenhouse glass intact yesterday?' he asked.

'Of course, Inspector. It was the noise of the glass breaking which roused me and drew me to the garden.'

'Thank you, Elinor. I would be obliged if I could speak with Mrs Jenkins, if she is receiving visitors.'

'She has received a number of visitors this morning who have come to express their condolences. She has been expecting you, Inspector. I was instructed to show you straight in once you were ready to speak to her,' said Elinor, as she led him once more to the drawing room.

Mrs Jenkins had recovered her poise. She was very self-possessed, confident, in control. 'You may ask me any questions you have, Inspector Bucke. But please do not be tiresome. My husband is dead, slain by a person unknown. I heard nothing last night, I saw nothing last night. There was no one here apart from Elinor and myself and there are no men living in secret cellars beneath the house, from whom I could extract an exorbitant rent. To my knowledge, at least. Will you take tea, Inspector?' He declined and she sighed. 'Mourning dress is so drab. I feel that the recommended two years is patently extreme and unnecessary. I may manage two weeks and my husband is fortunate to get that. You may notice, Inspector, that I have chosen bombazine rather than parramatta silk. The latter is too expensive and I only intend to wear it briefly. I have asked my solicitor, Mr Glascodine, to arrange the funeral, and he will have the good grace, I am sure, to let me know when it is.'

'I am pleased to hear that you have been able to concentrate on practicalities, Mrs Jenkins,' said Bucke.

She smiled without humour. 'It is important when you are married to an older man that you prepare yourself for his early death, particularly if he has intemperate habits.'

'And are you aware whether any of these habits he might have had may have exposed him to danger, Mrs Jenkins?'

She considered Bucke carefully, as if measuring what she was prepared to say. 'He had unexpected appetites, Inspector,' she said with sudden and unexpected candour. 'I made it perfectly clear some years ago that these would play no part in my life. Consequently, he has always found his comforts elsewhere, if that is what you mean. It was of no interest to me where he went or what he did or indeed who he did it with, although I believe his requirements took him into the darker parts of Swansea.

There was little I could do to advise him otherwise. He was not doing it with me and that was all that concerned me. I have no wish to embarrass you, Inspector, but his liaisons relieved me of what I always found to be an exceedingly unpleasant obligation.' Her eyes, fiercely blue, were cold and chilling. 'But I knew nothing of them. He came and went as he saw fit. I lived my own life and will continue to do so.'

'And so you do not know where he went last night? He said nothing to you?'

'I know that he went to his ridiculous little meeting at the Royal Institution, where no doubt he made an awful lot of noise for no possible purpose at all. What would it be last night? I wonder. The dishonesty of foreigners? The decadence of the French perhaps? The triumph of Empire? What about the birching of fallen women on a platform outside St Mary's Church? I have heard them all, far too often. It is odd to think that I will not have to listen to such rants again.'

'Why did he come home so late, do you think, Mrs Jenkins?'

'I cannot say. It is of no interest to me. He met someone. He went somewhere. It is what he did, often. Perhaps he merely wished to arrive home late so as to avoid me.' She looked exasperated. 'Perhaps there are others who are unfortunate enough to live in the town who you should ask. My husband was apparently a great captain of industry and his devotion to profit and enterprise was his primary concern. He was infrequently at home.'

'Did he have any particular enemies that he spoke of?'

Mrs Jenkins laughed. 'Just the whole world, Inspector Bucke.'

'Had he received any threats recently? Was there anyone you knew of with a particular grudge?'

'Please understand, Inspector. He was neither pleasant nor popular, but I do not know of anyone who wished him ill. Apart from myself, of course.' She stared directly, and without flinching, straight into Bucke's eyes.

He returned her stare. 'And are there any business rivals who might want him dead? Anyone to whom he owed money, for example?'

'It was becoming clear, Inspector Bucke, that his business affairs were of little consequence to anyone. Other people owed him money but were never going to repay it. Do not be misled in any way. My husband was on the very edge of bankruptcy. He might well have wished death upon those he believed had ruined him, but no one would ever have seen any advantage in murdering him. They had already had what they wanted.'

'What will you do now, Mrs Jenkins?'

'Live more easily, I suspect. I will sell Herbert's demeaning business. My solicitor, Mr Glascodine, has told me there have been people circling like dogs for some time, waiting to pick it apart. I await the future with interest.'

It was clear that her husband's parlous financial position did not concern her. Mrs Jenkins must have a plan and it must have been in place for some time. She nodded to him and stood up. She considered the meeting to have come to an end. 'Inspector Bucke, before you leave, may I congratulate you on the work of your constables. Their attention to domestic maintenance is to be commended.' She offered him a thin smile. 'You must excuse me.'

'Of course, Mrs Jenkins. It would be remiss of me not to ask whether your hand is making sufficient improvement. Cuts to the hand can be difficult and can take some time to heal.'

She looked down at the bandage on her right hand. 'Thank you, Inspector, for your concern. Broken glass from the greenhouse. A stray fragment. The cut has begun to heal and offers me no inconveniences.'

Chapter Nine

Chief Constable n was worried about the press. Publication day was tomorrow and he anticipated his reputation skewered by a headline. A town out of control, a murderer walking free, casually selecting his next victim, the police powerless and incompetent. He poked sharply at his wart and then turned his finger aggressively towards Inspector Bucke.

'It looks to everyone that we have a murderer loose about town, Bucke, and that we can't do nowt. Two in a week and you have detected bugger all. It's lookin' grim – and people from opposite sides of town. Must be same weapon, lad. Mayor says there's palpable unease. So empty them lodgin' houses and round up all foreigners. Tha' needs an arrest. And quick. You want my advice? Collar a sailor. Any Chinese in town? Or find Daniel bloody Guy. Then your troubles are over. Pin it all on 'im and suddenly you're a hero.'

It didn't seem like an acceptable solution to Bucke, who hoped that the career that was now coming to a close would be remembered more for its concern with a search for truth than with political expediency, but at that moment he had no idea how to begin the search. There was little doubt in his mind that someone was sheltering Guy, and as far as the Jenkins case was concerned, he knew he had absolutely no evidence to go on. They had the murder weapon that had killed Jenkins – but it was his own. And Punch? Whoever they arrested would inevitably be charged with both murders, anyway.

He gathered his constables together. Inspector Allison was busy with a weights and measures issue in the market, a responsibility he carried out alone and with great vigour, so Bucke was left to deploy the constables. Bucke told them briefly what he suspected – that Jenkins had surprised an intruder in his garden, had been assaulted, disarmed and then stabbed with his own sword. He was looking for information, unexpected comings and goings, bloodstained clothes, the sudden possession of money, drunken boasting – and also any news about Daniel Guy. Constable Davies shook his head and announced rather loudly, 'It's a rum do, sir,' and then looked confused at the sniggers of his colleagues.

They were to visit all the lodging houses in Swansea, and the constables coming on duty for the evening would then continue enquiries in the town centre. The constables grumbled, unhappy with their responsibility to carry out what they regarded as an unpleasant duty.

'My mam calls them nothing but "hotels for the accommodation of vagrants",' said Constable Davies with a scowl, but the offer of overtime, as it often did, calmed such irritations about the nature of modern police work.

Constable Davies had been assigned the lodging houses in the Burrows, behind the Royal Institution, where sailors frequently stayed whilst waiting to sign on to a new ship. His morning was reasonably untroubled. He found out nothing helpful at all. It was the sort of unchallenging, non-confrontational police work that he preferred, until he made his last call at Mrs Baum's in Gloucester Place.

She had once been married to the mate of the *Rosewood* who had been lost overboard during a storm in the Bay of Biscay a few years ago. She had then married a German sailor called Heinz Baum who was an infrequent visitor to Swansea, although their relationship seemed cordial enough, and they had opened a lodging house. The Baumhaus was generally clean, well run and, not surprisingly, popular with German sailors. Betty Baum looked after her lodgers well and did her best to keep them out of trouble. She took the visit by the police as a personal affront.

'What are you doing down here, Evan Davies? My house is a respectable establishment, as well you know, and I won't have you bothering those that is doing their best to maintain respectable habits with your questioning. I know you well enough, young Evan Davies, and I shall be having a word with your mam if you're not careful.'

'Just doing my job, Auntie Betty. That's all.' In view of the welcome he had received, he decided to simplify his enquiries.

'Is that so? And your job is about bothering people, is it?'

'I am not here to cause offence, Auntie Betty. I just need to know if any of your lodgers come from America.'

'My lodgers, Evan Davies, are hard-working men who don't need your sort of interference. You will find no trouble in my house. It is clean and my gentlemen pay on time, and we don't like policemen like you calling here and causing upset. I shall be telling your mam, don't doubt it!'

'I just need to know where they are from, Auntie, that's all. Any of them from America?' he asked a little desperately.

'I don't asks them, do I? No need. My gentlemen know what to expect and they give me no trouble. I hears lots of talking here. French, German, Italian. I don't know what they are saying but I don't need to. But I haven't heard anyone speaking American. Respectable we are, Evan Davies, respectable, and I won't have you saying otherwise. Get back up on to Tontine

Street, Constable Davies! All manner of things going on up there and right next door to the police station. Everyone knows, but instead you are down here, troubling the likes of me!'

'And so none of your lodgers have been to America then?' Constable Davies was nothing if not persistent.

'How should I know? And if I did, I wouldn't tell you, because it is none of your business.'

'It is not my fault, Auntie Betty, honest. Inspector Bucke sent me to ask you if I could look at your register.'

'Did he now? And how is Inspector Bucke these days then?'

'He thinks a lot, Auntie. Very deep. Will make himself ill, I shouldn't wonder.' He puffed himself up a little. 'We are working on a big case today. Tricky one.' Disappointingly, she already knew.

'Terrible business, so I hear. A husband murdered. A wife, a widow. I know too well what that is like. That is what you should be worrying about. Catching him what's done it, afore he does more. And worse. You can have a look at the register – it is all up to date – and then you can get off and do some proper work.'

The constables at work in the lodging houses might have added to the reassuring perception of an increased police presence across the town, but they had thrown up no new leads. Bucke listened to their inconsequential reports on their return. They had found one case of a contagious fever and so the poor sailor had been removed to the fever hospital. Constable Plumley had entered dreadful accommodation on the High Street, at an address which wasn't a lodging house at all, but a 'foul and filthy rat-infested slum used for immoral purposes.' Plumley did like a bit of drama. Constable Lewis had visited three lodging houses, all squalid and all overcrowded in contravention of the regulations, festering away on Tontine Street, within sight of the police station. His uniform was stained with goodness knew what, and, as Bucke observed, he was not the happiest of constables.

Additional enquiries at the railway station and at the harbourmaster's office had proved equally fruitless. The murderer was probably still in town. Perhaps it was Daniel Guy after all.

During the afternoon, Bucke considered the details of the registers as reported by the constables. It always fascinated him that men from all over the world found their way to Swansea. They probably never planned to come here, but a series of chance encounters and unpredictable circumstances had brought them to South Wales. They had arrived on one boat, been paid off and then looked for a position on another. Soon they could be far away, perhaps never to return. Whatever they did in Swansea, whether for good or ill, was quickly consigned to the past. He envied them. The whole world was theirs and they wandered freely. His inability to solve these killings would lead to his own departure. Perhaps it was time. Perhaps he had to be ready to accept an inevitable failure. And yet something about recent events troubled him. He could not help thinking that the two murders of Punch and Mr Jenkins were connected. He didn't know how but they were too similar. And how did Daniel Guy fit into it? Or didn't he? Was the man with the American gun an unrelated piece of insanity?

He walked around the town for a whilst trying to find a pattern that wasn't there and hoping that his measured tread could offer some sort of reassurance to sooth his anxieties or that, outside in the spring air, he could clear his mind. Instead, he watched dark smuts of soot floating from a grey sky, like poisoned snowflakes. It had become another fruitless day, full of sound and fury but signifying nothing. Something else he remembered from school.

By early evening, he was in Dynevor Place, wondering what he should do. Duty patterns meant nothing to Bucke anymore and he intended to walk the town again that night with his constables, asking unwanted questions – anything was better than the room on Fisher Street. Then the door to an undistinguished building which called itself the Swansea Languages College opened and Elinor Roberts came out. She stopped, surprised to see him, and a faint colour seemed to touch her cheeks, as if she had been caught doing something forbidden.

'Good evening, Miss Roberts. An unexpected pleasure indeed.' He could hear the faint but unmistakable sound of hymn-singing coming from Mount Pleasant Baptist Church at the bottom of the street.

'I am pleased to see you, Inspector. I have been on an errand for my mistress.'

'Please allow me to escort you some of the way to St James' Terrace. The night is dark—'

Elinor interrupted him. '*I am far from home; Lead thou me on!*' She laughed. 'One of my favourite hymns, Inspector. *Lead kindly light.*' She smiled brightly, her face fresh and natural, now that the constraints of control had been briefly lifted from it. 'We would sing it frequently when I was in...' Her sentence faded away.

They turned left and approached the Music Hall, where an audience was gathering for Mr Gilbert Legge's Grand Evening Concert, their carriages filling the road. 'I had not expected to see you this evening, Elinor. The Languages College is well regarded, I understand. A successful addition to the town, I believe.'

'I am an infrequent visitor, Inspector. I have no facility for languages but I must on occasion bring letters we have received from Mr Jenkins's business concern in Germany to be turned into English. I bring them to Professor Axmeyer and then take them home. Professor Axmeyer is a very learned man and has all the words which are required.' She glanced sideways at him. 'Please do not ask me what the letters are about, Inspector, for I do not read. Today, Mrs Jenkins received such a letter from Germany, and I must now take it home for her attention, though I assume she will ask me to take it to Mr Glascodine. Once Mrs Jenkins disposes of the factory, it will be a duty I will no longer perform.'

They crossed Mansel Street. He could see a constable ahead of them on the corner of Verandah Street. 'You seem very comfortable with your mistress, if I might say so.'

Elinor nodded. 'Indeed you may, Inspector. She is a good woman and I owe everything I have to her.'

Bucke raised his eyebrows in response. It was an interesting choice of words.

'It is true, Inspector. No one knows that as well as myself.'

At Verandah Street he wished her goodnight. He had to return to the police station to speak to the other officers and so asked the constable to escort her as far as the Tenby Hotel, after which there was little chance of her being harassed. He watched Elinor walk up the road for a moment in her confident, aloof way and reflected on how she had reacted when he saw her emerge from Swansea Languages College.

~

At the police station, Sergeant Ball told him that Joseph the Matchboy had been there asking to see Inspector Bucke. He wouldn't speak to anyone else. Bucke said he would try to find him later that evening. He joined his constables on the streets of Swansea – more questioning, more walking, more wasted time. If anyone knew anything, they were not saying. He had hoped to find Joseph, who was observant and reliable. He might know something, which was why he wanted to see him. But their paths did not cross.

Someone tugged at Inspector Bucke's sleeve in the crowd that had spilled onto Wind Street outside the Adelphi. It was Annie Taylor. He spoke to her briefly. No, she hadn't seen Dan Guy and he had better watch out because he still owed her money. 'I might have been sweet on 'im once, like, but he's not for me. Can't trust 'im.' It was Punch she wanted to talk about. Their sentences in prison had overlapped by a couple of days and Punch had told her about this "toff" who came to see her whom she didn't like but who paid well. Annie didn't have a name but thought it might help. He thanked her, gave her some pennies and told her to spend it on food. He knew she wouldn't.

But where had Jenkins been for those two hours or so on Tuesday night? Bucke was sure that this was a key piece of information. But none of the street women had seen anyone who resembled him. Or at least could remember seeing anyone like him. Perhaps he hadn't been in town to see a woman. Perhaps it was some meeting, something relating to his business? But why so late at night? It was all so frustrating and he was making no progress at all. He needed to go home and hope for sleep to settle his mind.

~

There was another meeting in Dynevor Place that night, in the dark rear garden of the Swansea Languages College. Axmeyer had a student, a clerk from a shipping insurance company on Wind Street, and there was thus no room available where they could sit.

'There was an inspector outside here this evening, talking to a woman,' said Guy. 'I could have shot him from the window, dead easy. Thought about it too. Thought you wouldn't like it.

Look, Pieter, I have been thinking. This place is no good. Too many people around. Every day there are people knocking on the door. Axmeyer don't talk to me often, but when he did last night, he told me there are people around the town asking about me. That bothers me.'

The truth was that Axmeyer frightened Guy. He was a rather stooped man in his late fifties, with spectacles which amplified a piercing stare, and Guy was convinced he was under constant surveillance – which was true. Axmeyer taught a range of languages with considerable proficiency and had a steady stream of students, largely wishing to learn French and German for business reasons, who spoke warmly of his patience. What Guy saw was not patience at all but carefully controlled intensity, and so he largely confined himself to an upstairs bedroom.

Axmeyer said very little. He merely looked at Guy over his glasses, seemingly horrified at the nature of the person to whom they had entrusted the conclusion of their plans. So it had been a long week, during which Axmeyer decided not to share with him the news of events in the town.

Guy was right, of course. He had to be moved from Axmeyer's rooms, though not for the reasons that troubled him. The Languages College had been the only alternative where he could hide once he had left Willrath's house in Hafod. But Moitch did not want either himself or the professor to be closer to Guy than was absolutely necessary. Daniel Guy represented a considerable difficulty for them. If he was detained as a result of his own stupidity, which was certainly a possibility, then Moitch hoped he would be able to implement their escape plan before he and Axmeyer were identified. But now that the police had carried out their search of the lodging houses, Mrs Baum could give Guy the place previously occupied by a sailor from Cologne. She was noted for her accurate registers, and the police were hardly likely to investigate Baumhaus again, unless they had information. Most of the sailors would be German-speaking and they would be unlikely to hold any meaningful conversation with Guy. He would be much more anonymous. As long as he did nothing stupid.

'Of course people are asking about you everywhere, Daniel. It is because you shot your wife. Perhaps they are hoping for a reward, I think. But I am having good news for you. It is no good idea to be keeping you in one place for too long. It will be better again to move you. I have a good place for you now, I think. The lady is a good friend of ours, but you must be discreet, always.'

'I am tired of sitting in a room all day, Pieter!'

'You may find your new place, I am sure, more agreeable. I will come to collect you tomorrow and I will show you also a place on the North Dock where, if things do not go well, you must hide. Then when you have seen, I will take you to your new lodging. Everything is now well. Everything will be fine.'

Chapter Ten

It was Friday night and the Sketty Debating and Dramatic Society was performing a night of amateur theatricals at the Theatre Royal on Temple Street. Every year, it was a policing headache. There was never much of a problem with the privileged cast. It was the audience they attracted.

The Society rehearsed their show thoroughly. It was a selection of sketches and comic performances presented to raise money for local charities. The children of the wealthy had spent long hours preparing for it with a handwritten script in hand, trying to learn their lines, remember their movements and think about their costumes; long evenings spiced with tantrums, arguments and discreet hand-holding.

The young men from the east side of town, however, did not see it in the same sort of way. For them, it was an opportunity to see the girls from the wealthier side of town perform willingly on stage for their entertainment and pleasure. The divine Alicia Southwell was appearing again this year, though it was not her acting talents that they came to admire. She was regarded as the Beauty of Swansea, and this evening was the nearest to her most of the audience would ever get. Her arrival at the stage door had been an exciting moment, with constables linking arms to hold back the leering, jeering crowd of beer-emboldened boys. Alicia and her friends hurried inside, simultaneously horrified and excited by such a reception. The young men who appeared in the performance and followed them through the stage door, were abused for their effeminacy, even though they had a proximity to the fragrant girls of Sketty which was forever denied the boys in the crowd. Apprentices and delivery boys desperately wanted to fight them to show, if only briefly, their superiority as males, before they returned to a grim world of drudgery, poverty and an early death.

It would later be generally accepted that Mr Cory Yeo was "particularly convincing" in the part of Barnaby Bracebutton and that Miss Southwell displayed a "happiness of insight and a grace of manner that are irresistible". Eastside opinion would similarly confirm that she was indeed "irresistible", though Eastside feelings about her insight and grace remained forever unrecorded. Some of the youths with more foresight than their friends had bought tickets for the performance and so sat in the dim light of the auditorium and exchanged loud and bawdy comments between themselves in the stalls. The leading families of Swansea, there to support their children, were horrified by such behaviour, and so a police presence was essential inside the theatre, where officers were required to look stern and unyielding and occasionally eject a ruffian.

Outside the theatre, excited and emboldened in the face of such unattainable charm and beauty, the boys did the only thing they could do – and that was to abuse police officers from the anonymity of the crowd. It was raucous and unpleasant, and policemen facing the scorn of an unruly public became impetuous.

Inspector Allison and Constable Lewis took up a position away from the crowd in front of the stage door and watched the bug-eyed crowd from relative safety, but there was no sanctuary. A butcher's boy from Morriston called Lewis a "mutton shunter", a derisive term for a policeman, referring to their harassment of prostitutes. Lewis angrily waded into the crowd to grab him, but the boys circled around him, and soon he had lost his hat and his handcuffs, which were waved before him like a trophy. Lewis retreated ignominiously, leaving behind those two items, along with his pride.

Bucke was inside the theatre when Sergeant Ball came to see him during the interval. 'You better come outside, sir. There is a deal of mafficking going on in the street and Constable Lewis might get himself into trouble, if we are not careful.'

'Thank you, Sergeant. I shall be there as soon as I can,' replied Bucke.

~

As the evening wore on, Allison and Lewis, like the boys in the crowd, sought solace in beer, in their case as a preferable alternative to considering their own incompetence in the face of an abusive crowd. The beer made them talkative.

'Bloody Londoners. Who do they think they are?' Allison announced and went on, without any trace of irony whatsoever, 'I'll wager he bought his way in. Or he knew someone. Everyone knows it should have been my job. Coming down here from the army. What does he know? Not suited to us. We are too clever for him. Even a man like Guy. Running rings round him.'

'Too right,' agreed Lewis, who was not paying as much attention as he should. 'No idea what he is about. My father should have had that job. Best man for it. Everyone knows.' He swayed gently and steadied himself with his hand on the flaking wall. He belched loudly.

Allison wasn't listening either. 'You see, I know where Guy is. Bucke hasn't got a clue. Daniel Guy is hiding in the cellar of a boozer in Sketty. Not a word, if you please.'

'You can trust me, Inspector.' He paused. 'How do you know?'

'I got my own team of informants, see,' he said, tapping the side of his nose. 'But don't ask because I am not saying. Let him try to find him for hisself an' then when he don't, I will slip in, see. Won't he look a fool!'

'Duw duw!' said Lewis, smiling at the cleverness of the plan. However, his mind, despite its fuddled state, was extremely busy. The credit for such a capture wouldn't do him any harm at all. They might be so pleased that the Watch Committee would promote him straight to Inspector. He stored the idea of a patrol through Sketty carefully away in his mind.

Bucke came outside and saw that the crowd, thankfully, was beginning to disperse as they became cold in the showers of rain that found their way to the bottom of the narrow street. He also saw that Lewis was drunk and a liability. He could see he had no hat and, without it, had lost what little authority he had. He sent him back to the police station. He would deal with his drinking later. Inspector Allison drifted away in the darkness.

The second half of the entertainment was mercifully shorter, and the cast, flushed with excitement and achievement, were taken back to Sketty for a celebratory party. The Eastside welcomed home their damp adolescents, and Temple Street had emptied at last.

Bucke was ready to go home when he heard someone running towards him.

'Oi, you! Get off home!' shouted Allison, pointing vaguely up towards the Castle, but a breathless Joseph skipped past him, his tray perfectly balanced.

'Inspector Bucke! Inspector Bucke! I been looking for you everywhere. I need to talk to you. About Punch. I saw who killed her. I was there. Honest.' He blew out his cheeks and straightened his ragged bow tie.

Bucke was immediately attentive. 'Very well, Joseph. What do you know?'

'It was late and there was not many people about and I thought it was time to go home and so I left that pub, sir, on the Strand because no one wanted to buy my matches. The Tiger Inn, it was. I walked along a bit and then I saw Punch and I thought she was talking to two men. But one of them walked away and the other one was wearing a hat and he had something in his hand and then she fell down. The man ran away up towards the Castle and then I went to see if I could help her but she was stabbed. She was my friend. She used to look out for me sometimes. I used to give her matches. But the man had killed her and I ran away in case he came back.'

'And you quite sure about this, Joseph?'

'Yes, sir. I've been frightened so I wanted to hide. But I knowed you would look after me, sir.'

'And would you recognise him again, do you think?'

'I think—'

There was a tremendous clap, and Joseph, unexpectedly, was sprawling on the ground. For a moment, Bucke was unsure what had happened, but then saw that Inspector Allison had slapped Joseph furiously on the cheek from behind.

Thomas Allison now stood over him, swaying slightly. 'Get up, you wretch! Don't you tell none of your lies to the Inspector. I know your ways. Get up and tell the truth!'

'I was telling the truth, honest I was. The man had something in his hand and it flashed in the light and she fell over.' Joseph stood up and secured his apple box. He was trembling now, he was hurt and he was frightened.

Allison slapped him across the face once again. 'Enough of your lies! Tell the truth!'

'I am telling the truth!' Joseph shouted, his cheeks red, with blood seeping from his mouth and staining his dirty chin. He was crying. 'It is the truth and the other man was Daniel Guy. I know him. He gave me a funny coin once. I saw him! But you'll never believe me!' He turned and ran off.

'Only thing they understand, Bucke. Wasting your time with all that fancy London talk. Show the filthy urchin who is in charge. You will never get anything from him otherwise. You can't trust scum like that. Just conning you for a bit of cash.' Allison grinned, his feet feeling unsteady on the wet, uneven cobbles.

Bucke said nothing, weighing up his options carefully. Then he walked across to him, grabbed him by the collar of his coat and threw him into the passage next to the stage door. Allison bounced off the wall and fell to the ground. Bucke picked him up and banged him against the wall. He pushed his forearm against Allison's throat and started to lift him off the ground.

Allison started to gasp, scrabbling at Bucke's arm with his hands to free himself. He hadn't realised how strong he was.

'Come on, Bucke. Don't be hasty... just trying to help... I know their sort... know how to handle them... It always works...

Still Bucke said nothing, his face ever closer to Allison's, pressing and slowly lifting.

He had killed men before, not only from a distance but also face-to-face, and he knew that it wasn't so simple to end someone's life with just your bare hands. But at this moment, Bucke was ready to give it another try. He'd hang, of course, but he didn't much care.

'Bucke... please... Rumsey... don't be soft on them... only thing that works...'

He silently lifted him a little more. Allison tried to force Bucke's arm downwards but did not have the strength. He tried to scratch at his face, but all he was aware of was that he was choking. His eyes were being forced out of his skull by the pressure; his tongue was too big for his mouth. Suddenly speech was an irrelevance. Instead, he snorted for air and desperately tried to keep his feet in contact with the ground. His head was scraping against the wall as Bucke pushed it upwards; his teeth were crushing each other. He could see nothing other than Bucke's eyes boring deep into his own. He felt Bucke's breath against his face and knew he was going to die.

And then Bucke let him go. Allison fell to the ground, gasping for breath and coughing. He rolled over and looked up to see Bucke glaring down at him with contempt. He still had not said a word. He turned and walked out of the passage. He searched everywhere for Joseph but he couldn't find him.

∽

Joseph ran up to the top of Temple Street with tears in his eyes and his hands in his box to secure his supply of matches and turned to the right. He stopped, breathless, at the top of Castle Lane, the dark, narrow gap next to the Castle Hotel that fell steeply down to the Strand. Never trust the police; this was what everyone had told him. Sell them information if you want to, they said, and when you do so, always remember that thieves have more honour. But he needed to tell someone about Punch and about Daniel Guy. He hadn't said a word to anyone so far, because he was waiting to speak to Inspector Bucke. Punch used to say he was all right, but he wasn't going back to find him now. He would go down to the Crown Inn. The barmaid there, Becky, let him sit in the lounge sometimes, if it was cold. He could ask her if she would speak to the inspector for him, then he could tell him about Punch. He walked down the familiar, uneven cobbles and then turned left towards the Crown Inn. He would be safe there.

At the dimly lit junction, two men came out of Baker Street and Joseph walked straight into them. He bounced back and suddenly realised he knew the taller man. He gasped, and the look he gave Guy showed beyond doubt that he recognised him. Pieter Moitch hit him once, very hard, in the face. Joseph staggered backwards and fell, banging his head hard on the wall, scattering his matches everywhere as he slumped to the floor. Guy was stunned by the speed of events, but Moitch had assumed control.

'Quickly. His legs you take, I think.' Guy did nothing, listening to the boy groaning. 'Come quickly now. He recognised you. Take his legs.'

Moitch held the boy under the arms and Guy picked up his feet. He was a slight, insubstantial burden. They carried him down Baker Street, across the railway tracks and then threw him into the North Dock. It was very dark and no one saw them.

Chapter Eleven

Rumsey Bucke spent the weekend contemplating his resignation. He couldn't stay here after nearly killing the Chief Inspector's son – and a colleague too. He had planned to go down to Mumbles on Saturday afternoon to look at the sea but, after searching fruitlessly for Joseph in the brisk wind all morning, any enthusiasm he once had deserted him. In the evening, he went into the pubs that Joseph frequented but there was no sign of him. He spent Sunday morning staring out of the window and then later in the afternoon he went to Danygraig Cemetery and stood with a hand on the headstone over the grave of Julia and the children for a long time.

It is not that he didn't want to resign; it was that the fuss which came with it would be tiresome. He tried to piece together his thoughts, but they remained fragmented and making sense of them seemed completely daunting. Perhaps the best thing he could do after he had been dismissed was to go down to the station and get on a train and see where it took him. In the absence of anything else, that seemed as good a scheme as any other.

So when he was summoned to the Chief Constable's office on Monday morning, he knew he was about to be dismissed and he knew that shortly he would be heading the short distance across the road to High Street Station. Allison, however, gave no indication that he knew what had happened at the Theatre Royal on Friday night; he was far more concerned with what had happened at church on Sunday morning and Bucke, a little confused, did his very best to pay close attention to what he said.

Chief Constable Allison had been approached by Mr Yorath the draper, who sold woollen goods from Commerce House on the High Street and was a voluble member of the local business community. Mr Yorath was anxious to express his concerns about the nature of the education received by his son, Morgan. He was a generously proportioned young man, who had always experienced considerable difficulties with the essential mysteries of reading and writing. However, it appeared that Mr Yorath had been persuaded by Vaughan Bristow that if he put his son's education in his hands, then Morgan was inexorably destined for a high-ranking position at the Bank of England, at the very least. Indeed, Mr Yorath had been very pleased with the reports he received on Morgan's progress, which spoke glowingly of the skills he had acquired, though strangely these newly acquired attributes were rarely displayed at home.

However, since last Wednesday morning, the school appeared to have been closed. Mr Yorath had paid in advance for tuition for Morgan, but this was not now being provided; Mr Yorath had dutifully sent Morgan to school every day since last Wednesday, and every day since last Wednesday he had been sent back home; Mr Yorath was understandably concerned that this might leave a gap in his son's education, which could result in that leading position in the Bank of England being offered to someone else. Intolerable. So the Chief Constable said he would look into it – and thus he told Bucke to go to Bristow's school – The Rugby College in Mansel Terrace – to find out what was going on. He would go, of course. There were plenty of trains.

There was no possible way he could have predicted that his world was about to be turned upside down.

He had not visited the school previously and was not sure what to expect. The building was a tall three-storey townhouse in an elevated position, with cellars beneath. It seemed quite imposing but closer examination would show that it was in need of some attention. Paint was flaking away from the walls and some of the plaster was cracked. At the bottom of the steps leading up to the front door, there was a man taking down the wooden sign which proclaimed "Rugby House". There was an untidy stack of school desks in the small front garden; and two boys were carrying them down the steps with difficulty, to pile them insecurely in a handcart. He struggled past them and knocked on the door.

It opened immediately, and Bucke, registering a female figure, said, 'Good afternoon. May I speak with your mistress?'

'I have no mistress, sir. I am the mistress, for what it is worth.'

'Please forgive me, madam. I assumed...' He was embarrassed more than usual and he was not sure why. He seemed unable to finish his sentence. He looked at the woman properly for the first time. She was short and slight. Her long dark hair, which had obviously been gathered up and pinned to the top of her head neatly and precisely at the start of the day, had started to fall loose. Her brown eyes appraised him coolly, looking at him down her small, slightly upturned nose from the top step, with her hand resting defensively on the doorframe. He noticed slender fingers, broken nails. Her head was tilted slightly to one side and she appraised him, quizzical and unafraid.

'You must be Mrs Bristow.'

'And you must be a policeman. As I can see from your uniform.'

He was transfixed by her eyes, large and bright, and with what seemed to him to be the longest eyelashes he had ever seen. He noticed her mouth and her generous lips.

'Yes. I am Inspector Rumsey Bucke, madam. I am here to speak to you about your husband.'

He found her quite striking and he identified in the way that she looked at him a considerable intelligence. She seemed flushed and her dark skirt covered in dust and dirt showed that it had been an extremely demanding day.

'Please excuse me, Inspector. Things have been unusually busy here today.' She looked beyond him at the man dismantling the school sign. 'Thank you for coming, Mr Pritchard. Particularly considerate of you, in the circumstances. Very kind! I shall lose no time in getting back in touch with you!' She offered him a cheery wave.

Mr Prichard said nothing, looked at her for a moment, and then returned to his work.

She lowered her voice. 'I can't pay him, you see; so he is taking back the sign. Not that I shall need it anymore. Unless I am also to be short of firewood.'

She blew away a stray piece of hair that wandered across her face. 'I think it might be best if I invited you inside. My dear neighbours have had enough to talk about this week already.'

She seemed disarmingly honest: a quality he generally admired, given the circumstances in which he usually worked.

'I believe it would be inappropriate to ask to speak to your husband, Mrs Bristow.'

'Indeed it is, Inspector. He is not here. He left here last Wednesday during the morning. I believe that my husband has deserted me. Perhaps you would like to come into the kitchen.'

The tall house was curiously quiet and bare. Their footsteps across the parquet floor echoed up through the building, making the impressive curved stairs and banisters seem abandoned, as if he was now somehow trapped within a ship of faded grandeur which had long been stranded on a distant beach.

'Most houses of this sort have frivolities such as dining rooms and parlours and the like, where you can receive honoured guests and important visitors. But because this house was converted to serve as a grammar school for boys, I am afraid that we have none of those desirable refinements. The kitchen here is all that I can offer.'

A school for boys? It seemed impossible to think that this was what it once was. Now it was quiet; the school had closed and now its soul had died. They sat in the kitchen at a scrubbed wooden table where a single half-empty teacup stood, lonely and forlorn.

Mrs Bristow sighed. 'Inspector, there can be no reason for pretence. Obviously, you are here to enquire about my husband. I imagine that angry parents have decided over the weekend that they were no longer prepared to pay for schooling that was not actually taking place. I cannot say that I blame them.'

He nodded. 'Yes, that is why I am here. Concerns have been expressed. Do you have any idea why he appears to have left Swansea?'

'Not at all. I had no reason to think that he was leaving. As far as I was concerned, last Wednesday was an ordinary day. He left in the middle of the morning. I saw him running down the steps with his Gladstone bag and then he turned to the left, down towards the Music Hall. It was the last I saw of him. I was more concerned with the boys who were parading around from room to room in an unlicensed fashion. I was forced to send them home, telling them that Mr Bristow was unwell. I did manage to maintain that falsehood until the weekend which, in the circumstances, I was quite pleased about. But now it seems, the news has travelled quickly.'

'And there are no pupil teachers here in the school?' asked Bucke.

'None whatsoever. It was an expense that my husband would not sanction and so taught all the pupils himself, though often the older boys supervised the younger ones. It was an arrangement which I always found rather surprising, since their parents had sent them here to be taught by an adult, rather than a child.'

'Was he worried about anything in particular before he left, do you think?' asked Bucke.

'Not especially. In fact, he seemed rather pleased with himself when he returned from his meeting at the Royal Institution. He spent the rest of the evening pacing around his study composing a letter to *The Times*. He liked to recite his words in the manner of an orator before he wrote them down,' she explained. 'I heard him.'

'And what was the subject of this letter? Do you know, Mrs Bristow?'

'I heard the sounds, Inspector, but paid no regard to the words. I had probably heard them before. It was just another happy evening in the Bristow household.' She smiled sardonically.

Bucke was certain that he had never met anyone quite like her before in his life. 'I see. What time did he return from his meeting, Mrs Bristow?'

'He was home at about 10.30 pm and, as I say, he took to his study. He had been drinking certainly, though not to excess.'

'And he did not leave the house again that evening?'

'Not for a moment, Inspector.'

'He was here all night?'

'Yes, Inspector. As I know to my cost,' she said.

He was shocked again by her unexpected frankness and he paused for a moment whilst he composed his next question. 'Your situation today would seem to suggest that the school has been experiencing some financial difficulties.'

'Oh yes indeed, Inspector. My husband has been living beyond his means for some considerable time. Bills have, of necessity, remained unpaid, and I have tried my very best to manage those debts and to pacify unhappy creditors. Since the news of his departure became public knowledge, there has been a succession of unhappy traders at my door, as you will have noted yourself. They will not be prepared to listen to my soothing words for much longer. The edifice he created has suddenly collapsed. I cannot express surprise, Inspector. It was always going to happen.'

'And Mr Bristow was aware of his perilous circumstances?' he asked.

She smiled contemptuously. 'Of course he was. Ridiculous as it seems, his concern has always been to promote a ludicrous image of himself as an intellectual giant in Swansea, leading public opinion whilst taking brandy in the drawing room with the great men of the town. Everything he ever did was about himself. Nothing else. Please excuse me for speaking in this way, but I cannot help but think that he has run away, Inspector, because he was disturbed by the prospect of being found out for what he is.'

'So he may have been frightened, do you think?'

'It is a possibility, Inspector. As you might expect, I have had plenty of time in recent days to reflect upon his actions. I have no doubt that running away when a situation becomes difficult is certainly within his character. The timing of his departure seems strange, that is all. He seemed to have persuaded himself that he would soon be able to resolve all of his financial troubles. So he told me anyway. But something clearly has changed.'

'Did he talk about how this transformation might happen?'

'Not in any detail,' she continued. 'He has been more agitated about this notion of a tunnel under the sea, as if that were in some way important. There were occasions when I tried to be the dutiful wife and I would listen with as much attention as I could muster, but I was not always as successful as he would have liked. He became very excited at times and spoke of armies marching beneath the waves that would destroy all that we hold dear. Apparently women would be outraged and sold into slavery, which seemed to me to be more of a particularly appealing opportunity than anything else, though usually my attentions were focused on issues that were much less lofty – like resolving household bills.'

Bucke paused again and considered what Mrs Bristow had said. She looked at him quizzically, with a confidence that he found rather appealing.

'Is there anything else I can help you with, Inspector?' she asked.

'Would you describe your husband as a violent man, Mrs Bristow?'

She considered her words carefully. 'It would be true to say that there were times when his insistence on domestic discipline took precedence over marital harmony.'

'And did such discipline happen often?'

'Not infrequently. I would say that generally it was always controlled, always quite deliberate.' She looked back at him steadily.

'Please do not misunderstand me, but on those occasions, did you considerate it proportionate?'

He realised immediately that he had said the wrong thing.

Her eyes flashed, then flamed in anger. 'Proportionate? What are you trying to say, Inspector? That it was justified? That it was acceptable?' Mrs Bristow's eyes fixed him steadily. 'To raise your hand because it was not the kind of fish you anticipated? Or because the newspaper was badly folded, since it showed I had been reading it before you? Is that what you think? Look at my arm, Inspector.' Mrs Bristow pulled up the sleeve of her dress and showed him a patch of puckered skin. 'Do you see that, Inspector Bucke? My skin burnt when he threw soup at me.

I protected my face. Such is the price of vanity. And you dare to ask me if it was proportionate?'

Bucke was mortified and stumbled a little over his words. 'No, of course not, Mrs Bristow. I do apologise. An unfortunate choice of words. Unforgivably clumsy.' He looked at the floor, his face flushed with embarrassment. 'What I should have asked you was whether your husband ever offered you extreme violence.' He looked up. 'I am sorry. I hadn't meant to imply...' He ran out of words.

'Are you married, Inspector?' Mrs Bristow asked aggressively.

'I am a widower.'

'And did you beat your wife?' she raged.

'Of course not.'

'So why...' she stopped suddenly. 'Oh.' Her hand went up to her mouth. 'I am so stupid at times. I am truly sorry, Inspector. I did not think.' She paused again. 'In answer to your question: no, he never threatened to murder me. I think that is what you wanted to say. But I am so sorry. Perhaps we should start again. Things haven't progressed very well so far, have they, Inspector?' She shrugged her shoulders and offered him half a smile.

'No, and that is entirely the fault of my own insensitivity. Thank you for your time this afternoon, Mrs Bristow. You have been very candid, but I think I should leave. I will show myself out. I will send another officer to see you.' He stood up.

She watched his face and the faint smile became more secure upon her lips.

'Please, Inspector. Please sit down. There is no need for you to leave. Perhaps we have both made mistakes. I would be happy to answer any questions you might have. Truly, God knows, it will stop me worrying about what happens next. I apologise, Inspector, for my blasphemous language.'

He found himself returning her smile. 'I hear much worse every day, Mrs Bristow.' He sat down.

'Did he own a sword-cane, Mrs Bristow?'

'I presume you mean a blade concealed within a walking stick. As far as I know, he had no such thing. He has a blackthorn walking stick of which he is inordinately proud. It has a knob at the end which he finds useful for disciplining the boys. He calls it The Basher.'

'Is that stick here, Mrs Bristow?'

'He would normally keep it in his study, but when Mr Maxwell arrived this morning to begin the recovery of the school desks which, as you will have noticed, continues apace, he began in the headmaster's study. It is now empty and the walking stick is not there. The Basher has deserted me too, it would seem. I would have been surprised if he had not taken it with him. I didn't want it. Never liked it.'

'Would you be prepared to speculate about where he might have gone? Any old friends perhaps?'

'I cannot say, Inspector. We have been in Swansea for three years now. Before then my husband had a school in Reading. He may have gone back there.' She paused. 'There was a woman, you see. Harriet Webb. She was my maid but she served my husband in a different way – with an affiliation order. She was one of the reasons why we moved here to Swansea and one of the reasons I now choose to live without any domestic help.'

'Are you suggesting that he may have returned to Reading? To Harriet Webb?'

'I do not know. I have no evidence that there has been any contact between them, but I would not know.'

Bucke stood up once more. 'Thank you so much for your time, Mrs Bristow. I know this might have been a painful discussion for you, but it has been very informative and very useful to me. Thank you. And I apologise unreservedly again for my insensitivity.'

She shrugged and smiled, tucking that stray hair behind her ear. 'You must think of it no longer, Inspector. I have a capacity for stupidity too, as you will have noted.'

They looked at each other in silence.

'You must return, Inspector,' Mrs Bristow said finally. 'I am sure you will have other questions to ask me in the coming days.'

'Thank you, Mrs Bristow. I shall not hesitate, should it prove necessary. I am sure I would find it interesting.'

She took him back through the house and opened the door.

'And you believe that he won't be back?' he asked.

'Yes, Inspector Bucke. I am quite sure of one thing, as I told you. That my husband has deserted me. He will never return.'

As Bucke descended the steps, dodging around a desk that had spilled from the stacked cart, he saw Baglow, a young reporter he knew from the Cardiff-based daily newspaper the *South Wales Daily Post*, walking briskly along Mansel Terrace. He looked purposeful, eagerly in pursuit of a story. The sight of a departing police inspector was just the sort of luck that he needed.

∼

Within a few days, all outstanding serious criminal cases in Swansea had been solved for, as far as the press were concerned, the police had finally got their man. Vaughan Bristow was a murderer, condemned by flight. Baglow's story was featured prominently in the *South Wales Daily Post* on Tuesday, and once it had been picked up and repeated by the weekly *Cambrian* on Friday, then Bristow would be a marked man. The *Cambrian* was seen as the oracle of all things in Swansea. What the paper said must be true always, although it was never to be troubled by concerns about evidence or motive.

Neither was Chief Constable Allison. All he had to say was 'Cracked it then,' which Bucke acknowledged with no more than a shrug. For Allison, any solution to a prominent crime like murder, no matter how implausible, was better than none. In his eyes, the truth had always been less important than his own reputation and that of the force he commanded. 'You've got your man. A shock to us all but you've got 'im. All you got to do now is find where the bugger's run to ground.' He said nothing at all about events involving his son outside the theatre.

Inevitably, it caused great excitement round town. Bristow had gone, fled, they said, after stabbing Jenkins during some murky disagreement or in a drunken rage. There had been an argument over goodness knows what. Bristow had followed Jenkins and ambushed him. They had been amicable enough at the meeting at the Royal Institution but that was a deception. He stole Jenkins's sword-stick and stabbed him. There were all sorts of theories and soon, of course, he was recognised as a double murderer. He must have killed Punch too, to slake his own depravity. Two stabbings on either side of a weekend? No wonder he had run away. The lack of any incriminating evidence was merely an example of his diabolical cunning.

Bucke was equally sure that Bristow hadn't done it, but he had to admit that the accusation helped him. The failure was now a shortcoming in a police department somewhere else, whichever one it was that today was accused of failing to catch him, which granted Bucke a little space in which to try to unravel what had happened.

He knew that Bristow had been identified as a murderer simply because it was convenient, although that didn't seem to trouble anyone. What motive did he have for killing Punch and Jenkins? Had he actually been present when the murders had happened, because if he could be shown to have been somewhere else, could he really have committed them? Did he have a weapon? Who cared? The case had been solved. Why else had a prominent head teacher disappeared immediately after

Jenkins was killed? The manner of his departure was sufficient to condemn him. Bristow's new status as a murderer was something in which many members of the general public were very eager to believe. The possibility was shocking and thrilling, showing that even a prominent professional man, like the head teacher of his own school, could harbour dark secrets and be tortured by the same passions as an ordinary man.

Bucke was certain he was just a distraction. Whatever he was, he didn't seem like a murderer. If he had been determined to kill Jenkins, what devious reason did he have for following him up to St James' Crescent to kill him in his garden, when he could have killed him in a passageway and saved himself the walk to the Uplands? Not only that, Mrs Bristow said quite clearly that he had been at home when Jenkins died. In the circumstances, what possible reason did she have to provide him with an alibi? None whatsoever. She must have been telling the truth.

Bristow was required to answer questions, and Bucke had to try and track him down. Perhaps he had information which would explain the unsettling events of the past few weeks. But there remained something about the timing of Bristow's disappearance which interested Bucke. Why run at that moment, if it wasn't in some way connected with Jenkins's murder? It didn't mean that he had done it, though.

The enquiries he led, however, were not productive. The great difficulty for the police was clear for all to see. Bristow had gone on Wednesday, and his flight was not confirmed until the following Monday, and in the interim no one had thought to mention it to them. But then why should they? Who could have guessed that he was a killer?

Bucke resisted Allison's instruction to bring in Mrs Bristow. He told him about the conversation and the statement she would give about him being at home at the time the murder was committed. 'Thing is, Bucke, why did she keep quiet about him buggerin' off then? Charge her with obstructing the police or summat. Anything. Then she will tell thee where he is.'

Bucke thanked him for his advice and ignored it.

A man who might have answered his description might have boarded the London train, and it might have been on Wednesday but no one could be sure. The ticket clerk at Swansea High Street station said that someone had bought a ticket who looked a bit like Bristow. But if he had caught the train, then where had he got off? No one could say. Did he buy a ticket to Neath? Or was it Cardiff? The clerk couldn't remember. So if it had been Bristow, did he travel to the end of the line in London or had he got off the train at an earlier station? No one knew that either. By the time Bucke had sent telegrams to London, to station masters and to police forces all along the Great Western Railway line, Bristow, wherever he was, had a considerable head start on him.

He hadn't been seen for seven days, which was long enough in anyone's reckoning. He could have gone to Bristol and have by now secured a place upon a ship heading goodness knows where. Or he could have changed trains in Swindon or Reading. How do you find out when no one knows anything? A man of unremarkable appearance had not been remarked upon.

The police in Reading could offer no help, which was a particular disappointment. They told Bucke that a number of businessmen in the town had come forward in the wake of the news, eager to resolve some outstanding financial issues with Bristow and would not have hesitated to inform the police if he had turned up, but no one had seen him. Poor Harriet Webb had experienced a rapid descent into poverty following her pregnancy and the death of her baby and was now working as a washerwoman. She had recently been arrested for stealing coal from the railway station and had thus been unable to offer Bristow help of any kind, even if she had wanted to. It seemed that he wasn't in Reading.

The anonymity of London might be an attractive proposition for an escaping criminal, but the idea that anyone might actually have recognised him in Paddington was laughable. His professional appearance would have allowed him to slip unnoticed through crowds of other professional-looking people and, of course, he had had that significant head start. There was little chance anyone would remember a gentleman determined to remain unnoticed. Bucke enquired nevertheless and was not surprised when he was told no one had seen him.

Inspector Bucke left the police station and wandered through the town in a vain attempt to clear his mind, calling in at the public houses to ask if anyone had seen Joseph but no one had. He did not appear to have been around for a few days. He stopped eventually, leaning against a wall on the corner of Plymouth Street, watching two dogs playing in the traffic, snapping at the horses' legs, and the people busy with their own lives hurrying past, all of them enclosed in their own worlds. Perhaps one of these strangers had a crucial piece of information which would make sense of everything. But how was he to find out, especially if they didn't know that they had it?

He tried to dismiss Guy from his mind and concentrate on the murder of Jenkins. If Bristow had been his murderer, then why did he do it? That was the central question in all murder enquiries. Why? He knew that men were not often killed by a stranger. If he had killed him, there must have been something that bound them together in a murderous relationship. All he could think of was the Swansea Society for the Acquisition of Useful Knowledge – and it was a ridiculous idea that such a pompous and ineffectual group could have nurtured murderous intent. Nevertheless, in Bucke's mind, something linked Bristow and Jenkins. They met, they spoke, they agreed. They had been together on Tuesday night; and twelve hours later, one was dead and the other had fled. Did Punch's murder somehow fit into all this? Bucke was sure that it did, but his mind could not tease out a pattern to any of these events. He was tired and he craved peace and rest; but Julia had not been to see him for quite a few nights now and he missed her dreadfully.

Chapter Twelve

When Bucke arrived at the police station the following morning, after another restless night haunted by shapeless fears, Sergeant Ball nodded a greeting to him and expressed his pleasure that the two murder cases had been solved.

'Never have thought it. Gentleman and a head teacher? Well, well. Takes all sorts. '

Ball then added, almost as an afterthought, that they had found Joseph's body floating in the North Dock. Ernest Leyshon, the superintendent, had fished him out with a boat hook. The body had been in the water for a few days.

Bucke sat down heavily, as if all the air had suddenly leaked from his body. Joseph had been looking for him. And now? He was another piece of Swansea's flotsam, his potential snuffed out forever.

'Doctor Beynon has got his body in that shed by Squire's Place, behind the Castle, Inspector. Probably fell in the dark. Terrible shame, a young boy like that. Constable Davies is down there watching the proceedings. There's no reason for you to go down. He can deal with it.'

Inspector Bucke thanked Sergeant Ball for his concern and walked across to Squire's Place. He owed Joseph something, an apology for the vicious behaviour of Inspector Allison, an apology for not being able to protect him, an apology for not being able to find him. He sent Constable Davies back to the station and took his place.

His apple box, empty of matches, had still been around his neck when they pulled him out of the water, and now it was beneath the wooden table on which the boy's body was lying. It wasn't a nice thing to look at. His thin, undernourished body was bloated now, almost colourless, apart from the heavy bruising around his eyes and the stains and the slime from the filthy water in which he had died. His bow tie was still in place, still untidy, still incongruous. No one really knew who Joseph was, where he came from or indeed how he had managed to survive for so long on the cold streets. But it didn't matter anymore. He was gone and no one would come to claim his body. Now he was nothing more than an abandoned fragment in poverty's cruel harvest.

'Broken nose,' said Doctor Beynon, looking up. 'Banged his head on something when he fell, I would suggest. He might have been drinking, but I would say it is more probable that he tripped and into the dock he went. There are ropes everywhere. Such a waste of a young life.' He shook his head. 'It is a cruel world that we inhabit, Rumsey.'

'How old do you think he was, Doctor?'

'Eleven, twelve, it is hard to say. I wonder what he was doing on the dock. I cannot imagine there was much business for a matchboy down here, especially during the weekend.'

'The weekend? How long has he been in the water, do you think?' asked Bucke.

'A few days, I would say. Three days? Four? He was obviously still alive when he went into the dock. He drowned. There is water in his lungs.'

'I have been looking for him since Friday, David. I saw him that evening but have been unable to find him since then.'

'That is because he was probably in the dock, Rumsey.'

'I know.' Bucke sighed. He knew that if Inspector Allison hadn't hit him around the head, Joseph might still be alive. But Allison had frightened him away and now he was a hollow shell, lying on a table in a dirty shed by the side of the dock. There had been neither goodness nor mercy for Joseph, ever. There had been no good shepherd to accompany him through his short life and save him from the water. He closed his eyes and lowered his head, breathing deeply to prevent the tears.

Doctor Beynon, concerned, leaned across and put a gentle hand on his arm. 'Is sleep still proving difficult to find for you, Rumsey? Perhaps I can offer you something which may assist?'

Bucke glanced up and shrugged. 'Some nights are better than others, David. Perhaps I will come and see you at the end of the week. Perhaps it would be better if I left this town behind and started again somewhere else.'

The doctor looked at him. 'You must not be too hasty. I would like your word that, should you decide to leave Swansea, you will come and see me first.'

'Time to arrange a funeral for a lost pauper, I think, David. He had nothing, no one knows where he came from, and I will never know if his dreams were better than mine. But now he is at rest, now he is at peace. I may come to see you, David. You have my word that I will consider it.'

He left the dock to the penetrating melancholy of a hooter from a ship, desperately trying to recall its missing seamen from wherever they were in the town. At the end of Baker Street, he stepped aside to allow two of its sailors to run past him at speed and, as he did so, he saw Mr Gallivan, Guy's neighbour, pushing a wheelbarrow full of bottles along the glistening cobbles to the Crown Inn. Bucke slipped back into the shadows so that he wouldn't be seen. And then he saw on the ground, kicked into the edge of the wall, a large number of matches. He bent down to examine them. They were wet following the rain but certainly unstruck. Were these Joseph's matches? If they were, then something had happened to him here. And then he had managed to cross the railway lines and stumble into the dock, leaving his precious matches behind in Baker Street? Unlikely. So had he been attacked? Had he been murdered? Why would anyone do such a thing? What did Joseph have? Nothing at all. Nothing that anyone would ever want to steal. Unless of course there was information inside his head. Which might suggest that Joseph had been silenced. Bucke's mind was racing, seeing links and connections, but aware also that he might be conjuring a story from the air. But he knew that Joseph had wanted to tell him about Daniel Guy. He said he had seen him. And someone could have killed Joseph in order to stop him. It was entirely speculative of course, he knew that; but this was another death in Swansea, another death that seemed to be haunted by the shadowy figure of Daniel Guy. He had to find the connections and piece all these elements together. Was Guy at the heart of it all? Why should that be?

~

He arrived late to the burial of Herbert Jenkins and listened to the barren words at the graveside in St Paul's Churchyard in Sketty. There was no rain. The sky chose not to weep for him, but the blustery wind blew Reverend Bolney's words far away, so that, separated and fractured, they lost all their meaning.

Virginia Jenkins, upright, haughty and displaying more than a hint of boredom, was inevitably attended by the quiet and alert figure of Elinor Roberts. The Chief Constable was there with his face, reddened by the wind, dramatically punctuated by that wart, which looked more and more like the bud of a grotesque flower. He was leaning heavily on a walking stick which had a green band or a stray piece of grass around it. His son Thomas stood by his side, holding his bowler hat in front of him and studiously avoiding Bucke by staring into the far distance in the manner of a madman. Bucke saw that the great men of Swansea were all present, hoping to be noticed. Their mutterings, of course, were about murder and were evidence of the sudden but unstoppable momentum that was gathering around the idea of Bristow the Killer. No one had expected that, which added to the frisson that crackled around the cemetery. Whoever Herbert Jenkins had once been, however tedious and self-important, that was far less significant now than the identity of the person who had pushed a sword deep into his torso. As the mourners dispersed, Charles Glascodine approached Bucke and took him to one side. 'Strange business all round, if you ask me. Might help both of us if you pop round to the office tomorrow morning, Inspector. Eleven o'clock, shall we say?' Bucke agreed. It should prove more useful than speaking to the grieving widow.

It had been a grim and unpleasant day. The sky had been unceasingly grey and malevolent and no one had enjoyed their work – it had been a day of death.

There had been a horrible accident involving one of the steam-powered Mumbles trams. A drunken seaman and oyster dredger called Edwards had been staggering home from Swansea by the side of the tramlines. For reasons best known to himself, he had been drinking somewhere, seemingly all night. A few people saw Edwards and some indeed had spoken to him and did their best to point him in the direction of home. All he was able to say in reply was, 'I am right drunk,' which of course he was. But at Lilliput Lane, he finally fell over onto the track, just in time for an early morning Swansea-bound tram to arrive and decapitate him. The driver, William Harris, didn't want to see the body, neither did the passengers, nor indeed did Constable Plumley; but it was his job to do so, and, when he recovered the corpse, he promptly vomited all over his uniform.

At midday, on the other side of town, Constable Lewis had found the body of a young man called Nicholas John on the railway line at Llansamlet and had the responsibility of informing his mother, a widow who relied completely upon the wages of her son. How could anyone ever tell a mother that the engine driver had reported that her beloved son had chosen to walk deliberately into a speeding train?

The two constables sat together in the corner of the police station, soiled and angry, their horror hidden behind their complaints about the difficulties and the indignities of the duties they had had to perform. As Bucke watched them, he knew that protesting like this was the only way either of them could ever deal with the immensity of the human tragedy that sometimes surrounded them.

It was an impossible job sometimes, Bucke knew that as well as anyone else, and as they sat around in gloomy commiseration, there came the news that another body had been pulled out of the North Dock. They groaned and watched with some relief as Constable Davies, who had wandered in to deposit some lost property at the desk, was sent off to deal with the corpse.

Bucke was aware that he really should speak to Lewis about his behaviour outside the theatre last week, but he did not think this was the right moment. However, he also realised that he desperately needed to talk to someone. He was a lonely man, lost in a featureless wilderness of despair and depression. Suddenly, quite unconsciously, he left the station and its dreary atmosphere of death and found himself walking towards Mansel Terrace. He realised immediately where he was going and knew that he was being foolish but he did not falter.

'Please come in, Inspector. You will allow me to serve you tea? It is something which I can still afford. I may even use my very best china, whilst I still have it, of course.' She took him through once again to the neat simple kitchen and he sat at the table, whilst she busied herself at the stove chattering away, also pleased to have someone to talk to. Bucke noticed that she was still wearing that grubby skirt he had seen before, though today it was covered by an apron tied at the waist. There was an open packing case in the corner.

'It is no better today. Things are not going well,' she said with surprising cheerfulness. 'The news has spread about my situation and has created some alarm. He has left behind so many unpaid bills, there is no money and I have had a series of visits from angry fathers. Did you know? Now there will be no Oxford education for young Edward, or so it appears. There was never going to be, but his father is demanding a refund. Not a nice man at all and neither is young Edward. Hit next door's cat with a cricket bat a few weeks ago. It is no wonder we've got mice.'

'I must assume there is no news of your husband?'

The lid of the kettle rattled and Mrs Bristow poured water into a teapot. 'No, Inspector. As I am sure I told you, I will not hear from him again. If he was to come back now, he would have to face up to what he has done – whatever that is – and Billy will never do that. He has gone.' She smiled at him. 'I must fend for myself the best that I can.'

'Billy? Who is Billy?' asked Bucke.

'It is my husband, Inspector. His name is William. I would call him Billy when I had a mind to irritate him, though to be frank it was often counter-productive. The name Vaughan was his invention to make himself sound more distinguished. As if in some way you can change your name and so change your character.'

She poured tea into the delicate cups and his rattled on its saucer as he picked it up. He was strangely nervous.

'Please be careful, Inspector,' she said, raising her eyebrows. 'It is hard to sell an incomplete tea service.' She dried a teaspoon on her apron and passed it across to him. 'Sorry, I should have placed this on your saucer first.'

'I am sorry too. My hands are shaking. I don't know why.'

'Had I realised, I would have used my second-best service.' She smiled reassuringly. 'You know, I was reflecting , just before you knocked on my door, about how unexpected are the paths that our lives must take. Now I am apparently married to a murderer. Perhaps I shall be notorious.'

'How do you respond to such a suggestion?'

'That I am married to a murderer or that I shall be notorious? Notoriety has a certain attraction, I think.'

Bucke smiled. 'I was referring to Mr Bristow, the murderer.'

'It is a ridiculous idea. He was never a murderer, however convenient that might be to your investigation. He did not have the courage. He was a bully, yes, and violent towards me, but with other men he craved their approval and wished for them to admire his intelligence. All a sham, of course. He needed important friends and social standing, but his dreams were built upon sand. His suitability for his job I have always questioned, but he told everyone, tirelessly, that he was an exceptional teacher so that, in the end, they seemed to believe him. He told them that he was the best person to prepare their children for university but he was no such thing. He knew nothing. You see, Inspector, my husband was a magpie. Forever picking up other people's knowledge to use for himself. He had not an original idea in his head. He just found many ways to say the same thing. He said he had influence in the universities which would enable him to find places for the boys, or find them employment within the government or commissions in the army. It was all a lie. Every word.' She paused to drink her tea, excited by this unexpected opportunity to express her anger. 'Do you know? I laughed out loud when I heard Billy boast that kindness and patience were the chief characteristics of his system of education. Kindness? Patience? A system? Heaven help us all. Did you realise, Inspector, that apparently, as a woman, I am emotionally unsuited to education? I am only allowed to teach dancing, music and deportment. Though, of course, I was expected to run a household.'

'You seem to have been unhappy in your marriage, Mrs Bristow.'

She did not immediately reply; there was no need.

'And you, Inspector? Were you happy in your marriage?'

'Yes, I was. Julia and I met at a Regimental Ball at Simla, and I think we both knew from the first moment that we had a future together. Her father was a Major and he was so pleased that Julia had found happiness. He died of malaria in India and I think it comforted him that he knew his daughter would be safe.' Bucke stared at the wall as though he could see Julia there, and gnawed in a distracted way at his thumbnail. Constance Bristow did not wish to interrupt this moment. He appeared distressed and vulnerable. 'I am sorry, Mrs Bristow. Did you say something?'

'I merely said that you were lucky, Inspector.' It was a small lie but it would not harm anyone.

'I know. We came to Swansea, we had two beautiful children and we built our home and our future. Then, without warning, death snatched them all away from me.'

'The children too? I am truly sorry. I did not know that.'

Bucke knew he should say something, but he wasn't sure he could find any words. 'Anna and Charles,' he said finally.

She looked at him carefully with her head to one side, tucking her hair behind her ear. 'It must have been a terrible moment. But you must always remember that you had all those happy moments that no one can take from you. You will never forget them. They are part of what you are and what you will become. Whereas I made one terrible mistake. I was young, of course, and the younger you marry, the longer you have to regret it. William was appointed as a teacher in my father's school in Bournemouth and he courted me, I suspect, in the hope that it would bring him advancement. My father was very sceptical of our friendship. He believed that I was too young – I was eighteen – and I am convinced he began to feel that William was a charlatan. But I was headstrong and my circumstances gave him little choice but to accede to my demands to be allowed to marry.'

Bucke nodded. 'I see.'

'Yes. My daughter Agnes was born soon after I was married. She has always proved to be my salvation, the one shining light in the treacherous darkness of my marriage. Now she has a position as a nursery governess with a family in South Africa. She was all too eager to get away. Agnes is eighteen, and when she left I advised her never to marry – and, given what she saw in this house, it is likely that she may never do so. Once she had gone, then I began to give serious consideration to my own future. I would have left myself, but my husband has been much more decisive, it would seem.' Mrs Bristow stirred her tea absentmindedly, though Bucke had noticed that she had not taken any sugar. She continued with her story.

'As I told you, there was an affiliation order served against William whilst we were in Reading. Poor little Harriet Webb, our housemaid, another of his victims – or so the newspaper tells me, along with all of its other readers. She is the reason we moved to Swansea, Inspector. But then, once we were here, he again consorted with another maid, so I had no alternative but to dismiss her and live, as you are aware, without the help of any domestic staff. There has never been room for a second mistress in my house. However unsatisfactory that position of mistress became, it was never a position that I was willing to share. You may gather, Inspector, that my husband was not a man to be trusted. And yet now it would appear that he has been awarded the status of a murderer who has terrorised Swansea. That is ridiculous. He is many things. He is a liar and a cheat, a fantasist, a cruel and unpredictable bully, I would say. But a murderer? Never. He has neither the resolve nor the strength to attack another man. He might beat a woman, but a man? Never. If you believe that William is a murderer, than you are completely wrong.'

'You have spoken of your husband's infidelities, Mrs Bristow. Were there any other occasions when you suspected he may have been paying for companionship amongst certain women in the town?'

She was amused by his careful choice of words. 'He did many things outside of the house about which, thankfully, I know very little. He saw no reason to tell me where he was going or where he had been. I often had no inclination to ask.'

'If it is of any consolation to you, I do not believe that he is the murderer, whatever the public seems eager to believe.'

'That must make your task all the more difficult. It is someone else who has been killing people, not Billy. But you must excuse me. Local tradesmen remain anxious to speak to me. They are unhappy but largely polite, and I smile as pleasantly as I can. How long their courtesy will last, I am not sure. Thank you for listening to me, Inspector. It has, in some small way, helped me. It would be a pleasure to see you here again, whilst I still have a roof over me. Though soon you may have to accept service in the second-best china.'

~

He returned slowly to Tontine Street. In the space of a few short weeks, three unhappy marriages had been revealed to him – the Guys', the Jenkins', the Bristows' – which had spawned an attempted murder, a death and a desertion. It seemed so unfair that his own happy marriage and family had been destroyed, whilst these others had staggered along in violence, acrimony and unhappiness. He paused for a moment before crossing Cradock Street, avoiding the manure glistening on the road. And the most foolish man of all? It had to be Billy Bristow. To be married to a woman like Constance and to treat her as he did, then to desert her? Inexplicable.

That night, a wave of unexpected emotions swept over him when he climbed into bed. He could not stop himself crying. He was wracked with guilt, smothered by the idea that these emotions were betraying his family. More than anything else, he wanted Julia to come to him. He concentrated and tried to make her appear from within his memories but she would not. She would appear only when she was ready, when she was no longer angry with him. How long must he wait before he could ask for her forgiveness? And then suddenly he fell into a deep, dark and dreamless sleep.

Chapter Thirteen

Constable Lewis was known for his cynicism, his arched eyebrows, his permanent sneer and a general lack of sympathy for those in difficulty. He was sometimes unreliable and frequently dishonest, but, however hardened he was to the misery which surrounded him on the streets, there were occasions when he was unexpectedly moved by what he saw. The death of Nicholas John he found particularly difficult. The memory of the poor mother, a widow living in dismal poverty and reliant entirely upon her son, who thanked him for bringing that awful news to her tiny cottage, would live with him for a long time. Why Nicholas had done what he did no one would ever know. He had worked quietly and unskilled in the tinplate works, breathing the filthy air for five years and then, so it seemed, had decided one morning to walk into a speeding train.

Lewis no longer had any wish to be a constable and deal with the chewed-up remains of unhappy people. Neither did he want to end up like his policeman father, who died under a collapsing roof whilst looking for an escaped prisoner in a derelict house in Pentrechwyth. He needed to get off the beat as soon as he could. The only escape he could see was promotion to an untroubled job as a desk sergeant. And he thought he saw a way to achieve that. He remembered, with incomplete but sufficient detail through the beery haze, the conversation he had had with Inspector Allison outside the theatre. Daniel Guy was hiding in a cellar beneath a public house in Sketty and Inspector Allison had been at a funeral somewhere yesterday, so he hadn't been able to do anything about it. But Lewis could. What a triumph that would be. A supposedly clever London inspector, out-thought by a humble Swansea constable. Soon to be a sergeant? Inspector, more likely. It would be good to have a choice.

So he persuaded Plumley to swap beats with him that morning. Make a change, he said, take them both away, for a short while at least, from places which held such graphic memories. Plumley was a little nervous about it since Sergeant Ball hadn't been consulted and it hadn't gone very well the last time he switched beats, but Lewis brushed aside his objections. He offered him guidance, recommending that he spend as much time as he could in Llewelyn Park. You could look busy there and be reasonably prominent, he said, but there was never anything to do. Whilst Plumley was thinking that over, Lewis headed up towards Sketty Cross.

Of course, his first problem was remembering to which public house Allison had been referring. There were plenty to choose from, though he was able in his own mind to reject those which did not have an obvious cellar. In the end, he decided that it must have been the Bush Inn, confusing complete guesswork with patient deductive analysis. He went round to the back of the house and announced to the landlady, Anora Crocker, who was busily pegging out her washing in the yard, that he had come to examine her cellar because he had heard that there were vagrants living down there.

'What? Are you mad, like? In my cellar? I am telling you, you are off yewer 'ead. Where is Constable Plumley? He never said nothing like that to me.'

'And I am telling you, Mrs Crocker, that I have received certain information.'

'Well, it is lies. Who 'as been saying these lies to yew? I want to know who they are.' If such people were ever to exist, they would find Anora's retribution fierce and unyielding.

'I am not at liberty to reveal my sources.' He was sure her reluctance was a clear indication of guilt. He tapped his policeman's staff on the doorframe. 'You better let me in or you will be in big trouble.'

'Go and 'ave a look if you want to be a dull bugger. There is nothing and no one down there, I am telling yew. But I want to know who 'as been telling stories, like. I'll have 'em.' Anora pushed past him into the kitchen and opened an insecure-looking door in the corner. 'Yew will need a light. It is dark down by there.' She passed him a saucer with the stub of a candle on it, which she lit with a spill from the kitchen fire. 'Here you are. Let me know when you is finished.'

He stood at the top of the steps, saucer in one hand and his staff in the other, and was suddenly very frightened. What if Guy was waiting at the bottom of the steps for him? Did Mrs Crocker know that he was there and had somehow deliberately lured him to his death? Did Guy still have a gun? But there was no going back now. He felt his way down, the candle creating sinister flickering shadows, suggesting movement. He was alert to every sound, but the loudest was his tread on each damp step, taking him inevitably to his doom. He reached the bottom and looked around. He could see nothing in the darkness around him, other than the dim shapes of barrels and bottles.

Suddenly there was a noise to his left. He spun around quickly in fear and his staff crashed into some bottles on the top of a barrel, which in turn smashed onto the floor. There was more scrabbling and scurrying. Rats. The smell of brandy filled the cellar.

'Are yew all right down there? What have yew done?' called Anora.

'Do not be alarmed. I am continuing with my investigations, Mrs Crocker.'

He leaned on a barrel and realised that he was shaking with fear. He sighed. Guy wasn't down here. Perhaps it was the wrong pub. He held the candle away from him and illuminated a pool of brandy slowly seeping into the cracks in the floor. One of the broken bottles – there were at least five of them – still had a bottom half that was largely intact. Lewis looked at it. A very useful cup, he thought. Tankard even, if he was careful. The brandy had gone, of course, but he was surrounded by beer barrels. Why not? He needed something to calm his nerves. No one would miss a little something from a barrel; no one would ever know. He picked up the glass and held it beneath a full barrel and opened the tap.

It came away in his hand.

The beer flowed out in a steady, unstoppable stream and emptied itself upon the floor. He desperately tried to replace the tap but he had no hope of reinserting it. He had no choice but to leave it to drain itself dry. He drank what had poured into his broken bottle, wiped the back of his hand across his mouth and put his makeshift tankard on top of the barrel.

Lewis squelched through the growing pool of beer and climbed back up the steps. Walking into the light was so much easier and he felt more confident. Mrs Crocker was waiting for him in the kitchen.

'Told you, dinteye? No one down by there. Who is it sent yew on this wild goose chase then? I shall be having a word with Constable Plumley when he comes back, yew can be sure of that.'

'My investigations are not complete. I may need to return. I would be obliged if you touched nothing down in the cellar, in case you interfere with important evidence,' he said, returning the saucer and candle to her.

'I hopes you have done no damage down there, Constable…
what did you say your name was?'

'As I said, you best not touch anything or you will be
answerable to the Chief Constable. Good day to you, Mrs
Crocker.' Lewis walked out into the yard and towards the gate.

'Oi! Constable! Why is your trousers all wet then? Had an
accident?' she laughed.

~

Charles Glascodine's office was 4 Fisher Street, a short distance
away from Bucke's room, and as he approached the door –
promptly at 11.00 am – the solicitor appeared, hurrying down
the street. He was breathless, as if he had been rushing. He had
an untidy collection of papers beneath his arm.

'Thank goodness. I thought I was going to be late. I always
think the world would run much more smoothly if people
reduced what they had to say by at least a half. Save an awful
lot of time. Please come in.' He battled up the stairs, pushed
open the door to his office with his back and dumped the papers
unceremoniously on the already cluttered desk. 'The Lord Mayor,
you see, is rather exercised by this tiresome visit by the French
engineer, de Lesseps. His office has taken over the preparations
for it and he is anxious that it should be a success. Whether it will
be easier or more difficult without the contributions of Bristow
and Jenkins remains to be seen, though personally I suspect the
former.' He sat down behind his desk.

'Thank you for seeing me, Mr Glascodine. I am sure you
have information which will help me understand what, to both
of us, appears to be a curious and unexpected murder.'

He brushed away Bucke's gratitude with a casual wave of the
hand. 'It does seem very peculiar, Inspector, I grant you, though
not quite as curious as this peculiar notion that he was killed by

Vaughan Bristow. It is frankly a ludicrous suggestion. I am not a police officer, but to me Bristow will always be more of a puffed-up buffoon than a murderer.'

'It does seem very unlikely. But it is convenient for some to believe it.'

'Bristow had enough troubles of his own, Inspector. Rather a hollow man, if you ask me. Skating on some especially thin ice, always on the edge of financial ruin.'

'In your opinion, capable of murder, Mr Glascodine?'

'Of course not, but one thing you learn in both our jobs, is that there is nothing men can do which should surprise you.'

Inspector Bucke inclined his head. 'I agree with you. You can be reassured that I have not yet abandoned my search for Herbert Jenkins's murderer.'

'Have you met Mrs Jenkins, Inspector Bucke? Virginia is a spirited woman, I think you will find.'

'Yes, Mr Glascodine. She does appear to be rather confident, although somewhat guarded, I think, in what she says to me.' He wasn't quite sure how much he should say and so followed her own example.

'It is not my place to tell you your business, Inspector, especially since you are regarded as the only police officer of substance we have in Swansea, but my advice is that you are very careful when dealing with her. She has a number of significantly powerful friends. No one is above the law, Bucke, of course not; but remain watchful, that is all I think I will say. But I would have no worries for her. She will survive these unexpected circumstances, of that I have no doubt. Of course, she may not be able to help you very much anyway, particularly with regard to her husband's business affairs.'

'She told me that his business affairs were in some difficulty. Is this true, Mr Glascodine?'

'Considerable difficulties, Inspector. There are two elements to this. In the first instance, the manufacture of the copper goods he makes now outstrips demand. Shipbuilders have found better quality – and cheaper – alternatives to his products. They are no longer required, is the simplest way of putting it. Secondly, his company sustained considerable losses in a contract with a shipbuilder in Marseilles. Jenkins supplied the items and was never paid.'

'I see. This might explain his antipathy towards the French, I suppose.'

'Certainly, Inspector. The factory in Hamburg is, oddly, sustained by personal loans granted to him by the German Government, but these I presume will now end. I have never understood what their interest could be, but Herbert was never prepared to discuss it with me. As his solicitor, it would have been useful to know, but he chose not to say. The Germans undoubtedly have better materials of their own, so what they wanted with his business, I do not know. Perhaps they will buy it now, although effectively they already own the factory in Hamburg and probably much of the one in Swansea. They have kept the business afloat, but it has sustained irreversible losses. I anticipate that the factory will close within days, but there are materials and machines which can be sold. It will all go. Virginia Jenkins has no interest in running the company or indeed any company.'

'And so there would, in your opinion, be no business rivals who might profit in some way from his death?' asked Bucke.

'None whatsoever. He had nothing anyone else wanted anymore.'

'And I am right to believe that Jenkins was aware of the financial peril his business was in?'

'Oh yes. He knew he had commitments and a position which he would be unable to sustain. He had been living beyond his means for quite some time. Virginia knew it too. His recent visit to Germany was an attempt to raise more money, I believe. The British Government were unlikely to give him any since his products no longer had any strategic significance. But then, they didn't to the Germans either. Strange.'

'The marriage did not seem a particularly happy one, Mr Glascodine.'

'Indeed not, Inspector Bucke. A significant difference both in age and in interests, and during the course of their marriage they have not grown together, but indeed have grown further apart. He brought his money to the marriage whilst she provided the status. She was the daughter of Lord Roberts of Presteigne and found herself inconvenienced following the attentions of his lordship's ostler. There was an unhappy procedure during which Virginia almost died.' Glascodine shrugged his shoulders. 'Herbert agreed to marry her, but neither of them has ever been very happy with the arrangement.'

'He seems to have been a man full of unhappiness and anger,' said Bucke, trying to prompt the solicitor to say more.

'Oh yes indeed, Bucke. He was a man of unsophisticated ideas, easily moved to unreasonable anger. The diversity of people, which in our professions provides interest and fascination, was a frustration to him. He could not entertain contrary opinions. Herbert was not a popular man, Inspector, though I would consider him to be more of an irritant than anything else. Undoubtedly a little obsessive and with strong opinions on issues which barely troubled others, but none of this was sufficient in my view to warrant his murder.' He paused and nervously rearranged some papers which were on his desk. 'Inspector. If I may be frank. If you are to find his killer, I am obliged to tell you that Herbert Jenkins had a fascination with the more dangerous parts of our town. I cannot say whether or not he created enemies there who might wish him ill, but it is part of his activities I had no knowledge of.

Where he went, who he met, is your world, not mine. Herbert and Virginia Jenkins always led separate lives, as I think you probably must now have realised.'

Bucke stood. 'Thank you, Mr Glascodine. This conversation has been most useful.'

'Incidentally, it would be remiss of me not to mention that there are a number of us in Swansea who have a concern. We are impressed by your work, Inspector, and your concern for all the people of the town, not merely the prosperous. However, recent unfortunate changes within the police force are to the detriment of you and of the town itself. Be careful, Inspector. But do not think you are alone.'

Bucke nodded his thanks and made his way down the narrow stairs into a thin but welcome sunshine. He realised that he was hungry and so collected a pie from David Jones, the bakers on Portland Street, which he ate outside, then wiped his greasy fingers on the inside of his pockets and considered what he should do. The conversation had provided a great deal of information, though, rather like one of Jones's pies, he was still not sure which parts of it would prove to be the most nourishing. The issues around the connection with Germany that Jenkins maintained were completely outside his own experience. What they added to his investigation he wasn't at all sure, but they obviously puzzled the solicitor. Since Professor Axmeyer had done occasional translation work for Jenkins, according to Elinor Roberts, he decided to discover what he could tell him about this part of the businessman's life.

~

When he arrived at the Swansea Languages College, a frustrated Axmeyer, unhappy at the interruption, asked him to wait briefly in a neat but sparsely furnished sitting room whilst he concluded a lesson. Bucke could hear faintly the tortuous mutterings of an early French lesson, as the professor patiently repeated the phrase *Je m'appelle John* every time his student mangled the sounds. The room was a space where students waited. It did not appear to be lived in – there was nothing to identify it as a place that belonged to anyone in particular – two chairs, a small table and the fireplace blocked with an embroidered fire screen.

He heard Axmeyer take the student to the door. '*Au revoir*, John.'

'Don't mention it, like. Much obliged. It was tidy.' The door closed and the professor came to retrieve Bucke from the waiting room. His bent and bony frame was wrapped unsuccessfully in a thin academic gown which seemed to be threaded with white hair from his copious, though wiry, beard.

'I do apologise, Inspector, for the delay. My work has its frustrations at times, not the least of which is the lack of progress made by my young shipping clerk. If only he could achieve even a rudimentary understanding of the English language, we might be in a position to venture with greater success into the intricacies of French.' He raised his hands in an expansive fashion. 'What can you do? Please excuse my melancholy. My name is Professor Axmeyer and I am the master here at the Swansea Languages College. How may I help you? I have a few moments which I can offer to you, for I always provision myself with a short gap between pupils as an aid to recovery.'

When he told the professor that he wished to speak to him about Herbert Jenkins, he raised his eyebrows and invited Bucke into his study.

Once inside, Bucke could see that this was the heart of the house. The walls were lined with books of all shapes and sizes. From what he could see of the tarnished spines, they appeared to be in a range of European languages. There were more volumes piled upon the desk, with the remains of a breakfast upon a chipped plate. Against the wall there was what looked like a kitchen table, on which rested one large and very old volume, along with an inkstand and a candlestick.

'I was most shocked to hear of the death of Mr Jenkins. The news came as a terrible blow to me,' said the professor as he sat down behind his desk. 'Please,' he indicated the seat opposite him.

'I believe that you undertook translation work for him?'

'Yes, indeed I did – business communications from Germany. His housemaid, Miss Elinor Roberts, would bring them to me and I would usually translate them as quickly as I could and she would take them back. They were not difficult papers to work on.'

'What was the content of these letters?'

The professor dismissed them with a wave of his hand. 'They contained inconsequential information, Inspector. About contracts and production numbers, about delivery dates, about transportation. Such tedium. There was little within them that would interest a stranger. There was so little within them that interested me. They were tedious but they were easy to complete and I was well paid.'

'And were you able to form an opinion of how the business was progressing? Did you see anything in the letters which you regarded as threatening or alarming?'

Professor Axmeyer was dismissive. 'Nothing quite so dramatic, I fear. It was merely business and alas, Inspector, it meant little to me. As you can see, I am a man designed for the rarefied atmosphere of the library and neither for factory nor for business. It was my facility with languages which was the basis of my employment, not my business acumen. Even an English policeman can understand that, I am sure.'

'Did you do all your business via Miss Roberts? Did you ever meet Mr Jenkins?'

'Occasionally, Inspector, there was a reason for us to meet. Whilst we may have shared little in our cultural interests or indeed from our family heritage, he has always been a good friend, an important friend, to Germany and we can ill afford to lose men of determination such as Herbert Jenkins.'

'Were you aware that he had been in receipt of money from the German authorities?' asked Bucke. 'Or indeed, that they continued to support his business even when it entered a serious decline?'

'As I said, Inspector Bucke, he was a respected friend and ally of Germany. Does that trouble you?'

'Not especially, Professor. But did such a friendship put him in a difficult position, in your opinion? Did he receive any threats from the continent as a consequence, of which you might be aware?'

Professor Axmeyer looked at him intensely over the top of his glasses, a cold stare which captured Bucke's eyes and would not release them. 'Such threats do not need to be written down. They are there all around us, for everyone to see. Bitter experience proved to Jenkins that his greatest enemies were the French, as they are for us all. They are truly the masters of betrayal. I am from Alsace and we know all too well how the French are not to be trusted.'

'I see. I am sure we are both aware that Mr Jenkins held strong views on the subject of Europe,' said Bucke.

'Indeed, Inspector. There were occasions when we talked at length of the great dangers which lie ahead for your country if you do not allow your eyes to be opened. If you proceed like sleepwalkers with a permanent link with France in the form of a tunnel, then the disaster will be yours. Herbert Jenkins saw this, and I like to think that I may have helped him towards an understanding of the inevitable conclusion of such folly. His greatest disaster came about because of the French, and the consequences of it are ones which he will have carried with him to his grave. I understood his rage. The French intend to annex Alsace Lorraine once again, and good men across Europe have a duty to unite to confront their tyranny.'

'Do you feel safe in Swansea, Professor?' Bucke wanted to unsettle him, to move him away from what sounded like carefully prepared political statements.

'Of course, Inspector. This is a strange question. Why should I not?'

'I wondered whether you found it necessary to carry with you any personal protection? A sword- stick, for example?'

'Why ever would I have need of such a thing? Of course not. I would admit that I walk slowly and that I require a walking stick, but I have no inclination to carry a weapon of any sort. I must be fortunate indeed, for I have never had the need to engage with footpads and ruffians. I never walk the streets in the night, Inspector. I have no desire to be confronted by the human frailty and desperation which must be your daily experience. During the day, I am busy with my pupils and I see some of them when their own working day is at an end, which means I must listen to the terrible shredding of language until quite late. It is then that I can continue with my own research.' He gestured at the table against the wall. 'It is the time of day I anticipate most of all. I am working to produce an annotated edition of the thirteenth century text *Le Tournoi du Chauveney* by Jacques Bretel, some of which was written in the dialect of Lorraine. Sometimes I work by candlelight – for I feel it is appropriate for such a historic text. I suspect that perhaps you are not familiar with it. Few people are, alas.' Axmeyer shook his head sadly. 'My work has become my quiet obsession but naturally it does not help my eyes.'

There was a knock at the door as another pupil arrived for a lesson. 'You must forgive me, Inspector, but this will be Mademoiselle Beynon. Her father pays for an hour of French conversation. *Bien sûr*, he will be discomforted if he were to feel that his daughter was receiving less than her allotted span. He is a doctor. He has great plans for her.' He shrugged. 'Perhaps they should not require any engagement with languages…'

'Of course, Professor. I quite understand,' replied Bucke. Axmeyer escorted him to the front door. 'Perhaps there will be an opportunity to continue this conversation on another occasion?'

'I would welcome that, Inspector. I wish you a pleasant afternoon.'

When he was outside on Dynevor Place, Bucke reflected briefly on his own shortcomings. He had never realised that Swansea was such a seething hotbed of European politics. He was amused by the idea. It is just a small town of small men pretending to be big men; important, influential men; but living a long way from anywhere else. Bucke walked down on to Gower Street. Something about Professor Axmeyer unsettled him. He knew that national struggles stirred up violent emotions, but he felt there was a controlled aggression about him which was at odds with his carefully studied academic persona.

As he walked through the door of the police station, stepping quietly around an angry mother berating her young son who had been detained for throwing stones at windows along the High Street, Constable Davies excitedly told him about a second body that had been recovered from the North Dock. He was sure that it had been crushed between a couple of ships because the head was a shocking mess, and he was equally sure the victim must have fallen into the water whilst drunk. Bucke, knowing that cautious reflection had never been one of Constable Davies's most obvious qualities, raised his eyebrows and was ready to suggest that he might be jumping to hasty conclusions, but the constable was desperate to present his own investigative triumph. A search of the pockets had proved fruitless but Davies was not to be deterred. He had examined the cap which had been tucked down his trousers. Inside were his name and his place of employment – Martin Willrath, the Morfa Copper Works. So Constable Davies, proud of his initiative, had gone there and discovered his address.

'Here's a thing, though, Inspector. I went to the house. On Odo Street, it was. But it was empty. All shut up. Nobody there, not even his wife or anyone. You would think she would want to know that he was dead.'

Chapter Fourteen

Constable Davies was not the only person who had been agitated by the death of Martin Willrath.

It was early evening when Moitch arrived at the Baumhaus after another tense day waiting in the shadows on Odo Street. He had seen the police officer arrive, which meant that they must have found a body. He had no reason to worry about the house. He had cleaned it himself on Tuesday and knew it contained nothing incriminating. He was more interested to see whether those who had abducted Martin Willrath came to the house. He was grateful that he saw nothing to alarm him. There was no reason for him to worry about Eva, who had been acting as Martin's wife. She had already departed for London where she would be met by members of a well-established cell which would smuggle her out of the country from Tilbury.

Eva hadn't been able to tell him much before she went. Neither she nor Martin had had any cause for alarm over recent weeks, although naturally they had always remained alert. When Martin did not come home from work on Monday, Eva had waited an hour, as agreed, then immediately implemented their emergency procedures. She told Axmeyer, who in turn alerted Moitch by placing a red vase in the bedroom window, meaning "Significant threat".

Moitch put Eva on a train from Swansea to London the same night, but he couldn't find Willrath. He had disappeared and undoubtedly not of his own accord. Moitch spent the rest of Monday evening wandering purposefully around Hafod, asking casual questions in the public houses. Willrath had left work on time, it seemed; that was all he could discover. He knew someone had taken him and was now questioning him. Sooner or later, he would tell them something; it was inevitable. Everyone did. There was, in reality, little that Willrath would be able to say, for their group was very self-contained, but Martin certainly knew that Guy was still in Swansea and he might feel compelled to offer this information. He knew Moitch too, but neither his name nor his lodgings. And only Eva, not Martin, knew the part played by Axmeyer. In his judgement, the mission was not fatally compromised but increased vigilance was essential. When he heard that the body had been pulled out of the dock on Wednesday, he knew that Willrath must have been questioned with frightful enthusiasm throughout Tuesday and he had been disposed of either when they decided he had nothing else to tell them, or after their enjoyment of their work had gone too far. Willrath had been a good man and Moitch wanted to believe that he had held them off as long as he could to allow Eva to escape and the others to regroup. He offered him his silent thanks. What was now obvious, though, was that someone was in the town determined to disrupt and prevent their mission. He had a good idea who it might be. How they found out about Willrath was immaterial. They were here, and Moitch knew he needed to adapt.

Moitch looked around the dining room in the Baumhaus with care. Steam, from the large metal tureen which Betty Baum was idly stirring on the stove, filled the room. A group of working men were sitting at tables, almost all of them with mufflers, eating soup, their caps politely on the scrubbed table rather than on their heads – Frau Baum was very particular about table manners. They were dressed for work in grimy waterproof jackets and leggings. In turn, they looked back at him. Everything seemed satisfactory. He did not get the sense that there was anyone here who might be an imposter. He could never be absolutely sure but they all seemed genuine. At the far end of the table there was Daniel Guy.

He was dirty and soup dripped slowly from strands of his unkempt beard. He saw Moitch but said nothing and continued to tear up a piece of bread which he dropped messily into his soup.

'*Guten Abend, Frau Baum. Ich hoffe, es geht dir gut,*' he said to her.

'Fair to middling if you please, sir. Would you care for a drop of soup? There is a cold wind out there, as my gents here can tell you.'

'*Nein danke.* I am looking for someone but he is not here. Some other time, I think.'

'Please yourself. Plenty here.'

He left the Baumhaus and went to the coal shed at the end of Baker Street to wait for Guy. He pulled the rags together which hung untidily next to the web-covered windows and served as curtains, lit a lamp and sat on an upturned bucket and waited. These were difficult conversations. Guy was their greatest liability, that was obvious, and Moitch wondered just how long it would be before he had to be eliminated. He was certainly useful as far as the overall objectives of the mission were concerned, but there would come a point at which his unreliability would no longer be tolerated. He was expendable, but then everyone was, even Moitch.

He remembered how he had been recruited by German Military Intelligence when he was arrested for murder following the incident in an alleyway outside a brothel in Bremen. He laughed to himself. The things a young man does, eh? He had no expectation of mercy, was certain that he was to die, for the extenuating circumstances of robbery would carry little weight in a German court for a man from the Baltic. But he had been unexpectedly offered a way out – the opportunity to work for new masters; ready to respect his considerable skills, but not sentimental enough to forget the debt he owed them. He knew that he was their creature, but he did their bidding without question. In their world of espionage, there was no moral compass and Moitch was their perfect tool. He questioned nothing, and for the first time in an aimless life, spent largely at sea, he showed loyalty to something other than himself. The Imperial German cause meant nothing to him, but they had saved his life and he knew his murder of a nameless thief had merely been put to one side, to be resurrected should the need arise.

Guy flung the door open. He looked like a man disturbed, a manic brightness in his eyes accentuated by their contrast with the ingrained filth on his face. 'What in God's name is happening?' he demanded.

'Please, Daniel. Calm yourself,' Moitch soothed.

But Guy wasn't listening. 'I stay in the house, just as you said. I know nothing. And then one of the sailors talks to me. He knows I am English and so he talks to me.' He paced up and down the coal shed in the flickering light, waving his arms around. 'And what does he tell me? He tells me he doesn't like Swansea. Tells me it is too violent. And why? Because a gent has been killed in his own garden, stabbed in the stomach, as if he was in a fight in a pub. And then I find out it is Jenkins! Jenkins is dead. You did not tell me! Did I not have a right to know? Was it you that killed him? Tell me!'

'Daniel, please. From the air, you are making fantasies, I think.'

'Jenkins has been murdered and you did not tell me!' He walked back to the door.

'It is just a coincidence. The world can be a cruel place. It has nothing to do with us, I think.'

Guy turned on him. 'You think? You think? You are always thinking! And what good does it ever do anybody? Jenkins has been murdered! Think about that!'

'It was just a robbery,' he said and waved his hands dismissively. 'Unfortunate it is. These things happen in a town such as Swansea, I think.'

'You expect me to believe that? Who did it? The police?'

'Daniel, listen to me—'

'Let me tell you something, Pieter, you are not the man you were when we worked together in America. Remember? We drank, we laughed, we had a good time. Let me take you back to Swansea, you said. Just what we are looking for. I have a job for you, you said. Easy. You will be a wealthy man. And what happens? You imprison me in a house full of Germans! You are my gaoler and all you give me are threats – and lies, I shouldn't wonder. I want no more of this. Find someone else to do your bidding. Tell Willrath to do it. Here is the gun.' He took it out of his pocket and waved it at him. 'Here you are. It is yours.'

'You cannot do this, I think, Daniel. You are committed.'

'Committed? No, Pieter. I have been chained but I will no longer do your bidding.'

'Listen to me, Daniel. You are having no choice.'

'Oh yes I have!' he shouted and pointed the revolver straight at Moitch's chest. 'I want out of this, Pieter. Or I will shoot you dead.'

There was silence. Neither man moved.

Moitch held his stare steadily, unflinching. 'And you think that this a difference will make?' He stood up and smiled like a dagger. 'Because you too a dead man would be. Do you think

166

that in all this I am alone? Do you not think that there are others behind me? Tell me, Daniel.'

Guy said nothing, breathing heavily.

Moitch lowered his voice slightly. 'There are many others. Much less understanding than me, I am thinking.' He advanced slowly towards Guy. 'You kill me perhaps, but you will die also. But much more slowly than I.'

Guy's hand started to shake. 'I am warning you—'

'And I too am warning you. Shoot me, Daniel. Aim well and kill me. Be pleased then, for a moment. But you will never rest again, I promise.' Moitch pulled his knife from his boot and came closer to him. 'The rest of your life you will spend waiting for my friends to come. And they will, be sure of it, and they will bring with them no forgiveness but the darkest of their skills they will show you, I think.' He stood in front of Guy, who was trembling, his eyes flicking around the coal shed, avoiding the threats in Moitch's eyes. He took the gun from Guy's hand and placed the long, sharp blade against his throat. 'There is no going back for you, Daniel. You must perform your duty and then be rewarded well. Or you will have chosen to die.'

Guy swallowed. 'Can't you tell Willrath to do it?'

'Willrath is dead, Daniel.'

His eyes widened. 'Dead? How?'

'Do not be troubled. He fell into the dock, that is all. Drunk. So he fell in, I think.'

'Willrath? Drunk? He wasn't a drinker. Not the type.'

'Such things happen, Daniel. A night in the town after a hard day at work. I am sad for him. But there will be no more disruptions to our plans now. Because you will be careful, won't you, Daniel? There has been only one murder victim in the North Dock this week and you helped put him there.'

'He was just an urchin. No one will miss him.'

'Possibly not, Daniel. But the murder of an urchin is still

murder. Perhaps I could be the witness who saw you, I am thinking. After all, they are already looking for you. And who would they believe? A man who tried to murder his wife? Pah!'

Guy said nothing. Moitch pressed the knife a little more firmly against his throat and Guy stretched his neck further up the wall. He swallowed with difficulty. 'Yes, Pieter,' he said finally.

'Do not forget, Daniel. You have made decisions. Some we did not like. Or perhaps are you forgetting? I think. You could have been at work and no one would have noticed you. But your wife you tried to kill. I have told you many times, I think that this was very stupid. But here, you are safe. What has happened here to you in the Baumhaus? Nothing. We are looking after you. Yes, you are safe.'

Moitch smirked and stepped back and put his knife back in his boot. He handed Daniel his gun. 'Look after it. The gun needs oiling, I think. It will soon be time to use it.'

~

There was a dead donkey in the middle of the High Street when Inspector Bucke walked up to the police station in the morning. The poor animal was emaciated and covered in sores. Some of the local dogs were taking more than a casual interest in the corpse. He wondered who the constable on duty was. How could they have missed something like that? He sighed. He would have to instruct someone to move it.

There were three telegraph messages which had come in from police forces in England, which all said the same thing. There were no reports of anyone matching Bristow's details being seen in Edinburgh, Leeds or Hull.

'Cunning man, this Bristow,' said Constable Davies as he handed over the messages. 'Very devious. Could be anywhere. Australia even.'

'Why do you think Bristow ran away, Constable?' he asked.

'Because he murdered Jenkins, sir.' Davies was doing his best to be helpful.

'And what is it that leads you to that conclusion?'

'Because he ran away, sir.'

'No one saw him do it. No one can say that he was actually there. By the very act of running away, he has thrown suspicion upon himself which otherwise might never be there. Constable Davies, why would we ever think that he had done it, unless he had fled?'

'The way I look at it, see, I think he was frightened he'd get caught, sir. That is why he did a runner. It is obvious. Two murders? It is the rope for him.'

'Now, you see that idea of him being frightened is one I am quite interested in. What would he be frightened of, do you think?'

'Of being caught, Inspector.'

'Perhaps there was something else before that. Why would you have run away, if it had been you?'

'I didn't, sir.'

'I know you didn't, Constable Davies. But what would cause you to run away from Swansea?'

The constable looked thoughtful. 'Well, sir, it would have to be if I had done something or if I was frightened that someone was going to do something to me. Then I would run.'

Bucke nodded. 'Exactly, Constable. And there you have it. Two possibilities.'

'But wouldn't it be easier to say that Bristow murdered Jenkins and Punch?'

'It would indeed be simpler, Constable. But it may not be true.'

'Does that matter, sir? We'd have an answer.'

'But it wouldn't be the right one.'

'You can't be sure of that; and the thing is, what you should be thinking about, sir, is that there have been no more murders since he ran away.' He nodded decisively, pleased to be pointing his inspector in the right direction.

'What about Joseph and the German they found floating in the dock this week?'

'Joseph fell off the dock and so did that German, because he was drunk.'

'You don't know that, Constable.'

'Well, he was a man from the copper works. Thirsty work that, sir.'

'How do you know he wasn't pushed in by a murderer?'

'That's easy, sir. Because your man Bristow has fled from the town, sir. We established that,' he replied patiently.

Bucke nodded. 'Thank you for your help, Constable. It has been most invaluable. If anyone is looking for me, you may tell them that I have gone to see Mrs Bristow. I have more questions for her.'

As Bucke left, Davies called out to him. 'It has been no trouble at all, Inspector. Glad I have been of assistance.' He was very pleased with himself, sensing promotion.

∾

Rumsey Bucke was quite breathless when he arrived at the school. He hadn't realised how briskly he had walked from the police station. Conversations with Evan Davies often made him want to run away as fast as he could. Bristow could well have fled Swansea simply because Davies threatened to talk to him. It was undoubtedly a possibility. Bucke had already decided it might be better to ask someone else to move the donkey.

'May I talk to you, Mrs Bristow?' he blurted out as she opened the door.

She looked at him in surprise. 'But of course, Inspector. Please come in. I am very pleased to see you. You have no news of my husband, do you?'

'No, I do not, but there are some things which I would like to talk to you about.' Unaccountably, he found himself staring at the floor. 'I do not believe that they... you see... it might not concern you directly but what I need to... you see, perhaps it will be that you can help me because...' He stopped and when he looked up, he saw her smiling at him. He felt himself blushing. 'I am sorry. I think sometimes that I have forgotten how to speak to people properly.'

'Inspector Bucke, if you wish to talk then I would be delighted to be given the opportunity to listen. But perhaps this conversation may better progress if we move from the doorstep and into the kitchen.'

'Of course, I am so sorry,' he replied.

'Inspector, think nothing of it. Please come in.'

He followed her through the house. If possible, it seemed emptier than it had been before. She had clearly reduced the amount of the house that she lived in, but at least the kitchen was an oasis of warmth amongst the cold echoes of the abandoned school. 'I won't be here much longer,' she announced, as she poured hot water into a teapot. 'The agent has instructed me to vacate the house, although he has kindly agreed to allow me to stay for a few days longer. I am busying myself looking for new accommodation. I will not trouble myself greatly about leaving this place. It was never a proper home. Now it belongs to another time.'

'You intend to stay in Swansea, Mrs Bristow?'

'For the moment, yes, Inspector.' She looked at him as she poured the tea. 'Please refresh yourself, Inspector, since you seem most anxious, and then I shall give you my full attention.'

He was so nervous he could barely keep still. The cup and saucer once again rattled furiously in his hand.

'I wanted to tell you that I have no reason to link any of the murder investigations to your husband. If you had thought that he had killed Jenkins, then you would have lost no time in telling me so. You haven't, though you have told me many other things. The only thing that implicates him is that he has run away. A foolish move, and one which, for me, is proving to be a distraction. The more he stays hidden, then the more his guilt is regrettably confirmed in the popular imagination. But he did not kill Herbert Jenkins and he did not kill Punch. I wanted you to know.'

'Who is Punch, Inspector?' she asked.

'I apologise. Why should you know? She was the unfortunate who was murdered on the Strand a few days before Jenkins was killed. The first murder.' He paused. 'She was the sort of woman who frequents public houses and attempts to engage men in conversation,' he added hesitantly.

'I see. How very forward are these prostitutes, Inspector Bucke.'

He hesitated again and took a deep breath. 'Call me Rumsey, please,' he said quickly. 'I would be most...'

'But I thought your name was Rumsey Bucke? Please is such an unusual surname.'

He did not hear what she said. He was embarrassed. He could not understand how he had been so foolish.

Constance filled the silence. 'Forgive me. I meant you no harm, Rumsey. You seem nervous today.'

He didn't notice her use of his Christian name. To what sort of madness had he succumbed, he wondered, that made him believe this was acceptable? 'Mrs Bristow. I apologise. How could I have been so... I shall leave at once.'

'My name is Constance.'

'Your husband... I mean, I should not have...' he stumbled on.

'Rumsey, please. Drink your tea and listen. My husband is no longer my husband. He has deserted me – and our daughter. Does such a man deserve my respect? With every day that passes, he is further away; and I find that most appealing, despite the difficulties he has left for me. Is his a torch I must still keep burning? I think not. I have, I think, been liberated.' She looked at him intently. He saw her eyelashes flickering magically.

He sat back in the chair. 'I do apologise. I should not have been so forward.'

'You have not been forward, Rumsey. You have been brave. You see? The worst is over now.'

He closed his eyes. 'Thank you, Constance. I apologise for being so inept.'

'There are worse things. You wished to talk, you said.'

'Yes. I do have a question for you. I am investigating three murders which happened so closely together, they are, in my mind, somehow linked.'

'Three murders, Rumsey?'

'Punch, Jenkins and then Joseph, a young boy from the streets, a match seller. He died after your husband left Swansea. I believe the poor child was murdered.'

'Why would anyone wish to kill a young child like that?'

'I have a suspicion.' He told her what little he knew of Joseph. 'I think he was killed because of what he knew, and what I want to know is whether there was a connection between Joseph and Herbert Jenkins, who, as you are aware, was murdered the night before your husband departed. Did you know him?' he asked.

'He visited my husband and I was required to be the dutiful wife. I gave them tea. I remember the gentleman being alarmed at the absence of a maid. What I remember most about his visit is that the top layer of his artificial teeth would slump down and his tongue would appear over the top of them. Fascinating and quite, quite repellent. I had the impression he was doing it deliberately. I cannot understand why.'

'What did they talk about, do you know?'

'Billy dismissed me to another part of the house after I had provided the tea, but that night I listened, of course I listened. They were excited, animated, as I remember. Talking about the ascendancy of the Empire, the criminal depravity of foreigners, our island state is our strength. It was the usual sort of thing that I listened to at the dinner table. I had heard it many times.'

'When was this?'

'January, I think. I remember that they sat in here because it was warm. The rest of the house was especially cold that night.'

'Does the name de Lesseps mean anything to you?' He hesitated. 'Constance.'

'Yes, it does. They talked of him a great deal, although they did not think that he was a worthy gentleman. A notable Frenchman perhaps, but not one of whom they maintained a high opinion.'

'What did they say about him?'

'There was a lot of talk about him coming to Swansea to speak to the society Billy was involved in, something about Knowledge. They talked about money and investments, but they were most alarmed about an undersea tunnel. And I remember very clearly Herbert Jenkins saying that if they could prevent this tunnel, they would be rewarded handsomely. When I heard that, I rather hoped it would be the means of settling some of our bills.'

'Did they say how they were going to prevent it?'

'The words he used were "As we discussed previously". That is all I know.'

'You see, Constance, it is the death of Jenkins which confuses me most. I cannot help but think that in some way it must be connected with the two others, but I cannot see what links them.'

'And you think that Punch and Joseph were killed for the same reason? They were both poor people who lived on the streets, you say.'

'Yes, I think so. Why do murders happen, Constance? It might be jealousy, envy, passion, madness. All those things. Often it is nothing more than money. But sometimes information is at the root of it all. The victim knows something and they are killed to stop them passing on that information to another person.'

'And you think that is why little Joseph was killed? He was a child. What could he know?'

'I am sure of it. It might be why Punch was killed too. Others want to believe that she was killed by one of her clients, perhaps even your husband.' Constance frowned but Inspector Bucke went on. 'That might be true but I do not think it was him because he had no weapon, only a stick for hitting boys. You told me so. Punch was stabbed. I believe that Joseph saw Punch killed by a prosperous-looking gentleman who was in the company of Daniel Guy. Your husband, as far as we know, was not acquainted with Guy. So it wasn't Bristow. But Joseph wanted to tell me about it, and someone killed him to stop him from doing so. And if that was the case, then it would seem to me that Punch was killed for the same reason – to stop her revealing the identity of the man who was in the company of Daniel Guy. After all, I was told by Eliza Keast, one of her friends, that she knew Guy through her sister, whoever that is. So she could recognise him. Guy didn't kill Punch. He had walked away, that is what Joseph said. So it has to be the other man, do you see?'

'I thought you knew that, Rumsey?'

'Yes, I did. And I also believe I know his identity. I cannot prove it, for I have no evidence. But nothing else makes any sense to me. It was no drunken sailor. She was killed by a gentleman – they do not often carry knives but they do carry sword-sticks. Joseph saw her stabbed and I saw the wound. She was killed with a long, thin blade that passed through her body. I believe she might have been killed by Herbert Jenkins. He had such a walking stick and he was known to frequent parts of the town where he could enjoy dangerous experiences. Joseph said that Punch was stabbed by a toff. Annie Taylor, one of her friends, said that Punch knew someone like that, an unpleasant man. The Chief Constable would say I was speculating – amongst other things – and he would be right because there are gaps in what I know, but it is what I believe.' He scratched his beard. 'Jenkins killed Punch. He fits some of the description; he fits some of the habits.'

'So what you are also suggesting, if I understand you, and of course I have no experience of these things, is that there is something which connects Jenkins and this Daniel Guy? Oh my!'

'Indeed, and someone is very anxious to keep this hidden, and that is why I believe they silenced Punch and Joseph. Knowing Guy seems to be very dangerous. But this cannot be why Jenkins died. Unless there was some kind of argument.'

Constance looked anxiously at him. 'Does this mean that you are in danger, Rumsey?'

'No more than usual, I would say. My frustration is that I cannot talk to Jenkins. I cannot talk to Punch. I cannot talk to Joseph. They are all dead. Each one murdered. I cannot talk to Guy because I don't know where he is.'

'And so Guy therefore has done his job well?' she asked.

'I would say so. He is still well hidden, somewhere in Swansea.'

'May I ask something? If Guy is so important in all this, what is he doing here? You say he has returned unexpectedly from America?'

'Yes. And when he came back, he shot his wife but failed to kill her.'

Constance looked very thoughtful. 'Allow me, Rumsey, let me speak of something I don't understand. Do you think he came all the way back from America just to kill his poor wife?'

'No, Constance.' Using her name was still new and it pleased him. 'I do not think he did. There was surely never any need to do so. He could have started a whole new life in America and no one would have any need to know who he was. No matter what she had done, he could have cast himself adrift from her, forever.'

'So therefore his wife was not the reason why he returned to Swansea. And so why is he, as you suspect, still here? Why hasn't he run away again? My husband did.' Constance watched him, enthralled by the way the story was unfolding.

'That is the question which puzzles me. Unless the shooting of Mary Guy was entirely separate from the purpose that brought him back to Swansea.' He pinched the bridge of his nose and looked out of the window, deep in thought.

'Which would mean that he hasn't done what he came back to Swansea to do, because he is still here in the town,' Constance said thoughtfully. 'Is he waiting for something, do you think?' Or someone? If he didn't come back with a gun to shoot his wife, then he might have come back to shoot someone else. But he hasn't found them yet. Who could that be? Did he have lots of enemies here before he left?'

Bucke turned his eyes quickly back towards Constance. He was suddenly energised. 'Wait, Constance! Wait! Let me get this clear in my own mind. He has come to shoot someone who hasn't yet arrived in Swansea. Of course! Why didn't I see it before?' He saw beyond all the fears and distractions that had obscured his thoughts and which Constance had now helped to dispel. 'He must have been sent back here to shoot an important visitor. And there is only one I can think of. Monsieur de Lesseps – about whom your husband and

Herbert Jenkins have been so agitated. If it isn't him, then I have no idea who it could be.'

Constance was wide-eyed. 'And you are saying that my husband was involved in this? Is that truly what you are saying? And that Daniel Guy is an assassin?'

'Though an unreliable one, it seems, since his attempt to kill his wife was so unsuccessful. But it explains why he is here and why someone is hiding him. And that is why your husband ran away. He may not have known Guy, but he certainly knew Jenkins. And he might have been frightened of what he'd got himself mixed up in. With Jenkins dead, he must have thought he was next.'

'Rumsey. This sounds like a cheap novel serialised in one of those magazines. Is it really true?'

'I know the truth is there, but I cannot lay my hands on it, for it slips always out of my grasp. I can invent a story which may explain everything but I need more evidence.'

Rumsey Bucke was shocked. He recognised that, in the presence of Constance, he had been able to formulate and express all the nebulous ideas that had been floating around his head and had uncovered a pattern which had previously eluded him. Ever since these troubles had started, everything had come back, always, to Daniel Guy. But why?

'Thank you, Constance. Talking to you has been extremely helpful. Do not think that I have told you the complete truth, because I do not know what that truth might be. But I have discovered more within myself than I knew was there before I came.'

'I have done nothing, Rumsey. What will you do now?'

'I must now work in the belief I am right until I know that I am wrong. I must still find Daniel Guy, and I must still try to understand the murder of Herbert Jenkins. If your husband did not do it and Daniel Guy did not do it, then who did? But thank you. You have listened to me, Constance, and in your presence the clouds seem to lift from me and...' He stopped, realising that he was saying too much.

Constance looked at him carefully and raised her eyebrows but said nothing.

'Please excuse me, Constance. I must return to the police station. There will be issues requiring my attention.' He stood up.

'Of course. But please remember, Rumsey, I will be especially honoured if, on occasion, you may see fit to call. I shall keep the second-best china available for just such visits.' She took him to the door.

'It would be remiss of me to observe, Constance, that I cannot help but notice that the tea service is the same as the one you used on my last visit. Nonetheless, I shall endeavour always to treat it with the respect that it deserves.'

She shook her head. 'Inspector, I must confess that I have been deceiving you. It is the only one I have. But I am impressed by your observational powers.'

As he walked away, he considered the extent of his observational powers. He realised that he had no memory at all of what Constance had been wearing. He could only remember her eyes and the warmth that they contained.

By the evening, he was able to reflect that he had had a better day than most of his colleagues, though it had not seemed likely at its outset. Inspector Allison wanted to carry out what he called a "raid" on Swansea Market to illustrate that he was taking his weights and measures responsibilities seriously, monitoring transgressions and collecting all income from trading licences personally. He was assisted by Mr Crockford, the market inspector, and deployed almost all the constables he had available that day. They were each given areas of the market that they were to assess simultaneously, checking weights and measures of all kinds. Sergeant Ball, who had plenty of experience of the market and its traders, would attend too. Inevitably, there would be fines and potentially a lot of unhappy traders, but for the police it would be an easy day, and Inspector Allison would have stamped his authority on this essential but difficult part of town.

The market had been there as long as anyone could remember; open to the grey skies, right in the centre of town, with entrances – and exits – onto Oxford Street, Union Street and Orange Street. It was a confusion of narrow alleys and tightly arranged stalls which represented, better than anything else, the town of Swansea in all its anarchic glory. Everyone, sooner or later, would be drawn into its embrace. It was full of character, embodying the inextinguishable spirit of the town, the defiant and independent attitude of a population determined to survive and living forever at the very edge of the law. There was good food to be had – and bad. The freshest dairy produce and the finest fish – but also on occasion, extremely questionable meat sold by some extremely questionable people. Here was where the town met the country, where the rural Welsh met a confusing urban mix. It was always vibrant and always just a few moments away from anarchy. There was sawdust on the slippery floor, there was the smell of yesterday's fish, the noise of squabbling dogs and the buzzing of flies. Terrified animals could smell the blood, the lungs, the lights, their death; and their howling distress was the background accompaniment to the operation of supply and demand without intervention. The stallholders were no different from their customers. They were all, customer and trader alike, living a hair's breadth away from poverty. Frequently, their transactions involved barter, when goods rather than money changed hands and had been doing so for centuries. And how could that ever be effectively regulated?

Naturally, Allison had not required Bucke's assistance. Weights and measures were his responsibility now, not Bucke's, and he was going to do the job much more effectively. He had gone out of his way to avoid Rumsey Bucke since the night outside the theatre. So whilst the constables all trooped off to wrestle with the slippiest of traders on the slippiest of floors, Bucke was instead leaving Rugby House and walking to St James' Crescent. There was a gardener he wished to meet.

Bucke recognised that he was more confident, more alert, more vibrant than he had felt for a long time. His mind was clear, no longer overwhelmed, and he was convinced once more that his job was worth doing. He was determined to part the fog which seemed to surround Daniel Guy, although a part of his mind that he could not control was calculating when next he could visit Constance Bristow.

His interest was, for the moment, focused on Herbert Jenkins. He was the feature in recent events which he could not square with the others. His previous visit to the garden had been undermined, but this time he would not so easily be frustrated. So he did not knock at the front door but instead went into the garden from the lane, since the gate was open. Bucke looked beyond the fluttering tablecloth at the greenhouse and saw that the broken glass had been replaced by a neatly inserted wooden panel.

There was an old man contentedly working away at a flower border, tidying up the daffodils and providing support for some of the longer stems. Mr Pettigrew, a man at peace, thought Bucke.

'It is mostly decorative work I do, sir. Maintenance. Madam has no interest in making the garden more productive, so I keeps it simple, don't I? She never comes outside. She don't bother me too much, fair play. But I must keep it looking neat and tidy for when she looks through the window.' He looked up at the sky. 'Nice work, see, when the clouds don't trouble you.' He was an old man with a deeply lined face, tanned and leathered by decades of windblown weather. 'There is a lot you could do here, if you were so inclined. I come along most days. Mrs Jenkins and Miss Roberts are very good to me. Done more than they need to, since Mrs Pettigrew passed away last year. Miss Roberts will on times give me a bite to eat or wash my clothes for me. They leave me alone to get on with my work and they seem to be quite pleased. I am not to go into the kitchen when the tablecloth is hanging on the line, which is a puzzle to me, but everyone has their little ways. Always washing tablecloths, they are, Inspector. Very clean.'

Bucke asked him about the murder. 'Terrible state of affairs. An important man like that.' He asked him if he remembered a fire in the garden. 'Yes, I do, Inspector. I lit it as Miss Roberts requested but she tended it. She had some items to burn. A very thoughtful young woman, Inspector. I remember clearly. She had washed my working clothes for me after I come to the house in the morning as normal on the day Mr Jenkins died, but I forgot to take them home with me. And do you know what? When I come back the next day and did them jobs the constables wanted, even though there was all the upset of the murder, blow me, she'd washed them again. There was no need but it just goes to show, doesn't it? Decent girl.'

Bucke thanked him and said he was going to speak to Elinor Roberts.

'Just about finished for today meself. Remember, best go round the front way. The cloth is out.' He winked.

Bucke nodded and wandered to the back gate, touching the tablecloth on the way. It was perfectly dry. He walked around to the front of the house and knocked on the door. Elinor, as always, opened it almost immediately. She did not seem surprised, but it was clear that she had no intention of inviting him inside. Bucke looked behind her and saw an upturned black hat on the stand with a walking stick, with what might have been a green enamel band just below the handle, balanced across the brim.

'Good morning, Miss Roberts. Would it be convenient for me to meet Mrs Jenkins? I have some questions concerning her husband's political views with which she may be able to assist me.'

'Unfortunately, Inspector Bucke, Mrs Jenkins is unavailable. She has gone down to Swansea for a meeting with Mr Glascodine to discuss Mr Jenkins's estate.'

Bucke raised his eyebrows. He knew this wasn't true. 'An unfortunate time to arrive, clearly. It is no matter. I shall return when my work allows it. Good day, Miss Roberts.'

~

The police were not the only ones heading to the market that day. So was Daniel Guy. He had being lying to Moitch, of course. He had been slipping unseen out of the back door of the Baumhaus when Frau Baum was assembling the daily soup, to do some casual work in the market as a porter, carrying lamb carcases for a few pennies and sometimes receiving a couple of kidneys or a bit of scrag end, which the barmaid at the Queen's Hotel would fry for him. It helped to fuel the ridiculous hope that perhaps he could earn sufficient money to facilitate an escape from Moitch and his plans, towards freedom and vitality. In the market, if anyone knew who he was, they didn't say, for his crimes belonged to another world. In the pubs nearby, he could have a quick drink, feeling confident that his dirty beard meant that he would not be recognised. In his enforced isolation, he yearned for this place where questions were rarely asked and where the world was full of colour and noise.

The police were not always welcome in the market and certainly not in the numbers who were there that day. They moved from stall to stall examining weights and checking scales for any dishonest arrangements. Measures and yard sticks were held up, rats' nests uncovered, snapping dogs avoided and their owners warned.

Constable Davies was enjoying himself. He had glanced in a cursory sort of way at the stall of Dai Rosser the butcher, but was much more interested in the attentions of a small group of traders and spoke to them wisely about the Guy case, as if he had actually been there when Mary had been shot. 'Duw duw, I am telling you. It was like Custer's Last Stand in that house. Bullets flying everywhere.'

A man with a sheep carcase flung over his shoulder, which obscured his face, interrupted him. 'I heard he only fired three shots and each one hit his wife. A right cow she is too, they say.'

'I was there. At least fifteen, I would say. I had to protect myself with a coal shovel in front of my face. They were pinging off like anything. Shovel is useless now, like a sieve. Thought we had him cornered in the kitchen, like a rat in a trap, but he got out through the window.'

Sergeant Ball approached. 'Come on, Constable Davies. Look to it. Dai Rosser's all right. I checked his scales earlier. Move on.'

He looked at the man with the sheep carcase across his other shoulder and their eyes met across the dirty butcher's stall, the sawdust and the rat droppings. Ball recognised him immediately as someone he had dealt with before – Daniel Guy. 'Oi! You! Stay where you are. You are under arrest!'

Guy spun round and heaved the carcase straight into Ball and fled. Dogs started to bark and snap, and chaos descended suddenly upon the market. As police constables advanced quickly to support Ball, they suddenly found their way blocked by barrows and by sacks of potatoes which suddenly split and tripped them. A large piece of rotten ox liver found its way beneath Constable Plumley's feet and he slipped and fell. Dogs began to fight over the liver and one of them got hold of Plumley's trousers. Davies knocked it away with his staff. Somehow a pair of putrescent rabbits found their way onto Constable Lewis's shoulders.

It was a brief moment of rebellion. The traders didn't know what Guy had done or who he was, but this was an opportunity to strike back at today's oppressors – the police. And how could one of them stand apart from the others and assist the police, today of all days? It wasn't possible. So they subtlety hindered the pursuit or kept out of it completely.

Ball ran after Guy, who headed desperately towards the Oxford Street exit. He leapt over Mrs Eynon's bread but misjudged his jump and landed with his back on her stall, which collapsed under his weight, her loaves scattering everywhere. Ball had him, he was sure, but as he went towards him, Bucke's old foe Elizabeth Dacey wheeled a heavy barrow of bones straight into him and then let go of the handles. 'Sorry, Sergeant Ball. Bit heavy for me at my age, see, my lovely.' It was the intervention that Guy needed. He scrambled to his feet and ran out onto Oxford Street, as Ball struggled to remove his rattle from his belt and then began to revolve it.

As he returned towards the police station, Bucke heard the police rattle and quickened his pace. The alarm seemed to be coming from the market and so he hurried down Heathfield Street. At the junction with Portland Street, a man running blindly and at speed crashed straight into Bucke and knocked him to the ground. He looked up and his eyes met those of the man who was leaning against the wall, catching his breath. Something told him it was Guy. He was certain. Their eyes locked for a moment and then Guy stepped over him and was away. Bucke, winded, struggled to his feet, but he realised that Guy had a head start on him and that he couldn't catch him. He could only watch as he disappeared into the narrow streets in the northern part of the town. There were no constables around – they had all been deployed in the market – and he knew he would never find him. So a chastened Guy was allowed to find his careful way back to the Baumhaus, using the sort of circuitous looped route which enabled a dirty and unkempt man to blend into the impoverished districts of the town. He knew he had to lie low for a little while now. Certainly, there was no need for Moitch to know about this little adventure.

~

Back in the market, William Mabe was busily employing a dirty rag to wipe away the sawdust from the carcase that Guy had dropped. He was the one who had given him a casual job as a porter and he was answering Ball's questions with as little detail as possible. 'I don't know who he is, do I? He turns up now and again. Works hard. No need for me to ask questions. Why should I? I tell you what, you lot would be better off if you found out who killed poor old Punch, than persecuting them as is trying to earn an honest living.'

William Mabe had never had an inclination to cooperate with the police, his regular and despised adversaries. His offences were many and various. Selling unfit meat, driving his horse and cart furiously along Oxford Street without care for pedestrians, riding the railway to Neath without buying a ticket, fighting with other traders and drinking. Always drinking.

'What do you call him then? What's his name? Where's he live?' asked Ball.

'I have told you. I don't know. I don't care. If he turns up again, I will give him honest work. Simple as that.'

'No, you won't, Mabe. You will tell me.'

'Is that a fact, Sergeant?'

'You listen to me. Inspector Bucke would like to know where he lives, see.'

'Would he now? He has become a very curious man as I hear, our Inspector. Very enquiring. A great deal he wants to know. He wants to be a very knowledgeable man. But all that knowledge can be the sort of thing that might get him into trouble, I shouldn't wonder.'

Constable Lewis came up to them. 'Those rabbits of yours stink, Mabe. You shouldn't be selling them. All over my uniform too. How am I going to get that smell off? I don't think they are fresh.'

'Well, well. An expert.' He sniggered. 'Listen to me, sonny. They stop being fresh when people stop buying them.' He saw Inspector Bucke coming towards him along the alley and boomed out a greeting. 'Welcome to the Music Hall, Inspector. Come to see what your fine police officers have been doing, have ya? Wouldn't believe it if I told ya.'

Bucke looked at him. 'And William's been playing his part too, has he? I don't doubt it.'

'Naturally.' They were both Londoners and consequently Mabe treated him marginally better than he did any other member of the police. 'Want a sausage, copper? A little bit of something to take home?'

Bucke grinned. 'Why in God's name would I want to sample one of your little bags of mystery?'

'You never know, copper. Might have a prize in one of 'em.'

'And what might that be? A piece of meat? That would certainly be a prize worth talking about.'

Mabe went back to the carcase, muttering, and Ball explained to Bucke what had happened, about how he had come so very close to apprehending Guy.

'These things happen, Sergeant. If it was him, then it proves that he is still in Swansea. Where is Inspector Allison?'

Ball raised his eyebrows. 'Out on Union Street, they say. With Mr Crockford. Measuring a barrel of herrings.' He glanced carefully around him then lowered his voice and added, 'I shall tell him what happened and remind him what he is supposed to do when the police rattle sounds.'

As Bucke was about to turn onto Oxford Street, one of the old established traders stopped him. She was known to everyone as Beryl Butter and she wanted to talk. She was an honest and hard-working woman who, every week, went to Carmarthen to collect the very best cheese, bacon and, of course, butter. Her stall was one of the finest in the town and her goods were highly regarded. But today she was very unhappy and worried. Inspector Allison was threatening to condemn her scales and fine her unless she paid him an additional fee every time she came to the market. And she could not afford it. Bucke was horrified, though not at all surprised. He promised that he would look into it for her. Encouraged by what she saw of their conversation, Nellie Damms, who ran a stall selling household linen, also called him over and told him that a young man had tried to sell her a bag full of slippers earlier in the morning. She had declined, knowing full well that they were stolen.

'You know that Maggie Cleary? The one who sells onions over by Orange Street? It was her son John. A right villain, he is turning out to be.'

Chapter Fifteen

He didn't like doing it. He wished he did not have to. But it was his duty. The police force had its procedures and he had to follow them. So Inspector Bucke was obliged to speak to Chief Constable Allison and tell him what he had discovered and the direction his investigations had taken.

Afterwards, he wished he hadn't bothered.

First of all, he told the Chief Constable about the unease amongst the market traders. He didn't tell him that his son was behaving illegally, because he wanted more evidence, but merely said that some of the more honourable and trustworthy traders were being targeted. As he anticipated, Allison was unimpressed and not prepared to listen.

'Them down at the market ? Had it easy for far too long,' he sneered. 'Of course they is going to complain, now someone is doing a proper job. Just gossip. An' another thing. Where were you then, when that fiasco in the market were going on? Why weren't you there wi' Inspector Allison then?'

'I was continuing with my investigation into the murder of Herbert Jenkins, who himself has started to feature in my—'

Allison interrupted him eagerly. 'You are wastin' everybody's time and you are talkin' nonsense, lad! Bristow killed the tart and Jenkins. Everybody knows. And that urchin? Fell in the dock. And you're still wasting that time wi' all o' this?'

He realised that it was not a good idea to tell the Chief Constable about his belief that Jenkins had murdered Punch but still continued to offer Allison an updated report, in spite of the overwhelming evidence against such manifest futility.

'I have strong evidence to suggest that Guy is still in Swansea, and I think he is in some way connected with the recent murders. Sergeant Ball saw him in the market and there is a suggestion that from there he fled up towards Greenhill. I saw him running away.'

'How do you know it was Guy? You've never seen him. That's what you told me. Take no notice of Sergeant Ball – mistaken. I mean, his eyes are rubbish. No idea. Guy's gone, Bucke. Another one you've lost. Shot his wife, she din't die, he has buggered off. What's tha' problem?' He pulled at the wart and his face flinched with the discomfort.

Bucke closed his eyes briefly and tried to continue. 'I am particularly concerned about the visit of the Frenchman Monsieur de Lesseps. I think I may have uncovered a conspiracy to kill him...'

This was clearly a step too far for Allison. He banged his hands on the table. 'What are you talkin' about, Bucke? What kind o' nonsense is this? Conspiracies? There is real crime happenin' in this town and you are doing bugger all about it. You listen to me. Lord Mayor's office has taken over the arrangements and it's all goin' well. Everythin' organised. You need to get down there and get policin' sorted out – crowd control, that sort of thing. Keepin' smelly buggers away from that Frenchman. Don't want him thinkin' we is all beggars, do we? But don't say no word of this ridiculous idea of yours. I mean, who is going to kill this Frenchie then? Come on, tell me.'

He had no wish to tell him. 'My enquiries are continuing but I think you should know—'

'Enquiries continuin', you say? That means you haven't got no idea. You have got no bloody evidence at all. And don't tell me Daniel bloody Guy. He could barely shoot his bloody wife. I'm telling you, Bucke. Am watchin' you. And I will tell you something else as well. There has been a burglary while you have been messin' about. Glanmor Terrace at Reverend Manning's school. A good friend of mine, Manning, and some urchin has smashed kitchen window at the back and got in. Tampered with the locks on the desks and nicked a pair of boots and nine pairs of slippers. That's the sort of thing you should be worried about, not made-up stories. Inspector Allison is up there now lookin' into the burglary. Good officer. Gets things sorted while you are doing nowt. I am warnin' you. Look to yourself and get some proper work done.'

'I shall value your advice as much as I always do, Chief Constable,' replied Bucke, the contempt in his voice unheard by the Chief Constable. 'I think Inspector Allison may find it profitable to speak to John Cleary. His mother has a stall in the market selling vegetables. We arrested him last year. He did seven days for assaulting Constable Davies when he refused to leave the Glamorgan Arms. Good day, sir.'

As he left the police station, he was once again frustrated and angry. Policing was a team operation or it was nothing; yet his senior officer displayed a closed mind daily and entertained an incompatible perception of duty. So, if his investigation had any hope of success, then he needed to go to a place where he could speak and be confident that what he had to say would receive proper consideration and an intelligent response. And he knew precisely where he should go.

$\backsim$

The visits by Rumsey Bucke had become Constance Bristow's salvation. She knew that people liked the face she showed the world, one of competence and good humour; but in the quiet of the night, her uncertain future filled her with anxiety. How would she ever survive as a single woman? Her only consolation was that at least Agnes was living independently and was not part of what was both her Great Uncertainty and her Great Adventure. But her spirits lifted whenever Rumsey came to call, and she waited in pleasurable anticipation for his visits. He was intelligent and sensitive and she valued most of all that he treated her as an equal. He listened to what she said and reflected on it before he spoke. He did not demean her or belittle her. He also involved her in his work – entirely inappropriately, of course. She knew things she had no right to know, but Constance was moved beyond words that he chose to trust her in this way. As her life changed, she came to realise the true nature of her subjugation during her marriage. William had never seen her as a person, merely as a prize, as a symbol of his social advancement.

Now Rumsey gave her courage and restored her self-belief, which had previously been only barely sustained by those petty victories paid for in bruises and abuse. Here was someone, finally, who respected her.

She realised that she had wasted eighteen years in a marriage which had brought her nothing but Agnes. She knew she had to live with those consequences. This was the path she had once taken and she could never go back and take a different one. But perhaps the awareness she was gaining as her independence blossomed provided some comfort, for it meant that she was more able to make important decisions.

There was one thing she had no choice about. She had no alternative but to leave Mansel Terrace and find rooms. She realised that the very act of doing so was an act of liberation, and she began to feel that she would now be able to make her own decisions about her own destiny. What did William used to say? *Carpe Diem*? Seize the day? Well, that is what she would do. She would make use of almost the only two things she possessed – apart from a tea service – her maiden name and her ability to play the piano tolerably well. Thus, the Constance White School of Pianoforte was born where, one day soon, she was sure, young ladies would also be able to learn dancing and deportment to add to their musical achievements. Constance hoped that in this way, with good fortune, she would be able to achieve a professional status which she could not attain in any other occupation. She gained confidence daily, finding rooms on St Helen's Road and work for two mornings a week teaching piano at Miss Higginson's Select Day School for Girls on Eaton Terrace.

But, of course, word of mouth would never be enough for a new venture like this, and she was very moved when Rumsey paid for an advertisement to be placed in the *Cambrian* newspaper: *Miss Constance White. Pianoforte lessons given to a limited number of pupils.* She had accepted his gesture of support with grace. Why shouldn't she? She knew it was offered with honour and it had touched her to see the embarrassed way in which he had stumbled through his offer of support.

A piano? Now there was an essential item for a pianoforte teacher. They cost £15 from Thompson and Shackell's Music Warehouse on the High Street but she knew she couldn't afford that. So she used all the money she had to buy a cottage piano at an auction of "well-preserved household furniture" at the Auction Mart on Waterloo Street, though her unfamiliarity with procedures meant that she almost bought the previous lot which was a dog kennel and a double-barrelled shotgun. She enjoyed herself, finding it all rather thrilling, though she did suspect that others had stopped bidding to allow her to buy it. But the piano was small enough to be accommodated in her reduced circumstances and fitted nicely against the wall. It had a rather attractive tapestry front which she could one day imagine herself studying closely whilst some of her less talented pupils found unusual ways in which to dismember Bach. It was sometimes hard for her to grasp the enormity of the whirlwind which had suddenly embraced her in a few short weeks.

~

These new rooms were much smaller but they were more comfortable, more relaxed. The spirit of William Bristow which lurked in Mansel Terrace had been dispelled and Rumsey Bucke felt less of an intruder. He sat at the scarred deal table which she had brought with her and enjoyed the warmth which came from the kitchen range. He told her about his meeting with the Chief Constable and how that had made him feel.

'Whatever he says, I am determined to solve these riddles. The more I talk to you, the more I feel I understand what is happening. Allison still believes that your husband was the killer, but he is nothing of the sort. He ran away from Swansea because he was frightened – I have believed this for some time, but I thought it was because of some indiscretion or a concern for his solvency. But I was wrong, I am sure of it. After the murder of Jenkins, he fully expected to be the next victim.' He then counted off the points he made by grasping the fingers on his left hand as he made them. 'Your husband believed he was under threat and he was frightened. It is easy to express strong opinions about all manner of things, but not so easy to accept that in doing so you might be putting yourself at risk. He had entered a dangerous world and found himself out of his depth. He was shocked to learn that his opinions might make people angry. So he fled.' He paused. 'Sometimes I think it is wrong for me to criticise your husband, but that is what I think.'

'I have told you, Rumsey. He is now a stranger to me. I know him as a liar and a coward. Not as a husband. Please don't forget that.'

'There is something else I must tell you, Constance, a conclusion I have drawn to which the Chief Constable was not prepared to listen. I believe Virginia Jenkins has been acting as a courtesan to some of the leading individuals in the town, whether with or without her husband's approval, I cannot say.'

'Oh my goodness! Gentlemen callers! How scandalous!' Constance clapped her hands. She was suddenly relishing every possibility, her eyes sparkling. 'I apologise. What I meant to say was… How unsavoury!'

'A tablecloth hanging on the clothes line in the garden is a sign to any visitor that Virginia Jenkins is already engaged with another of her gentlemen. One must presume that they all know about each other.'

'It is what I would do,' nodded Constance thoughtfully.

'Pardon? '

'The tablecloth. Rumsey, think about it. It would be most unseemly to have one's gentleman callers patiently making small talk in the drawing room whilst watching the clock.'

'I am pleased that you approve of her arrangements,' said Bucke.

'And these are eminent men, you say?'

'Naturally. Are you not shocked, Constance? Perhaps I am shocked that you are not shocked.'

'Why should I be, Rumsey? We should hear more of this sort of thing. The skull beneath the skin. Are such people better than your women along the Strand and their clients? I do not think so.'

'You are right, I believe. She is very much the same.'

He thought of all those women doing what they had to do, using the only currency they had, to survive on the dangerous streets. They had not created those dark and dangerous areas in the town. They were its victims. He realised too that Constable Sprague's theft of that important tablecloth had been so unfortunate, because it allowed Virginia and Elinor to discredit his evidence about a man in the garden and disguise their activities for a little longer. 'Have you met Mrs Jenkins, Constance?'

'Once, at a musical soiree. I think my husband knew something about her because he was fussing around her all night. You don't think... No. I don't want to think about that. I certainly didn't like her very much. She was very superior. I was nervous and tipped sherry down my bodice. She was certain that I was much beneath her, though now I am not at all sure what she has to feel superior about.'

She paused thoughtfully and Bucke wondered whether she was speculating that she might have had to make a similar choice, if it was the only alternative to starvation. 'She is the same as the rest of us, and she has no right to assume superiority over anyone else, no matter who they are. I would imagine that Elinor Roberts must be acting as her maid in all things. Receiving callers, taking hats, smiling nicely, making tea, closing doors.'

'Indeed. She is fully involved in everything that goes on in St James' Crescent. She must know far more than she has told me. Elinor will certainly know who was in the house prior to the murder of Herbert Jenkins. She might have seen it happen.' He ran his hands through his hair.

'And so you think she might be hiding the identity of an eminent man in the town who is a murderer? You do realise, don't you? It could be the Mayor. Or the vicar. It might even be your Chief Constable. What are you going to do?' Constance asked.

'What I always do, Constance. I shall be patient. I shall not rush into anything at all. After all, such arrangements cannot be my concern until an offence is committed. And, so far, there has been no criminal activity – or at least not until I can understand the death of Herbert Jenkins. The indiscretions within the Jenkins' house might be moral ones perhaps but not necessarily criminal ones. I would look foolish if I tried to prosecute her for running a brothel or a disorderly house because I would receive no support from my superiors. So I must be certain of the information I have. In these circumstances, it is inevitable that she has acquired powerful friends who will not like their own identity to be revealed. I now understand that I must be very careful of how I proceed or I may lose my employment.'

'Do you think that is why Herbert Jenkins went in through the garden when he came home on the night when he was killed?'

'I believe that it is a possibility. If he thought she was entertaining on the evening that he died, Herbert might have gone around to the back of the house to check the tablecloth. Did he want to catch her with another? Or did he wish to avoid an embarrassing scene? I don't know. I don't know how much he was involved in her affairs. But I must now consider that the murderer might not have been waiting for him in the garden or had not followed him home. The murderer could have come from within the house – it could have been one of Virginia's gentlemen who killed him, either accidentally or deliberately. I shall need to speak to Elinor, I think. She must tell me who was there, but she may not. Why should she? But you see, the more I find out about what might have happened, the less I seem to know.'

Chapter Sixteen

He slept fitfully again, the details of the case rebounding around inside his head. There was a key to the whole affair, he was sure; but it was always just beyond his reach. Then he was aware of pressure at the bottom of his bed and sat up. There, sitting cross-legged and looking expectantly at him, were Anna and Charles, just as they always did. They were smiling at him, willing him to wake up because they had something important to say or perhaps a game they wanted to play. He tried to speak to them, but he was unable to produce any sounds. And then behind them he could see Julia, and she was smiling too. She was dressed to go out, in her hat and the elegant coat he insisted she bought. He wanted to ask her where she was going but he couldn't. The children hopped off the bed and stood either side of their mother, holding her hand: a defining image of love, contentment and safety. Charles waved at him but neither of Bucke's arms would move. He wanted to go with them, but he knew that he couldn't.

And then he woke up.

He cried again, he often did, and watched the sun rise above the roofs opposite, lost in his memories. He got out of bed, took the doll and the wooden sword from the chair and put them in his wardrobe.

It was the sort of beautiful day for which May is renowned but which it doesn't always successfully deliver, and, though his mind was on more sinister matters, Bucke did stop briefly and look towards the sky to feel the warmth on his face as he went down to the Mayor's office in the Town Hall. If he truly believed in the possibility of an assassination attempt, he had to familiarise himself with the arrangements for de Lesseps's visit – and even if he didn't think it was likely, now that the idea had flashed across his mind, he had an obligation to prepare for it. The sudden collapse of the Swansea Knowledge Acquirers, useful or otherwise, had quietened the frenzied excitement about the visit for a while but now, as it came closer, interest was building once more. All the tickets for the dinner in the Mackworth Hotel had been sold, and there would be a respectable audience of one hundred eager Welsh investors, each of them hoping to make a fortune from a monumental engineering project to dig a canal through 45 miles of swamp and mosquitoes on the other side of the world.

As far as Bucke was concerned, the event was well organised, and, of course, he would offer the mayoral assistants no suggestion whatsoever that there might be even the remotest suggestion of danger. Their distinguished guest, together with his seven-year-old daughter Ferdinande, known to her family as Nandi and who was accompanying him on his European tour, would be met by dignitaries at the Mumbles Road Station. They would be accommodated by the mayor, Alderman John Jones-Jenkins, and offered the opportunity to refresh themselves after the train journey from Liverpool. After all, Monsieur was over seventy years of age. A carriage would then take de Lesseps and Nandi to the Mackworth Hotel on Wind Street for dinner, where afterwards, he would deliver a speech – in French – on the advantages of the canal. Presumably, translations would be muttered throughout the dining room as he spoke. At the end of the evening, a carriage would take the party to High Street station to begin another journey, this time to Amsterdam, where he would deliver the same speech, in French, but to a Dutch audience. These were the arrangements that Bristow had announced those weeks ago and which Jenkins had so loudly dismissed. And where were they now? Did their loud and hectoring objections actually matter anymore? How things can change.

As far as Bucke was concerned, the old gentleman would be vulnerable throughout his time in Swansea. A determined assassin could strike at any moment, but he reasoned that the most dangerous points were the entrances and exits, where uninvited guests could get closer to de Lesseps, whilst sheltering within a crowd. That would be the only way they could even hope to get close enough to kill him. They were unlikely to try and shoot him from a distance, assuming they were going to use a gun.

He would deploy officers at the two stations and outside the Mackworth. Bucke didn't think anything was likely to happen at the dinner table itself, but had a particular concern about the lobby through which de Lesseps must walk. He needed constables who were alert and observant. He was not sure that he had any. He thought he would recognise Guy if he saw him and so would Sergeant Ball. But the others? If the greatest risk was in the lobby, he would have to place himself there, along with Ball. And then? Hope for the best. And that was never the most convincing of plans.

Someone asked whether they should provide each guest with a shovel so that they could begin immediately the construction of a tunnel beneath the sea and they all laughed heartily. The words of Jenkins and Bristow had clearly had an impact, though no one seemed to be taking them too seriously.

Bucke had enough information to enable him to make his plans for the visit, though he would have been far more comfortable if he could arrange the arrest of Daniel Guy before the end of the week. There was no contribution he could offer them which would advance their plans. They seemed competent and organised and he decided to return to the police station. As Bucke walked down the stairs, he met the borough treasurer. This was fortuitous. Bucke had wanted to see him but had been unable to make an appointment.

Mr Islay Young was a quiet, rather anxious man, who found ledgers much safer and infinitely more reliable than people. He avoided eye contact as much as he could. He was short, bald and overweight and had the admirable virtues of scrupulous honesty and efficiency. Bucke rather liked him.

'Good morning, Inspector Bucke. I understood that you wished to see me. A pleasing coincidence, for I believe that I may need your help – urgently – and in regard to a rather delicate matter. I took the liberty of speaking to Ada last night and she was in full agreement that I should speak to you. Perhaps I should not have spoken to her about this but, to be quite frank, I find myself in a difficult dilemma and I am able to rely entirely upon her discretion.'

His wife, Ada, a large and ebullient character, did a great deal of work in supporting the orphans of Swansea, raising money, trying to find them employment and providing meals and clothing in the winter. Bucke had always regretted that she had been unable to do anything for Joseph.

'You know very well that I have the utmost respect for Mrs Young and I know that any advice she would give would be worth serious consideration.' It was the polite thing to say but Bucke meant it. She was a decent person and he had always found their devotion to each other admirable and touching. 'I am sure I don't have to tell you that I have always valued what she says.'

'Thank you, Inspector. I appreciate your words very much. I should be grateful if you would accompany me to my office.' He led him a few steps along a corridor, opened the door to a small room and invited him in. Everything was neat and ordered, systematically arranged, a bit like his mind, mused Bucke. Through the window, he could see dockers unloading sacks from a ship in the dock a short distance away. There was shouting and the rattle of pulleys and chains, but when the borough treasurer began to speak, all those noises seemed to fade away.

Young sat down and fidgeted nervously. 'I have no wish to bore you but I have been looking at the income Swansea derives from the market licences for traders and from fines for non-compliance with regulations concerning weights and measures. I have compared the income we received for the last twelve months, whilst it was part of your responsibilities, and then calculated a weekly average figure. You must understand, Inspector, that I know this all sounds rather tedious, but it has proved to be especially revealing. You see, since Inspector Allison has been responsible, the income has reduced dramatically. And yet there cannot have been such a dramatic change in circumstances to explain this reduction. It should remain reasonably constant.' He paused. 'I cannot imagine our market traders are suddenly better behaved than they were when you were watching over them.'

Their eyes met. They knew exactly what was going on. 'Mr Young, you have no alternative but to take this matter to the Mayor.'

Young sighed and briefly removed his glasses. 'I know, Inspector. I want you to know that I have no wish to compromise your position, but, as Ada said, we value your opinion and I wanted to make sure you did not think I was acting rashly or disproportionately.'

'Not at all. I have had my own concerns for a while. You know that you must do what is right. Siphoning away the income due to the Swansea corporation and, heaven forbid, keeping it for yourself – well, it is a serious crime. '

'Indeed. You will appreciate my difficulties, I know you will, but they are compounded by the fact that these weekly accounts have been countersigned and approved by the Chief Constable.'

There was another, significant, pause.

'Oh dear,' sighed Bucke. 'Perhaps he just didn't read them.'

'But he signed them, Inspector, and that, I am afraid, is the point. We must assume that he read them. What other assumption can we make? And you can confirm that you know of no reason why the income should disappear so rapidly that there has been a dramatic reduction in the region of 75%?'

'None at all. Especially since I know that fines have been collected and that licences have continued to be issued.'

Now it was Mr Young's turn, 'Oh dear.'

'It will not be pleasant, Mr Young, but we both understand what you appear to have uncovered and what it is that you have to do. We must always do our duty, and I want you to know that you will always have my complete support, for I trust your judgement implicitly.'

Young looked firm and resolute. 'Thank you for your time, Inspector, and for your kindness.'

Bucke could sense that there was something more, so he waited, knowing that there were other things Young wanted to say. Suddenly it all tumbled out. 'I know the stupidity of others is a daily feature of your employment, Inspector, but I cannot comprehend how anyone could be so obviously deranged as to believe that they could keep such a deception hidden. And if I am honest, Rumsey, I am even more angry that Inspector Allison seems to believe that I am so incompetent that I would not notice. If they had tried to bribe me, it would have made more sense. But to assume that I would not discover it...' He sighed angrily. 'To be frank, I find it hurtful. Allison seems to believe that I am as inadequate as he is, and that reason alone would have been sufficient to ensure that I would never shirk from my duties.'

'I never had any doubt that you had the courage to do your duty, Islay. Should you need anything from me, you know where to find me.'

He rose and Mr Young shook his hand. 'Thank you, Rumsey. I am greatly obliged for your time.'

He walked along the High Street, which was pleasantly quiet at this time of day. Of course, Bucke was not at all surprised that such behaviour had been uncovered, for Thomas Allison had brought with him a reputation for dishonest practice. But how could he have ever imagined that a man as assiduous, professional and virtually incorruptible as Young would not be able to see what he was doing? That was an act of the most arrogant stupidity. He wondered what would happen now. A huge scandal scattered throughout newspapers across Wales? Or quiet repayment and a discreet resignation? And where would that leave him? A couple of weeks ago, it would not have mattered greatly. Now though? Rumsey Bucke suddenly had pressing reasons to stay in Swansea. All he could hope to do was to try to ensure that he was not personally compromised by a collapsing police force.

He had intended to tell Sergeant Ball that he was going to St James' Crescent to have another conversation with Elinor Roberts, but those plans were completely derailed when he walked in through the front of the police station and found Anora Crocker waiting patiently for him, holding a large hessian sack. She had plenty to say and he thought that he ought to listen to her in his office, in his own space. He soon realised that this had been a sensible decision.

'Now I don't want to waste your time but it is like this, Inspector, see. But you have got to understand that Mr Crocker, well, he is saying I should let it go, isn't he? Don't worry about it, he said. Accidents happen, like. But I do worry about it, don't I? I mean, you would, wouldn't you? Anyone would. It was a whole barrel that went. Last week it was, and Mr Crocker said I should let it go; but I am telling you, it was a whole barrel, honest to God. And all these bottles. It is money I don't have a mind to lose, my lovely.' She dropped a hessian bag onto his desk, and it crackled with the broken glass. She sat opposite, waiting for a reply.

'I see,' nodded Bucke, thoroughly bewildered. 'Perhaps if you tell me the story right from the beginning, I will be more able to offer you the kind of help that you might need, Mrs Crocker.'

'Do you want me to start with the constable or with Mr Crocker?' she asked.

'Start with whatever came first, Mrs Crocker,' said Bucke patiently, as he stuck his hand into the hessian bag. He touched broken glass and suddenly had an intuition what this might be about. He pulled a piece out and examined it carefully as she spoke.

'Well, Mr Crocker came first but really that isn't why I came here to talk to yew. We all make mistakes and that is a fact.' She cackled. 'No, yew can't help me with Mr Crocker. There is none that can. I reckon he is allergic to arsenic, see.' She cackled again. 'Yew be careful in that bag, lovely. Don't want you cutting yourself, do we?'

'Mrs Crocker, as I remember, you and your husband are the tenants of the Bush Inn in Sketty, am I correct?'

'Yes indeed, sir, we are so. We run a clean and reputable house, sir.'

'I take great pleasure in hearing that, Mrs Crocker. So why did you feel the need to come down to the police station to see me today?' He pulled out another, larger, piece of glass.

'Oh well, that will be the constable, won't it, Inspector?'

'And which constable might that be?' he asked.

'The one that isn't Constable Plumley. The one that come up to the house and looked in our cellar, isn't it? That one. Said he were looking fer people living down there. Stupid notion and I told him so, but he wouldn't listen, so I give him a candle and down he went. Said he was carrying out investigations.'

As Bucke turned around that larger fragment of glass in his hand, his suspicions were confirmed. 'Where did these bottles come from, Mrs Crocker?'

'They had brandy in 'em, didn't they? And—'

'And where did these bottles full of brandy come from, Anora? In a wheelbarrow perhaps?'

There was a long pause.

Bucke could see in Anora's face the dawning realisation of the terrible mistake she had made. He knew that she now understood why her idle and feckless husband had dismissed out of hand any possibility of reporting such vandalism. He had already accepted that this was a price they had to be prepared to pay. But it seemed that she knew better and now it was too late. Anora's anxious eyes flickered around the room, avoiding Bucke's steady gaze. Outside, a cart went past, rattling along the cobbles. A child shouted. A dog barked.

Bucke folded his arms and rested them on the desk, leaning towards her slightly. 'Mrs Crocker. Anora. It might be easier to talk to me about what has been going on.'

Mrs Crocker's forehead was suddenly more damp than it should have been. 'Nothing's been going on, Inspector. Don't know what yew are saying. They are broken bottles, like, and yewer constable broke them, but I think it might rightly be best if I went home, since yew are not willing to listen to me...' She reached out and tried to get hold of the sack, but Bucke laid his own hand upon it and shook his head.

'I am more than happy to listen to you, Anora, once you decide to talk about the things I wish to hear. Tell me about these bottles of brandy that are brought to you in a wheelbarrow by Mr Gallivan of Little Gam Street. You see, they are plugged with rags, not wax seals. I have seen them. Look carefully, Anora. There is no sign of any wax on any of the glass in the sack. That is because no one has paid any duty on the brandy. It has been smuggled into Swansea on a ship. Came in a barrel, I imagine, and the Galllivans put it in bottles and then sold it to you and to others. This is a crime you know, Anora.'

'I am much obliged for your time, Inspector, but think it is best for me to be going now...'

He shook his head. 'Not yet, Anora. You stay right here. We have quite a lot to talk about.' He asked Sergeant Ball to dispatch a constable to the Gallivan house whilst he spoke to Anora Crocker. She couldn't tell him anything he hadn't already worked out, though he eventually identified the constable involved from her garbled description. Bucke was aware that he should have acted sooner on what he knew and surprised himself once again when he realised that he was suddenly more inclined to do his job properly. He kept her with him long enough to prevent her getting a message to the Gallivans, then he sent her home to face her husband.

He brought in Constable Lewis who was obviously delighted to learn that his careful investigations had uncovered a smuggling ring, though he became a little uncomfortable when he was asked to explain why he had been in Sketty in the first place, since Bucke made it very clear that as far as he knew, no one had heard of any arrangement between Lewis and Plumley to swap beats. He noted with some interest that Lewis decided not to engage with that issue at all.

'I thought the arrangements I uncovered in the cellar of the Bush were suspicious, Inspector, but I did not want to trouble you when you are busy with other issues. So I have been continuing with my investigations and I was confident that I was getting near to a breakthrough. A devious bunch of dissemblers, without a doubt. Another few hours and I believe I would have cracked it open like an egg. The fact that she came in and made a confession to you just shows that my investigations had put her under such a strain that she had to confess. I thought this might happen, Inspector. She knew that I had trapped her. Painstaking work: that is the secret.'

'I am delighted to hear of your success. You may find that a visit to the cellar at the Crown Inn on the Strand may assist you in your enquiries, Constable,' offered Bucke. 'Additional evidence. Very important.,' He nodded.

The colour drained from Lewis's face. 'You want me to go to that den of thieves and villainy on my own?'

'Take Sergeant Ball with you, Constable Lewis. I am sure he will keep you from harm and allow you to collect the vital evidence that you require. Make sure that he takes his handcuffs.'

It was not a difficult assignment at all. The landlord of the Crown Inn was delighted to be given the opportunity to help the police in any way that he could, once he knew that the renewal of his licence might now depend upon it. Of course, he was completely shocked that duty on the brandy had not been paid. He thought someone else had done that. His eager confession outlined that it had been a very simple operation, one that was both effective and profitable.

William Bonnell from Newfoundland, the mate on the *Gazelle*, brought in brandy in barrels from France. Gallivan collected it from the docks. It was transferred into the washed bottles by Mrs Gallivan and sold to publicans around the town, with John Phillips and Mr Gallivan making the deliveries. It was straightforward, profitable and illegal. Bonnell was detained at the docks just before the *Gazelle* set sail, and the Gallivans and

Phillips picked up on Little Gam Street, their flirtation with the acquisition of easy scraps of money at the very edge of the law suddenly at an ignominious end.

Of course, Lewis was very pleased with himself and was delighted that four people had been thrown into prison, awaiting their appearance at the police court in a few days' time. He told anyone who would listen that his assiduous investigation had shown the rest of the police force how these things should be done, though his drinking companion Inspector Allison was not available to share in his triumph.

Inspector Bucke thought this might be a good moment to visit Mary Guy once more. He needed to confirm that her husband had not been in touch, especially in the light of his escapade in the market. She was lucky that she too was not in prison, and Bucke hoped this good fortune might encourage her to remember information she had previously omitted.

He found Mary particularly anxious. 'I only washed bottles, that is all I was required to do. I helped Mrs Gallivan in return for a few pennies. I didn't know what they were going to do with them. How could I know? It was none of my business.'

'Even though your brother was making deliveries for them, Mary? I find that hard to believe. You must have realised what was happening. Did his employers know what he was doing?'

'That is no affair of mine. A woman deserted by her husband must survive the best she can. Isn't that so, Inspector?' She looked at Bucke defiantly.

He acknowledged her words and inclined his head. News travels fast, he thought.

She stood up gingerly in order to stretch her back. She was still in some pain and obviously found it easier to stand. 'What do you think will happen to them?' she asked.

'There will be a fine. Evading duty is a crime but I would not expect a prison sentence. It might deter others, but it would do nothing to recover the lost income for the corporation. It is going to be a problem for a large number of publicans too. They could be in danger of losing their licences. The effects of this crime could range far and wide. Many people could be involved.'

'What if they cannot pay, Inspector?'

'The courts will decide what will happen and sometimes it is hard to predict what they will do. But if you do not commit a crime, there is no price to be paid, Mary, I am sure you understand that. The very least I would expect is that it will prove expensive for them. If Gallivan has any sense, he will plead guilty and say that neither you nor his wife knew what you were doing. You should get off with a warning – you can say you didn't know why you were washing the bottles. That should be enough; after all, neither your brother nor Gallivan are publicans, and I assume you never met the sailor Bonnell.' She turned her head away from him. 'It will be harder for Mrs Gallivan, I fancy. If she was the one filling the bottles from the barrel, then in such circumstances she can hardly plead ignorance. They might then decide that the Gallivans will face a heavier fine. I would suspect that it is something they can ill afford. Recently, the courts have been very firm. They might have to pay three times the value of the brandy they had, three times the duty that would normally be attached to the brandy and three times the court costs incurred. I wouldn't want to have to pay it. Let us hope you will be lucky and they treat you kindly. You have had much to deal with of late.'

'Have you found my husband yet?' she snapped back at him. 'Is not that more important than punishing those who have nothing?'

'Someone is sheltering him, Mary. Unless I have information, it will take me a little longer to find him. Who knows how long it might take me? But I am sure he remains in Swansea.' He shrugged his shoulders. 'Have you seen Daniel?'

'No. Would I be alive if I had? I have told you before. I don't know where he is. What else can I tell you? I need him to be arrested so that I can sleep at night, Inspector.'

'You can tell me where he might be. He is in Swansea. I need to arrest him. Because if he remains free in Swansea, he may come back to see you, Mary. I can only stop that happening if you tell me what you know.'

'But I have told you already! There is nothing that I know. I would tell you if there was. Why should I want him to stay at liberty and wait for him to return with his gun?'

'You said to me that Daniel once left you for another? Who was the woman?'

'Woman? She was a girl, a child. It wasn't right. People like you should have stopped it happening. Her name?' She paused and thought for a moment. 'It was Nell Owen. Something happened and she lost her mind. They put her away in the County Asylum. Still there, as far as I know.'

The following day, whilst Lewis excitedly continued to unravel the smuggling ring and made himself especially unpopular in a number of public houses, Inspector Bucke took the train to Bridgend to visit the Glamorgan County Lunatic Asylum. There he met William Stockwell, the steward of the asylum, who found for him the information he required. It wasn't difficult. Everyone remembered Nell Owen. She had been popular and helpful and her quiet suffering had touched everyone there. She had been a resident for many years until, as her condition improved, she was released into the care of Virginia Roberts, the daughter of Lord Roberts of Presteigne.

Of course, Bucke knew immediately who she was.

Chapter Seventeen

On his return from Bridgend in the afternoon, he attended the court for the trial of Robert Sprague. He watched as William Jones, a ginger-beer maker, was sentenced to two months for stealing three chickens. Henry Evans was accused of stealing an iron wagon wheel but was acquitted. And then he watched as the disgraced policeman, blinking defiantly in the dock and occasionally smoothing his hand over the scars on his face, was sentenced to six months in prison, with hard labour, for stealing a tablecloth, the property of the late Mr Herbert Jenkins of St James' Crescent, Swansea.

There was a sombre mood at the police station at the conclusion of the proceedings, and Bucke feared that it could only get worse when Mr Young's discoveries were acted upon. How could they possibly police Swansea effectively when the force itself was so discredited? How could they deliver the law to the town when they themselves were no better than the criminals they were supposed to pursue? Late in the afternoon, as he was about to leave to walk up to St James' Crescent to see Elinor, he received a visitor who had been sent by his mother to see him, with unexpected news of William Vaughan Bristow.

A young man, Tom Vernon, who worked as a steward for the Dominion Line, sailing between Liverpool and America, had returned to Swansea to see his mother in Foxhole, and, before he returned for his next trip, she had persuaded him to go to the police station. He told Inspector Bucke that there had been a man from Swansea on the last voyage who, recognising Tom's accent, had introduced himself as a local head teacher called Professor Vaughan Bristow. He told Tom he was heading west to open a school in Chicago. Or north to Canada, he hadn't decided. Tom thought such indecision a little strange but found nothing particularly memorable in the conversation. However, the meeting stuck in his mind because there had been a bit of a problem when a young Irish woman travelling in steerage accused Bristow of being over-familiar. The captain had managed to calm the situation down and kept Bristow safe from her angry relatives for the rest of the voyage – three long days. The crew were glad to see the back of him when they finally docked. Tom's mum thought the inspector might be interested.

It was quite late when Tom finally left the station, and Bucke knew it might be regarded as improper for him to call upon Constance at such an hour, particularly with this piece of news. But he went to see her as early as he could the following morning. The visit to see Elinor Roberts would have to wait.

When he arrived, Constance was dressed for work, nervous and excited. She was wearing a white high-necked bodice with the sleeves buttoned tightly around her wrists, ready for the piano. Her fingernails, slowly restored, were neat and trim. When Bucke told her what he had discovered, she was quiet for a long time, looking out of the window at nothing at all, with tears welling in her eyes. Her hair was still loose and Bucke watched her gather it up in her hands and pull it backwards to look at the ceiling.

'I should be pleased, I suppose. I know he is not going to come back. He has gone and I have started a new life. It is so much better than my last one… and yet it all seems so final. I may never see him again, but he has left his mark. I will never be able to dismiss all those memories of my wasted years.'

He leaned forward in his chair and took her hand. 'You will, Constance, with help. Perhaps you need a little time to reflect upon this news. I shall leave you now and I promise faithfully to return later.'

She breathed deeply. 'Do not concern yourself, Rumsey. I will compose myself, I promise you. I have my first pupils this afternoon and so I must begin to present myself to Swansea as Constance White, the pianoforte teacher. Don't misunderstand me. I am relieved. Perhaps I wish that it had happened sooner, that is all.'

But Rumsey returned far sooner than either of them expected. As he stepped down onto the pavement from the house, he saw Elinor Roberts walking towards him along St Helen's Road, away from the town centre, with a basket over her arm. She had clearly been to the market. She could not avoid speaking to him.

'Good morning, Inspector. Mrs Jenkins wishes to eat fish today and so I have been to collect a haddock.' She held the basket towards him in which a fish stared back, glassy-eyed, mouth open.

'Yours is a busy life, Miss Roberts. I wonder if you could spare me a few moments of your time before you return home. There is something I am anxious to talk to you about.' He paused. 'I have an idea. Please come into the house. I have an acquaintance here who I know would be able to accommodate us for a few moments.'

This wasn't something that he had planned, but some instinct told him that he should speak to her in the presence of Constance; that Elinor might be more comfortable and perhaps speak more openly if there was a woman with him and if she was away from the influence of Mrs Jenkins.

Constance, her eyes still glistening, had the good sense not to be surprised. She greeted Elinor warmly and took her through to what was to be her teaching room, raising her eyebrows in questioning surprise as she passed Bucke. He nodded imperceptibly and then called Constance his "assistant", and she looked surprised but pleased.

Elinor looked around warily, unfastened her bonnet and placed it on her lap.

'Please, Miss Roberts, you must not alarm yourself. I wish to talk to you about the murder of Herbert Jenkins, for I believe you may be in great danger. You may be assured that you can speak freely before Miss White. She considers the information I receive and helps to formulate the proper conclusions. She knows as much about the case as I do myself.'

'Inspector, I fear you overstate—' He raised his hand to help Constance realise that her sentence had finished.

Elinor Roberts said nothing, watching them carefully.

'Elinor, you must tell me what you know. I know that Mrs Jenkins entertains gentlemen at the house. Constance is aware of this too.' He nodded at her. 'So are many more people, I fancy. Elinor, there is no profit in you keeping silent about something that I already know. You could be in danger.'

'I am not in danger, Inspector.'

'I believe that on the night of the murder, someone came out of the kitchen and murdered Mr Jenkins. If it was one of Mrs Jenkins's visitors, then they may return to do you harm.'

'They will not come back, Inspector.'

'They could want to kill you, Elinor.'

'They do not want to kill me.'

'You seem strangely confident, Elinor. You speak as though you know who committed the crime.'

She looked at him blankly. 'There was no one with Mrs Jenkins that evening.' She paused. 'Apart from myself.'

'Then if that was the case, why was the tablecloth hanging outside? I know what Virginia Jenkins does. I know about the tablecloth, Elinor. I know what it means.

'Because the tablecloth was damp and needed to dry. That is why you place washing on a line outside. To dry, Inspector. I thought you would have known. I then took it in when the policemen came.'

Bucke persisted. 'Someone was with Mrs Jenkins. That man could have killed Mr Jenkins.'

'Inspector, please.' Elinor sighed with exasperation. 'There was no man with Mrs Jenkins. Consequently, that man, who was not with her, could not have killed Mr Jenkins. I do not know how I can express it more simply. It must have been someone else. I am not in danger, I assure you.'

Bucke knew that the moment had come. 'Elinor, you should know that yesterday I paid a visit to the County Asylum in Bridgend.'

There was a long pause. 'I see.' She stared down at the floor, avoiding his eyes.

'They speak very highly of you there.'

She nodded in acknowledgement but did not lift her head. She began nervously to twist the ribbon of her bonnet.

'I know who you are.'

She looked up. 'No, Inspector, you do not. You might now simply be acquainted with who I used to be.'

'You are Nell Owen, Punch's sister.'

'My poor sister, yes. As children, we were very close, but then we followed our own chosen roads to sorrow. '

'Has life been unkind to you?' asked Constance with sympathy.

'I believe that life is unkind to everyone, Miss White. In some way or another. We all have difficult times which are often impossible to bear.'

'Yes,' she replied softly. 'We do. But some times are more difficult than others.'

Elinor said nothing.

'It was a man, wasn't it? It is always a man.'

Again, she did not reply and looked away at the wall, wrapping the ribbon tightly around her fingers.

'Elinor,' said Inspector Bucke softly, 'tell us about Daniel Guy.'

Elinor looked at him and as she began to speak, she drifted far away from them, deep into her own past, into those memories that she could never hide, which were always present, no matter how much she fervently desired them to disappear.

'We were intimate, Inspector. It was unrestrained but I never thought that I would be with child. I was barely fourteen but I believed I was much older. I believed I was ready for the world. And then my baby was born. And Daniel Guy took him from me. It was a boy and I called him George. But Daniel Guy was older than I was, and he said we could not marry because I was too young and because he was already married. We had to wait, he said. And he took my little Georgie from me. He said that he knew a rich woman who would pay him well so that she could finally have a child. George would want for nothing and I would see him grow as a fine young man. So Daniel Guy took my sweet boy from me. But the husband would not allow his wife to hold George and Daniel Guy could not sell him and had to come away.'

'Do you know the details of the—'

'Inspector! Please!' said Constance sharply. 'What happened next, Elinor?'

'Daniel Guy took Georgie to the beach and buried him in the sand. I saw Daniel Guy walking on the street with a shovel. I asked him where my little Georgie was. Daniel Guy laughed at me. Told me Georgie was a sickly child. That he had died on the way home and so he had buried him. He was lying. Georgie was not sick. Georgie was a fine and healthy child and I loved him. I took the shovel from him. I was in a frenzy. I dug everywhere I could on the beach but I could not find my own little Georgie. Then the tide came in and I dug even more, but I could not fight the water. I tried to turn back the sea, but it would not listen to me.' Her head slumped and her body shook. Elinor's breath shuddered from her.

Constance had covered her mouth with her hand, confronting, Bucke knew, a pain beyond her imagining. He also knew perfectly well that Elinor must relive this moment every night in her dreams.

Elinor lifted her head. 'I am sorry. I have no more tears. It is strange, but I can no longer cry.' She tried to compose herself. 'Soon a policeman came and took me away. They said I had buried George in the sand myself and placed me in the County Asylum. I was not well, Inspector. I was troubled in my mind for a long time. I could not stop thinking about my poor baby. I had dressed Georgie in a new gown for his new home. That is how always I saw him. It is how I see him still.'

He watched Constance lean across and enclose Elinor's hands in her own. 'Oh, you poor, poor woman,' her eyes damp once more. Bucke said nothing, his own eyes moist, his own sorrow reawakened.

'There were many times I wished to be dead, Miss White. I started to believe them when they said that I had put my boy in the sand. I tried many times to take my own life and there were many times I was restrained. Once, I ran away and walked into the sea, to plead for George to be returned to me. The sea is cruel and does not listen.' Elinor closed her eyes tightly and bit her lip. 'But as the sickness in my mind became less, I was allowed to carry out some duties in the County Asylum and I learned many skills. It is a good place, whatever some might say.

In my time, the health of the institution was very satisfactory, the mortality was low and there were no epidemics of any kind. I know that because I heard Dr Pringle tell a visitor, and that is why I knew I was in a good place. After I had been in the hospital for eleven years, I was fortunate indeed to obtain my position with Mrs Jenkins. She took pity on me, for she had a similar burden in her life and because of what her husband did. She has been a generous and loving lady and has given me much encouragement. I owe everything to her.' She paused and looked around the room, as if remembering where she was. 'Virginia Jenkins is the blessing of my life and I will never say or do anything to betray her. She gave me my new name and brought me to a new world. Catherine Owen was my sister and I was truly sorry that she was killed, but now I am Elinor Roberts. Roberts was Virginia's maiden name and I was happy to take it as my own.'

Bucke was about to speak when Constance caught his eye and shook her head. She sensed there was more to come.

'Daniel Guy came to the house in March, Inspector. He came with Professor Axmeyer to see Mr Jenkins. As soon as I opened the door, I knew who he was but he did not recognise me. I was a child when I served his purposes. I am different now. When I saw him, I knew then that I must kill him. So I have been looking for him in town. I could have asked Professor Axmeyer where Daniel Guy was, but I do not think he would have told me the truth. I think it might have been a dangerous thing to do. He is not a gentleman to be trusted, sir. Today, I was looking for Daniel also, for I heard that he had been seen in the market but I still could not find him.' She rubbed her eyes and then gazed at Bucke with perhaps the most piercing eyes he had ever seen.

'As you can see, I lived for many years in death's dark vale. But I am recovered now. So if you find Daniel Guy, I would be obliged if you would allow me to kill him, Inspector Bucke.

Please. His death would mean little to a hangman, but I myself might then find rest.'

~

Elinor Roberts left soon afterwards, with the haddock apparently required to satisfy at least some of the appetites in St James' Crescent safely in her basket, her bonnet in place, her self-possession restored.

Bucke leaned against the wall next to the piano. There was so much in what Elinor had told them, much that was unexpected, shocking. He needed time to think. She had confirmed that Guy and Jenkins knew each other and were at the heart of a plot. She had provided the proof that he needed. And now Axmeyer was implicated. The three of them had met. That was interesting, but what did it mean? Some of the words she chose when talking about Mrs Jenkins were especially unexpected, he thought. She had also mentioned something that Herbert Jenkins had done. He wondered what she had meant.

Constance was sitting on the piano stool, absorbed by the human tragedy she had heard. Eventually, she suggested that if Elinor were not available to deal with Guy, then she would be happy to do so on her behalf. 'You say the law forbids it? But justice demands it. How do you deal with that, Rumsey?'

He told her, as gently as he could, what he had learnt a long time ago, that only a fool would think that law and justice were the same.

He must go to see Professor Axmeyer again, this time aware of his essential unreliability. He could arrest him perhaps – on what grounds, he was not sure – but he could not see how that might help. He needed to uncover the whole of the conspiracy, not just a part of it, or its members might slip away to re-form later. He had been looking for Guy for weeks now – and that had not changed. But now perhaps Axmeyer would lead him to Guy and he might then be able to solve the murders. Although his mind was racing with all the implications of what Elinor had said, he still knew enough to try and be systematic.

In the police station, he asked Sergeant Ball to request a message be sent to America using the transatlantic telegraph cable, asking for William Vaughan Bristow to be detained. It was impossible to believe that this might actually happen but he had to try.

'Trail will have gone cold, Inspector,' said Sergeant Ball gently. 'You know that. And it is a big place they say, America. Never catch him now.'

Bucke spread his hands. 'We don't know, do we? They might have already arrested him for some crime or other. Let's see what happens.' In fact, since he was convinced that Bristow was no murderer, he was not sure at a personal level that he wanted him to be detained at all. He had his own reasons for wanting him to quietly disappear into the vastness of North America.

Chapter Eighteen

As Inspector Bucke made his way to Dynevor Place to question Axmeyer again, he saw Evan Davies coming out of a chemist shop with a package. There was guilt upon his face, as if he had been found doing something particularly embarrassing.

'Fresh supplies of laudanum, I presume, Constable?' He knew he shouldn't tease Constable Davies, but sometimes he could not resist it.

The constable shook his head seriously. 'No, sir. Certainly not, sir. Far from it, sir. It is Epsom salts for my mam's special foot lotion. Moses Boyce the chemist keeps some for me. It never fails. Best cure ever for sweaty feet. You take an ounce of salts and then mix it good and proper in some boiling water. Then when it is cold, you slap in a half-pint of gin. Then drink a glassful when required.'

'And you drink it?' asked Bucke.

'Certainly, sir. Makes you feel a little more sprightly, sir.'

'And you don't wash your feet in it, Davies? You see, I would have thought that—'

'Certainly not, sir,' interrupted Davies. 'Not if I was going to drink it, sir.' He looked at Bucke and was bemused, as if

Bucke had been suddenly possessed and had started to speak in tongues. 'I wouldn't want to drink it if I had put my feet in it, sir. They are proper smelly when I get home.'

'Very wise, Davies. I don't think I would drink it either.'

'You should try it, sir. Proper reviving, fair play.'

'I shall waste no time in doing so.' His mother's medication might explain some of those issues surrounding Davies which frequently troubled him, thought Bucke. This was, however, all his own fault. He should never have started the conversation.

'I'll mix some up for you, if you like, Inspector. My mam would love it if I did.' Davies was nothing if not generous.

'No, no, Constable Davies,' said Bucke desperately. 'That would be exceptionally kind but please do not trouble yourself. I must go out immediately on important work. A clear head will be essential.'

'I will have some ready for you when you come back, sir, so don't you concern yourself.' Davies winked and tapped his nose.

~

Bucke arrived deliberately just before the hour, the time at which Axmeyer usually admitted a new pupil. When the professor answered his knock at the door, Bucke held his gaze for a long moment, an indication that their relationship had changed. He saw in Axmeyer's unflinching and contemptuous response, a silent acknowledgement that they were now adversaries.

'You would wish to speak with me, it seems,' said the professor. 'I have a few moments before my next pupil arrives and I am eager to help you in any way that I can. Please come in, Inspector.'

The sitting room was as cold and unwelcoming as before. They sat down and faced each other across the small table, and Bucke defied the intensity of eyes eager to intimidate him by maintaining eye contact. This was certainly a man with something to hide. There seemed to be a controlled intensity about Axmeyer. He denied any knowledge of Guy, of course. He couldn't really do anything else. He confirmed once again his professional contact with Jenkins and agreed that he had visited the Jenkins' house. After all, his facility with languages was well known. But in the company of a man he had never met? This was absurd.

'I know nothing of this man of whom you speak. Guy, did you say? And who is he, may I ask?'

'A fugitive with whom I am anxious to meet, Professor. He may be able to help me and so I am speaking to everyone who may have had contact with him.'

Axmeyer smoothed the end of his beard with his hand. 'I must, I fear, disappoint you. I do not know of this criminal. What has he done? Broken the windows of a public house on the High Street?'

'He is wanted in connection with at least one murder, as well as other crimes,' snapped Bucke quickly. He was cross with himself for reacting to his goading.

'And you believe that I have been consorting with such a person? So ridiculous. And who would say so?'

'Elinor Roberts, Mrs Jenkins's maid, saw the two of you together at the Jenkins' residence in March, Professor Axmeyer.'

Axmeyer laughed and sat back in his chair. 'And why do you choose to believe the word of a lunatic housemaid? The woman is deluded, Inspector. Herbert Jenkins told me about her. It reflects the considerable charity of the man that he was prepared to give such a fantasist a position in his own house, in spite of her considerable mental derangement. Who else saw me? No one, of course. That is because it did not happen. She is lying,' he said with scorn. 'As I told you on your previous visit, Inspector Bucke, I am a simple and uncomplicated person. I spend my time here working within the simpler world of my monograph, which is so much more attractive than consorting with *räuber und mörder*. I apologise, Inspector, I should have said robbers and murderers. Sometimes German comes to me unbidden.'

There was a knock at the door. 'My pupil, I anticipate. My very own Mademoiselle Beynon. I am sorry I cannot help you with your search for Daniel Guy. In a town as small as Swansea, Inspector, it is hard to imagine that anyone could remain hidden for any length of time,' he said with a smile. 'You must excuse me.'

'Of course, Professor. If I have any more questions for you, I hope you will furnish me with another meeting.'

'Naturally, Inspector. But I am sure your attention will be taken by the imminent arrival of Swansea's illustrious guest. It will require careful preparation, I believe, to prevent disruption of the Frenchman's orchestrated, but dishonest, overtures to your people. He lies and he means you harm.' He took hold of Bucke's forearm and squeezed it tightly, his eyes burning brightly, his hostility briefly forgotten. 'You must understand, Inspector. Educated men in both our countries need to come together. It is imperative that we form a German-English axis to confront the French and their Russian allies. The greatest threat to us all comes from the east. Surely you can see that, Inspector? Agree to a tunnel beneath the sea and within a year you will have Russians marching through your Trafalgar Square. Do you understand what I am saying? The future of the world depends on men of the most exalted mental capacity, and yet we live in a time when there are too few of them.'

As he walked through the town, Bucke wondered whether it mattered a great deal, but he could not remember referring to Guy's full name. Where had Axmeyer heard the name "Daniel", he wondered? He decided it didn't matter. He knew that the professor had been lying. This conspiracy might also be the reason why Jenkins had been murdered. He sighed. Nothing changed. The more he found out, the less he knew.

As he turned into Waterloo Street, he met Sarah Rigby, who was heading for home with a small loaf of bread. She was a little more educated than most of the other women who worked on the street. She had come from Bristol intending to find work in the town, but had eventually found only one way in which she had been able to survive. She was well-known as someone who did not drink, and the money she earned she saved. She had no intention of spending the rest of her life like this. When he saw her, Bucke remembered that Constable Lewis was eager to suggest that the two of them were in some kind of loose relationship and that they intended one day to marry.

'Good afternoon, Inspector Bucke. It is quiet here on Waterloo Street today. I have been wondering where your constables are. There must be some sort of crisis which demands their attention elsewhere in the town. I haven't seen one at all, and there was a man just now who deposited his orange peel on the pavement with no regard for the safety of his fellows. You can never find a policeman when you want one.'

'There is nothing going on which I am aware of, Sarah, although as far as I have been told, you yourself can always find a constable when you require one. I have heard Constable Lewis say that you have an understanding.'

'Indeed? Gethin says many unexpected things, Inspector Bucke.' A breeze suddenly fluttered the faded ribbon which circled her straw hat and she flicked it away from her shoulder. She smiled at him. 'As you know.'

'Do you really intend to marry him?'

Sarah laughed. 'Inspector, it is not that kind of understanding, no matter what he says. Gethin understands that if he wants me to do anything, he has to pay first.'

Bucke smiled. 'I feel a sense of relief.'

'As I do myself. Even I, in my reduced circumstances, believe I can do better than Constable Gethin Lewis.'

'Tell me, Sarah. Why do you persist in this dreadful occupation? It is dangerous, unpleasant and unhealthy and condemns you to ridicule and abuse.'

'You might need to see the world as we see it, Inspector.' She sighed. 'There are far more women working on the streets than I suspect even you will ever know. Some rarely, some secretly, some frequently. But no one does it because they want to. Or because they enjoy it. None of us do. But many of us have run out of choices. Who amongst us can say they would never stoop so low? When you have stooped as I have stooped, then you will know that it isn't that low at all. It might kill many of us, but it allows us all to live.' She began to walk away but hesitated and turned back to him. 'But, Inspector, since we are talking like this, I would like to tell you that there are some dark and shadowy men around the town these days. We have all been cautious since the murder of Punch. But we see such men in the town now. They don't trouble us; they are not interested in any of the girls, it seems. But there is something sinister about them. I don't know where they are from or where they go. But they are around all the time.' She spoke very carefully. 'You take care, Inspector. Things are not right in the town at present. There is something violent about these strangers in the shadows and I am sure there is something in motion. All of us need to be vigilant.'

He knew that she was serious. Women like Sarah knew more than anyone else about the dark underbelly of Swansea. 'I believe you are right, Sarah. But I believe it is a temporary difficulty. Please remain careful. You must not hesitate to tell me if you are ever fearful.'

'I shall, Inspector, though I do not think these shadows threaten any harm to those like me, but I will be careful, as I always am. I do not intend to live my life in this way for much longer. I have saved a little money; and in Bristol, the ships sail for Australia. I know there will be a new life for me there.'

As Bucke watched her walk away with her bread, her ribbon waving behind her, he thought about what she had just said. Was it not true? What did almost everyone he had met really want, above all else? A new life. And who, out of all of them, would be granted such a rare opportunity? Sarah perhaps? Or himself?

∼

When he arrived at the station, he found things strangely quiet. He had hoped to talk to Chief Constable Allison about mounting a surveillance operation outside the Swansea Languages Academy but he was unavailable. Locked in a meeting, all morning apparently, with Islay Young, the County Treasurer. No one was quite sure where his son Thomas was either, which was awkward because as Sergeant Ball was eager to tell him, he had taken a complaint from Maggie Cleary about the treatment of her son when he had been arrested. Maggie had been adamant that Allison had been rather heavy-handed with John, and that the heavy bruising to his eye and the loss of hearing in his right ear were injuries inconsistent with the official explanation of an unfortunate stumble in the cells.

Bucke realised quite suddenly that he was the senior officer on duty and thus, in the absence of anyone else, he permitted himself to authorise the deployment of constables to watch upon Professor Axmeyer. He briefed them carefully about what they should do, trying his best to keep it simple.

If Professor Axmeyer left the premises, they should follow him and report on where he went. If there were callers, they should note any identifiable features and the times when they came and when they left. They would start immediately because, as he told them, he knew the professor was inside.

Lewis, energised and confident following his recent success with the smuggling ring, was eager to be involved in surveillance duties and was given a later watch, just before midnight. The other constables were less enthusiastic. Squatting behind the hedge of an overgrown garden in Dynevor Place in a thin drizzle, watching a house where nothing seemed to happen was, very soon, singularly unattractive. When it was Constable Plumley's watch, he had the great excitement of seeing the professor place a glass vase on the windowsill of the upstairs bedroom and then light a candle in his study, presumably to facilitate his nightly journey into the past where he would continue with his research. It was an extremely tedious evening which did nothing to lighten his gloomy disposition, and he was glad to hand over to Constable Lewis.

All seemed quiet in Dynevor Place. The professor had not yet gone to bed. The candle still flickered. Inspector Bucke said that he worked late. Axmeyer had not shown himself at all after his brief appearance at the window earlier, and it was hardly likely that he would go out at such a late hour. There didn't seem any advantage in allowing the damp of the garden to penetrate his boots any further and chill his weary feet. Lewis decided it would be a better use of his time if he went to look for Sarah Rigby.

Chapter Nineteen

Axmeyer had left a glass vase in the window and Moitch had seen it on his habitual evening patrol past the Languages College, when he had also noticed the police constable lurking clumsily in the bushes. The surveillance was so obvious that it had almost made him smile. But with Axmeyer calling a meeting and a policeman in a hedge, he realised that something was amiss. It did not surprise him, for he himself was becoming uneasy. There had been scurrying shapes in the shadows for a few days now, and they were not the normal figures of a Swansea night time. He immediately recognised their skills. There were occasions when he had been followed, he was sure of it – and professionally too. Tonight, he was being watched by a team, not by an individual. It took all his considerable skills to lose them in the dark, narrow streets. Moitch pulled down his cap even further, as if this would increase the darkness around him, for it always provided him with some comfort. He was convinced that French agents were in town, and he was angry with himself for not recognising it sooner.

By the time he had returned to Dynevor Place, he was sure he had lost them and then realised that any additional evasive action was not required, since the constable in the undergrowth had gone. Nonetheless, he went to the back door of the house and slipped into the darkened kitchen when Axmeyer opened the door. He led Moitch to the study.

'We can talk in here. The police believe I am working at my research so they are not alarmed by a light.' They sat at the table and Professor Axmeyer produced a bottle of brandy. 'There are some French things which I am prepared to tolerate.' He poured a measure into two small heavy glasses.

'Do not worry. There is no constable outside at the moment, Professor. They are so incompetent, I think.' He sipped from his glass.

'It seems to me, Pieter, that the police in this town are entirely incapable. An officer has been to see me – for the second time. I believe that he suspects something but he does not understand what he suspects. Like his officers. When the constables are watching the college, they do not know what they see.'

'It is the French who must concern us most, Professor, I think.'

'Naturally. But it is no surprise, surely, that they are here, when their great engineer is coming to the town. They are obliged to be here to protect him. You must not be unduly alarmed.'

Moitch bit his lip. 'Of course not, but I worry, because about something they must have a suspicion. Why else would they have killed Willrath?'

'A good man. We shall miss him.' Axmeyer shook his head.

'I believe they are like the police inspector. These Frenchmen are anxious, but they do not know of our plans. They know that I am in Swansea but their knowledge is incomplete.' He emptied his glass. 'I do not think they know you are here. So I expect them to continue to observe me, as much as they can. They will not strike yet because they cannot find Guy, even if they know about him. Even then, he only knows what we have chosen to tell him, which is very little. But he is a weakness, I think.' Moitch chewed anxiously at a fingernail.

'Of course he is. In my experience, such conspiracies as this never work for long. They are only as strong as the weakest part. And Guy makes our arrangements frail and fragile.' Axmeyer poured more brandy.

'Would you like me to deal with this police officer, Professor? I believe he lives in rooms on Fisher Street, opposite where I was until most recently. I have moved once again, this time to a place called Walstrom's Boarding House.'

'At this stage, I do not think that it is necessary. The death of a police inspector is a complication we do not require at the moment, when we are but two days away from our conclusion. It would make our task harder if we had to deal with an angry police force. And besides, you clearly know where to find him should it prove necessary. He told me that the Jenkins' maid recognised Guy when I first took him to the house. This is how he has connected myself and Guy. It is a mistake I should not have made and I am sorry for that. Had I known sooner, you could have dealt with her too, but not now. We must not be distracted.' He leaned across the table and placed his hand on Moitch's arm. 'Do not worry. Guy will be dead soon and the police inspector may then question his body for as long as he wants. And I am sure the inspector knows nothing about you.'

'I worry that our operation is not secure, Professor, and it is Guy that makes it so. He is truly an unworthy vessel, I think.' Moitch sighed.

They drank in silence for a moment and the sound of the choir rehearsing in the Baptist Church drifted into the room.

"*If you but trust in God to guide you,*
And place your confidence in Him,
You'll find Him always there beside you
To give you hope and strength within."

Moitch gave a derisory snort. 'There is only one thing I trust, and God is not that thing.' Moitch bent down and pulled his knife from his boot, which he placed gently on the table, the blade glinting in the light of the candle.

'Consider, Pieter. What is our objective? Remember, it matters little whether Guy succeeds or fails. The death of de Lesseps would be an additional success, but our objective is to disrupt the relationship between England and France by creating distrust. We can undermine this tunnel idea.' Axmeyer smiled at his choice of words. 'We will thwart French ambitions. All we need is an attempt on his life by an impressionable madman, unbalanced by the things he has heard, fuelled by the intense patriotism of the fool. You see, even his remarkable stupidity in attempting to murder his wife is to our advantage, however much it has made the mission difficult for you. He will become a newspaper item. The man the police could not find. "And please tell me," asks a reporter, "what is this tunnel idea that has distressed him so? Oh my goodness, what a ridiculous notion!" You must not become anxious, Pieter. You know that Guy will die, whether he succeeds or fails.'

'I understand those things, Professor.' He put the knife back in his boot and drained his glass again. 'But I think now we should go. There is no constable outside. Each of us must move away from our current accommodation, I think. It is time for us to take up residence in the attic of the Baumhaus for these last two days – the police will not find us and we can make sure that we do not lose Daniel Guy. The police do not know me, and perhaps they will tell themselves that you have fled, perhaps even with Daniel Guy. I agree that it is not ideal, I think, but we have come so far and with such difficulty. Frau Baum has been watching him well, but now we must have the responsibility to prepare him for the part that he must play.'

~

It was a time most respectable people would have been taking a relaxing breakfast, preparing themselves for another busy day. Except that Cathleen McDonald was not respectable and never took a relaxing breakfast. She was still drunk from the night before and had, for no reason anyone else understood, attacked Constable Smith with a rolling pin as he walked up the steps of the police station. He had received an unpleasant cut above his left eye. It could have been much worse, but, once they had managed to bundle her into the cells, Sergeant Ball still had no alternative but to send the constable to the hospital for treatment.

It was whilst Sergeant Ball was cleaning off some of Smith's blood from his uniform that Evan Davies reported that, when he had turned up for his watch at the Swansea Languages College in the early hours, Lewis had not been there to carry out a handover.

'I was early too. Thought I'd give Gethin a bit of a break, like. I did my watch but nothing happened, see, and I handed over to Constable Smith. Has there been a problem, Sergeant? There is blood all over the steps.' Ball looked at him in exasperation and sent Davies straight through to see Inspector Bucke.

This report was followed almost immediately by the appearance of Constable Hughes, who had been on watch. Hugh Workman, a clerk at the Metropolitan Bank on Wind Street, had arrived for a lesson and knocked firmly, but Professor Axmeyer had not answered the door. Hughes had checked the back of the house. The kitchen door was locked too. There was no sign of life at all inside. What should he do? He had left Workman watching the place, who was concerned that the professor might have been taken ill.

Bucke hurried to Dynevor Place, fearing the worst. He thought it highly unlikely that Axmeyer was lying unconscious on the floor, but the possibility that he might be was reason enough for him to enlist the support of Hughes to break down the kitchen door, with Workman's enthusiastic assistance.

The college was abandoned, it seemed. The professor's book and manuscript had gone from the table – and Bucke was certain that Axmeyer would never have willingly chosen to be separated from them. He had fled.

Bucke looked round the rooms carefully. Without Axmeyer, the whole college seemed a shell. It was a place where he received pupils, but otherwise there was nothing there; no character or even identity. Closer examination of the books on the shelves revealed to Bucke that there was little of substance behind those dirty spines. They were just cheap novels, generally in French and Spanish, bought by the yard to fill the shelves. They were the perfect representation of the nature of the college. Everything about it was hollow. It was all a sham.

Bucke wasn't angry; his feelings had gone far beyond anger. He recognised this crisis as a defining moment. He had been betrayed. Scorned. His own position and that of the police force as a whole had been seriously compromised. He saw no possible reason why anyone should continue to excuse or accommodate Lewis's casual approach to his duties. His own instructions had been treated with contempt and ignored, and the consequences of Lewis's idiocy were incalculable. Bucke had no reason to assume that Axmeyer had left the building before Lewis replaced Plumley. Subsequent officers had reported nothing. It seemed likely therefore that he had left during Lewis's shift. So, as a result of his wilful negligence, they had lost all contact with Axmeyer and now had no idea where he was. Officers like Davies and Hughes had been watching an empty building.

It was a turning point, Bucke saw this clearly. There was a choice to be made, but he could not be sure what direction the police force would now take. To support Lewis would be an act of supreme folly, for it would permit anarchy amongst those whose job it was to enforce law and order in the town. He knew what he had to do. He wondered whether he would be supported.

∾

Bucke found Chief Constable Allison sitting behind his desk in his office, a much diminished figure after a day spent in the company of Islay Young, a man with precise, neat and accurate ledgers. He told Allison that he had uncovered a serious example of the dereliction of duty and would be obliged if the Chief Constable would attend a meeting to be held with Constable Gethin Lewis.

He appeared uninterested and shrugged. 'Whatever you want. Get on with it.'

Sergeant Ball was asked to intercept Lewis when he was about to leave after his shift and bring him into Bucke's office. Allison sat behind his desk, rubbing his wart with his thumb, his hooded and downcast eyes, further hidden behind his spectacles, suggesting a lack of interest in the proceedings. Bucke sat to his left. Lewis was allowed to remain standing.

Lewis, the great investigator who, apparently single-handed, had cracked a brandy-smuggling gang, could not see what all the fuss was about. Heavy fines had been imposed on all members of the gang, and the praise he had received in court from the magistrates had emboldened him. When Bucke confronted him, he was initially defensive but then suddenly became more assertive. He was aware that he had been backed into a corner but decided that the best form of defence was to attack. Perhaps now was the ideal moment to discredit Bucke and implement his careful plan, one which would deliver the final revenge for his overlooked father – and his own promotion.

Lewis was bold, confident, contemptuous.

'Listen to me, Inspector Bucke. There is no point you banging on, blaming me. How do you know this professor of yours legged it when I was on duty? You don't.'

'But your colleagues were there. You were not,' Bucke said patiently, gripping the chipped edge of the desk as an aid to concentration – and to keeping his temper.

Lewis sneered. 'Your professor could have gone any time, my friend. I mean to say, I could see that it were no good me standing outside there all night. My boots were covered in mud and there were leaves on my uniform. There were better things for me to be doing. It happens that I had heard of an illegal drinking den in Inkerman Street and I decided that it would—'

'You decided? What right did you have to make such a decision?' Bucke was sure that if he encouraged Lewis to continue to talk, he would inevitably condemn himself.

'Common sense, matey. And anyway, someone has to make decisions when their inspector's off consorting with a married woman. It's not right, Chief Constable.' There was no need for him to hide the dislike he had for Bucke any longer. He was now determined to press home his assault on the inspector's integrity.

Bucke ignored the slur. 'It is your duty to follow orders, Constable. Your refusal to do so sabotaged the work of all your colleagues. A consequence of your negligence is that we have lost track of an important suspect.'

'Important?' He laughed. 'What are you on about? It was a waste of time. He were just an old man. You have no idea what you are doing, Inspector.'

'Constable Lewis, I have no alternative but to request that disciplinary action is taken against you for dereliction of duty, being absent without leave during a surveillance operation in Dynevor Place on 2 June 1880.'

'Is that a fact?' he said, with calculated contempt.

'You will be reported to the watch committee who bear responsibility for such transgressions, Constable Lewis, and until then—'

Suddenly Allison interrupted. It was as if he had just woken up. 'So what have you got to say, lad? Serious business, this. Your job's on the line.'

This was Lewis's big moment, the one for which he had planned for such a long time. 'Well, see, Chief Constable, it is all about what standards are set, and I am sorry to bring this to your attention, like, and I have been meaning to mention it, see, but well, this isn't easy, but I have to tell you, Chief Constable, that early last year—'

'By this you mean 1879, is it, Lewis?'

'It is that, Chief Constable. As I was saying, I saw the great inspector here, Inspector Romsey Bucke—'

'It is Rumsey, actually,' corrected Bucke.

Lewis rolled his eyes. 'The great London inspector. Well, I saw him steal a yew tree from a garden in Henrietta Street.' Lewis nodded for emphasis.

There was a perplexed silence. Allison scratched his head. 'Yew tree?'

'That is right, Chief Constable. A yew tree. I saw him do it with his bare hands. I saw him grip the trunk and rip it from the ground.' He waited for the impact of his revelation.

'And where were you at the time, Lewis? When, as you claim, Inspector Bucke attacked this tree?'

'I was in a garden across the road, receiving important details about a crime from one of my informers.'

'Would this happen to have been a woman, Constable Lewis?' asked Bucke.

'It is not my practice to reveal the identity of my informants, Inspector,' he said proudly.

'And this would have happened in the early hours of the morning, would it, Constable?' asked Bucke.

'You should know, Inspector. You were there.' Lewis was confident, believing that now he had him cornered.

'And you haven't mentioned this afore?' asked Allison.

'No, Chief Constable. I thought it best to wait before I brought this to you, to be sure of my information.'

'I see, Constable Lewis. So let's just be clear. You saw the inspector here steal some kind of shrub, over a year ago, and did nowt about it?'

'Well, I was shocked, Chief Constable. I thought the inspector should be setting an example to the rest of us, like.'

Allison paused for a moment and then pressed the palms of his hands on the desk with surprising delicacy. 'As I am sure you will understand, Constable Lewis, this puts me in a very difficult position.'

'I do understand, see. I am sorry it had to be me who told you. It must be a big shock.'

Allison shrugged, indicating that his own feelings were irrelevant. 'And you kept quiet about it?'

'Yes, I did, sir, on account of me being astonished by the inspector not upholding the values of the police force, sir. As I see it, Chief Constable, he has betrayed your confidence. You deserve better. Always said so.' Lewis puffed his chest out and rocked up onto his toes to look authoritative.

'Bucke, what do you have to say about this then?' asked Allison.

'It is plainly ridiculous, Chief Constable.'

'Well, he would say that.' There was scorn in Lewis's voice. 'It might have been dark; it was two o'clock in the morning after all, but I could see what he was doing, plain as anything.'

'Hmm. You see, Constable, as I was saying, it leaves me with a big bloody problem, if I am honest.'

Lewis couldn't stop himself smiling. 'I am sure it does, sir. A trusted colleague like the Inspector. A Fancy Dan like him and everything, and then he goes and lets you down. Terrible.'

Allison shook his head. 'I don't think you understand, Lewis. Problem is you, old lad.'

'Me, sir?' Lewis was utterly bemused.

'Yes you, sir!' Allison banged the table for emphasis. 'You see, Constable, when you looks at this carefully, what you are tellin' me, is that you saw a crime bein' committed but did nowt about it. So you see, you withheld information from the Chief Constable about a felony. Which is me, Lewis. Serious offence, that.' He dropped his head slightly and then looked straight up into the constable's eyes. 'You never know. Praps you are implicated. A yew tree-stealing racket, was it?'

Lewis was suddenly confused. Everything seemed suddenly to be going wrong and he could not understand why.

Allison gave him a mirthless smile and then continued, 'See, there are no witnesses, except yourself and whoever this lassie was who you were in that garden with, and until now you've not told me nowt about it. Watch Committee will take a serious view, Lewis. Very serious. You've let the force down. You've let yourself down. An' let's not forget you've been in front of them afore for not doing your job properly.'

'Chief Constable, please.' Suddenly Lewis saw his schemes lying in dust before him.

'Nowt I can do, I am afraid, son. You didn't report a crime. I've got a job to do now. And you've just admitted it. It won't go well for you. I tell you now, son. Next meeting of Watch committee, you'll be dismissed. '

'Mr Allison, sir. Chief Constable, please. The inspector is a thief and—'

'If I were you, I should bugger off home. This is not the place for the likes of you. Give your handcuffs to Sergeant Ball as you leave, son. He will be pleased to see 'em.'

Chief Constable Allison sank back in his seat, removed his spectacles and massaged his eyes with his thumb and forefinger as Lewis, shocked by the sudden turn of events, left the office. He bowed his head and tried to compose himself. 'It is a rum do, Inspector. Mind you, I reckon someone must have said that afore.'

'They have, sir, many times. May I just say thank you for—'

'No need, Bucke. No need. I probably owe you an apology, any road. On account of our Tom.' Allison turned to face the window, to avoid looking at him. 'You see, Bucke, he's been a bit daft. Been helping himself to bits of cash. Well, he is not a bad lad but... it were just small change really... Should have checked, I suppose, but I didn't think...' He rubbed his eyes again. 'I have promised to pay the money back and our Tom, well, he will have to go. I mean, I think he has gone but he is not talking to me at present. He will come round. Sure he will. It is just that... well... I shall be offerin' me resignation. Wanted you to know. Thought I should. Things have been a bit harsh for you recently. Don't suppose I have done much to help. But you see, I trusted him and the responsibility might have been too much for him and I made a mistake by not checking his figures and, well, Mr Young has had a word and...' There was a long pause. 'I will be around for this blessed visit, Inspector, but I will be gone soon after that's done. I will square everything with t' Watch Committee afore I go. Still, me and Mrs Allison have had our eyes on a public house for a while now. The Jersey Hotel in Briton Ferry. Lookin' to take it on sooner than we thought.' He paused again. 'I would be obliged if you said nowt for a while. It is going to be a difficult couple of days. But our Tom never meant no harm. An' he was a good officer, isn't that right, Bucke? Isn't it?'

His words trailed away, a desperate pleading in his eyes. But there was nothing he could say that would ever rescue his son or indeed salvage his own career. Rumsey Bucke almost felt sorry for him.

Chapter Twenty

Constance listened carefully to Rumsey's news. Her own morning had gone well. Her pupils seemed pleasant; one was particularly talented, and she enjoyed teaching at a more advanced level after two painful sessions with beginners. She was calm and sympathetic as Bucke paced around her teaching room, ignoring the tea and the bread and cheese she had prepared for him and telling her about the rather more difficult morning that he had experienced. The byzantine intricacies of office politics were not something she had ever had to deal with herself, but she understood about human behaviour. When Rumsey told her about the yew tree, she couldn't stop herself laughing – it was such an absurd idea – and then stopped herself. He might be offended; he might think that she wasn't taking this seriously. But there was no need to worry. He grinned too.

'It is good to see you laugh, Constance.'

'How could I not? Why a yew tree, for heaven's sake?'

'I suspect that he had trampled over the poor thing during an energetic encounter with his beloved. I was living on Henrietta Street a year ago and Julia… my wife,' he added with embarrassment, 'my wife, yes, well, she told me the neighbours were concerned about Mrs Biddle who frequently entertained a gentleman friend in the early hours after her husband came home drunk from the Tenby Hotel and fell asleep in front of the fire. But only, of course, when it wasn't raining.'

She laughed again. 'I could never have anticipated such debauchery on a respectable street where police inspectors should be striking fear into the hearts of the dissolute.'

'It will be almost impossible to strike fear into anyone's heart at the moment. There is a serious lack of policemen at precisely the wrong moment.' He went on to tell her that not only had Gethin Lewis been dismissed and Constable Smith delivered to hospital, but also that Inspector Allison had been sent home and that the Chief Constable was on the verge of resigning. 'And we have got Monsieur de Lesseps arriving in three hours. I haven't got enough officers.' And, though he didn't say so directly, he believed there was an active assassination team stalking the streets.

'And the Chief Constable is resigning, you say?'

He nodded.

She looked at him carefully. There was something troubling her and he realised it. 'And do you think you would like the job of Chief Constable, Rumsey? You are now the most senior policeman they have left. They may well ask you to do it.'

He shook his head. 'And I should spend all my days in meetings and become a portly bore, sitting behind a desk, writing reports and taking tea with the Lord Mayor. No, Constance. It is not what I wish.'

'I am glad. I do not think it would suit you. It will separate you from your people. The poor people, those on the streets, those in difficulty. They need you, Rumsey. People like Elinor. Like Joseph. Like me.'

They exchanged a long look in silence, for words were not required.

He cleared his throat. 'But I need police constables. I have deployed all I have, but there are too few of us.'

'I read about Monsieur de Lesseps in the newspaper earlier.' She picked up a copy and read from it. 'He is over seventy years of age but is possessed of all the vigour and energy of a man of fifty.' An eminent and wealthy man like that would certainly be worth meeting,' she said with a smile.

'Constance. This is especially serious.'

'So am I,' she smiled, her eyes bright.

'You are not intending to attend, are you? Do you have a ticket?'

'Why would I have a ticket, Rumsey? What good would it be to me? This is an occasion for the great men of Swansea. Women, whoever they are, will be not required.'

'I thought perhaps your husband...'

She laughed. 'No, I don't have a ticket. Blond Billy Bristow never ever buys. He blusters and he boasts. Hmm. Perhaps I should devote myself to poetry. Billy would have been there, of course, centre stage, on the top table, and then there would be a fuss because the waiters had unaccountably not laid sufficient places. But Billy would have been gracious and accepted their apologies. An oversight. These things happen. Please pass me the salt, monsieur. But not for him the tawdry business of paying for a ticket. I think I would like to observe this great man, a vigorous Frenchman too. How exciting. I think I will go to the Mackworth to see him.'

'Please, Constance, I don't think you should. It could be very dangerous. There are unknown forces at work in this town today.' He tried to sound strong and firm, but he was, in truth, a little tentative.

'I appreciate your concern, Rumsey, of course I do. But please do not try to control me. I will make my own decisions now. I have found independence, with your help and with your trust. I am a new person and I look to the future with great anticipation. But I will not be controlled, Rumsey. Not anymore.'

Bucke acknowledged defeat. 'I know that, Constance. I am only concerned for your safety. But I also know that only a foolish man would ever try to control you. And I have no wish to change any part of you.'

'You must not worry. I have no intention of being a distraction, Rumsey. Perhaps indeed I can be of some help.'

∼

Ferdinand de Lesseps arrived by the three o'clock train from Liverpool and stepped off the train at the Mumbles Road Station, to warm applause from a large crowd, who were craning their necks to see their famous visitor. As he observed from a vantage point in the signal box, Bucke could see that he need not have worried about security. Monsieur de Lesseps was surrounded by burly figures who seemed to emerge from the crowd the moment he stepped off the train. It was on time too, to the minute; a triumph of British engineering and punctuality. Bucke hoped someone had made a note of it.

De Lesseps was a portly but elegantly dressed man, with neat white hair. A fine exuberant and waxed moustache reached out towards those elongated ears which are the speciality of older males. He had the prosperous air of a man from a privileged and comfortable background. He seemed confident too, after a successful career as a diplomat in different European capitals. He looked around him, smiling at a scene which confirmed his own celebrity. His eyes took in the dignitaries and the security, appearing to assess and analyse arrangements which had been made for him. By his side was his youngest daughter, Nandi, neatly dressed and with the self-confidence born of wealth and status. She too looked around her at the scene on the platform, such attention and ceremony a normal, unremarkable, part of her life.

They were greeted by the Mayor with the Chief Constable, who escorted de Lesseps and his daughter, with her governess, to a waiting carriage which took them to the mayoral residence where they could refresh themselves after their journey. Constable Williams was particularly pleased to have been asked to ride alongside the driver to provide security. Other constables had also been placed along the route at significant points to provide Williams with any necessary support. It was going to be a long day for all of them.

~

Elsewhere in Swansea, in the attic of the Baumhaus, Daniel Guy was being prepared.

Axmeyer watched as Moitch washed Guy and then shaved him. Guy looked particularly apprehensive when Moitch approached his throat with a razor, and, as far as the latter was concerned, it was a missed opportunity. Nevertheless, he did his job well. Guy's face soon looked red and raw. Parts of his skin were experiencing daylight for the first time in years. Layers of grime were removed and he seemed more presentable, although he still didn't look much like a waiter.

They showed Guy the uniform he would be required to wear, which they had obtained from a Portuguese waiter with roughly the same build, who had worked at the Mackworth and was now trussed up, with bricks tied to his hands and feet, at the bottom of the Swansea Canal. Moitch did not, however, show Guy either the advertisement for an earlier meeting of the Swansea Society for the Acquisition of Useful Knowledge or one of Bristow's letters about the Channel Tunnel, torn from a copy of *The Times*, which he had hidden carefully at the bottom of a trouser pocket. Guy would not understand what they were, since he could not read, but they could be important. They were small details perhaps, but they would help to point a discerning investigating officer in a particular – and wrong – direction.

They would dress him and take him to the rear of the hotel and then he would appear to take Moitch into the lobby and then escort him outside as if he were an intruder, efficiently apprehended. He was then to position himself in a corner of the lobby and advance only when de Lesseps left the dining room in which he was speaking.

Moitch reminded him of his duties once more. 'Please understand, Daniel. I want you very carefully to listen. The Frenchman you must kill in the lobby of the hotel – on no account are you to go into the dining room where he is speaking. There is more chance of you being discovered when they see you are unskilled when serving at the table. You will spill something. They will look at you. So in the lobby you stand. Look as if you have been positioned there. Direct people, if you have to. But do not choose to speak to anyone. Stand by the wall and plan to shoot him as he approaches the exit from the hotel. Move purposefully when the time comes. Do not hesitate. Do not think. You must shoot him and then continue your movements and run outside before anyone has time to react. You have not so far to go to escape outside. I will be there. But it must be in the lobby. You understand. Tell me you understand, Daniel.'

'I understand, Pieter. I shoot him in the lobby just as he is about to leave.' He appeared sullen. His face looked sore.

'Outside, I will be waiting and I will get you away and onto the ship. You must come through the door immediately. I will expect you when the gunfire I have heard. If you do not come through the door immediately, I will not be there. But I am sure you know that we have made careful plans to help you. We will all be calm and efficient and you will be in no danger, I think. Of our plans the police know nothing. They are entirely ignorant, I think. You shoot. You run. It is easy.'

'And I will get my money? On the ship or before?' He held the gun in his hand, as if daring to threaten him.

'Of course, Daniel,' said Moitch soothingly. 'Your payment you will receive. We agreed. We are honourable people. You will receive everything that you deserve, I promise you.'

'That is all right then.' Guy continued to look at the gun as he thought through his own intentions. He had virtually dismissed the idea of shooting Moitch immediately, because he was reliant upon the escape plans he had prepared. Once they were at sea, he could throw him overboard. That shouldn't be too hard. He still hoped to find time to tidy up his business in Swansea before he disappeared, never to return. A new life in America beckoned once more. This time he would have money, but he knew he would feel more content if he killed Mary. Could he do that before the ship sailed?

'Daniel, now you must dress. The Frenchman begins his dinner at 5.00 pm and so you must be in place so that people are familiar with you being there. They will see you once and then they will forget about you if you do as we have planned, I think. They will eat and they will talk and they will propose many toasts. His train leaves Swansea at 9.00 pm and so I expect no later than 8.30 pm he will leave the dining room. There may be sufficient light enough outside for you to see me. And I will take you far away.'

They waited outside the attic door whilst Guy dressed himself. Axmeyer and Moitch shook their heads.

'This Daniel Guy is unworthy of us,' sighed Axmeyer, rubbing his hand up his neck and pushing his beard outwards. 'But perhaps he is perfect for our purpose. It is not often we must build a plan that is based upon failure. But it is true and its failure will be our success.'

Moitch voiced his deepest fear. 'There are times, Professor, when I am thinking that perhaps he is not what he seems. Perhaps he is a French spy, placed here to betray us all.'

Axmeyer was reassuring. 'You worry too much, Pieter. That would require him to be a very clever man who is pretending to be stupid, one of the greatest actors of the world. I do not believe this. He is as stupid as he appears. There is no plot here, other than our own. I am sure of it. These are the doubts that assail us all whenever a mission is approaching its conclusion.'

'I am sure you are right. I hope you are right. He is stupid but he should do enough to sow the confusion and the doubt that we need. But if he is a French agent.... I worry, I think.'

'We can stop this now, Pieter, if you are not sure, if you are uncertain, if you think the operation is too dangerous for us. You must feel that it is right.'

Moitch looked thoughtful. 'I worry too much.' He made his decision. 'We go on. We shall do it.'

The two men embraced warmly.

'Fear not. I am ready to play my part should I be required. The evening will belong to us. Take care, Pieter. I will see you in ten days' time as we have planned, in Hamburg. I am sure of it.'

Chapter Twenty-One

It would be a tedious evening of speeches; of toasts proposed and accepted; of loud, pretentious conversation, fuelled by decent Bordeaux from the cellars in honour of Monsieur de Lesseps. Businessmen from across Wales had turned up to be seen and to feel important, drawn by the prospect of extreme returns on small investments in a project far away. It was very tempting. You give a little bit of money to a world-famous engineer, and then he gives you a lot of money back a year or so later. How good it would be to become a successful investor.

Constance, like many others, had managed to squash into the lobby, which was full of the curious. She realised that she had no reason to be there. It was nothing to do with her at all, but she enjoyed the sense of occasion, and this new-found freedom to make her own decisions, tonight filled her with confidence. It was a considerable pleasure and it was good to be a part of this civic excitement. Now she was here, however, she wasn't really sure what she was going to do. She asked a tall man who looked a little like a hotel porter what time the reception was expected to finish, but she had a rather unsatisfactory grunt in reply. Standards at the Mackworth were clearly slipping. But she couldn't leave now. She believed that she would, in some way, be letting Rumsey down.

~

Bucke could see her as he tried to monitor what was happening in the hotel. He was not at all happy with the arrangements. He realised he should have planned ahead for this moment more carefully, but he hadn't, and there was nothing he could do about it now. He was constantly checking entrances, looking behind doors. There were too many people in the lobby and they had spilled out onto the pavement outside. It was disordered and unmanageable, and he did not have enough constables. Drinkers from the nearby public houses joined in too, curious about what was happening in the Mackworth and suddenly needing to be part of it, whatever it was. If it was good enough for the wealthy, then it was good enough for them. Bucke wanted to clear the lobby completely, but there were not enough officers to monitor every entrance and exit. People wanted to see the famous man, and if he took the unwelcome out of one entrance, they would come in through another.

He had stationed a police van outside the hotel, around which customers from the Adelphi gathered to tease the horse and irritate Constable Hughes. Bucke had also deployed Constable Plumley down at the bottom of Wind Street, where he could also monitor part of the Strand and Quay Parade, just in case. He shouldn't really be on his own in that part of town. But it was a chance he had to take, for resources were thin. The other officers were spread around the hotel. He had placed two inside the dining room itself, though he did wonder if it were necessary, since de Lesseps was accompanied everywhere by silent guards, squeezed into ill-fitting dress suits. He asked Constable Davies and Sergeant Ball to monitor the crowded lobby as best they could.

He slipped quietly into the dining room now and again to keep an eye upon proceedings within. His attention was drawn repeatedly to the little girl. How many times had the poor child listened to speeches like this? How many more times would she have to endure the pomposity of local civic worthies as she was trailed from town to town, from country to country?

De Lesseps was greeted with great applause when the formalities had ended and he was ready to speak. He spoke in French, and Bucke's own familiarity with the language was limited so he could only keep up by straining to listen to the murmured translation which passed around the room like the hissing of rain. De Lesseps explained that he had some understanding of English but for him it was more important that he spoke confidently, without using barely-understood words which might create unfortunate misunderstandings.

His project to build the Panama Canal, he said, would make England and France great allies, just as the Suez Canal had done. Seven thousand men could dig it in six years and then the dangerous voyage around Cape Horn would be no more. This would have particular benefits for the copper trade which was so important to Swansea's wealth. The dangers of disease and death in Panama had been exaggerated. He and Nandi had been there and they had survived quite well indeed, as everyone could see. If a man in his seventies and a girl of seven could thrive, then surely fit young men, working with the latest technology, would be fine? The audience responded politely, murmuring their approval. But this was not all that he had to say. He reflected that perhaps this great project of a tunnel beneath the Channel would further unite the two countries of England and France in a lasting and productive marriage. It was such a considerable opportunity. He would not build it but he would support those who could. There were a few murmurs as a translation of these words spread around the dining room, but if he understood the reaction, he ignored it and continued.

Bucke nodded to the constables and slipped out of the room. Everything seemed ordered and secure in there. It was the lobby and the street outside which still worried him more. There was no pattern, no order. Few of the faces were familiar. He tried to find Constance but he could not see her. Constable Davies was leaning against the wall, looking serene and disengaged. The light was starting to fade outside and the cool evening air was welcome when it drifted into a lobby overheated by so many bodies.

There was applause inside and then the doors of the dining room were flung open to signify the end of the presentation, and the guests gathered on either side of the door to applaud de Lesseps as he left, holding his daughter's hand. There were shouts of 'Congratulations' and 'Well done' and a deal of mutual back-slapping. Behind him came the Lord and Lady Mayor and the Chief Constable. There were people everywhere, just a mass of bodies pushing and straining, enough to provide anonymity to anyone. Then he heard Ball shouting out 'Inspector!' He couldn't see Ball anywhere but as he looked for him he saw a hotel porter pushing his way through the crowd towards the dignitaries. It had to be Guy, but there was such a crush in front of him and he had to fight and push his way in his attempt to get closer. He saw Guy reach down, probably to his waistband, and he saw, quite clearly, a revolver in his hand.

Bucke threw himself between two guests and leapt upon Guy, grabbing desperately at his arm. It was enough to deflect his aim. He fired but the bullet cracked the top corner of the mirror next to the dining room door. They fell to the floor, with the gunshot ringing in their ears. Bucke slammed the revolver into the floor and the gun went off again, searing the carpet as it gouged its dark furrow.

He pinned his arm and hit Guy repeatedly, kneeling on his chest. He was aware that a space had cleared around their struggle. He desperately tried to direct the barrel of the gun away from anyone, but in the chaos of the lobby that was impossible. A third shot rang out. Bucke had no idea where that one went. He thought he might have to break his fingers to get control of the gun.

Suddenly a hefty boot pinned Guy's wrist to the floor.

'It's over! Let go of the gun or I will crush your bloody wrist, sonny!' the Chief Constable shouted. 'Can you hear me? I shall count to three and then your hand is splintered, but you still won't get away. Understand? You have been collared. One...'

Bucke felt Guy's chest subside as he stopped struggling. He knew he had been caught. 'All right! All right! Stop it! Stop it, please! You are hurting me!'

'Let go of the gun. Let go of the gun,' repeated Bucke as calmly as he could. 'Daniel, listen to me. Let go of the gun. It is over.'

His fingers relaxed and Bucke was able to pull the revolver away from him.

Constable Davies knelt down beside him. 'All under control, sir?'

'I believe so, Constable. Thank you.' He bent closer to Guy and lowered his voice. 'Listen to me, Daniel. Listen to me carefully. Your case is serious. The charge against you is a very serious one. I feel it my duty to caution you that you should be particular in what you say, as what you do say I shall have to repeat, and it may be used in evidence against you.'

Guy laughed bitterly. 'I have got such a tale to tell you, copper, such a tale. Let go of my arm. You are hurting me.'

Bucke pulled Guy to his feet and pushed him firmly into the wall. As he gathered his hands behind him, Sergeant Ball appeared by his side.

'Hang on, Inspector. I've got my handcuffs out.' He attached them with practised ease. 'There we are. I will take him back to the station with Constable Davies and the gun, sir. You must stay here and calm nerves. It is your duty. Don't worry about the prisoner. He is handcuffed. He is mine. You did well, sir.'

'Thank you, Sergeant. When you have him locked up, leave Davies there in the station and you come back down here to me.'

'Yes, Inspector. And I will bring my handcuffs back with me.' He took Guy's arm. 'This way. Don't try to be clever.'

With his prisoner secured and ready for the police van, he was able to look around the lobby. He saw two large French bodyguards bundling de Lesseps outside. A thin haze from the gunfire drifted in the air, men waving and shouting, people pushing desperately towards the exit, the cracked mirror hanging at a slight angle and then, in its distorted reflection, he saw Constance lying on the floor. The third bullet! It took him a moment to locate where she was. In dread and horror, he blundered towards her.

Then Bucke saw that one of the French bodyguards was standing over Constance and he watched him gently lift her up. She shook herself and smoothed down her dress, whilst the Frenchman lifted up the small shape which had been beneath her. It was little Nandi. He held her and she buried her face in his shoulder. The guard looked at Constance and gave her a brief but clearly sincere bow and then carried Miss de Lesseps outside through a gap in the crowd created by two of his colleagues.

Bucke fell to his knees in relief. Constance saw him and alarmed, squeezed rudely between others to reach him quickly. 'Rumsey! Are you hurt?'

'No, Constance, I am fine. I slipped.'

'Exciting, wasn't it?'

He raised his eyebrows. 'Please, Miss White, there is work to be done,' and he stood up. Bucke was the man in control now;

he was energised. His confidence had been restored; he was a policeman once again.

'Chief Constable, I should be grateful if you could ensure Monsieur de Lesseps is safe at the railway station. I believe he has already gone for his train. There are constables there, but it might be politic if you could go and acknowledge his safe departure.'

'Of course, Inspector. Need to show 'im we are still in control. If I can find the mayor, I shall take him with me.' He approached Bucke and looked as if he was about to shake his hand but then thought better of it.

Bucke turned to Constance. 'Miss White. I should be obliged if you would attend to the Lady Mayoress. Her hysteria is becoming a distraction to us all.'

Constance put her hands to her head and tried, without success, to restore her once carefully arranged hair. She blew a loose strand away from her face as always and then, shockingly, winked at him and smiled. It was a private moment; and in the confusion, he was sure no one else saw it. When next he saw her, she had gathered up the woman, had administered brandy and was stroking her hand soothingly.

He looked around the lobby. Frightened guests, who had either spilled out onto Wind Street or taken shelter in the dining room, were now returning to the scene of the excitement and were disappointed that there was little to see, apart from the mirror and the effects of the third bullet which Sergeant Ball pointed out to Bucke on his return.

'It went into the fruit bowl on that table over there. Smashed one of them pineapple things. A right proper mess. But that's your three bullets, sir. Mirror, carpet, pineapple. No one hurt and you've got Daniel Guy. He's in the cells. A good night's work.'

Slowly, order was restored. Sergeant Ball managed the carriages as they came to pick up guests, and Bucke chivvied them out of the hotel bar where they had gone to restore their courage. Local drinkers abandoned their sightseeing, disappointed that no local worthies were bleeding in the gutters, despite hearing any number of gunshots, and returned to their public house of choice.

Constance crossed the lobby to say goodnight. The Lady Mayoress had offered her a lift home in her carriage. She thought the mayor was probably in a meeting with Chief Constable Allison and she wasn't prepared to wait for him in the hotel. He watched them depart from the hotel steps and failed to suppress a smile when Constance gave him a discreet wave. At last, everything was ordered and calm. Now he could return to the station and question Daniel Guy. There were so many questions he had for him.

'Well, Sergeant Ball, a rather unusual evening but—'

Ball interrupted him by putting his hand on his arm. 'Listen, sir.'

It was the dreaded sound of a police rattle, once again disturbing the night. And then the faint shouts of 'Murder! Murder!'

'The Strand! Must be Constable Plumley, sir!'

They ran.

Chapter Twenty-Two

As soon as he heard the gunshots and the commotion, as soon as he saw de Lesseps and the governess bundled into a carriage by the French agents, followed a few moments later by Nandi, Moitch knew it was time to go. Guy wasn't coming out. He watched the de Lesseps' carriage leave at speed, heading straight up Wind Street to the station with the bodyguards running alongside it, then walked as briskly as he could, without attracting attention to himself, straight down to the Strand. He had brought a sack with him from the Baumhaus which, once slung over his shoulder, would transform him into a seaman. Axmeyer would be fine, he knew it. He would get himself to Dover and then across the Channel. And they would meet once more in Hamburg, a job well done, leaving Swansea a long way behind them. And what would they think of their mission? Had it been a success? Probably. There would be no tunnel beneath the Channel; he was sure of it.

Moitch rarely left anything to chance. He knew that a ship, the *Tritone*, was planning to sail on the high tide just before dawn, heading for Ostend. It had an Italian crew who would spend the night before their departure in the public houses of Swansea, a final moment of release before the sea took them back once more. All Moitch had to do was to tag along and then slip aboard the *Tritone* as if he was one of them.

He followed the loud and unmistakable sounds of an Italian shore party to the Crown Inn, where a fiddle player was imperfectly scratching out simple dance tunes and all was crowded and excited. He was sure that he wasn't being followed.

Soon Moitch was moving amongst the drinking sailors with practised ease, grasping their hands and forearms in lasting friendship, laughing and buying them drinks, moving lightly and easily across the sticky floor. Thick clouds of smoke were ballooning up to the ceiling, mingling with the unmistakeable smell of unwashed sailors and spilled beer. Suddenly the Italians had a new best friend, this small dark man who seemed to know them and yet who they could not quite remember. Perhaps it was the drink. His name would come back to them, given time; of course it would. He was such good company and so generous too. Wave your pot and he would make sure it was filled once more. He grabbed hold of Becky the barmaid and spun her round. He kissed her and she laughed and called him a saucy devil. He was quite a character, this new friend of theirs.

Moitch drank nothing. He worked the crowd, placing himself at the heart of the group. If anyone was to ask, well, of course, he had been with them all evening. Life and soul. Such good company. A great friend of everyone. It was hard work, but Moitch was good at it. He had done it before. You find someone who had drunk too much. You put your arm around him. You help him stagger down the dark streets and then onto the ship. You must make plenty of noise. You must make sure that everyone sees you. Then, when you had him safely on board, slip away and hide in the hold until the ship is far out to sea. Then offer to work your passage. Easy. Just keep your wits about you and make sure everyone else is properly drunk and...

And then he saw him, and Moitch knew he was doomed.

Moitch was at the heart of a maelstrom of drinking and noise, playing some sort of inane practical joke involving a sailor's hat, when the crowd parted for a moment and he found himself looking straight into the eyes of another man dressed as a seaman. Moitch didn't know him but he recognised him, nonetheless. He was a large, powerful-looking man with the froth from his beer fringing his bushy moustache. He held that eye contact for a moment and then, with a faint smile, raised his tankard to him, one professional acknowledging another. Perhaps there was a momentary hint of regret in his expression; there might even have been a brief shrug. An apology perhaps? This is what I must do. In other circumstances, we would surely share a drink together and exchange amusing stories. But alas, tonight, things are different. I must do what I must do.

Moitch looked around. The man would not be alone. He would have a team with him. He couldn't recognise any of the other agents who must surely be there, but in the thick air of a crowded, dimly lit pub, it could be anyone. If there was a back way out of the Crown, then it was unlikely that it would bring him any greater safety. Suddenly he knew he had been trapped. The Italians were starting to leave, shouting to each other and waving vigorously at Becky. One of them tried to take her apron, but she slapped him and his friends cheered and laughed. Two of them at the door gestured towards Moitch, apparently calling him over. It seemed that the protection of this crowd was his only hope of salvation, and so he slipped into the middle of them as they spilled out onto the Strand. The raucous group began their slow and unruly procession down towards the dock where their ship was waiting impatiently for them. He was desperate to make sure that he was always surrounded by them, drunk and unsteady though they were.

There were slurred shouts of concern. 'Francisco!' someone called, as a sailor staggered into a gas lamp. Moitch took hold of him to act as a support. Perhaps he could use him as a shield. The Italian looked at him, grinned with his wet mouth, and then planted a kiss on his cheek. He started to say something which Moitch could not understand, but the Italian's unfocused attention was drawn by one of the other seamen who decided it would be a good idea to climb the lamp post. The group re-formed itself around the base and began to cheer his efforts. 'Casettari! Casettari!' they shouted, watching him creep slowly to the top like a large beetle. Someone started to sing. Moitch struggled to keep Francisco upright.

And then there was a whisper in his ear. 'Pieter Moitch.' Someone held his arms and Francisco fell to the floor. There was a sharp blow to the small of his back. Moitch wasn't quite sure what had happened. Had he been struck in the kidneys? He didn't know. It seemed unusual; the pain seemed to be deeper and his eyes were becoming blurred. The gas light seemed to dim. He was sure the lamp post was bending. And then the man from the Crown appeared in front of him, his black moustache looking like a large bottomless pit beneath his nose, with a man on either side of him. Moitch wanted to lie down but he was held tightly. He looked him in the eyes and tried to speak, but the words wouldn't form and then the man produced a large knife and disembowelled Pieter Moitch.

They released him and he fell to the floor. His legs shook violently and his hands grabbed feverishly at the treacherous cobbles, trying to find comfort where there was none. And then his head rolled against the wall at the end of Baker Street and Moitch was still, with two wet unused matches clinging to his hair.

Chapter Twenty-Three

Bucke and Ball found Plumley with a particularly unpleasant dead body and a drunken Italian sailor who he had handcuffed to a gas lamp. Three other constables, returning to their beats at the end of the Mackworth operation, had responded to the rattle and were doing their best to keep a group of intoxicated and angry Italian sailors at bay. It had the potential to become a very ugly confrontation very quickly.

Bucke was anxious to clear the area as soon as possible, before a policeman was attacked by a reckless mob. A single assault might serve to embolden the others and provoke a violent situation which would be impossible to control. He sent for a wheelbarrow from the Crown and requisitioned a room there. Whilst the constables waited, he patrolled the edge of the excitable crowd, trying to calm their anger with soothing tones and hand gestures, since effective communication was impossible. He had no idea what they were shouting about. They were pointing in at least two directions, probably suggesting that the police would be better advised to follow such obvious lines of enquiry, except that there was no consensus about which direction was the right one.

He listened to what they were shouting and assumed that the Italian in the handcuffs was called Giardinieri. His head was slumped against the lamp post, with his hands wrapped around it in a bewildered embrace. Bucke could see that, in his drunken state, Giardinieri was finding it hard to understand this inexplicable drama, one in which he had unexpectedly become the leading character. He watched, his head nodding in fascination and confusion, as two constables reluctantly balanced a heap of spilled pink gore on top of the corpse, which they gingerly manoeuvred into the wheelbarrow, cursing at the staining they received and the terrible wet sounds the corpse made. Bucke advised them that it was better to focus on the sightless eyes rather than the gaping wound and those unstable, liberated entrails.

The body was wheeled to the Crown Inn and guarded, whilst Doctor Beynon was invited to attend on the Strand with, naturally, Bucke's sincere apologies. He also sent a policeman to the harbour office to prevent the sailing of whichever vessel these angry seamen crewed, which would give him a little more time to question them – once he had found a translator.

Then, when all was as well ordered as he could hope, Bucke and Ball took Giardinieri and Plumley back to Tontine Street, one for questioning and the other for his own safety. The Italian sailors followed them up the hill and then gathered together outside the police station, shouting, threatening and occasionally banging on the windows. Although this jeering mob did not appear so emboldened that it might be prepared to go inside and affect a rescue, he still believed it prudent to lock the door of the station.

Constable Plumley, still shocked and agitated, confirmed that he had heard a commotion from his post on Wind Street and, on attending the disturbance on the Strand, had found the group of Italian sailors engaged in a confused and horrified lament. He had no real idea what was going on until he saw the butchered body lying next to the wall, looking like something abandoned after a robbery at an abattoir. So he had arrested the person nearest to the corpse. 'I mean how was I to know which one did it? They were drunk and none of them could speak either English or Welsh. I tried them both but there was no hope. So this one will have to do. We've got him. Let's wait for one of them to tell us what happened.'

Bucke could not be happy with such an apparently arbitrary approach to police work, but he knew that it was the one that Chief Constable Allison favoured. In all their dealings with foreign seamen over many years, language difficulties always proved to be a barrier to justice, as well as to communication. He had a duty to apprehend the real killer, but he could only do that if he could understand what a group of very drunk Italian sailors remembered, which no doubt was very little. He knew there was a significant amount of work to be done if anyone was to form a picture of what had happened, and Giardinieri wasn't in a position to help him at that moment. He was slumped in a chair next to the counter. Sergeant Ball sat with him, though it didn't seem likely that he would attempt an escape. The only thing that did seem likely was that he might be about to vomit. They all hoped that he wouldn't, but they provided him with a bucket just in case.

Constable Davies leaned forward on the counter, looking very much at home. 'Things got a bit busy after I left, by the look of things, Inspector. Everything is satisfactory here, nothing to worry about.' Bucke exchanged a glance with Sergeant Ball who shifted slightly in his seat as Giardinieri made retching noises.

'And how is Daniel Guy, Constable?' Bucke asked Davies.

'I am sure he is fine, sir. As Sergeant Ball requested, I removed his handcuffs which I then returned, and then, once Daniel Guy was placed in his cell, the door was securely locked. Since then, I have not been near him at all.' Davies was confident. He wanted to give the air of a man in control, of a man who had finally found his natural place in the order of things. During the course of the evening, it had become clear to Davies, without a doubt, that the job of desk sergeant would now be his. He'd be good at it, he knew. It was the job he had always been looking for, the job for which he had been designed. Dealing with lost property. Keeping the cells clean. Important work, neat and predictable.

Bucke was relieved. He had finally detained Guy. He was the indispensable piece in a puzzle he had been trying to understand for such a long time now. 'And nothing unusual has happened since you locked him up, Constable? No requests for medical attention or food or anything like that?'

'No, sir. Nothing at all. He has been quiet, sir. I imagine he would have been surprised to see the priest, though. Turning up like that. I'll wager he gave him plenty to think about, Inspector.'

Bucke was alarmed. 'I am sorry, Constable. What are you talking about? I am not sure I understand what you are saying. Who was this priest?'

'A Catholic priest he was, sir. I am a chapel boy, me, Adulam on Cefn Road, so I didn't know who he was. Not seen him around town anywhere, but then I wouldn't. I expect he keeps himself to himself, busy doing his confessions and whatever else it is they do. He was all dressed up in them fancy clothes and everything. Had a Bible, I could see that. To be honest, I have no time for papists myself, so I took particular notice of him, in case he tried anything underhand. First off, I could see he was a bit old, sir.' He was proud of his powers of observation. 'He had a big thick stick to help him walk. I also noted that he had a bit of a stoop, a big beard and he wore big thick glasses. I would recognise him anywhere. You can rely on me at all times, sir.'

'Did he say why he was here in Tontine Street, Constable?' The chill feeling of dread was seeping through Bucke's veins as

Davies went through his story, apparently blithely unaware of the implications of what he was saying.

'Well, Inspector, I made a careful note, because I thought you would want to know that he had done his job proper, like.' Constable Davies consulted his notebook which he produced from his breast pocket. 'He said he wanted to see the prisoner Daniel Guy. He said that you had sent him. He thought Guy might have more to say to you if he put the fear of God into him first. Make him confess, like. It is what they do, isn't it?' He snapped the notebook closed decisively. 'Well, it seemed like a tidy idea to me. Might save you a bit of time, I thought.'

'Did I mention this to you before, Constable Davies? Did I talk to you about the possible arrival of a clergyman of any kind?' Bucke was trying very hard to remain patient and calm.

'No, Inspector. I remember quite clearly what you said. However, I thought you might have changed your mind.' Davies knew very well that initiative was frequently rewarded.

When he reflected on this moment later, Bucke realised that he already knew what the answer was going to be. But he also knew that he had to ask the question, just as he knew that he dreaded hearing the reply.

'But you didn't do this, did you, Constable Davies? You didn't take him to see Daniel Guy, did you? Even though he asked. Tell me you didn't.'

Constable Davies looked around at his colleagues with the confident air of a man who knew his duties, one who could never be accused deserting his post. 'Of course not. I couldn't leave the desk unmanned, could I, Inspector? That would be wrong. So I gave him the key.'

'You did what?' Bucke felt physically sick.

'I shouldn't worry, Inspector. He wasn't there long. He was a priest after all, sir.'

'A priest? I don't understand, Davies. Are you— '

'You know. Like a vicar or a minister, sir. Don't you fret yourself, Inspector Bucke. He brought the key back. I have it here.' He held it up in triumph.

Bucke snatched it from him. 'Come on, Ball!' He ran down the stairs, two at a time, though he wasn't sure why he was hurrying. He had a very good idea of what he would find.

The door of the cell was indeed locked, and when they flung it open, Bucke noticed first a pair of boots, then a pair of trouser legs and then a small overturned table.

Daniel Guy had been hanged.

Two straps had been torn from the hammock which usually hung from hooks on the wall but was now lying on the floor. The straps had been attached to the iron water pipe which passed through the cell close to the ceiling and then had been fastened in a slip knot. Guy was suspended by his neck, with his back resting against the wall. He was dead, his blackened and protruding tongue a final gesture of contempt for those who had spent such a long time looking for him. Sergeant Ball cut him down with a knife and together they lowered the body to the floor. They noticed an ugly red mark to the side of his head, but that might have happened when he had been restrained earlier in the hotel lobby.

Inspector Bucke leaned back against the wall, rather like Guy but without the straps round his neck, and closed his eyes. He was sure there was a conspiracy here to stop him finding out what was going on. The men he had wanted to talk to – Jenkins, Bristow and Guy – were now all beyond his grasp. He was certain that Axmeyer had done this, that Daniel Guy had been murdered in order to silence him. He banged the back of his head against the cell wall. At least de Lesseps had escaped uninjured. But Bucke had been at the heart of all of this swirling confusion and had never once understood what was happening, and it seemed unlikely that he ever would.

Now he needed urgently to find Axmeyer. But he was sure that he had disappeared. He had been one step ahead of Bucke for at least the past few days, probably longer. Was he still disguised as a priest? Unlikely perhaps, for that might make him too distinctive. He would be as unremarkable as any old gentleman with a walking stick and thick glasses. The beard could disappear in a moment. Bucke would, of course, send officers to search the railway station and to question the staff. They would also check the docks. They would contact their colleagues in Neath and Cardiff and all points east. Any information, please? We have a killer on the loose. But then was he a killer? If he was, how had he done it? What evidence did they have that could condemn him? A mark on Guy's head that suggested he had been struck with something? But with what? A stick or a Bible? And Bucke himself had been wrestling with Guy on the floor in the Mackworth. He might have caused the injury himself. He was certain they would never find him. He was much too clever, whoever or whatever he was.

Constable Davies, however, was untroubled by the news of Daniel Guy's death. When he went down to the cell and looked at the corpse, he shook his head wisely. 'Don't think he liked what the priest had to say to him, did he? Oh, and the Italian has thrown up, sir. Missed the bucket too.'

Chapter Twenty-Four

The next morning, two inquests were held at the police station. It was quite early and no one wanted to deal with any complications at this time of the day, least of all the coroner, Mr Strick. After all, everything was very straightforward. The jury sensibly allowed themselves to be guided by him and thus they found that Daniel Guy had taken his own life. They all had other, more important, things they hoped to do before lunch.

Guy had been identified informally by Sergeant Ball and then formally by his wife, Mary, who was brought to see the body. She looked at it briefly and displayed no emotion at all, providing the positive identification the law required. She left immediately without speaking to anyone, apparently deep in her own thoughts. Bucke wondered if she would now be able to sleep peacefully.

The court listened diligently to Inspector Bucke's report of events at the Mackworth and those back in the cells. Guy was a wanted man who had attempted murder before and had, once again, failed. Bucke described him as a troubled and unhappy man and then retired to the back of the room where he listened to the rest of the proceedings with a curious detachment.

He listened as Mr Strick, determined to be as helpful as possible, honoured the jury with his own observations on Guy's actions and death. His motive for attempting to shoot Monsieur de Lesseps had become clear when two newspaper cuttings were found in his otherwise empty pockets. They should, he observed, be regarded as the key to his behaviour. They suggested that Guy's opinions had been inflamed to a considerable degree by the suggestion that foreigners intended to invade the country he held dear from under the sea, with the collusion of traitors. Acting alone, using a revolver he had brought back as a souvenir from America, he had attacked de Lesseps in the Mackworth Hotel in the grip of exaggerated patriotism. He was a man inflamed by what he regarded as a betrayal of the country he loved. His subsequent suicide merely confirmed that the balance of his mind had long been disturbed. Members of the jury nodded. Bucke stared out of the window.

Guy had injuries which were consistent with struggle and restraint at the hands of the police who had detained him following the failed murder attempt. No one could be quite sure when he had died, but it was hardly likely to have been before the priest came to visit. Even a Catholic friar would surely have noticed if he had been dead. There was some polite and grim laughter from the jury, to which Mr Strick smiled in response.

Beyond that, who could possibly say that Guy killed himself whilst he was in the company of the priest? This was almost impossible to believe, unless the police, on no evidence at all, were going to pursue the idea that the priest was an imposter. Indeed, Mr Strick added, the visit of a mystery priest, acting out of concern for the prisoner's well-being, might have given him cause to consider his criminal activities and his sins. And whilst taking your own life was indeed a sin, it was perfectly possible that in his remorse, following the guidance of his confessor, his mental derangement had followed its inevitable course. He must therefore have died by his own hand after the visit had concluded.

As it was, the respected French gentleman had safely departed by train, after having been escorted to the station by the Mayor and the Chief Constable, who had offered their sincere regrets for the evening's unfortunate turn of events. Nonetheless, the jury should not worry unduly.

'It was clear that Monsieur de Lesseps had formed a high opinion of the town and of the efficiency of its operations. He confirmed that he was indebted to Chief Constable Allison for saving, not just himself but, in addition, his young daughter. I think we may safely conclude that he will look upon Swansea with particular favour when he begins his momentous canal through Central America.'

Mr Strick looked over the top of his glasses towards the inquest jury. 'It was unfortunate indeed for the police that on the same night, in an entirely unrelated incident, an unknown seaman was murdered on the Strand. I am told that inquiries are continuing into his identity but, as I am sure you must have heard me say before, I am convinced that the safety of all our citizens requires that the terrible scourge of the knife is removed from our streets as a matter of urgency. Foreign seamen should be made to understand that the knife must always remain on board ship. It has no place on Welsh streets.'

The seaman's body had been delivered to the police station and Bucke led the jury out to see it, displayed in the old stable in the rear courtyard. Dr Beynon had, in deference to their sensibilities, tidied up the exposed organs and reassembled the abdomen as best he could. It wasn't a pretty sight, but it was more acceptable than the one which had greeted Constable Plumley the previous evening.

Doctor Beynon confirmed that the man had been stabbed twice; initially, it seemed, in the right side of his lower back, and this had been followed by the catastrophic injury to his abdomen from which there could be no recovery. The wound was consistent with that which would normally be associated with a long, broad-bladed knife. The blow was probably delivered at close quarters by someone standing in front of the victim. He could offer no explanation for the initial wound in his back, unless the man had been attacked by two men at the same time.

Constable Plumley then gave evidence about finding Giardinieri sitting on the ground next to a dead man 'who had spilled his lights' and that, whilst the murder weapon had yet to be recovered, his proximity was such that he must be regarded as the prime suspect. The wound was of a kind that was normally associated with the knives that Italian seamen carried with them as a matter of course. Italians, he advised the jury, were 'sudden and quick in quarrel and addicted to the use of the knife. In my dealings with them, I find them hardly more than half-civilised.'

The inquest concluded with a summary of all the things they didn't know, which hardly pointed towards a confident and considered verdict. No one knew anything about the identity of the dead man on the Strand, even if there were few secrets about his body, since the entire contents of his abdomen had been glistening on the cobbles for all to see. There was nothing to identify him at all. He had been in the company of a group of Italian sailors but no one, whether drunk or sober, knew who he was. They were sure he wasn't an Italian and they were positive that he wasn't part of the crew, but they did not know where he had come from. His sack contained no clothes, no papers. It had been bulked out with a threadbare blanket.

The mystery had deepened when the corpse had been examined. His pockets were entirely empty, but he had beneath his clothes, resting against the small of his back, a homemade money belt which was now soaked in blood. It contained a significant number of banknotes in a wide range of European currencies, though it seemed impossible that they could ever be used to track his recent movements with any success.

Giardinieri was unable to offer any explanation of what had happened, though it was doubtful if he understood what was happening to him. Bucke watched him and saw that he had persuaded himself that the court was just a formality and that they would acknowledge that it had all been some sort of terrible mistake and he would be released with a handshake and a cheery wave. How wrong could he be?

The verdict was one of wilful murder found against Francisco Giardinieri and he was committed to trial at the forthcoming assizes. He must have killed the unknown sailor in a drunken dispute, now forgotten by everyone, and would now be condemned to death. Of that, there should never be any doubt.

The inquests had been a shocking travesty for Inspector Bucke. A simple solution to both cases had been regarded as more desirable than the truth. He had his own incomplete version of the murder of Daniel Guy, but the complete injustice of the arrest of Giardinieri gnawed at him. As far as the *Cambrian* and its readers were concerned, all outstanding issues had been resolved. There had been yet another night of violence on the streets, with foreigners once again using Swansea as their own deadly playground, one in which they felt free to stab each other with impunity. An example needed to be made. A hanging was what they needed to send out a proper message. The *Cambrian* welcomed the inquest verdict and looked forward to an example being made:

More murder on the streets. Brawl leaves seaman dead.
Italian arrested.
De Lesseps suspect commits suicide in police cell.

~

The crew of the *Tritone* were hanging around aimlessly in Swansea, awaiting permission for the ship's departure. They were still enraged by the apparently arbitrary targeting of their colleague, but, as Bucke learnt when he found an English-speaking sailor from Genoa on another vessel, they could remember little of the events on the Strand. Between them, the only recollections they had were fractured and chaotic.

Poor Francisco was terrified. The more he was told, the more that was translated, the worse it became for him. His loud laments, which echoed through the county gaol, were understandable but irritated both inmates and officers alike. The fact that one of the residents of the police cells had died there, had not encouraged Francisco to take a positive view of Swansea's law enforcement or of its concept of justice. His considerable distress when Canon Wilson from St David's on Rutland Street sent young Father Ware to offer him solace and confession, was loud and prolonged. He was sure he was about to be treated to the same sort of pastoral care that Daniel Guy had received.

Casettari, who had looked down from the top of the lamp post, remembered seeing Francisco and the mystery man lying on the ground and three others – or perhaps four – whom he didn't recognise – calmly walking away down the Strand. He could not remember whether they had been with them in the Crown Inn or not. They were just sailors and he had lost sight of them when his imperfect hold on the lamp post had started to waver. No one knew anything about the dead man. He had suddenly appeared amongst them, as if he had been hiding all night beneath a table and had suddenly chosen to emerge. He had been good company, friendly and generous. He seemed to get on well with everyone. There were no arguments at all.

One thing all his colleagues were sure of, though, was that Giardinieri was so drunk he could barely stand, let alone stab someone. He was incapable of carrying out any crime that you might mention. Giardinieri had been in a daze for most of the evening. He enjoyed his drink when he was on shore leave, but no one regarded him either as violent or tempestuous and he had never been known to carry any sort of weapon with him. He was a married man with children; all he ever cared about was getting home safely with his wages as intact as possible. He and his wife were planning to buy an olive plantation so that he could retire from the sea. Giardinieri a murderer? It was impossible. If he had done it, where was the knife?

The police had searched the streets in the gloom of the gas lights for the murder weapon but found nothing themselves. However, at lunchtime, a large vicious-looking knife was brought into the station. Two children had found it early in the morning when their mother, Mrs McCarthy, had sent them to a sawmill to get sticks to light the fire. It had been lying against the wall near Padley's Yard, and the children saw it because it was being pecked at by two argumentative seagulls. The boy, Timothy, had been using it to cut up an apple for his sister until Mrs McCarthy had taken it off him because it looked much too sharp and because she believed that it belonged to a tradesman who probably could ill afford to lose it. There were traces of blood around the hilt and it was especially sharp, so it needed very careful handling.

No one ever came to claim it and Sergeant Ball often wondered what sort of profession required a man to carry such a serious blade, an expensive one too, broad, well-balanced, twelve inches long and deadly sharp. A slaughterhouse man? A fisherman? A hired killer? They kept it in a drawer for a while, but anyone could cut themselves inadvertently if they were not careful and so it was moved. After a while, no one could remember where they had put it; and then it soon slipped from everyone's mind, as did the memory of the man whom it had once killed.

Early in the morning, on the day after the inquest, the unidentified seaman was laid to rest quietly in the cemetery at St Matthew's, a short distance from the police station. Bucke got there just in time and stood opposite Reverend Underhill as he went through a brief service, offering the dead man a moment of dignity. The two gravediggers who had been leaning on their shovels a short distance away, impatient to complete their work, soon enclosed the coffin in the earth, just another unknown sailor who had died a long way from home with no one to mourn him, and who would now rest for eternity in a cold grave in Swansea. Bucke had brought flowers with him, but these were for a different murder victim. He placed them gently on the grave of Joseph the Matchboy.

Daniel Guy was buried in the grounds of Swansea Gaol. Mary Guy chose not to attend.

Chapter Twenty-Five

*T*he *Tritone* was finally released from the dock, for there was no reason to detain it any longer. Bucke had heard from the crew what little they could remember, and so he allowed them to leave their colleague behind them. They lined the deck as they left, staring reflectively at the receding town. There were tears, for Francisco appeared to be trapped and there was no prospect of them ever seeing their friend again. He had not murdered anyone, but someone had done it and an example needed to be made. Enquiries continued along the Strand and around the town, but, after a week, it seemed that all possible avenues had been exhausted. The Italians were blind drunk, the victim had been buried, and Bucke was sure that the murderers had walked away.

As Constance suggested when he spoke to her, he had in fact found out all there was to discover about the murder. 'A small group of unknown killers has killed an unknown man on the Strand for reasons that are unknown. I mean, it is none of my business, Rumsey. I am just a piano teacher – and a mere woman too – but you might sleep better if you was not quite so fixated on it, because really there is nothing else to know. That's it. You know all that, and that is all there is. You prevented the assassination, and now you need to concentrate on preventing this execution.'

What she said made perfect sense, but she didn't have the idea gnawing away at her like an obscure medieval torture, slowing eating its way through his skin. And perhaps if Giardinieri was not facing execution, he would be more ready to accept that there was too much he would never know. But he could not let an innocent man die so casually. No one seemed to care very much; after all, most people had more pressing things to think about.

Without doubt, there was still a great deal to concern him, even without an imminent miscarriage of justice. Whilst Inspector Bucke had been alerted to Chief Constable Allison's resignation, the announcement came as a shock to everyone else. *Saviour of de Lesseps Resigns* proclaimed a headline in the *Cambrian*, and there followed a detailed analysis of how the brave Chief Constable saved the day and, in the process, the reputation of the town. Following this moment of triumph, he was resigning to fulfil a long-cherished ambition to manage his own public house, away from the stresses and dangers of police work. *He deserves our thanks for what he has done to keep our town free from the very worse consequences of frailty and corruption*, the newspaper concluded pompously.

The eulogy was a moment's dignity before the truth inevitably emerged and publicly reshaped his reputation. His son Thomas Allison had already resigned from the force and had gone to ground, apparently in Llansamlet, where he had taken a job as a shearer in the tinplate works and was now refusing to speak to anyone. The consequences of his fraud would be left to his father to manage whilst absorbing the public wrath. He had, of course, done a deal. The Chief Constable would pay back the missing £300 and resign, and, in return, they would allow Thomas to leave the police force untroubled. It wasn't right of course, but it was expedient.

~

Late on Thursday afternoon, as Inspector Bucke examined a list of overtime payments due to the constables following the de Lesseps visit, he was asked to attend a meeting in the Mayor's office in the Town Hall, and, as he walked through the town, he prepared himself carefully for it. He would not accept the job of Chief Constable. He would be adamant about this. It wasn't a role that would suit him, whatever they might say, and he spent some time rehearsing phrases and sentences that, he was sure, would present a convincing argument whilst remaining suitably bland and diplomatic.

On his arrival, he found that all this careful planning had been entirely irrelevant.

When he was shown into the mayoral parlour, it wasn't the mayor who was waiting for him. Instead, it was a distinguished man with a confident military bearing. He was well dressed, upright and correct; the sort of man Bucke remembered from his service in India, a well-bred soldier. He introduced himself as Colonel Grey and shook his hand warmly. 'Been sent down by Her Majesty's whatnot. You know, Whitehall. Sent me down to have a word.' He was affable and welcoming but clearly not a man to be underestimated.

They sat opposite each other on either side of the fireplace. 'Sorry to arrive unannounced, Inspector, but needs must. Have to tell you, we have made enquiries with your senior officers. Served with distinction in India; well done. They speak highly of you – educated and intelligent, they say. Certainly not the sort of person we would expect to find working down here,' he said knowingly. 'Hell of a journey, even on the train. But anyway, we wanted to say we are grateful for the steps you took to save Her Majesty's Government from what would have been considerable embarrassment during the recent visit by Monsieur de Lesseps. Very sensitively done.'

Bucke was surprised. 'Thank you for your kind words, Colonel, but I don't think I did a great deal at all. I was fortunate to be able to prevent Daniel Guy killing de Lesseps, but then we lost any opportunity to question him. As far as I am concerned, our enquiries are no more advanced than they were before the evening in the Mackworth began.'

'Too hard on yourself, Rumsey. You see, in my line of work, you can never know everything. You have to muddle through sometimes without a complete picture. And that is what you did. Well done, I say. You see, I have spent some time thinking about this case. Quite an interesting one, though we were particularly remiss at the beginning in not seeing any of the implications of the de Lesseps visit. Caught us on the hop. Would have enjoyed an opportunity to have had a word with the Latvian, mind you, but you can't have everything.'

'I am not sure I understand...' Bucke was thoroughly bewildered.

Grey threw his arms out expansively. 'Course not. Forgive me. That is why I am here. We owe you an explanation. By the way, before we go any further, about this Italian of yours, the one who now languishes in your prison awaiting trial and his inevitable execution. He is entirely innocent, as you know. Italian Ambassador is understandably quite agitated about it. Home Secretary is minded to ask you to hand him over into the Ambassador's care and he will be quietly repatriated. No need to go to the assizes. Such a waste of money.'

'I am relieved, Colonel Grey but—'

The Colonel talked over him. 'You could not have known it, but you were dealing with a plot by German agents to disrupt the construction of a Channel tunnel. How could you know it? Think we have worked it out now, finally. Wasn't easy, I must tell you. A German agent, a Latvian called Pieter Moitch, probably recruited your man, Guy, in America when they discovered he could speak Welsh, that is my guess anyway. Could pass as a resident, you see. Makes sense, doesn't it? Then they used men like Herbert Jenkins to persuade de Lesseps to come to Swansea. If that part had failed and de Lesseps hadn't come, they would probably have disposed of Guy and you would have found him floating in the dock. But he succeeded – or someone did. It was an impressive operation, although all our plans are liable to be wrecked on the rocks of human frailty. Your Daniel Guy was, it seems to me, a particularly unreliable person, but nothing he did could have ever implicated the Imperial German Government. Everything could have been denied and that is what they wanted most of all.'

'Who is—'

'Pieter Moitch? Someone who we have had an interest in for some time. Certainly a skilled agent. We knew he had arrived in Liverpool from America, but after that we lost track of him. We did not know that he was in Swansea for quite a while. We knew nothing at all about Daniel Guy at the start. Bit of a failing on our part, I suppose. The French knew where Moitch was but didn't choose to share that with us. It was his misfortune that on the night of the assassination attempt, he came up against someone equally as good as himself. Their top man at that sort of thing is François Iché. We are certain he was the one who sliced open the man you found. No one else. He likes a bit of theatre, does Iché. Imagines it acts as a warning, I shouldn't wonder. They brought him in to carry out the murder and then took him out the same night on the *Supreme Sagesse* for Le Havre. It means 'Supreme Wisdom' – a quality we are not privileged to possess . When the Italian said he had no idea what was going on, then he was absolutely right. Poor man. Entirely innocent.'

The Colonel stretched out his legs and then stood up. 'Please excuse me. Long morning on that beastly train.'

'But why Swansea?' asked Bucke.

'You are some distance from London in Swansea, Rumsey. Should it be your desire, you can bring people into the town and take them out again with the utmost simplicity – that is what the French did. They were in and out on the tide. No one would ever know. Something else you need to know: discovered there has been a German cell operating here for some time. Very pleased to have shut it down. Brought agents into Swansea to Mrs Baum who was running a guest house down on the docks somewhere and then they were able to deploy them across the country, like your Axmeyer. Interesting man. Not a professor, but an interesting man. My opinion, for what it's worth? The French consul has been keeping an eye on Axmeyer. We detained him in Brussels, by the way.'

'What will happen to him?'

'Axmeyer? Probably try to persuade him to work for us. Speaks fluent Russian, which might be of some help to us. If that does not suit him, he will be quietly hanged.' Grey looked around the room. 'Nice if we could get some tea. Is anyone around, I wonder? We think Axmeyer and Moitch were managing the mission, though there might have been someone else too, we aren't sure. I suspect the Latvian's real purpose was to silence Guy when the assassination attempt was over. Clean away the dirt such plots always leave behind. Guy was always just a small disposable part of a much larger game. Once Guy had agreed to carry out the murder, then he was doomed. I imagine his attempt to shoot his wife caused his controllers to revise their plans rapidly; but in terms of his credibility, it probably helped. Could never be presented as anything other than a lunatic who had listened too closely to Jenkins and your letter-writing head teacher. And you see, that was the point.' He pulled on a bell by the fireplace. 'Think this rings in the kitchen, do you?' He started to wander round the room, enjoying this opportunity to tell a story. 'Don't think the Germans were ever too concerned whether Guy succeeded or not. Even a failed attempt to kill de Lesseps would have shone light upon the tunnel idea which so vexes them. Truth of it is, they fear a supply line under the Channel which they could not attack and which could re-arm France during a German invasion. It isn't going to happen now. It has energised retired admirals and shopkeepers across the Home Counties, who have already written impassioned letters to the editor of *The Times* about perfidious foreigners and the supremacy of the Empire. And so in that respect, the Germans got out of it entirely what they wanted – and none of it could be publically attributed to them. Is there anyone else here, or are we alone in this building?' He pulled the bell again. 'I could make it myself, you know. Done it before, actually.

'You see, it all started when opportunity came their way,' he continued. 'The Jenkins' factory in Hamburg was probably the key. Jenkins was never motivated by some kind of misguided patriotism. It was all about money. The Germans knew all too well that he had money difficulties and was on the edge of ruin. He was motivated to save his business and his status here in Swansea. They paid him to get de Lesseps here in the town and at the same time to create hostility towards him.'

'And Jenkins knew about the murder plot, do you think, Colonel?' Bucke was fascinated by the story. He realised he had known some of what had happened but only a fraction of it.

'Oh, he knew, but he had issues with the French, as you know, so it probably didn't trouble him. Was promised a fee for mobilising anti-European sentiment, didn't care about anything else. He, in turn, recruited this Bristow buffoon. Their words would prove to be the cover for the attempt on de Lesseps; words that would inflame an unbalanced killer. You see, we invent these clever little stories around the fireplace in our cosy little offices, with a glass or two of whisky; but of course, when they get out on the streets, they never quite work out as we planned.' He smiled ruefully. 'It's a game, you know. I doubt very much if either of them ever received any money, and the Germans have now gained control of the Jenkins' business in Hamburg. No idea what they are going to do with it. Never any good.' He became exasperated. 'Is there a shortage of domestic help here in Swansea? As far as we are concerned, the episode is over. This little German cell was closed down when your Mrs Baum was put on a ship to Germany. As I said, Rumsey, you have prevented considerable embarrassment for Her Majesty's Government, and what has been noted is that you have done so without the full information at your disposal. Thank you.'

Bucke was not so pleased. 'I do not feel I have done anything, Colonel. I stopped nothing.'

'It is in the nature of my work, I fear. We always know when we have failed. But we can never know about what we have prevented.'

'People died and I have arrested no one,' he replied.

'Ordinary people, Rumsey. They died. They always do. You served in India. You know what happened there. It is wrong and it keeps me awake at night. And if there was anything you could show me that would prevent it, then I would become your disciple. But until then, I try to console myself by this strange idea of the greater good. If a prostitute and a matchboy have to die in order to keep a hundred others alive, then I have to think that it is acceptable. In my world, it is usually agents and informers who pay the price.' He sighed. 'I should have confirmed the domestic arrangements before I came.'

'But surely you could have acted earlier. Or the French could have. It would have stopped unnecessary suffering.'

'Why didn't we act sooner?' He shrugged. 'Standard practice – leave it as long as possible so that you can apprehend as many of the plotters as you can. You can see that, I am sure.

I also think, strictly off the record and all that – I know you understand – that my masters were not at all interested in this tunnel nonsense. They were quite happy for someone else to make it disappear and never once get their hands dirty. The French had it all organised. De Lesseps was carefully guarded. I doubt if he was ever in danger. The French let him flush Guy out. No point in scaring him off, and those French agents do seem to have dealt with the lot of them in the end, though we have never been convinced by the murder of Jenkins. I think that is something for you.'

'May I ask something, Colonel Grey? How do you know all this? It sounds as if you were here all the time.'

The colonel smiled. 'The French and the Germans are not the only ones with agents, you know. Perhaps ours are the better, because they don't know who ours are. You would be surprised, I think. Just let me say, we always get the best information from the ladies, though as individuals, not one of them has a complete picture of what's going on. We have had agents watching events in Swansea for the past few weeks, once we had a sniff of things, but it can be hard to make sense of all the information we receive, and it can take quite a while to put it all together. Sure you appreciate that.'

Bucke looked thoughtfully at the fireplace. *We have been nothing but puppets*, he thought. *Unimportant pieces to be sacrificed in a game no one ever explained to us.* He did not say these things. Instead, he asked, 'I have wondered, Colonel, if Jenkins was murdered by Guy. It is a possibility I have considered.'

Colonel Grey looked at him very carefully and then scratched behind his ear reflectively. 'It has the benefit of being convenient, does it not? It is possible.' He paused and raised his eyebrows. 'An argument? Money? Who can say? In such business there is no honour.' He looked at him knowingly. 'As I said, it remains an issue for you.' He paused again. 'I repeat. We have no interest in the death of Herbert Jenkins.'

'I know,' replied Inspector Bucke. He returned his eyes to the Colonel. 'Thank you. This has been most helpful.'

'It was the least we could do. Of course, it is for your own ears only. I know you understand that. Your position becomes exceedingly difficult if you are indiscreet, but you know that too. Sorry about the tea, by the way.'

'Please, Colonel Grey. Do not trouble yourself. Let me see what I can do.'

∾

Once he had found Colonel Grey a cup of tea, Inspector Bucke walked slowly up to St James' Crescent, thinking carefully, once again, about the death of Herbert Jenkins. It was early evening. This would be as good a moment as any, he thought. He had heard that Mrs Jenkins was planning to leave Swansea and he could not leave it any longer. He saw two boys rolling a hoop along Walter's Road, beating it with a stick, dodging the carts and the pedestrians. He had left such simple pleasures behind him a long time ago, but at times like this he regretted their loss very much.

As he approached the crescent he could see a wagon drawn by two horses turning up the hill towards the Uplands. It must be carrying away some of the house contents, and the men would probably return tomorrow to complete their task. He was alarmed, thinking that Mrs Jenkins had already left, but she and Elinor were still there, though living now in a restricted number of rooms. He noticed that the entrance hall echoed when Elinor admitted him, in the way that Bristow's school had once sounded hollow. She said nothing to him, as if their previous conversation had never happened. She took him into the drawing room, where there was still some furniture, although the walls were bare, and a table was piled with the prints that had once decorated them. The dog was in the hearth. It lifted up its head to look at him briefly and then went back to sleep. Virginia Jenkins did not invite him to sit down. He could sense no one wanted him here. Not even the dog.

'I heard you were leaving us, Mrs Jenkins. I feared I was too late. I can appreciate that this might be a difficult time, but I am very eager to speak to you before you depart.'

'We are moving to London, Inspector. We require a place to live with more sophistication and more opportunities for grieving widows. This is a small town, a backward and dirty location, full of its own self-importance and wallowing with pleasure in its own ignorance. We will be pleased to put this place far behind us. I imagine you will be happy to remain here in a town which suits you.'

He ignored her insult. 'It is important that I speak to you both before you depart. About your husband's death, Mrs Jenkins.'

'Indeed, Inspector Bucke? And you are here to tell me about dramatic developments in the case? That you have apprehended the killer?' She snorted derisively. 'I do not think this is so, Inspector, is it? Because this is Swansea. In others towns, this crime would have been solved a long time ago. But not here.'

He welcomed her clumsy provocations. They showed that she was apprehensive about what he might say. 'Mrs Jenkins, I have to tell you that I have been considering the death of your husband in some detail and I think it is only right that I share with you my conclusions.'

'How interesting, Inspector. Fascinate me, please do. It has been a tedious day.'

'You see, I have always found it hard to believe that Mr Jenkins's murderer followed him through the streets and finally murdered him in the garden. It always seemed more probable to me that he was killed by someone hiding in the garden or by someone from within the house, by one of your gentlemen friends, who may have thought that, as Mr Jenkins approached the house through a dark garden, he was not the homeowner at all but, indeed, an intruder. This left me with the disturbing possibility that your husband was killed, by accident, by a prominent member of our community.'

Mrs Jenkins leaned forward slightly in her chair. 'Gentlemen friends? Really, Inspector. I am sure that there are other ladies, even in Swansea, who might take considerable objection to such an implication. It is entirely offensive, but since I am leaving Swansea, perhaps you have determined to speak without the normal restraints. How unconventional you are! I suggest to you that in the future, Inspector, you would be better advised to take no notice of ill-informed gossip.'

Bucke shook his head. 'But you are not like other ladies, Mrs Jenkins, are you? If we consider for a moment that tablecloth the officer stole some months ago – you had no particular interest in it. But you needed to deflect attention away from your departing companion, who you feared had been identified. You have a long and distinguished list of gentlemen who have regularly visited the house, and they require from you absolute discretion. I am ashamed to say that Constable Sprague hinted at this and I chose not to listen. I think poor Punch tried to tell me too. I listened but I did not hear.'

She waited for a moment before she replied. 'Inspector. I seem to remember telling you that Elinor and I were at home alone on the occasion when my husband was murdered. I have a distinct memory of that, Inspector.'

'Indeed , Mrs Jenkins, and so do I. And so, if that is the case, if as you say you were alone and there was no one else here, then it must have been one of you who murdered him. You see, for a short time I wondered whether the company he kept had killed him – foreign agents perhaps or money lenders or criminal gangs. But I now know that I was wrong. I remembered something too. I remembered that there was no tablecloth hanging on the line when I arrived here that morning, but there had been earlier, which Elinor removed to apparently assist the police, but which was there to lure him into the garden. And, as you say, Mrs Jenkins, you and Elinor were alone.' He waited for her response.

'How interesting, Inspector Bucke. I would have thought that the immense volume of your work with the depraved would have given you insufficient time for such fantastical speculation. I cannot fail to be impressed by your imagination. But please, Inspector. This is laughable. Foreign agents? Criminal gangs? The town is stalked by a murderer. He attempts to murder his wife, or so the press would have us believe. He shoots at her brother; he attempts to shoot a visiting dignitary. Two people are stabbed to death and then a third appears to have been selected as a Polynesian sacrificial victim and disembowelled to appease some pagan god,' she snarled, snatching up one of her prints from the table next to her and waving it at him, before throwing it back down. 'There might indeed be other victims lying dead across the town, about whom neither we, nor indeed you, are aware. Who can say? And then you come here to confront a grieving widow and her maid? It would seem to me, Inspector Bucke, that you must look to yourself and examine your own sad litany of incompetence, rather than lose yourself in your dreams.' Her eyes were blazing now and her hands were gripping the arms of her chair tightly.

Bucke remained calm, pleased that he had started to unsettle her. 'You killed your husband, Mrs Jenkins. I know it.'

Her face, like her knuckles, was white now and she shook with anger. 'Complete nonsense of course but let us speculate,

Inspector, since indeed you enjoy telling such stories.' She stood and faced him. 'Let us think of my dear, dear Herbert. And let us just imagine that he had raped me. Again. Here in this room. Again. His open sword-stick a threat upon the occasional table, pushing my face into the wall, next to The Savages of the Pacific. Do you still like that idyllic picture, Inspector? Still appealing, is it? Imagine how that might feel, inspector. If, of course, such a thing could ever happen. And we know that it did not. But perhaps then Herbert laughs and leaves for his meeting. Imagine what thoughts might run through your mind at that time. Imagine, Inspector Bucke, just imagine how soiled you might feel.'

Elinor had left her place against the wall and approached her. She laid her hand upon her arm. 'Virginia—'

'No, Elinor! I will not stop. I am telling our inspector here a story. He likes a story. Tell me now, is this better or worse than the stories you make up in your own mind? Tell me, Inspector! Tell me!'

'Virginia, please,' soothed Elinor.

She glanced at the maid, then closed her eyes tightly and composed herself. 'But of course I didn't do any of that. Daniel Guy killed my husband, didn't he? He was waiting in the garden, was he not? Everyone knows he was. The man was deranged. And in his guilt at such a terrible crime, he killed himself in the police station. We all know that is true, don't we, Inspector?'

Bucke looked at her steadily but said nothing.

'Remember, my husband was a man who left behind him a trail of agony and destruction from the moment he was born and finally, after many years, came home and found justice waiting for him. Should I regret that? My only regret is that I didn't do it myself.'

Elinor spoke now, a strange determination on her face. 'You must not listen to Virginia, Inspector. You must listen to me. I must tell you that when Daniel Guy took my George from me to give him to a childless woman, it was here that he brought him. George should have become Virginia's son. But Herbert Jenkins would not allow it and so Daniel buried him. He dug a hole on the beach and filled my son's face with sand. His mouth, his eyes, his ears and his nose, all full of sand. And then he died.'

Inspector Bucke said nothing. He had not expected this.

'I killed Mr Jenkins for two reasons, Inspector,' she continued. 'First, in revenge for the murder of my sister, because he killed her, even when she did not deserve to die. And then in revenge for stopping Virginia from taking my little boy Georgie. He would have been alive still, such a wonder he would have been, here in this house. This should have been his home, look at it! His alone! All this was stolen from him. I did it, Inspector. I stabbed him until he was dead. I am proud of what I did.'

He waited for a moment before he spoke. 'Thank you for your confession, Elinor. You are loyal and devoted to your mistress beyond measure. But you didn't do it. It is not possible. You knew Jenkins had been murdered, of course you did. Because you were there. Perhaps you struck him on the forehead with the frying pan. I cannot be sure, but I think someone did. After that, there were tasks you had to carry out – you washed and cleaned the blade and you washed Mr Pettigrew's clothes which Mrs Jenkins had been wearing. But you did not kill Jenkins because he killed Punch – because at the time you didn't know that he had done it. None of us had the evidence of the child Joseph who had seen them together.' All the time he said this, he watched her carefully.

Elinor stared straight at him. 'Of course it is possible, Inspector. I stabbed him. Three times I stabbed him. And then I burned my gloves so that no one would know. He would not let Virginia adopt my little boy and so allowed Daniel Guy to kill him. I have cursed him every day for it. And yes, I did know he had killed my sister, Inspector Bucke. Because I saw his walking stick. I washed the blood from it as he requested. He said he had stabbed a dog which had tried to bite him that night, but I knew his habits. I knew where he went. I knew what he did. And I knew who he had killed. Did anyone else die that night? You have no need to examine your records, Inspector, I can tell you. No one.'

'And so why did you wait so long to kill him, Elinor? I am not sure that it makes a great deal of sense. You will have to explain this if you want me to believe you.'

She continued to look at him impassively. 'Because I had buried his sins deep within me. I had to. But when Daniel entered my life again, that made them real once more. It was Daniel who killed Georgie, but Mr Jenkins was responsible too. And then he killed my sister. He had forfeited his right to live.'

'I do not believe you,' he said gently.

'You should, Inspector. I killed him.'

Virginia had heard enough. 'Stop it, Elinor; there is no need,' she urged.

'There is every need, Virginia. I owe you everything. I owe you my life, my love; it is a debt I am willing to pay.' She was full of fearful resolution. 'I killed him, Inspector. You know now why I did it and when and how. I must now offer myself to you for arrest and committal.'

Virginia walked up to her and held both her hands as they looked deeply into each other's eyes. She spoke to her so gently, in a voice Bucke had not heard before. 'There is so much that brings us together, Elinor. We have shared so much pain. We have lost so much. And yet we have found such love. I won't allow you to do this.'

She turned to Bucke, still holding Elinor's hand.' I went to the County Asylum to find her. I knew she was there; Doctor

Pringle told me so. He has always been a special friend of mine. I knew I bore a responsibility for her. I needed to atone for what my husband did. And now he has paid the price. Daniel Guy began this tragedy and he has ended it. Now, Elinor and I can leave for a new life in London.' She lifted Elinor's hand and kissed it. 'You are such a clever man and you have such a love of fantastical tales. But of course, Inspector, as our leading and respected policeman, you will know more than anyone else that you have no shred of evidence for your speculations upon the death of my husband. Daniel Guy did it, not me. But think of this. If it were true, who would blame me? The world is a better place. You know that. Who is it that mourns Herbert's passing? No one. Elinor did not do it either, though she had cause. She is often a troubled woman. You can place no credence on her confession.'

'She did not do it, Mrs Jenkins. We both know that. You did. You killed your husband.'

'I confess, Inspector,' said Elinor. 'I repeat what I said. I killed Mr Jenkins. I hit him with a frying pan, I took his sword and I stabbed him. Twice, the sword bounced off something inside him and would not go in. The third time, nothing stopped the blade. I killed him.'

He said nothing more and waited.

'This is all nonsense, Inspector Bucke,' said Virginia. 'I would not have permitted Elinor to have done it. But if I had done it, I would have wanted to see his face. The English Way, I believe he called it. To look into his eyes and then to pierce his soul. I would have wanted him to know. I regret that I did not do it. Such a pleasure denied.'

Bucke was relentless. 'You put a tablecloth on the washing line to make sure that he came in through the garden. You knew that he would not run the risk of meeting one of your visitors in the hall. So you waited for him in Mr Pettigrew's clothing.

You hit him hard on the forehead, probably with a frying pan, unless Elinor indeed did that. You stabbed him three times, Mrs Jenkins. The blade became stuck. So you put your hand on his chest and pulled it out hard. You cut your hand as a result. Then the blade went between his ribs and you left it there. Elinor burned your bloodstained gloves.' He paused. 'Did you speak to him, I wonder?'

She smoothed her bodice. 'If I had found myself in such an unexpected situation, there might have been much I would have said. Who knows what words I might have found? I am sure that if he had fallen backwards, I would have stood over him and exulted in his death.' She smiled. 'But of course I didn't do it. How could I? The opportunity for such pleasure was cruelly stolen from me by Daniel Guy. He is not only a murderer, but also a thief. He stole from me the sight of the man to whom I was married, choking on his own teeth. Spitting them across the garden path. Desperately seeking his own breath. Then the blood frothing from deep within him. His legs thrashing, breaking glass. That a lady such as myself, a mere woman, should do such a thing? Frankly, it beggars belief.'

'Passions run deep in all of us, Mrs Jenkins. We are all capable of things which may shock and surprise us. And then we find that the noose does not discriminate.' He could hear Elinor gasp by her side, but he did not take his eyes away from Virginia.

'I think you will find that it does. Are people from the west side of Swansea often hanged?' She looked at him in disdain. 'You must be disappointed that your fantasy has no natural conclusion. I am sure there are other more pressing matters for you to deal with. The sale of rotten meat in the market, for example. Mad dogs. They are more worthy of attention than your remarkable tissue of dreams, fit only as a melodrama at the Music Hall. Put your fantasies to one side, Inspector Bucke, before they take root and consume you.' She took Elinor in her arms and held her close.

~

He walked thoughtfully down the steps and a short distance along St James' Crescent. He knew that he had the power to ruin more lives; whatever he chose to do, he could never bring Herbert Jenkins back. And why would he want to do such a thing? Why, in pursuit of the irrelevant truth, would he ever wish to destroy pure love? Why would he even contemplate such a thing?

Then he turned. They were still together on the doorstep, watching him. They stood side by side, facing an almost certainly disapproving world together. All that he could ever be was the law, and sometimes it was blind. And perhaps it was his turn now. He stood still and watched them until they turned into the house and closed the door behind them. Yes, Daniel Guy had killed Herbert Jenkins. How could he ever have believed otherwise? It was obvious. The man was insane and he had committed suicide when the balance of his mind was disturbed. How foolish he had been not to have seen it until this moment. Daniel Guy's wish had been fulfilled; he had finally become a murderer.

Chapter Twenty-Six

He sat quietly whilst Constance practised at the piano. She needed to improve now that she was a professional, that was obvious, but it had become particularly urgent since she found herself tutoring a talented pianist. She was going to enjoy it, but it required some additional effort on her part; she could not allow herself to become complacent. So new pieces were needed and these had become a symbol of her new determination. When she saw them, she remembered how her life used to be, so she treasured them and then worked hard to master them.

Rumsey Bucke listened as he picked his way haphazardly through *The Times*. The paper still featured letters which condemned the Channel tunnel and proclaimed Great Britain's sovereignty and Empire in the face of continental envy and subversion. The attempted assassination of de Lesseps and those provocative scraps of newspaper in Guy's trouser pocket had become national news and the tunnel had suddenly achieved the sort of prominence that it had previously been denied. It was no longer a bold and exciting engineering innovation, but something which would fatally compromise national security. If de Lesseps had no intention of building it, then what had it got to do with him? What was the purpose of his enthusiastic endorsement? For many letter writers, consumed by prejudice and rumour rather than by understanding and fact, the tunnel was simply a plot devised by France, a country which could never be trusted. The German plot to discredit and disrupt appeared to have worked.

It had been an emotional day for Rumsey Bucke. The Watch Committee never asked him if he wanted to apply for the position of Chief Constable, at which he was oddly quite offended, even though he never had any intention of doing so. Vanity, he supposed. He was quietly amused. Was vanity better than his previous lack of interest? He thought it probably was. The new Chief Constable was Captain Isaac Colquhoun from Carmarthen whom he knew vaguely and who seemed to be generally respected.

Constance sighed loudly and banged her hands upon the keys in discordant irritation. She flexed her fingers and then started the piece again. Bucke remained anxious about this developing friendship with Constance. Not because she was married to another man, however inadequate he had proved to be. It was because he could not dismiss from his mind the possibility that he was betraying his family, even though they were no longer with him. He still missed them terribly but increasingly accepted that he would never see them again, perhaps not even in his dreams. It was a long time since they had been to see him.

He would tell her about his meeting with Colonel Grey eventually, just as he would tell her about his final conversation with Virginia and Elinor. Would she be shocked? He doubted it. Constance was sensible, tolerant and sympathetic. He enjoyed talking to her; he valued what she said. Most of all, he liked being with her. Just like now. They were not talking, they were busy, each in their own preoccupations. But they were together.

It was the comfort and the security he experienced when he was with her that he valued most of all.

He watched Constance closely, knowing that she could not see him, as he kept putting off the moment before he had to return to his room on Fisher Street. She had stopped playing again and made a note on the score and then started once again. It was the fourth time she had restarted this particular sonata, and it was proving to be a tricky piece.

He listened and wondered what it would be like if he could start again, just as easily as her. He could have saved Punch if he'd known then what he knew now. And Joseph.

But that was not how it was. Once you started, there was no going back. One incident led to another, inexorably to the next and onwards, through a whole series of incidents which eventually took you to an unexpected place. You never knew where that place was going to be. But Constance could start again. She always knew the beginning and the end, and the notes provided a map by which she could navigate her way. She could rectify her mistakes, whereas he had to live with his and she could always recognise hers immediately. The notes sounded wrong, discordant. He often didn't know how discordant he had become until it was too late.

He thought about what he had done. He still didn't think he had prevented anything, as far as he knew. He had merely reacted to incidents that had nothing to do with him, without any idea of direction, without any musical notation, without the benefit of any kind of map. And whilst he had been stumbling along in ignorance, Punch and Joseph had died without any understanding of why it had to be that way.

Constance abruptly threw down her pencil. 'Mozart can be so irritating at times, damn him! Come, Rumsey, take me for a walk before you go home. I can't get this part right at all and anyway, it is a lovely evening. I think I should like to look at the sea.'

He got out of the chair and Constance smiled at him as he helped her into her coat. He knew there would be times to come when he would find himself on the dark side of the street, but he knew that he could now choose to cross over into the sunshine and enjoy the light.

Afterword

This is a work of fiction but it uses many historical events which have been brought together to create a narrative.

I have tried to be as accurate as I can with place names. All streets, shops and public houses are real.

De Lesseps did visit Swansea in June 1880, bringing with him his young daughter Ferdinande in an attempt to recruit investors for his ultimately unsuccessful attempt to build the Panama Canal. He often spoke in support of the plans to build a tunnel beneath the English Channel.

The Jenkins family, the Gallivans, Betty Baum and Joseph are my invention, but Bristow the head teacher and professor of domestic violence, was real enough. He did abandon his wife and flee to America. Charles Glascodine was a solicitor and an eminent public figure. Maurice Theophilus Axmeyer was a teacher of languages in Dynevor Place; and in 1879, he found himself in difficulties after touching women in the streets.

Daniel Guy returned from America, just as he does here. He did shoot his wife Mary three times in his brother-in-law's house on Little Gam Street and she did survive. He took his own life in prison, using straps from his hammock, after his arrest (not in the police station).

Catherine Owen, or Punch, did appear in court dressed as a sailor but she wasn't murdered. I do not know if she had a sister.

Peter Moitch, a Baltic sailor, was killed in a brawl with a group of drunken Italian seamen and Giardinieri was sentenced to death for the murder in 1865. He was later pardoned because he had been wrongly identified.

Martin Willrath, a furnaceman from the Hafod, appeared in court in August 1880 for wounding another worker in a fight. As far as I know, he never fell into the North Dock.

Francois Iché was a French sailor who was shipwrecked and drowned off the north Devon coast in December 1852.

John Allison was Chief Constable and resigned once his son's fraudulent behaviour was uncovered in 1877. He did become a publican in Briton Ferry, and Thomas did leave the force to work in the tinplate factories. Constable Robert Sprague was imprisoned for stealing a tablecloth from a clothes line in 1859.

The Swansea Society for the Acquisition of Useful Knowledge did flourish briefly in the 1840s. We miss them still.

Nelly Damms in the market? Well, she was my grandmother.

And Rumsey Bucke? He was a police inspector in Swansea and he was forced to resign from his post in 1872 following accusations by Constable Lewis that he had uprooted and stolen a yew tree, a charge he always denied. I have always believed that he deserves better. So I offer him, through this novel, a different life.

April 2018
Swansea